THE
LIGHTNING
ROD

ALSO BY BRAD MELTZER

FICTION

The Escape Artist
The House of Secrets
The President's Shadow
The Fifth Assassin
The Inner Circle
The Book of Lies
The Book of Fate
The Zero Game
The Millionaires
The First Counsel
Dead Even
The Tenth Justice

NONFICTION

The Lincoln Conspiracy
The First Conspiracy

THE LIGHTNING ROD

A ZIG & NOLA NOVEL

Brad Meltzer

WM

WILLIAM MORROW

An Imprint of HarperCollins*Publishers*

THE LIGHTNING ROD. Copyright © 2022 by Forty-four Steps, Inc. All rights reserved. Printed in the United States of America. No part of this book may be used or reproduced in any manner whatsoever without written permission except in the case of brief quotations embodied in critical articles and reviews. For information, address HarperCollins Publishers, 195 Broadway, New York, NY 10007.

HarperCollins books may be purchased for educational, business, or sales promotional use. For information, please email the Special Markets Department at SPsales@harpercollins.com.

FIRST EDITION

Designed by Nancy Singer

Library of Congress Cataloging-in-Publication Data has been applied for.

ISBN 978-0-06-289240-9 (Hardcover)
ISBN 978-0-06-325216-5 (International Trade Paperback)

22 23 24 25 26   LSC   10 9 8 7 6 5 4 3 2 1

For my grandfather Ben Rubin,

my Poppy,

whose unrelenting kindness

helped me realize who I want to be

ACKNOWLEDGMENTS

I celebrated my fiftieth birthday while writing this book. Simultaneously, the global pandemic hit. These two events, at least for me, became instant reminders of what the characters in this book have been telling me for the past three years—that we as human beings are utterly fragile and outrageously resilient. So I'm just happy we're here together, dear reader. I missed you. Welcome home.

Speaking of home, I owe massive thank-yous to the following: My first lady, Cori, who reads it first, tears it apart, and somehow always leaves it better. In many ways, she's done the same with me. I've loved her since ninth grade, and every year, that love expands. Jonas, Lila, and Theo are my blessings. All the love that Zig has as a father comes from my love for them. They'll understand one day. Jill Kneerim, my friend and agent, is a true gift. This is a book about figuring out who you really are. Over two decades, she's helped me do just that. Jennifer Rudolph Walsh gave me new life at my original publisher. I owe you forever for that and much more. Jay Mandel, you've been wonderful since the moment you picked up the ball. Special thanks to Hope Denekamp, Lucy Cleland, and all our friends at the Kneerim & Williams Agency.

As you'll see in these pages, there's nothing like the bond between siblings, so I need to thank my sister, Bari, who understands me like no one else. Also to Bobby, Ami, Adam, Gilda, and Will, who are always by our side.

For more than twenty years, I've still got the same crew reading my early drafts: Noah Kuttler gets it at the start, imbuing it with his own voodoo. Ethan Kline brings a level of sophistication from the other side of the ocean. Then Dale Flam, Matt Kuttler, Chris Weiss, and Judd Winick tell me all the parts they love and hate, as well as all the jokes that aren't funny. But c'mon, I'm always funny. And did I mention I'm fifty? That makes me exceptionally wise.

The characters in this book were born because a few inspiring people let me into their lives. So let's start with William "Zig" Zwicharowski who, a few years back, retired from his position as the Port Mortuary Branch Chief at Dover, taking care of our fallen troops and making sure they were treated with honor, dignity, and respect. To every person on the Dover team, thank you for what you do for Gold Star families. The same is true for former Dover man and funeral home expert Matt Generaux, who makes sure I don't mess up the details. Special thanks to Sergeant Major Amy L. M. Brown, the real-life Army Artist-in-Residence, for sharing her adventures. Zig, Matt, and Amy, you are my moral compasses. (Heart!) Finally, the ringleader for all the military details—and one of my oldest childhood friends—Scott Deutsch. Every book, I ask him hundreds of impossible questions about the military. He gives me all the right answers. So any mistakes are mine.

I also need to thank everyone at Dover, including Christin K. Michaud and Major Ray Geoffroy.

I leaned on one of my dearest friends, the incredible Dr. Rachel Nonkin Avchen, who helped me navigate the details of the CDC and gave me some of the coolest things to write about (and yes, I know the SNS left the CDC). Additional help came from Gregory Hand, Jason McDonald, Mark Moynihan, Mona Patel, Paul Renard, and the very kind Lisa Dillard. My police chief and dear pal Jimmy West is the absolute best, and so is Dr. Lee Benjamin, for the best ways to murder people, as well as Bob Gourley, the CTO of all my work. Special thanks to Art Roderick for details on the amazing mission of the U.S. Marshals; Samantha Vargo for help on forensic photography; Mike Workman on all things that go boom; Ben Becker for the gun expertise; Steve Whittlesey, for the beekeeping help; and Mike Hayes for his friendship and advice on key military details. Additional details came from Abbey Gau and Patricia Evans at Longwood Gardens, Rosa Flores, Susan Generaux, Mynor Rosa, Rob Scheer, and Mark Whitworth. And thanks to everyone else who anonymously added details to these pages. You know who you are.

Whenever Zig refers to his mentor, that's me leaning on the advice of the great Mary Roach. Go buy her book, *Grunt*. It's spectacular. The book *Raven Rock* by my friend Garrett Graff was especially helpful, as well as articles including "Autopsies of the War Dead Reveal Ways to Save Others" by Denise Grady, "In the Hands of God," and "Maneuvers" by Kristin Henderson, "The Mercy Girls" by Jennifer Miller, "Inside the Head of a 'Bad' Kid" by Bonnie Marie Laabs, and some of the best confession stories on Reddit. Special love to Master of the Book, who deserves to be acknowledged, but will only do it with a code name.

Super big thanks to the rest of my inner circle, who I bother for every book: Jim Day, Chris Eliopoulos, Jo Ayn Glanzer, Katy Greene, Denise Jaeger, Katriela Knight, Jason Sherry, Marie Grunbeck, Nick Marell, Pansy and Rob Price, Staci Schecter, Liz Sobel, and Maria Luisa Venusio; everyone at the USO and HISTORY, including Nancy Dubuc, Paul Cabana, Mike Stiller, and Russ McCarroll, for helping me find Zig and Nola, and of course, my family and friends, whose names forever inhabit these pages. Finally, major thanks to everyone in the military and veterans community, especially their family members. Your sacrifice is never forgotten.

More than two decades ago, my publishing life started at William Morrow and Rob Weisbach Books. So massive thanks to Rob Weisbach, for being the first to say yes. All these years later, I'm now right back when I began, and I couldn't be more grateful. As a result, I need to thank everyone there for welcoming me home with such kindness and grace: Liate Stehlik, for being a leader who I trust and follow (you've truly been incredible), Jennifer Hart, Kaitlin Harri, Sam Glatt, Kelly Rudolph, Christine Edwards, Stefanie Lindner, Carla Parker, Tessa James, dear old friends Andy LeCount, Sharyn Rosenblum, and Ian Doherty, as well as the kindest and hardest-working sales force in show business. I've said it before, and I'll never stop saying it: they're the real reason this book is in your hands. I need to add a final thank-you to David Highfill. Every book has a champion. He's been far more than that to me. Let me say it as clearly as I can: he helps me be the writer I've always wanted to be. It means more than I can express, and I express for a living. Thank you, David, for your faith.

In each of us there is another, whom we do not know.

—*Carl Jung*

THE
LIGHTNING
ROD

PROLOGUE

ELMSWOOD, PENNSYLVANIA

These were the last fourteen minutes of his life.

"Wojo, you're up," a valet with watery eyes announced as a midnight-blue BMW turned the corner and crept up the driveway.

Anthony Wojowicz was older—thirty-two, which made him practically geriatric in the valet scene. But with parents who worked in the mine—truly *in* the mine; his stepdad worked days, his mom used to work the hoot-owl shift overnight—Wojo wasn't afraid of hard work.

Ever since he was little, Wojo had considered himself a lucky guy. When he was a kid, a pickup truck hit his friend as they stepped off the curb, missing Wojo by inches. It was the same when his older cousin stole Wojo's Halloween candy one year, then got sick from a pot brownie that was accidentally distributed. As Wojo got older, his overstyled messy black hair starting to recede, everything didn't go his way—his ex-wife was proof of that. But he was lucky to have his new girlfriend (he'd met her in an elevator, of all places), lucky that they found that mole on his back early, and especially lucky that when he got fired from LensCrafters, he found this job, parking cars at Barron's Steakhouse.

During his time at LensCrafters, Wojo's child support was deducted directly from his paycheck. Here, as a valet, he got tips in cash, which not only gave him some breathing room, but also gave him a way to save up for that birthday party at the indoor skydiving place in Philly that Gabriella, his ten-year-old daughter, was begging for. His ex said no to the party. But with what Wojo was going to clear this weekend? He'd have enough to say yes.

With a quick rub of his crooked nose, Wojo jogged toward the BMW, forcing a smile at the driver. Years ago, his stepdad had told him that anyone who drives a BMW has a small penis. Wojo always liked his stepdad. And the fact that the car here was a 2013 128i coupe? C'mon. There were Camrys more expensive than that.

Small fry, Wojo decided. Not nearly big enough for what he had planned.

"Good evening," Wojo announced as the door to the BMW swung open. "Welcome to Barron's Steakhou—"

"Don't readjust my seat," a commanding baritone insisted. The fortysomething driver was big—built like a bulldozer—and the car seemed to tip as he got out. Stubborn lips. Military posture. The buzzed blond hair made Wojo think of Captain America. But it wasn't until the man stood up straight that Wojo spotted his seven-thousand-dollar Panerai watch.

Before Wojo could say a word, the driver slapped his keys against Wojo's chest.

Fwap.

That was the moment—as the keys smacked him in the chest, as Captain America brushed past him without any eye contact—that Wojo made a fatal decision.

"After this, I'm on break, yes?" Wojo called out to his watery-eyed boss.

Watery Eyes nodded. That would give Wojo twenty minutes.

Sliding into the BMW, Wojo readjusted the front seat and put the car into drive. The interior was pristine, but Wojo's eyes were on the rearview as he waited for Captain America to disappear into the restaurant.

With a tap of the gas, the car inched forward, toward the valet lot. But as soon as Wojo arrived in the lot, he headed for the lot's back exit, made a quick left, and hit the gas, out onto Route 1.

On the steering wheel, he pressed the small button that showed the cartoon headshot of a little man with three tiny parentheses coming out of his mouth. There was a loud beep. Voice command.

"Go home!" Wojo announced.

The center screen lit up and an address appeared. *2678 Ocean Avenue.* Wojo grinned. Like anyone else in middle age, Captain America was too old to realize nothing good comes from putting your home address into your car's GPS.

"Start Guidance," Wojo said, hitting the button again.

"Plotting a route to . . . home," the female computer voice replied.

Nine minutes away. Not bad at all. Lucky, lucky.

Wojo thought again of the seven-thousand-dollar watch. Good sign. So was the address on Ocean Avenue.

Even now, as he turned off Route 1 and passed the golf course that marked the edge of Elmswood's oldest suburb, Wojo told himself he was a good person. He didn't think of himself as a thief. But he was. His rationalization was his daughter, of course, and that he was always a gentleman about it. When it came to picking marks, he only chose the snobs, the ones so caught up in their own self-importance, they couldn't muster a simple *hello* or, God forbid, a *thank you.*

Manners. Decency. What the hell was wrong with the world these days?

More important, Wojo was smart about it. He wouldn't run in and rob people blind. If he did, it wouldn't take long for the police to figure out that all the victims had eaten dinner at the same restaurant.

He had rules and he stuck to them. Trips like this were only once a month (twice during that month when his sister was going through her divorce). And instead of grabbing everything in sight, he only took one item: A ring. A bracelet. On his best night, a sapphire necklace.

When a single piece of jewelry goes missing, people don't call the cops. They blame themselves and assume it's lost.

Seven months in, with eight jobs done, Wojo still hadn't been proven wrong.

"In one thousand feet . . . make a right," the computerized female voice announced as he blew past the white painted-brick colonial where he'd grabbed that four-carat heirloom ring a few months back.

Four minutes left to live.

Pausing at a stop sign, Wojo glanced around at the black leather interior of the BMW. His stepdad was wrong. This car was nice. So was the neighborhood, though that wasn't a surprise. With a menu that had a $145 tomahawk ribeye chop, Barron's Steakhouse attracted the best around.

"Destination ahead . . . on the left," the female voice added.

Cul-de-sac. Naturally. The mainstay of every suburban ecosystem.

Wojo shifted in his seat, feeling that tingle in his crotch. This wasn't better than sex. And certainly wasn't better than sex with Darla, the energy drink sales rep who he'd met in the elevator and did that thing with her tongue. But it was close.

Pulling into the driveway and squinting through the dark, Wojo took a good long look at the tasteful yellow ranch-style house—four bedrooms at least, maybe five. Nothing breathtaking, but that inlaid brick front path and the freshly planted flowers out front? Captain America was doing just fine.

As Wojo shut off the car, he waited a few seconds, double-checking that all the house lights were out. No one home.

Clipped to the sun visor was a small gray remote. Garage door opener. He pressed it with his thumb. If Wojo was really lucky . . .

Rrrrrrrrrrr.

The garage door yawned open, revealing storage boxes, bicycles, a spare freezer, and a workbench that looked like it hadn't been touched in years. If Wojo had looked closer, he would've spotted the empty gun safe along the back wall.

Ducking into the garage, Wojo pounded the Door Close button on the right-hand wall, and suddenly, he couldn't get the song "Total Eclipse of the Heart" by Bonnie Tyler out of his head. *Turn around, bright eyes!,* he mentally sang as the garage door lowered, swallowing him whole.

Even in the dark, Wojo could see the keypad for the alarm. As always, he reached for his phone, which held an app that would help him unlock it. For years now, every alarm company had had to file their particular transmitter frequencies with the FCC, which made them publicly available. For real. Publicly available. Most door and window sensors operate at 315.0 MHz, so all you have to do is copy that frequency to jam it. But as Wojo got closer to the keypad (still singing in his head how forever was gonna start tonight), he saw that a bright green light was on. Alarm wasn't even armed.

Lucky night for sure, Wojo thought, picturing his daughter Gabriella in skydiving pose, arms outstretched, the wind widening her smile so much, she was nothing but teeth. All that was left was . . .

Wojo gave the doorknob a twist. Locked. But not for long. From his pocket, he pulled out a key ring filled with bump keys, the same ones locksmiths used. It took two tries to find the right one, then . . .

Click.

The door swung open, and Wojo was hit with the whiff of a stale mop and bleach. Laundry room on his left. In his pocket, Wojo slid his hand around the small black stun gun he always carried on these trips, just in case someone jumped out of the dark.

Inside the house, everything was silent. No barking. No obvious pets. A good sign.

In two and a half minutes, the blood would be everywhere.

Right now, he was slow-walking through the family room, eyeing the cherry floors and the built-in bookcases that were filled with kids' DVDs and far too many Tom Hanks movies. Captain America had a wife and teenage kids, by the looks of the photos on an end table.

When it came to décor, the family had spent money on the couch—a modern chocolate-brown leather sectional—but everything else—rugs, coffee table, shabby-chic slipcovered chairs—was like a Pottery Barn, West Elm, and Crate & Barrel bomb went off. All of it in its prime a decade ago, just like the BMW. Every life has a peak. Ten years ago was when Cap was really making money.

Along the far wall was a framed revolver—an antique buccaneer-style flintlock pistol from the 1700s, complete with a wide brass barrel like something from *Pirates of the Caribbean*. Worth at least three grand, Wojo knew, though he walked right past it. Something that big goes missing, the cops get called. Besides, he knew where the real rewards were.

Following the house's main artery, Wojo made a left toward the master bedroom. He wasn't walking gingerly anymore. Too excited. Down the hallway, he saw the way the bedroom opened to the right. Toward suburbia's real prize. His and hers closets.

According to home security experts, during a break-in, the very first place that criminals go is the top drawer of a woman's dresser. As a result, women are never supposed to hide their jewelry there. But most women did it anyway, not wanting to deal with the headache of moving their favorite items in and out of a safe.

A flush of adrenaline lifted Wojo's chest. Yet as he stepped over the threshold and made a right toward the closets, he was surprised to hear . . .

Kllk.

A light in the room popped on. Wojo squinted, blinded.

"You really think we wouldn't find out?" asked a man wearing a latex Oscar the Grouch mask. He was on the opposite side of the bed, which was drowning in throw pillows. In the man's hand was a gun—an M1911 military pistol—aimed straight at Wojo's face.

"This isn't—" Wojo said. "I wasn't—"

"You should know better! I know you know better!" Oscar the Grouch exploded, his voice muffled by the mask, which was deflated and misshapen, wobbly on his head. Even with his navy sweatshirt and baggy jeans, it was clear he was well built, though he had a natural impatience in his stance, ready to spring. His hands were bony and pale white.

Wojo backed up into the wall, his face burning with fear. A single thought filled his brain. He didn't know the *why* or the *how—Did they follow him?*—but one thing was clear: This was no longer a robbery. It was a *trap.*

Two minutes to go.

"I-I'm a good person," Wojo insisted. "This wasn't— My daughter—"

"Down! Now!" the Grouch shouted, his finger on the trigger.

Wojo dropped to his knees, keeping his head toward the floor. "I didn't take anything. Just let me—"

"Stop talking!"

Wojo lowered his head farther, practically curling into himself.

When bombs go off and horrors happen in the real world, people say that time seems to slow down. That's not true. It actually seems to go faster, but it's happening at such an accelerated rate, the human brain can barely register everything it's experiencing. At this moment, that's where Wojo was.

The Grouch was shouting now—*"You know what you did!"*—but Wojo didn't hear it. As the Grouch came closer, Wojo noticed a noise, a deep . . .

Ka-klaak.

The hammer on the pistol. The Grouch had pulled it back, and now, all Wojo could see was his daughter, crying, sobbing . . . her birthday . . . she'd forever link his death with her birthday.

Ninety seconds to go.

"Look at me!" the Grouch shouted.

Wojo refused, his brain catapulting back to his ex-wife, to their first apartment, to Gabriella being born, to standing outside the steak house and the burst of ego and anger that brought him to this r— Wait. In his pocket . . . the stun gun. He still had the . . .

The Grouch was close now, so close that Wojo could smell the latex of the mask . . . could smell the way the man's jeans reeked of sawdust and—

"Pick your head up!"

Wojo still didn't pick his head up. He was curled tight, his hand snaking down to his own pocket. Seventy-two seconds.

"You do realize this is *your* doing?" the Grouch added, pressing the barrel into the crown of Wojo's head. A plump vein swelled on the Grouch's hand as his finger tightened on the trigger. "You understand that?" he asked, like he was waiting for an answer.

In one minute, Wojo would be dead.

But he still had a minute.

"I asked you a ques—"

Wojo pulled the Taser from his pocket, squeezing the trigger so fast, he felt an electric snakebite in his own leg as he whipped out the weapon. The stun gun had two metal fangs at the end of it, which Wojo stabbed straight into the Grouch's left thigh.

The Taser's blue light crackled like a mini lightning storm.

"*Guuh* . . ." the Grouch shouted, his leg going limp, his whole body falling sideways, like a cleaved tree.

Forty seconds to—

Go, go, go, Wojo thought, scrambling to his feet. The stun gun would buy him a moment.

Wojo ran from the room and darted through the house, back toward the front door. As he ran, he was still squeezing the trigger, the blue electricity crackling as it lit his way.

In seconds, Wojo was outside, the summer air licking his face. Until that moment, he didn't realize how hard he was sweating. His heart punched in his chest. Up the block, he spotted the red rear lights of a car leaving, though he barely registered it.

He looked around, panicked, lost, like he'd awoken in a strange hotel and couldn't quite figure out where he was. *There. The car he came in.* The BMW!

Sprinting for the car, Wojo ripped open the door and slid inside. He pulled the keys from his pocket and threw the stun gun aside. But just as he went to start the car, from the back seat . . .

A thick forearm wrapped around Wojo's neck. Behind him . . . in the back seat . . . someone was already in the car, waiting for him. Wojo caught a glimpse in the rearview. That buzzed blond hair . . .

"*You think I'm blind!*" Captain America roared, tightening his choke hold. "I forgot my jacket in the car, and when I came out— *You think I wouldn't see you leave!?*"

"P-Please . . . you don't understand . . ." Wojo pleaded, realizing that the car he saw leaving was a taxi. Cap was a man of action. He'd jumped in a cab to race back home.

"*Please . . . Inside . . .*" Wojo added, twisting wildly, fighting to get loose, clawing at his own neck. Cap's grip was too strong. Wojo was thrashing now, his face a pale purple, tears squeezing out behind his eyes. He could picture Oscar the Grouch and his misshapen mask. By now, the Taser would be wearing off. He'd be here soon.

"*You steal my car . . .*" Cap roared.

Ten seconds.

"*. . . and break into my house!?*"

"If we don't— Please . . . He's—" Wojo begged. *"If we don't go, he'll kill us . . . !"*

"He?" Captain America asked. "Who's *he*?"

Tink. Tink.

Outside the driver's window, a knuckle tapped against the glass.

In perfect sync, both Wojo and Captain America turned left, looking up at a saggy, askew Oscar the Grouch mask. The man in the mask raised his gun.

Pffft. Pffft.

Two quick shots. Then a third when he saw who else was in the back seat.

Anthony Wojowicz wilted sideways. A small burn mark from the bullet appeared in his temple and sent a spray of blood across the passenger seat. Dead at thirty-two years old.

Behind him, Captain America—an Army veteran named Archie Mint—slumped forward, a matching burn mark on his cheek.

Wojo's luck had finally run out. But when it came to Archie Mint, well . . . even in death, Mint still had a bit of luck coming.

1

Four hours. He spent four hours working on her body.

"Ziggy, let her be. She looks good."

"Good?" Jim Zigarowski asked, standing over the coffin, makeup brush in his hand. "Not *great?*"

"Let me rephrase. Great. Beautiful. Michelangelo would say you're Michelangelo," said Puerto Rican Andy. Zig never liked the name, but Andy had been calling himself that since fourth grade, when there were three Andys in his class. Today, at three hundred pounds, Puerto Rican Andy lumbered through the viewing room at Calta's Funeral Home, carrying a metal easel with a bushel of bright daisies that he placed at the foot of the coffin. "She hasn't looked this good since Reagan was President."

"Don't listen to him, ma'am," Zig whispered, leaning down toward the dead elderly woman with high cheekbones and pale pink lipstick. Fallen #2,546. Mrs. Leslie Paoli, ninety-three years old. Dead from stomach cancer and whatever else you catch when you spend your last decade in a nursing home. "You look even more beautiful now, Mrs. Paoli."

Zig meant it. For four hours, he'd polished her nails, cleaned her dentures, used putty and makeup to cover the bruises on her neck and arms from all the machines at the hospital, and washed and re-styled her hair, which probably hadn't been shampooed in months. He even put her in the same dress—gold sequins with a crystal butterfly pin at the shoulder—that she was wearing in the photo next to her b—

"Bossman, they're here!" Puerto Rican Andy called out, sweat running down his shaved head, skating toward his neck tattoo—a phoenix—that poked out from the collar of his white dress shirt. Andy was big and looked like a convict, but as his parole officer had told Zig, the phoenix referred to Dumbledore, Puerto Rican Andy being the biggest Harry Potter fan in rural Pennsylvania. *Ravenclaw,* Andy would say to anyone who asked.

"Bossman, y'hear what I—?"

"One more sec," Zig said, adding some final blush to Mrs. Paoli's cheeks.

As always, the hardest part was getting the coloring just right. People think corpses are gray, but by the time they arrive at a funeral home, they're white. "Like geishas," Zig's mentor used to say. Once your heart stops and your body is on its back for a few hours, gravity sets in, blanching your face, chest, and legs—that is, unless an artful mortician gives you back your color.

"I told you, ma'am, we'll take care of you," Zig whispered, moving a stray silver hair from her forehead and flashing that charming smile that had gotten every mah-jongg group gossiping back when he first moved to the small town of Wonderly Square. Zig's silver-and-black hair was shorter now, for summer. Across his jaw was the hairline scar that he'd used to his advantage during those wild years after his divorce.

For most of his adult life, Zig had been a mortician at Dover Air Force Base, home of the mortuary for the U.S. government's most high-profile and top secret cases. On 9/11, the victims of the Pentagon attack were sent to Dover. So were the hostages who were killed in Beirut, the victims who were shot at Fort Hood, and the remains of well over fifty thousand soldiers and CIA operatives who'd fought in Vietnam, Afghanistan, Iraq, and every secret location in between. In Delaware, of all places, at Dover Air Force Base, was America's most secretive funeral home.

Two years earlier, Zig had left it all behind. There was too much pain—too many old scars torn open from spending every day with dead young soldiers. Within a month, he'd found the job here at Calta's Funeral Home, in a building that, back in the seventies, had been a Dairy Queen, complete with a red mansard roof that was now painted beige. Zig took it as a sign, hoping things could be a bit more nice and easy. But really, when was anything in life nice and easy?

"I'm looking for Jim Zigarowski," a man in his late thirties called out, stepping into the viewing room, then taking a half step back once he spotted the coffin. He wore a shiny blue suit, no tie, like he was going to a beachfront wedding.

"You must be Mr. DeSanctis," Zig said as the man took off his Mercedes baseball cap, which he'd clearly gotten from the dealership.

"Is he actually wearing a Mercedes hat?" Puerto Rican Andy whispered. "Ten points from Slytherin."

"Is that—? Is she—?" DeSanctis motioned to the coffin.

"Your mother is—"

"Mother-in-law. She's— Mother-in-law," DeSanctis insisted.

"My apologies," Zig said, putting on his funeral home voice, which made him sound like an NPR host. "As you'll see, we got her all cleaned up, so if you want to take a look—"

"Y'mean at the *body*? No. No no no." DeSanctis laughed nervously. "We'd rather remember her how she lived, not how she died," he explained, glancing around at the chairs, the flowers, even at the framed vintage metal sign from the funeral home's original 1908 location. *Offering Understanding*, it read in antique lettering. He glanced around at everything, really, except Mrs. Paoli. "Anyway, if you wouldn't mind . . . y'know . . . closing it . . . ?" he said, pointing with his fancy baseball cap toward the coffin.

"Of course," Zig replied with a polite grin.

DeSanctis stood there an extra few seconds. "Gotta be a horrible way to go, right? Like I told my own kids, don't ever put me in a nursing home. Last thing I want is to spend my final years collecting dust."

Zig nodded, still faking a grin. But as he looked around the ancient funeral home, Zig was surprised by how much the words stung. *Collecting dust.* Was that all he was doing these days?

DeSanctis headed out to his family, as Zig felt a buzz in his pocket. His phone vibrating. To his surprise, caller ID showed a familiar number.

302-677 prefix: Dover Air Force Base.

The life he'd left behind.

"Ziggy, it's Wil! What's cooking, good looking?" Wil-with-one-L announced.

Enthusiasm was always Wil's major. But Zig and Wil weren't buddies. Or even acquaintances. In the two years since Zig left Dover, Wil had called him a grand total of zero times. Still, Zig was so surprised by the call, he didn't give it much thought. That was his first mistake.

"How's private practice?" Wil asked.

"Wonderful. Couldn't be better," Zig said, eyeing Mrs. Paoli, frozen in her coffin.

"Listen, sorry to bother you, but we got a case that just came through—a lieutenant colonel, one of our own," Wil explained, meaning it was someone who worked at Dover. "The point being, the funeral's near you—just a few towns over—and we want the body treated perfectly, so . . ." He put on his best *Godfather* voice. "You up for letting us *pull you back in*?"

"Wow. Al Pacino impression. Topical. Wanna hear my Mr. T?"

"I'm serious, Ziggy. We could use the help. It's a good case. Funeral's tomorrow. You up for this or not?"

Zig stared at the coffin, at Mrs. Paoli and the crystal butterfly on her dress. Outside, down the hallway, DeSanctis was grabbing a handful of mints from the welcome bowl and stuffing them in his pocket.

"Yeah. I'm in," Zig said, thinking maybe this was just what he needed.

THE FOLLOWING MORNING, ZIG LEFT his house at 5:00 A.M., his camouflage backpack stocked with his mortician kit: baggies, modeling clay, makeup, and all his tools, including scalpels, forceps, draining tubes, and even a sternal saw, just in case.

Running down the front steps, he felt good to be in the mix . . . to be helping a family that truly needed his expertise. Zig was a sculptor. With bullet wounds to the face, you need to be prepared for the worst. And he was.

But the one thing Zig wasn't prepared for and didn't see was the man with the buzzed hair and pointy face who was parked diagonally across the street.

From his own car, the man watched Zig leave his house and head down the front steps, a travel mug of coffee in his hands.

If Zig was smart or even a bit suspicious, he would've checked over his own shoulder. But the only ones who do that, the man thought to himself, are those who know they're in trouble.

2

Mmmmmmmmmmmmmmmmmmmmmmmmmmmmmm.

Zig knew that sound, the low mesmerizing hum vibrating through the building. It was coming from the school's gym, the only place in town big enough to hold the nearly one thousand mourners who were packed into the bleachers, waiting to pay their respects.

It was the same in every small town. Fallen soldiers' funerals were community events. Outside, fire engines lined the streets, flags hung from every storefront, and folks lined up early. From the rumble, the crowd was restless.

"You got a prep room for me?" Zig called out, moving fast, like he was in an emergency room scene on one of those doctor TV shows, both hands on the metal rolling cart that held the flag-covered coffin.

Fallen #2,547. Lieutenant Colonel Archie Mint, forty-eight years old. *Almost my age,* Zig thought, steering the coffin down the long hallway of Elmswood High, pretending it was normal to push a coffin down the corridor of a high school.

"End of the hall, make a left," said the man who was running just ahead of the coffin.

Clifford. *Like the big red dog,* Zig thought, nodding thanks as he followed the thin, six-foot-four-inch, sixty-year-old man with a mediocre handshake and the build of a Q-tip. *God, why's the head of every local funeral home always look the part?*

"A prep room . . . ? Is the damage really that bad?" Clifford asked.

Zig stayed silent, spotting a stray blue thread on the American flag. He reached down to grab it. Whether it was a ninety-three-year-old civilian or a forty-eight-year-old lieutenant colonel, every one of the fallen deserved the very best.

"We'll take care of you, Archie," Zig whispered toward the coffin.

The tricky part was that in summer heat like this, the coffin acts like an oven. Makeup on the fallen soldier begins to melt. So does the wax that's used to smooth over bullet holes or other wounds in the victim's face.

"Mr. Zigarowski . . . I should warn you . . . Mint's family . . ." Clifford said. "His wife wants an open casket, but maybe we should just tell her—"

"She's getting an open casket," Zig insisted, picking up speed.

With a sharp left, Zig turned the corner, leaving the narrow hallway. Royal-blue metal lockers with built-in combination locks lined one wall; a colorful hand-painted mural of Martin Luther King Jr. lined the other, along with an educational poster that read, *Don't Quit Your Day Dream!*

As Zig looked around, something clenched in his chest.

"You okay?" Clifford asked.

Zig nodded, taking a half step back, his heart feeling like it was made from a thin-stretched cloth. *This school . . . My daughter went to this school,* Zig thought, though he knew that wasn't quite right.

The layout . . . the bright blue lockers . . . even this exact gray-and-white checkerboard linoleum floor . . . It was the same layout the Pennsylvania Department of Education used for dozens of local high schools, including the one in Zig's hometown, where he used to take—

Magpie, Zig thought. His daughter, Maggie. Images flooded forward and there she was. He could see her—back from the dead as old memories were laid over this new one: young Maggie walking down the hallway, running her fingertips across the combination locks, sending their dials spinning like pinwheels, each of them losing steam, slowing, returning to their lifeless, inert state.

Maggie was only twelve years old when she died, but right now, Zig could see her so clearly—the light freckles on her nose . . . the smell of Thin Mints on her breath . . . and of course, that night at the Girl Scout campout, when a soda can exploded in the campfire, sending shards of metal straight for Maggie's face.

On that night, fellow Girl Scout Nola Brown shoved Maggie out of the way, saving Maggie's life and giving Zig an extra year with his daughter. The time went too fast, Zig suddenly picturing Nola when he saw her two years ago, on that case they worked together at Dover.

The hardest part was seeing Nola fully grown, a reminder of what Maggie never got to experience. He could still see his daughter now, walking hallways just like this every Tuesday and Thursday afternoon so she could take singing lessons with Mrs. O'Keefe, the choir teacher.

"—igarowski, you hear what I said?" Clifford asked, Zig now humming that song she'd been practicing in choir. "La Vie Bohème" from *Rent*. Even then, Zig knew that Maggie's favorite part was watching Zig squirm when she sang all the curse words.

Six days after her final choir practice, Maggie was dead on that night that Zig could still conjure so quickly. It was the most potent weapon in grief's arsenal: the speed of its return.

"Yeah . . . no . . . I'm fine," Zig insisted as they reached the double metal doors at the far end of the hallway.

WEIGHT ROOM
Athletes Only

One of the few rooms with a doorframe wide enough for a casket.

"We tried cleaning it up," Clifford said, motioning to the bench press and squat rack that were shoved into the corner. But all Zig could focus on were the two men across the room, blocking the doorway to a connecting conference room.

Both were beefy, late twenties, in tight suits that they hadn't worn since high school. *Local firemen,* Zig wagered. *Or cops.* With big funerals like this, you hire all the local help you can get, though the way they were standing at the threshold—like Secret Service agents—their real job was to protect—

"*Oh, Tessa!*" a woman's voice called out.

"Tessa, I'm so sorry!"

There was a chorus of sniffling and nose-blowing.

The family.

Zig could feel them, even from here.

Before Zig could react, the door slammed shut, the two beefy guys following Clifford into the room with the family, which left Zig alone. No surprise. No one wants to be with the body.

"Okay, Colonel—it's just us now. You can tell all the dirty jokes you want," Zig whispered, locking the wheels of the rolling cart and taking off his camouflage backpack. "By the way, your family loves you. A lot."

With a gentle tug, Zig removed the flag from the coffin and folded it carefully, making sure it never touched the floor. "I saw your wife next door. Lucky man," Zig said, now thinking of his own ex, which caught him by surprise. They'd been divorced for nearly fifteen years. "Just remember, sir—your wife was lucky to have you, too."

Zig snapped on a pair of nitrile medical gloves, then lowered his head for the quick prayer he said in every case. *"Please give me strength to take care of the fallen so their family can begin healing."* Yet no matter how much strength Zig prayed for, he knew the grieving family would always need more.

At that moment, Zig thought that the government was taking extra good care of Mint. But as he was about to find out, he had no idea what the government was really up to.

Unhooking the coffin's wooden latch, Zig lifted the lid and got his first good look inside—at Archie Mint's broken body.

3

A clear plastic bag covered Lieutenant Colonel Mint's face, like he was suffocating. Standard Dover procedure—to make sure that in transit, makeup didn't get on the fallen soldier's uniform.

Zig pulled out his phone and some earbuds. Fighting the urge to put on "La Vie Bohème," he instead went with Paul Simon's *Graceland*. "Diamonds on the Soles of Her Shoes." Zig's best work was always done with music.

"There you go—just like that," Zig said, gently removing the plastic, then carefully lowering the colonel's head back onto the satin pillow.

"You earned your rest, sir," Zig said, taking a longer look at Mint's face. Chiseled features, jaw like a movie star. Handsome, even now, Zig thought, noticing the ribbon rack on Mint's chest, decorated with medals. Among them, one stood out—the Soldier's Medal, which was awarded for a heroic act that didn't involve enemy combat, like saving someone in a fire. "Real superhero, huh?" Zig asked as Paul Simon sang in his ear about a poor boy who was empty as a pocket with nothing to lose.

Whoever prepped the body at Dover had done tremendous work. The problem was, so had the heat. With the high temperatures in the hearse, the molding clay that'd been used to rebuild the colonel's face was now waxy and melted, revealing the outlines of the bullet hole in his cheek, as well as the pockmarks from the glass that had torn through his skin. According to the medical examiner's report, Mint was shot through a car window.

"Um . . . Mr. Zigarowski? I'm sorry to do this, but in terms of timeline . . ." Clifford called, sticking his head in the room. He motioned to Mint's family behind him. "They're . . . uh . . . they want to know when they can begin."

"Five minutes," Zig said as Clifford shut the door.

Turning up the Paul Simon, Zig pulled out a bottle of . . . "Got you some lighter fluid," he told the colonel, wetting a makeup brush with one of the few liquids that would break down the wax and make it more pliable. "Don't tell the suburban moms—this is the cheapest face-lift of all."

With a few artful swirls of the makeup brush, Zig slowly redistributed the wax, meticulously resculpting everything back into place. This was Zig's gift: no matter how bad the damage, he could put back together what had been taken apart, giving families a sense of closure they never thought they'd—

"*Ahem!*" someone coughed.

Zig looked up, pulling out his earbuds.

"The family— She has a question for you," Clifford explained, stepping aside and revealing a woman with chestnut-colored hair that was pulled back in a faultless bun. She was petite, compact, but solid in her shoulders, radiating strength. *Definitely military,* Zig thought. Lieutenant Colonel Mint's wife, Tessa.

"We were just hoping . . ." Tessa motioned to the body. "These are— For the coffin," she said, handing Zig an Adidas sneaker box with no lid. Inside were a few old photos, a worn leather baseball glove, and a single yellow Post-it with a handwritten note that read, "YOU CAN."

Tessa started to explain, but she didn't have to. Behind her, frozen in the doorway, were two kids: a lanky seventeen-year-old boy with blond hair like his dad's and a neck that curved like a comma, and a black-haired girl who was clutching a cell phone with two hands, like she was strangling it. The girl was twelve, with doubting eyes and dark scabs on both her knees and elbows. Zig liked her immediately, especially when he saw what was written on the child-sized baseball glove.

Make sure I win this week, Daddy. Love, Violet.

"If it's okay, I'd like to see him now," Mint's wife said, leaning hard on the word *I*. She wasn't letting her children any closer, standing in front of them like a lioness, one arm blocking their way.

"Of course, ma'am, lemme just . . ." Tearing off a strip of gray masking tape, Zig wrapped it around his hand, sticky side out. With a steady, almost reverent stroke, he rolled the tape—which was stronger than any lint brush—from Lieutenant Colonel Mint's chest down to the white gloves on his hands, which were, as always, positioned left over right, so the wedding hand had prominence.

As the tape kissed the wrist of the colonel's white gloves, the lip of the right glove lifted, revealing a plastic glove inside—another Dover custom, to keep body fluids from seeping out. Inside that glove, Zig noticed a spot of blood—from three deep scratches on the back of the colonel's hand.

Zig made a mental note. Bodies get scratched all the time, but in the Dover report that Zig saw, there was no mention of it. To make sure the family didn't see the blood, Zig quickly readjusted the colonel's hands—to make sure the left completely covered the right, moving the colonel's thumb just so.

"He'd appreciate your sense of perfection," Tessa said. "When he ate, he wouldn't let any of his food touch each other—even spaghetti and meatballs," she explained, her voice catching as she laughed and cried in the same breath.

She was strong, trying to use humor as armor. But as Tessa stepped forward to finally see her dead husband up close, well . . . at the real ground zero of it all . . . there's no protection strong enough.

"I thought he'd— They told me he wouldn't look this good," Tessa said, her face lighting up with . . . it could only be described as relief. It's what military families understood better than anyone: the simultaneous terror and joy that comes from seeing your loved one one last time. "His face . . . they said the bullet . . . *He looks beautiful*," she blurted, the tears now rolling down her cheeks. "You got his smile right, too. He was a terrible smiler." Even the kids started to laugh. "Thank you for this."

He deserves no less, Zig thought to himself.

"I'm serious," Tessa added. "What you did was magic."

"I used to work at Dover, too," Zig explained. "I appreciate his service there."

"Who, *Archie?* Archie was in the reserves. He never worked at Dover," Tessa said, looking confused. "I think you—"

"Ma'am, we should really get going," one of the funeral employees—a man with a flat nose—interrupted, cutting in front of Zig.

Zig backed up out of respect, but was lost. Yesterday, when Wil called, he'd insisted that Mint was *one of ours*—a Dover employee.

"Ma'am, the crowd's waiting," Flat Nose added, Zig now noticing the fresh shine on the man's shoes. Zig had thought he was a fireman or a cop, but a shine like that . . . that was military polish, like he was wearing the rumpled suit to blend in. There was a bulge at the back of Flat Nose's jacket. Definitely carrying a gun.

Flat Nose gave a nod, and a phalanx of volunteers appeared from nowhere, swirling around the coffin, carrying flowers, picture frames, a new American flag. There was even an eighty-year-old man with a trumpet, who would play taps at the end. Within seconds, the coffin was moving, the family following behind, everyone on their way.

"We got it from here," Flat Nose said to Zig, raising his hand like a crossing guard.

For Zig, the job was done. Yet as he stared down at Flat Nose's gleaming shoes, as he replayed the confusion on Tessa's face when she heard her husband worked at Dover, and especially as he noticed the way Flat Nose was gripping Tessa's arm, practically yanking her away from the coffin . . .

"Actually, I was thinking of attending the service," Zig said to Flat Nose.

"I told you, *we got it from here,*" Flat Nose insisted.

"I'm sure you do," Zig said, flashing a grin. "But y'know . . . out of respect." Sidestepping around him, Zig stayed with the coffin—

and Mint's wife, who held tight to her daughter. "See you inside," Zig added, following right behind them.

"AND NOW, PLEASE JOIN ME as we pray," the chaplain began.

"*Almighty God . . .*" the crowd began to read from their prayer cards, their voices echoing through the bleachers.

Zig stood just inside the door of the gymnasium—never taking a seat—so he'd have a better view of everyone inside. On the far side of the gym, past the bleachers, Flat Nose stood inside the opposite door. When the service first started, the other funeral employees were handing out prayer cards and ushering people to open seats. But even now, Flat Nose just stood there, scanning the crowd, like he was looking for something. Or someone.

Something clearly wasn't right. *But what the hell's got you so jumpy?* Zig wondered, following Flat Nose's stare to the crowd. Even in the packed bleachers, the funeral looked like it always did: family members in the front row, mourners in the other rows, and a few strangers in the back rows, stealing glances at their phones. There were local politicians in nice suits, local press in cheap suits, and photographers and cameramen in even cheaper suits, all packed in the corner, a tiny firing squad, just waiting for Mint's wife to give her eulogy so they could get footage of her sobbing as everyone muttered words like "so young" and "so unfair."

And of course, there was a smattering of elderly vets—the Veterans of Foreign Wars—decked out in their old military caps, waiting to do the twenty-one-gun salute at the cemetery and then go to the local bar to tell war stories. Zig wondered if maybe today was the day he'd go with them.

"*Ahuuuhuuuh,*" a voice rang out. Twelve-year-old Violet started to cry, and now her brother was shaking, too. Silently, breathlessly, they tried to hold it together, Tessa clutching them both—one in each arm—as every person in the gym stared their way while trying not to look like they were.

Zig caught himself doing the same, then looked away.

It was the only reason he noticed the door as it opened on the opposite side of the gym. A shadow flickered. At first, Zig thought it was Flat Nose, but it was someone new. A woman with caramel skin. Zig assumed it was another mourner, maybe a reporter, someone running late.

The shadow moved again, and as the light revealed the woman, Zig's eyes went wide. Those pointy features . . . the silver, moon-colored hair with a black streak . . .

"Nola . . . ?" Zig whispered, not even realizing he was saying the name. He'd known her since she was little. The woman who once saved his daughter's life. *"What the hell're you doing here?"*

4

Nola.

That was definitely Nola.

At the sight of her, Zig's windpipe clenched. Earlier, he'd been thinking about her saving Maggie's life . . . but two years ago, on that case at Dover . . . she'd saved Zig's life, too. Swallowing hard, he could taste that bitter coppery tang. Blood. He'd never forget the taste of his own blood.

On that night, Zig was beaten with a metal crowbar. Broken ulna, two black eyes, a severe orbital rim fracture, and fourteen stitches between his forehead and chin. It was this woman—Sergeant First Class Nola Brown—who saved him . . . they saved each other actually . . . from Royall—Nola's foster dad—who had tracked her down, trying to murder her.

It'd been two years since Zig had last seen her.

As she made her way toward the bleachers, she moved like she always did—slow, determined, with unmistakable presence and power for someone in her late twenties. Nola didn't walk; she lurked, like a hunter, her willful lips pursed, her chin tucked into her chest, like she was forever trying to avoid being seen.

It wasn't working. Behind her, hidden by an honor guard holding an American flag and an Army one, Flat Nose glanced her way, then lifted his wrist to his mouth. Handheld mic. Like the Secret Service. He was calling it in. This whole time, that's who he was waiting for. Nola.

"Amen," the crowd said at one of those prompts where everyone knows what to say.

For a moment, Nola stood there, studying the mourners who packed the bleachers, scanning them, her eyes sliding left to ri—

She glanced back over her shoulder, turning toward the honor guard. Even from here, Zig could tell—something was wrong. Her eyes narrowed. He'd seen that look before—that uncomfortable mental tug when someone feels like they're being watched.

Flat Nose looked away, shrinking back behind the flags.

If Nola noticed, she wasn't reacting. She continued her search, eyeing the coffin, the chaplain, the flowers—then quickly turning her attention to Zig's side of the gym.

Zig stepped backward, out of the doorway. Did Nola see him? Not a chance. He was too fast and she was too far.

But then Zig remembered . . . Nola saw everything.

Peering back across the threshold, Zig spotted her leaving, rushing out. Yet as she reached the door, Nola glanced back over her shoulder. Like she'd known he was there the entire time.

Their eyes locked.

Contact.

Zig stood there frozen, and then, like a child, raised his hand and . . . waved. *Oh, God, did I just wave at her?*

Nola's black eyes narrowed. *Stay away,* she warned with a dark glare.

Then she ran, dashing out into the hallway, a few people turning, but most barely noticing.

Before the door slammed, Flat Nose was moving, weaving his way through the honor guard, whispering something into his handheld mic while striding after her. As Flat Nose darted through the doorway, Zig noticed that the bulge in his jacket was gone. He'd pulled his gun.

Nola . . . ! Zig wanted to call out. It wouldn't help. She was already out the door, with no idea what was coming.

Don't jump to conclusions, Zig told himself. *For all you know, Flat Nose is one of the good guys and Nola did something wrong.*

But across the gym, as the door slammed shut, Zig was replaying that moment two years ago when the metal crowbar collided with his throat. A burst of blood had flooded forward. He couldn't breathe. He thought it had crushed his larynx. Nola's foster dad—Royall—wound up again. This was it. Curled on the ground, Zig closed his eyes and muttered a final prayer . . . until Nola rushed in and fired three quick shots. She'd come back—putting her own life at risk to save Zig. *How the hell can I leave her now?*

Zig started to move, then stopped himself. *Walk away, avoid her problems.* But when it came to someone in trouble, and especially when it came to Nola, he could never just walk away.

In a burst, Zig darted up the hallway on his side of the gym and reached for the knife in his pocket. *Dammit dammit dammit,* he thought, knowing full well that he'd regret this.

5

Running now, his knees already aching, Zig followed the hallway around to the right. He passed a janitor's closet, a half-empty trophy case, and even the driver of the hearse—a young private with a moon-shaped chin—who was waiting in the hallway, ready to take the coffin to the cemetery.

"Mr. Zigarowski, is everything . . . ?"

"You see anyone run this way?" Zig yelled.

"Mr. Zigarowski, are you . . . ?"

Zig blew past him, picking up speed. Nola and Flat Nose couldn't have gotten f—

Turning the final corner, Zig was moving so fast, he nearly stepped on a coat that was on the floor. He jumped, hurdling over it. But it wasn't a coat. It was a man—Flat Nose—facedown on the gray-and-white linoleum, his arms and legs splayed outward, his body motionless.

Mothertrucker. If she killed him . . .

Zig slid on his knees, even dropped his knife as he felt for a pulse. Thank God. Still breathing.

On Flat Nose's forehead were two red welts, one on each temple. Zig had seen those before, from Nola's favorite weapon—a homemade insulated glove with metal pins, just a centimeter long, at the thumb and pinkie. When she pressed the pins into your temple, your body vibrated with more electricity than a military-grade stun gun. Whoever Flat Nose was, he didn't have a chance.

"Okay, big man, don't vomit on me," Zig said, tugging Flat Nose onto his side, into the fetal position. He tilted the man's head just right, to open his airway and make sure he wouldn't choke if he threw up.

"Nola, you still here!?" Zig called out, rummaging through Flat Nose's jacket, searching for ID. Better to know who he was—or at least who he worked for.

Nothing. The ID was gone. So were his wallet, gun, even his radio. Nola had picked him clean.

So what the hell does this have to do with Colonel Mint? Zig wondered, putting away his knife and remembering the Dover report. Two nights ago, during what seemed like a home invasion, a robber had shot Archie Mint in the face, and murdered a valet named Anthony Wojowicz. *Did Nola come here for Mint . . . or did she know the valet?* Mint seemed more likely—he and Nola were both military.

But as Zig rolled the facts through his brain, he couldn't shake the feeling that if the government was sending armed agents to a funeral— and hiding Mint's real assignment from his own wife—this was about far more than a petty robbery.

So what was Nola's stake? Zig took another look around. On this side of the gym, the long hallway was empty. Straight ahead was a doorway that led outside; on his left was a staircase that led upstairs.

Wherever she went, Nola was gone.

Of course she is, Zig thought, still reeling from the sheer coincidence of—

Wait.

Zig closed his eyes, replaying it again.

God. How could he be so blind? For Nola to be here *at the exact same time, in the exact same spot* that Zig was . . .

No way was this all a coincidence.

Pulling out his phone and stepping over Flat Nose to give himself some space, Zig clicked to *Recent Calls.* Dover Air Force Base. He gave it a tap. It rang twice.

"Mortuary Branch Chief," Wil-with-one-L answered. "How can I—?"

"You think I'm a damn moron?"

"Ziggy? Is that—?"

"I know you have caller ID, Wil. And I also know you're full of manure," Zig said, still scouring the hallway and shoving open the door that led outside. There was a parking lot with scattered orange traffic cones. The practice area for driver's ed. Fenced in. If Nola came this way, she'd have to go up and over the fence. Zig let the door shut and headed for the stairwell. "This case, Wil. No more lies. Why'd you put me on this case?"

"I told you—"

"Please don't say it's because I'm the best sculptor."

"I swear on my mother's eyes, Zig, that's the truth. When the weather gets this hot, stiffs melt and—"

"Don't call them *stiffs*. They're our fallen."

"You know what I'm s—"

"There were armed agents here, Wil—quiet operators from the look of it—at a funeral! They were whispering in their sleeves like the President himself was coming."

"Ziggy, I have no idea what you're—"

"That's strike two. Oh, and I spoke to Mint's wife. According to her, her husband never spent a day working at Dover."

"Can you please listen?"

"I saw her, Wil. I saw Nola."

There was a pause on the line. A long one.

"You were looking for her, weren't you? That's why your men were here—she's the one you were hunting," Zig challenged, shoving open the door to a pale yellow stairwell, realizing it was the same color yellow as the original morgue at Dover—to reduce stress and keep employees calm. It wasn't having its intended effect here.

The stairwell was quiet. No sounds of anyone running.

"You knew she saved my life—that I knew her when she was little," Zig added. "So you figured *what*—that bringing me in would somehow distract her and knock her off balance? Then you could send in the big guns and they'd—"

"Ziggy, you have to understand, we had no—"

"Who's *we*?"

Wil paused again, then blurted a single name. "Whatley."

Air Force Colonel O. J. Whatley. Dover's new wing commander, in charge of the entire place. A year and a half ago, when Colonel Hsu was promoted and Master Guns retired, O.J. took over the mortuary and its homicide investigation team.

"Why's the head of Dover looking at Nola?" Zig asked, hearing a noise on his left. At the far end of the hall, a uniformed policeman was kneeling over the still-unconscious Flat Nose, checking his vitals.

Zig's eyes narrowed. According to the funeral plans, security was being run by the Pennsylvania State Police, all of them in gray formal ceremonial dress uniforms and Smokey Bear hats. This officer was in a dark blue beat-cop uniform. The only one in the whole gym dressed like that.

"Sir . . . can I help you?" Zig called out.

The cop stood up, quickly walking away, leaving Flat Nose behind.

"Come to the office," Wil said through the phone. "Colonel What-ley can explain."

"How about *you* explain instead?"

"Just come to the office."

Zig hung up the phone. If he wanted answers, the beat cop was the far better bet.

"Officer!" Zig called out.

The cop didn't stop. Instead, he ducked into a nearby stairwell, the door swinging shut behind him.

Picking up speed, Zig sprinted after him. At the stairwell, he shoved his hip into the door and—

"You had a question for me?" a flat voice asked.

Zig tried to hit the brakes, but instead slammed directly into the chest of the police officer, who barely moved at the impact. The cop was short—five foot eight—but built solid, like concrete.

"Mr. Zigarowski, yes?" the cop said, his voice deliberate and mea-sured. "You're looking for her, too." It wasn't a question.

"Excuse me?"

"I apologize for eavesdropping. I was . . . I heard your conversa-tion," the officer said. "Nola Brown. You know her."

"Who the hell're *you?*"

The officer smiled a broken smile that looked more like something he'd memorized than something he actually felt. "Roddy LaPointe." He smiled wider, working hard at it. "I'm Nola's brother."

6

This was Roddy when he was seven.

He was a boy who was good at hiding things. This knife was a perfect example. He'd stolen the switchblade with the pakkawood handle from Gary Dubursky's older brother.

Holding it now in his open palm, Roddy liked the weight of the knife—it had heft, like it mattered—and though he couldn't verbalize it yet, he knew that not everything in life mattered.

With his thumb, Roddy pressed the knife's silver button. The spear blade sprang out like a Nazi salute.

"Roddy, you dumb shit, we're not even looking for you anymore!" yelled twelve-year-old Ellen P., the one girl on the block who everyone was afraid of. "No one cares!"

"I bet he's out of bounds," clucked Chad, a mouthy ten-year-old.

Back before he and Nola got rescued from the group home in Arkansas, Roddy had learned the consequences of being out of bounds. Here, he wasn't out of bounds. He was twenty feet straight up, well hidden by the leaves of the crooked red maple tree that served as home base for their game, a hasty merger of freeze tag and hide-and-seek.

Standing on a branch that curved like a hammock, he stared down at the tops of Chad's and Ellen's heads, watching them move around like ants. Roddy stretched his arm straight out, dangling the knife from his fingertips.

A few weeks ago, someone had lit a fire in the newspaper vending machine outside of Margie's Luncheonette. Two weeks before that, one of the girls in Roddy's class had come home crying, saying her knapsack smelled like pee. And last week, a neighbor had accused Roddy of using a stick to poke out her cat's eye. Roddy swore on Jesus he didn't do any of it.

In response, Roddy's new foster dad, Mr. LaPointe, told him, "There's both a Good Roddy and a Bad Roddy inside you—but you need to feed the good one. D'y'understand?"

Roddy shook his head. He didn't understand.

"Try it like this," added Mr. LaPointe, a devoted churchgoer. "We each have a little monster inside us."

"A real monster?"

"Kinda real. Sorta real. Like the Bad Roddy versus the Good Roddy. You have to look inside and— Try it like this. In those moments where you want to figure out good from evil, well . . . y'know that little whisper that you hear at the back of your head? That's your conscience—it'll always lead you right."

It was wise advice. Lately, though, the whisper at the back of Roddy's head was starting to get louder.

"I bet he quit," Ellen P. said, clearly annoyed as she took a seat at the base of the tree.

Roddy wouldn't quit. Not when he was having fun like this, pinching the knife between his pointer finger and thumb, letting it dangle, the blade pointed straight at Ellen P.'s head.

"Hey, Nola, your brother run away?" Ellen P. called out to the little girl with the black eyes who was standing there with the group, but somehow also standing there by herself.

"Who you think's weirder—him or you?" Chad added.

Nola stood there, eyeing a big rock on the ground, wondering what sound it would make hitting Chad in the teeth.

Up in the tree, Roddy shifted his outstretched arm to the left, now dangling the knife over Chad's head. All he had to do was let go. He didn't even need to aim. Gravity would do the rest. A smile lit Roddy's eyes. An erection expanded in his pants. There was a deep thrill that came with thinking about the silver blade plummeting straight into

Chad's skull, but there was also something else . . . something Roddy didn't quite have a word for.

"You're definitely the weirder one, ain't you, Nola?" Chad asked.

Nola still didn't respond, didn't move, didn't do anything, still staring at the rock.

Fight back, Roddy tried to tell his sister, his fingers moistening with sweat, the knife still dangling above Chad's head.

"She's *definitely* the weirder one," Ellen P. taunted, Roddy now moving the knife over Ellen, then back over Chad, and then, to his own surprise—in a perfect swirl of rage, embarrassment, and helplessness—Roddy shifted his arm so the knife was directly above his sister Nola.

For the rest of his life, Roddy would think back to this moment. It was here—as the knife dangled from his plump fingertips . . . as he held it above his twin sister's head—that seven-year-old Roddy LaPointe finally understood the electric charge currently coursing through him.

This switchblade knife with the pakkawood handle wasn't just a cheap thrill, or a childish impulse, or even a self-destructive whisper at the back of his head.

It was power.

That was the word for it. This knife . . . it gave Roddy *power*. And dear God, after all he'd been through in Arkansas, it felt good to have power.

"Roddy, where the hell are you!?" Ellen P. demanded.

I'm right here, Roddy thought, staring down at Ellen's head, at all their heads, tiny targets that taught him what none of his future therapists or court-appointed counselors would ever take the time to explain: that the most potent power in the entire world came from having power over someone else.

Naturally, at seven years old, Roddy couldn't articulate any of that. He just knew he felt good. Better than he'd ever felt in his life.

He wanted that feeling back again. And soon, he'd get it.

In the distance, the jingle of an arriving ice cream truck sent the kids, including Nola, scattering up the block.

Their hiding game was over. Roddy put the knife away, his adrenaline levels returning to normal. His foster dad was right, though. We all have a little monster inside us.

7

"I don't mean to be rude," Zig said, "but let me be rude. Since when does Nola have a brother?"

"Um, I guess since birth," Roddy said, adding a puffy little laugh. Zig didn't laugh back.

"We were— They split us up as kids," Roddy explained, standing there, one hand on his police baton, the other fidgeting with the tip of his black tie. He had spidery fingers that stood out even in the poorly lit stairwell. "I stayed with our foster family—the LaPointes— but Nola got sent to—"

"How'd you know my name?"

"Huh?"

"Before. You called me *Mr. Zigarowski*. Who told you my name?"

Roddy swayed there a moment, blinking slowly, like his wiring was slightly off. He had a nasal voice, high in pitch, but he also spoke slowly and precisely, like he had a plan, or at least knew what happens when there's a lack of one. "From the story. In the newspaper. I saw it online a few years back," Roddy said with another slow blink. "Nola's foster dad—"

"Royall," Zig said.

"Yes. Royall. According to the newspaper, foster dad Royall was running some sorta scam against the military. Nola shut it down. They gave her a commendation and everything."

That was the sanitized version that the military released to the public, though it left out the most important part. To save Zig's life, Nola had put a bullet in her foster dad's head. She disappeared soon after.

"She's my sister—my twin," Roddy added, Zig now doing what everyone does when they hear someone's a twin: looking for the resemblance, trying to decide if it's there or not.

"You don't believe me," Roddy said, taking off his police cap and revealing caramel skin, a pointy face, and a nose that had clearly been broken. He was young, late twenties, though as with so many cops and soldiers, his weary eyes—clones of Nola's, black with flecks of gold—looked like they'd lived through a few extra decades. "I haven't seen her since we were— We must've been seven."

"So a few years ago, you saw a mention of her online—and then, what? You've spent all this time trying to track her down?"

"Ever lost any family, Mr. Zigarowski?"

Zig stayed silent.

"I'm sorry. I offended you. Because your daughter passed away," Roddy said, Zig now realizing Roddy was missing that filter that stopped him from saying every loose thought in his head. "I read about your daughter, Maggie, when I looked you up."

"Maybe it's better if we stay focused on Nola," Zig said, now replaying his call with Wil from Dover. For some reason, the head of Dover, in charge of all their homicide investigators, was looking for Nola. Now her brother—a cop—shows up, doing the same. Whatever was really going on, it was bigger than anyone was saying, enough to bring Nola out of hiding.

"I'm not stalking you, Mr. Zigarowski. Nola's my blood relative—the only one I have. And I know this sounds a bit nutty, but it's . . . it's like I can feel her out there, y'know? Like she's my twin in ways that . . . Again, a bit nutty, but it's like my pieces aren't pulled together until I—" He took a breath. "I just really want to find her."

It wasn't completely nutty. Anyone with a missing twin would do the same. But as Roddy's spidery fingers pinched the brim of his police cap, Zig could feel that twitch in the back of his brain, the same one he'd get when he was reading the morning paper and saw a young person's obituary that was conspicuously silent about the cause of death. *There's more to that story,* Zig would think, which was exactly what he was thinking right now.

"Roddy, how'd you know Nola would be here today?"

Still staring over Zig's shoulder, out into the hallway, Roddy said, "You don't trust me, do you, Mr. Zigarowski? You think I'm here to hurt her."

"I met you two minutes ago. It's a little early t—"

"I had problems when I was little. Real problems. But I've turned those around. I got help."

"I'm glad you did, Roddy. But that still doesn't tell me—"

"They knew each other."

"Pardon?"

"Nola and Colonel Mint. They weren't strangers."

Zig figured as much, but it was time to get more info. "According to who?"

"I'm police," Roddy said, pointing with his chin to the badge on his chest. "That's my job—finding things that aren't meant to be found. Nola and Mint . . . they spent time together."

"Meaning they served together? Or they had something more—?"

"Huck! Huck . . . please . . . please just wait!" a female voice echoed from the hallway.

Zig turned just in time to see a lanky boy with a long neck— Mint's son—as he burst through the gym doors, his mother, Tessa, chasing behind him.

"Ican'tIcan'tIcant," Huck pleaded, moving quickly, shaking his head over and over. He wasn't running. He was stumbling, practically falling, crashing on his knees, nearly slamming into the trophy case.

Behind him, in the gym, the crowd was singing a hymn—"How Great Thou Art"—their voices reverberating up the hallway.

"Ican'tIcan't . . ." Huck repeated as his mother caught up to him, dropping to her knees and wrapping her arms around him, like he was a grenade and she was willing to take the impact.

"Huck . . . sweetie . . . I'm here . . . right here," Tessa said. She started to say something else, but immediately knew words weren't what mattered. *"I'm here, I'm here, I'm here,"* she repeated, hugging him tighter than ever, young Huck twisting and turning, his face bright red, his teeth gritted, his long neck trying to stretch out of her grip, like his head was about to unscrew from his body. "We'll get through this," Tessa insisted.

Watching from the stairwell, all Zig could picture was his own daughter's funeral, right as it started, as they were about to walk out from the private receiving area and enter the room that held the waiting crowd. As Zig had stepped forward, he reached over to hold his wife's hand. She pulled away. Right there, Zig knew that Maggie wasn't the only thing being buried that day.

"I-It's too hard, Mom," Huck said.

"It is," Tessa agreed. "But I'm still here. I'm not going anywhere. Now let's go make Daddy proud." And just like that, she tugged her son to his feet and they headed back toward the gym.

"God bless strong mothers, huh?" Zig said, still in the stairwell.

When Roddy didn't reply, Zig glanced over his shoulder.

The stairwell was empty. Roddy—and Agent Flat Nose—were both gone.

8

This was Nola when she was fuming.

She was sketching, of course, sitting on the roof's parapet, which was covered in bird shit. She didn't care. Her pencil was moving in a blur.

Four floors down, the crowd exited the funeral, streaming into the street like an ever-expanding octopus. A few were crying and hugging, but the majority were making small talk, checking their phones, picking out where to go to lunch. *No surprise,* Nola thought. Death was terrible company. Three steps outside the funeral and most people just wanted to get back to their lives.

"To those joining the procession, please put a magnet on your car and put your bright headlights on," a funeral employee announced. "Also, with a crowd of this size, please be aware of your surroundings."

Nola was most definitely aware.

On her sketch pad, she drew every detail she remembered from the gym—the coffin in front, the pastor at the podium. She added some crosshatching to his chin, trying to get his face just right. He had watery eyes, cataracts coming. But the rendering . . . something still looked wrong. It was the same with every other face in the bleachers—from the man with the feral eyes and overgrown mustache to the forty-year-old woman whose kids sat next to her in size order—everyone looked too angular. Her line work was short and choppy.

Nola knew why. This was how she drew when she was distracted. Angry, if she was being honest. Fuming.

She took a breath, closed her eyes.

Mongol . . . Faber . . . Staedtler . . . Ticonderoga . . . Swan. Nola flipped through the mental list the psychiatrists gave her for when her rage was too much. *Mongol . . . Faber . . . Staedtler . . .*

She tried picturing Lieutenant Colonel Mint, then the so-called funeral employee with the flat nose who she put down in the hallway. But all she kept seeing was Zig.

Such a pain in the ass. She didn't like Zig, didn't like the way he always looked at her with pity in his eyes, like she was someone he was there to rescue. It made her feel like she was twelve again . . . and if Nola wanted one thing in life, it was to never feel twelve again.

The question remained, though: *What the hell was he doing here?* She sketched his face, the deep worry lines and wide eyes. He looked confused, almost as surprised as she was.

Even when Nola was little, when she was drawing, she saw things—things she didn't even realize were there. When her pencil hit the page, the full image appeared. Her art teacher, Ms. Sable, called it a gift. Army psychologists saw it as a different sort of asset, selecting her to be the Army's Artist-in-Residence.

Since World War I, the Army had kept an artist—an actual painter—on staff, to document everything from the beaches of Normandy to Vietnam to 9/11. With Nola's ability to spot things as she painted—like an elderly Iraqi man who was strolling through a village—she could find what everyone else overlooked, like the phone the old Iraqi was carrying. On that day, Nola looked up mid-brushstroke. The village had no cell service. Moving in close and putting a knife to the man's throat, she confirmed that what he was really holding was a detonator.

According to her supervisors, Nola saved at least a dozen lives that afternoon. From there, the Army quickly realized that her observational skills were something they could use to track and kill those who did harm in this world, which was fine by Nola, since, my God, did she excel at that.

Now sketching the edges of Zig's shoulders, Nola added two straps: a backpack for his mortician tools. Was that why he came? To work on Mint's body? That made some sense—still, for it to be Zig of all people. No way was that coincidence.

In her pocket were the ID and wallet that she'd swiped from the flat-nosed "funeral employee" she hit with the electroglove. Sergeant First Class Malcolm Green, at least according to his CAC, the ID card carried by all active military. Twenty-nine years old, from South Carolina. Like a careful soldier, he didn't keep any mention of his unit or who he worked for in his wallet, though as Nola flipped through his photos, she found a family pic from a recent holiday ball.

Around his blond wife's neck was the same type of gold charm so many spouses get from Rhudy's Jewelry in North Carolina. The charm had a hand grabbing two lightning bolts. In gold sparkly letters were the words *Semper Vigiles,* Latin for *Vigilant Always.*

"Fuck," Nola whispered, suddenly feeling like there were ants under her skin, crawling from the back of her neck and fanning out down her arms. That unit . . . she knew that unit. Of course it was them, her past back to haunt her. *Vigilant Always.*

She started to sweat, scribbling harder now, searching to see who else they might've hidden in the crowd. Shifting the sketch pad, she took another look at her drawings of the pastor, then Mint's wife and kids . . . the crying boy with the thin neck and the daughter with the scabbed knees—Huck and Violet—there was something in their faces . . .

Nola leaned closer, recognizing that cocktail of loss and anger in both their eyes. They'd never be the same. But in the daughter's eyes, there was something else, too. Defiance? Disobedience? Nola didn't have the word for it yet, but she'd seen it before in her own life. Loss was always the best tutor.

In the distance, dozens of car doors slammed all at once, a chorus of mourners headed to the cemetery. Nola turned at the sound; her pencil broke on the page. Mint's kids didn't deserve this. Pulling a new pencil from her bag, Nola added a few extra lines to the flag on Mint's coffin, replaying that day all those years ago when she first encountered that unit back at Warehouse 3, or as the military codenamed it, *Grandma's Pantry.*

Nola scribbled the words below Mint's coffin, not even realizing she was doing it. *Fool. You're a novice fool,* she told herself, erasing them just as fast. *When did you get so sloppy?*—though she knew the answer. This close to home, this close to her old life, to Mint and what he did for her . . . then to have Zig show up . . . That was why they'd sent him, wasn't it? The dumb old dope was so excited to come back, he didn't even realize he—and she—were being used. As always, the unit had a simple goal before they attacked: Make her emotional. Careless.

Nola was usually too smart to let things get personal, but the way her blood was starting to churn . . . *No. Don't let them dictate your path. Find your calm and you'll find who's behind this.*

Forcing herself to keep drawing, she held her pencil tight, sketching bystanders in the bleachers. She tilted her head, taking notice as one in particular came into view. The man was squat and wore a uniform . . . a cop, Nola realized. But as she started filling in his face—those eyes . . . she knew those eyes . . . they were just like hers—

No.

She hadn't seen him in decades. But there he was. In the crowd at the funeral.

Her twin brother. Roddy.

Nola's pencil stabbed through the page, nearly puncturing his face. He was polished and clean now—a cop—but at his core, she knew who he really was.

Nola was moving now, scrambling, bits of gravel spraying across the rooftop, her brain churning through all the possibilities.

The fact that Roddy was here— That meant he knew. *He knew the truth about Mint . . . that she and Mint—*

Get out! Now! she told herself.

Bursting into the stairwell, Nola darted down, down, down, praying she had it wrong. She needed to run, leave, get answers. Jumping down the last three steps, she hit the push bar at full speed, sending the metal door swinging wide. Someone was crying, and a few mourners still lingered in the parking lot.

Nola lowered her head, speed-walking toward the lot. She thought she'd had it figured out, even the Zig part, but with Roddy in the mix . . . the way he was hiding there, lying in wait . . . A darker thought filled her brain.

Mongol . . . Faber . . . Staedtler . . .

She didn't want to think it. Her head was still down, trying to stay out of sight. When Nola first heard what happened to Mint, she immediately came running, like this was one of her old missions. But it was time to admit: This wasn't a mission. It was a trap—and she was standing at the center of—

Kllk.

"Sergeant Brown, you seem like a reasonable person, so I'm going to make a reasonable request," a man whispered behind her, pressing his gun to the back of her head. "Show me those hands."

Nola started to turn, reaching for her electroglove.

"And don't think I'm gonna let you zap me in the head. Malcolm's still pissed about that," he said, yanking the glove from her hand, the speed of his attack sending her colored pencils flying across the asphalt, his gun still at her head. He was massive, but spectacularly fast, in a cheap suit just like the other so-called funeral employee. The giveaway was his weapon.

"Please just make this easy, Sergeant Brown," he added, pulling down on the bolt release.

Nola knew that sound. Submachine gun. Special Forces.

Without a word, Nola raised her hands in the air.

Smiling, he pulled out his handheld mic. "I got her. Package en route," he said. "Yeah. Don't worry. I'm on it."

Shoving her forward with his gun, he reached for his handcuffs. "I don't know what you did, Sergeant Brown, but damn, is my boss excited to see you."

9

"He's a big fat liar," Waggs said through the phone.

"You don't know that," Zig replied, gripping the steering wheel, the small earbud microphone swaying near his chin.

"I *do* know that, Ziggy. And y'know how I know?"

"Because you looked him up."

"Because I looked him up . . . and more important, because of what I *found*," Waggs said. As head of the FBI unit that gathered terrorists' biometrics from explosive devices, Amy Waggs was a master at uncovering what people left behind. As Zig's first friend at Dover, back when her husband had decided he was gay and asked for permission to date his law partner Andrew, she was also a master at Zig.

"Can I make a prediction, Ziggy?"

"Is this a real question, or is this like that time when you tried to convince me that oatmeal cookies were real cookies, even though we both know they're cruel insults made of cardboard?"

"Wow, going with an old joke about oatmeal cookies," she said, well aware of how Zig always dealt with nervousness.

"That's a new joke."

"And an old habit. Remember that night on the first anniversary of your divorce," she said, "when Charmaine posted all those Facebook photos of her and her friends at some bar, all of them making horrible kissy faces and toasting with their fruity pink drinks like it was some middle-age bachelorette party? Y'know how many jokes you made that night, Ziggy?"

Zig stayed silent, remembering the photos perfectly, especially the one where Charmaine, his ex, was smiling wide, looking genuinely happy. On that night, Zig didn't call anyone. But Waggs called him.

"This is me, Ziggy. No more jokes. Whoever's chasing Nola, however she's tied to Colonel Mint's death, I'm telling you . . . the more you dive into this, the more you're gonna get hurt."

"Waggs, I appreciate the concern, but—"

"You're not listening. This is what Nola always does. The moment someone puts their neck out for her, she chops their head off."

Glancing in his rearview, Zig spotted a black Acura. Washington, D.C., plates. Not a big deal. D.C. was barely an hour and a half away. "Can you please just tell me what you found about her brother?"

"No. Not until you open your eyes. I know you and Nola have a history—she grew up in your hometown, and more important, was friends with your daughter . . ."

"This has nothing to do with Maggie!"

Waggs let out a laugh. A real one. "You really can't make peace with her, can you?"

"Who? Nola or my daughter?"

"There's your problem, Ziggy. Sometimes I'm not sure you can even tell the difference."

With a tug of his sweaty hands, Zig pulled off at the exit for his small town of Wonderly Square. *Where Nature Smiles for Five Miles,* read the homemade wooden sign. On his right was the town's main strip mall, which always reminded Zig of the Twin Pines Mall from *Back to the Future,* where the DeLorean first hits eighty-eight miles per hour. Doc Brown had it right. Time travel was risky.

"By the way, Ziggy, in case you haven't noticed, Nola didn't ask for your help. In fact, near as I can tell, even after they tried to nab her, Nola actively *avoided* your involvement. So let's start again: Why're you suddenly so obsessed?"

Hitting the brakes at the end of the exit ramp, Zig eyed a heavyset Hispanic woman on the side of the road. She was dressed in a ratty

Philadelphia Eagles T-shirt, selling flowers from a white plastic bucket. Locals called her Big Philly. Zig called her Luciana.

"Gerbera daises," Luciana mouthed to Zig, pointing to her beat-up assortment of red, orange, and yellow flowers that everyone knew were the week-olds from Bouquet of Sun, the local flower shop. As usual, Zig rolled down his window and gave Luciana a dollar. As usual, he didn't take any flowers.

"I asked you a question, Ziggy," Waggs said through the phone.

Hitting the gas and watching Luciana shrink in the rearview, Zig noticed that the flower lady was waving—not at him, but at the next car that had just come off the exit. Black Acura. Washington plates. Zig squinted, trying to get a better look at the driver. The sun visor was down, blocking the driver's face.

Zig made a quick left. The Acura went right. Other side of town. Zig kicked himself for being so paranoid.

"Waggs, what number date are you on?"

"You're trying to change the subject."

"I'm making a point. You and the Deuce," Zig said, referring to the guy Waggs had been dating for the past few months—the first real boyfriend she'd had in almost a decade.

"His name's *Mikel*."

"Don't insult the Deuce like that," Zig teased, using the name that Waggs instantly regretted telling him was on Mikel's personalized license plate—*TheDeuce*—named after the '32 Ford coupe that his grandfather used to drive. "So date number six with the Deuce? Number seven?"

"Date eleven," Waggs said. "Today's our two-month anniversary. He sent me a corsage."

"Wait. An actual corsage? Like for prom?"

"Don't make fun," Waggs warned, Zig now hearing a soft pop through the phone.

"Waggs, I need to know right now—did you just open that little plastic corsage box? Because I'm currently picturing you sniffing it like you're wearing a puffy dress in the back of a limo."

There was a long pause. And a soft snap.

"You just put it back in the box, didn't you?"

"Zig, you said you had a point."

"My point is simply that even someone new in your life—like the Deuce—if he was in trouble, you'd want to—"

"Nonono. Don't you dare try to use my good thing to make your bad thing look good. You don't even know Mint."

"My job is to take care of our fallen troops."

"That *was* your job. Not anymore. You left it, remember? So please spare me the high-and-mighty speech."

"It's not a speech."

"I know—it's your mission. But you heard what his wife said. According to our records, Mint's last assignment wasn't at Dover. He was a reservist, doing security work at FIG," she said, referring to the Pennsylvania military base known as Fort Indiantown Gap.

Zig didn't say a word.

"Wait," Waggs said. "You already looked him up, didn't you?"

Of course he had.

"Who'd you sweet-talk? Esther in Veterans Affairs?" Waggs challenged.

"Connie in Personnel."

"You called Connie before you called *me*?"

"I used to work there, Waggs. I can name Connie's grandkids by heart, including the little one who they dressed like a Harley-Davidson biker for Halloween."

"So she told you? Mint was assigned to Dover only since last night. They gave him pencil orders."

Zig nodded. He'd seen it before. When a government spy was killed overseas on a secret mission, Dover sometimes used pencil orders to hide where they were really stationed. Giving them orders that were "penciled in" made it look like they worked at Dover.

"That doesn't mean Mint was Spec Ops or some secret squirrel," Zig said, remembering the medals on Mint's chest. The average spy had far fewer. "Sometimes when a government big shot dies, like a senator," Zig added, "they can also get pencil orders to bring them into Dover—so they get our good morticians, rather than some local funeral home."

"Either way, your so-called friends at Dover were lying to you, Ziggy. And when you called Wil to ask him, he kept that lie going!"

"Maybe he's just trying to protect Mint's privacy."

"Or maybe they know it's the best way to suck you in—*Mint's one of us*—and now you'll come running, which is exactly what you did, isn't it? Then all you had to do was spot Nola, which—no surprise—you did that, too. I love that you're one of the kindest people on the planet, Ziggy, but I've seen teenagers in horror movies who're less predictable . . . car washes that were less predictable . . ."

"I get the point, Waggs."

"*Ferris wheels* that were less predictable!"

"Now you're rubbing it in. And being overdramatic."

"No. I'm being smart. I know what getting that phone call meant to you. I know the past few years haven't exactly been packed with excitement—"

"You didn't see the look on Nola's face, Waggs. She knew she was being followed. Whoever's chasing her . . ."

". . . is now potentially focusing on *you*! Is that your grand plan—put the bull's-eye on yourself?"

Zig stayed quiet, making a left on Citrine Avenue, a narrow street dotted with beat-up birch trees. Within half a block, houses started popping up—most of them one-story bungalows—with little front porches that people actually sat on, rather than just used for ornamentation.

"Ziggy, if you think there's something fishy with Mint's death—"

"He was shot in his own driveway—of course it's fishy."

"Then call in help!"

"And tell them what? That the head of Dover didn't tell me everything about his private investigation? That's not a crime, that's a—" Zig's mouth stayed open as he turned onto his own block.

Halfway down, a police car had pulled diagonally into the street, blocking Zig's way.

"Ziggy, you okay?" Waggs asked in his ear.

"Unclear," Zig said, slowing down and bucking to a stop.

The door to the cop car swung wide. A short man in a dark blue police uniform stepped out.

"Mr. Zigarowski, nice to see you again," said Nola's brother Roddy as he flashed a broken smile. "You got a few moments to chat?"

10

For the rest of his short life, Conrad Benn would regret this moment.

"He's in, yeah?" Conrad called out, rushing past the secretary, a middle-aged Asian woman with smoker's lips and Velcro carpal-tunnel wrist braces that everyone knew were just for show.

"Don't," Ms. Li warned, barely looking up.

Conrad was still moving, his squatty legs pumping, his square face sweaty, his fist about to knock on Mr. Vess's cherrywood door. "Mr. Vess said if I found something—he said to interrupt."

"Young man, I'm trying to help you here," Ms. Li said. She called everyone *young man* since employee retention wasn't exactly Mr. Vess's strong suit. "Perhaps you should start again and ask me who Mr. Vess is in there with."

Conrad froze, his knuckles now inches from the door. He knew that tone. "His daughter?"

"His daughter," Ms. Li said, undoing her Velcro straps—*zzzt. zzzzt*—then redoing them.

Born in a spotty Armenian neighborhood outside of Cleveland, Conrad was a big guy, but never a bright guy. As a high school football player, he'd earned the nickname *Volcano* when, during a steroid rage in the school parking lot, he punched his fist through someone's driver's-side window, and of course required surgery. Definitely not bright. But that didn't mean he was dumb.

Putting his ear to the door, Conrad heard electronic beeps and boings. "Are they—?"

Ms. Li nodded. A few weeks back, for his daughter Nessie's birthday, Mr. Vess had bought an upright vintage video game—Frogger— original console, original paneling, refurbished joystick. Every day after school, this was their ritual. Daddy and daughter time.

"Yet if you think it's worth bothering him," Ms. Li added, like she was enjoying herself, "I guess I really can't stop you, can I?"

Conrad glanced down at his phone, a single bead of sweat skiing down his square face. "He said to interrupt," he whispered, more to himself than anyone else.

Ms. Li offered nothing but a shrug. *Zzzt. Zzzzt.*

"This is stupid. Mr. Vess told me if we found something—" Never finishing the sentence, Conrad rapped his knuckle against the office door.

The video game went silent. There was a shift in the air. Conrad took a half step back. He could feel it through the door. Like when the T. rex turns your way in *Jurassic Park*. Something was coming.

"It's the turtles—I hate those turtles," a slow voice grumbled through the door, using two distinct syllables for the word *tur-tles*. Mr. Vess always spoke slowly, every sentence expanding and filling the room, like he was daring people to interrupt.

"Mr. Vess?" Conrad asked, leaning in toward the closed door. "You talking to me or your d—?"

"Speak. Quickly," Vess's voice insisted, though it took five full seconds to get the words out. The door was still shut. He wasn't opening it.

"Sir, I . . . uh . . . I found— That thing you—" Conrad paused, careful of who else was listening. "You should see this, Mr. Vess."

The door opened just a few inches, Mr. Vess's knife of a nose and yellow teeth glowing through the crack.

Conrad slid his phone toward the gap. It was yanked from his hand, the door still barely open.

Conrad could hear Mr. Vess breathing through his nose as he studied the photo on the phone.

"Who's the cop?"

"You don't wanna know," Conrad said.

"And the guy with him?"

"That's who Dover called in. Still trying to figure out why. From what we can tell, he's got a personal interest in Mint's case. Already making calls and sniffing everywhere."

"He got a name?"

"Jim Zigarowski. They call him Zig."

Mr. Vess continued staring at the photo, the glow of the phone lighting his face. He tended to see things in black and white. You're good or you're bad. Smart or dumb. Loyal or a rat.

"Dad, cmooooon," his daughter pleaded, the beeps and boings of Frogger starting up behind him.

"Call in the Reds."

"Sir, you sure that's a—?" Conrad stopped, started again. "There are easier ways t—"

Vess shot him a look. Argument over. As Vess had learned years ago from his grandmother, some businesses succeed by making noise; others profit only when there's quiet. "Call in the Reds. And I assume you have an address for Mr. Zigarowski?"

11

"Ziggy, say the word and I'll send help," Waggs said in his ear.

Zig stayed silent as he got out of his car in his driveway. His right hand skated toward the knife in his pants pocket, while his other hand tucked his phone into his shirt pocket. Even as Roddy approached and Zig slammed the car door, Zig didn't shut off his phone. If things went south, better for Waggs to be listening in.

"Roddy, what a true joy to see that in addition to invading my personal space, you've driven over an hour to show up at my home," Zig said, adding an extra scoop of charm, hoping it would defuse whatever was coming. "Though if you're here for the block party, you're actually two weeks early," he added, loud enough so Waggs could hear.

Roddy didn't laugh, didn't even grin, like he was still processing the—

"Oh. Heh. I get it. You're making a joke. That's funny," Roddy said, his odd smile back in place. He took his cap off his head, revealing short black hair that was shaved to the scalp on the sides. Big yellow letters on his car door read *Jersey City Police*. A Jersey cop out in southeastern Pennsylvania. Whatever Roddy was up to, he was crossing state lines to do it.

"Would you mind hanging up your phone, Mr. Zigarowski?"

"My phone isn't—"

"I can see you're midcall," Roddy said, holding up a small high-tech tablet. The kind that usually only feds had.

Zig still didn't hang up his phone.

"Mr. Zigarowski, I'm obviously here to talk about my sister—and I have a feeling you want to hear what I'm about to tell you. I can't do that if there's a stranger listening in."

Zig stood there a moment. He didn't have much choice.

"Ziggy, don't hang up!" Waggs called out.

Click. She was gone.

"Mhmm," Roddy said, making a satisfied noise as he stared at his tablet. The line was clear. "My foot fell asleep two times today. Y'ever have that happen? Twice in one day?"

Zig just stared at him. "Roddy, back at the funeral, you said you had problems when you were younger. I'd like to know what those were."

Roddy barely moved, staring up at Zig's gray clapboard bungalow with the white trim that needed painting. "You worry about her, don't you, Mr. Zigarowski? Nola. Your body shifts when I say her name. You're her friend. I didn't think she had anyone who cared for her."

"If you have a specific ques—"

"You understand that she and Colonel Mint—they knew each other," Roddy said, his voice slow and methodical.

"Knew each other where?"

"From one of Nola's first assignments. Where she did one of her first paintings. At a place called Grandma's Pantry."

12

This was Roddy when he was seven.

Once again, he was hiding. And chewing gum, Juicy Fruit. They were all hiding and chewing gum—him, his foster sisters, and his foster brother—huddled together at the top of the stairs, spying down, like they were trying to spot Santa Claus on Christmas.

But this definitely wasn't Christmas.

"She in trouble?" one of them asked. *Chew, chew, chew.*

They all chewed back. They didn't have to answer. Nola was always in trouble.

"It looks like . . . I think she's eating," said the oldest, Anne Marie, squinting through the slats of the banister toward the kitchen, where their mother and father, Barb and Walter LaPointe, were serving Nola dinner. "Mac and cheese."

Not just any mac and cheese. *Space Jam* mac and cheese, plus the rest of Nola's favorite meal: chocolate milk and Oreos—Double Stuf, of course.

"Here you go, sweetie pie," Walter said.

That was the tip-off. Nola was never *sweetie pie.* Only his three biological kids were.

Knocking the Oreo plate aside, Walter slid a vanilla-icing sheet cake in front of Nola. From upstairs, the kids couldn't read the bright green letters:

WE WILL MISS YOU!

Nola looked around, confused.

"This will be your last night with the family," Walter told Nola matter-of-factly.

"Wh-What's going on? Why're you doing this?" Nola asked.

Upstairs, at the back of the pack, young Roddy was silent, tucking his gum under his tongue. He knew why they were doing this.

A year and a half ago, twins Nola and Roddy had been rescued from a brutal group home in northern Arkansas. Someone had shown Barb LaPointe a fax with their photos. She took it as a sign from Jesus, driving to meet the adorable twin three-year-olds. To her surprise, Roddy and his sister—with identical bowl haircuts so that predators wouldn't know Nola was a girl—were three years older than the group home had disclosed, with behavioral problems omitted.

On his first night in Texas, Roddy refused to get undressed, sleeping in his clothes on the couch. He did the same on his second night, so Barb slept on the chair next to him. When Barb woke up, Roddy was at her feet, like a loving cat. *Progress,* she thought.

The twins had matching black eyes with flecks of gold and the same honey-colored skin. But Roddy's disarming grin made him more charming and likable than sullen Nola. And also more dangerous.

At the end of their first week, Roddy's foster sister Anne Marie noticed that one of her gold bangle bracelets was missing. Roddy found it in Nola's room.

"Thank you!" Anne Marie said, pulling him so close, his cheek was pressed into her breast. "You're the good one," she whispered.

Over the next few weeks, a window in the house was broken. Toys began to disappear, then were found in Nola's room, always smelling like urine. In no time, the LaPointes were worried about the safety of their own children, a worry that deepened when someone set fire to the living room carpet.

Therapists came to visit and things went back to normal. Then Nola came home with a black eye (and a ruthless hospital bill) from a ferocious boy in fifth grade, whose front teeth she'd knocked out with a steel thermos.

"Miss Nola," Walter said in that tone no one argued with, "it's time to go."

"N-No," Nola replied, tears swelling in her eyes.

Walter seized her arm.

"No! Please don't do this!" she yelled, trying to pull out of his grip.

At the top of the stairs, the other kids curled together, watching helplessly.

"What're they doing?" the youngest, Paulette, whispered.

"Keeping us safe," Anne Marie replied.

Behind them, Roddy kept to the back of the pack, his head down so no one could see the joy that was spreading across his dark eyes.

Ten minutes ago, when the LaPointes said they wanted to speak to Nola alone, Roddy thought they'd found out the truth: It was him. Roddy was the one who'd broken the window and peed on the toys. Just like he was the one who stole Anne Marie's bracelet and hid it in Nola's room. It was even Roddy who picked the fight with Thermos Teeth, telling the ferocious fifth grader that he'd spit in the boy's backpack. Roddy was about to get his face punched in until Nola came to his aid.

Sure, Nola was the one who set fire to the carpet—a rushed and poorly considered plan to protect the family dog, whom Roddy was chasing around with a candle—but right now, that was the least of Nola's worries.

"Someone . . . Roddy . . . *help! Roddy . . . please!*" Nola begged, fighting to break her foster father's grip.

At the top of the stairs, Roddy didn't move, didn't make a sound. He was just a kid. He could never have engineered, much less foreseen, all this. But to watch it play out . . . naturally, he felt bad. But if the choice was between Nola taking the fall, or Roddy confessing everything? Well, that was no choice at all.

"Don't make this harder than it is," Walter LaPointe said, tugging Nola's wrist.

"Please! I'll be good!" she yelled, bits of Oreo spraying from her mouth. She was clawing at his hand. Her foster mom was crying. *"We'll both be good!"*

"Don't look," young Anne Marie whispered at the top of the stairs, covering Paulette's eyes.

Roddy didn't take the advice. Leaning between his foster sisters, he gripped the wooden guardrails like jail bars, chomping on his Juicy Fruit as something new filled his chest. He thought it was another rush of power, but it wasn't. It was a thrill—that was the only word for it. The thrill that comes from getting away with something. A dark grin spread across his face. No matter what Nola said, no matter the proof, would they ever believe Roddy was the guilty one?

They would. For months now, the LaPointes had known the truth. They knew both twins had problems, but it was Roddy who needed more help. Money was tight. With three other kids to take care of, they could help one of the twins, but not both. Barb LaPointe prayed on it for a week. The decision was clear: Find Nola a new home. She was the stronger one. The resilient one. She'd be okay.

"I'll be good! We'll both be good!" Nola begged. *"We won't bother anyone again!"*

Duh-duh-ding-ding-ding-ding-DING-DING. The doorbell rang, playing "The Yellow Rose of Texas," though Roddy never knew the name of the song.

"No, please . . ." Nola begged as Walter scooped her up. She grasped at the kitchen chairs, the phone cord, anything to get a handhold. Barb was sobbing as she followed them to the living room, prying Nola's grip from the threshold. *"Please, Mom—don't give me to them! Don't give me to them!"*

But it wasn't *them.*

It was *him*.

To this day, Roddy could still remember every detail—the diagonal view from the top of the stairs, the curve of the wooden guardrails in his hands, even the sweet smell of the Juicy Fruit—as the front door opened.

"I'm here for . . . er . . . for the . . . I'm the . . ." The man never finished his sentence. He had a pitted face, greedy eyes, and incredibly long eyelashes. "I'm Royall Barker," he explained.

Walter went to shake his hand, but he was still holding Nola, like a thrashing bride on the threshold.

Royall cocked his head at the sight. "You must be Nola."

"Dad, please," Nola begged, trying to grab at the door. *"I'll be good! I swear, I'll be good!"*

It would be twenty-one years before Roddy saw his sister again.

13

"Grandma's Pantry," Zig repeated.

"You don't know what I'm talking about, do you?" Roddy asked. He was smarter than Zig first thought. When Roddy stared at you, his black eyes fixed like an anchor, it was easy to think he was socially awkward—which he was—but he was also clearly analyzing every detail he observed. "What about Rashida? Have they told you about her?"

"Roddy, you just drove really far to get to my house. If there's something you want to know, can we just get to it?"

Out of nowhere, Roddy turned to his left, staring up the block. All was quiet. A second later, a black car zipped across Citrine Avenue, just as Roddy knew it would. The car was gone in an eyeblink. Zig now noticed that Roddy was wearing a hearing aid of some sort. Were Jersey cops allowed to serve with hearing aids?

"Have you seen this painting, Mr. Zigarowski?"

Roddy held up his tablet, swiping to a photo of a canvas covered in watercolors—grays, drab browns, and at the very center, a mix of yellow and black. The painting was of someone's cubicle, but it looked like it'd been painted years ago: Big gray computer monitor. Messy desk. The focal point was a soldier in a black windbreaker, sitting in profile, working at the computer. Two other, younger soldiers—a Black woman and a Black or maybe Hispanic man—wore matching windbreakers and stood behind him. All three of them were studying the big monitor. A black-and-yellow patch on the woman's shoulder showed a barely readable scribble underneath. *Semper Vigiles*. Latin for *Vigilant Always*.

"I assume you know who painted this?" Roddy asked.

Zig motioned to the bottom corner of the painting, which had a signature line in white block letters: *NBrown*.

"When was this painted? It looks old," Zig said, though it wasn't just from the outdated computer monitor. The art itself . . . the soldiers at the center—it looked more . . . rudimentary than Nola's usual paintings.

"When she was Artist-in-Residence, you know what her job was, right?"

"She painted disasters."

"Sometimes disasters, sometimes total horrors, sometimes the mundane," Roddy explained, shaking his leg like it was asleep again. For over a century, the Army had had a painter on staff documenting the country's greatest battles. "Five years ago, when they hired Nola as Artist-in-Residence, the Army told her she could go wherever she wanted—Afghanistan, Syria, anywhere. War painters get full clearance. In fact, on the day this painting was created, a Pave Hawk Medevac helicopter crashed in Bahrain. Eight service members, including three doctors and a reporter, were killed. *Time* magazine made a cover story of it."

Zig remembered the story—and the bodies when they came through Dover. Zig had worked on the copilot, a Marine, whose head was cracked open like an eggshell. Zig spent nine hours wiring the man's skull together, then personally polished his wedding ring, which somehow had gotten looped onto a cracked rib. When they presented the ring to the Marine's family, his wife threw it back in Zig's face, screaming that this wouldn't bring back her dead husband.

"Why're you telling me this?" Zig asked.

"That Medevac story was impossible to ignore. It was national news. Most war painters would've headed straight to Bahrain. Instead, for some reason, on one of Nola's first days on the job, she headed *here*." He pointed at the painting.

"Grandma's Pantry," Zig said.

"*This* was one of the very first pieces of artwork she painted."

Zig took another look. "So what was the mission in Grandma's Pantry?"

"It's the title of the painting. But recognize any of the soldiers?"

Zig looked closer at the painting. The soldier sitting at the desk—his face was in profile. But his forehead . . . his hairline . . .

Mothertrucker. "Lieutenant Colonel Mint?"

Roddy swiped to a new photo—the back of the canvas, where Nola always ID'd her subjects. Onscreen, three names were hand-written in block lettering:

ARCHIE MINT
RASHIDA ROBINSON
ELIJAH KING

"From what I could find, all three were in the same unit," Roddy explained, swiping back to the painting and enlarging the photo to enhance the logo on Mint's jacket. A hand grabbing two lightning bolts. *Semper Vigiles.*

"Army Security Agency," Roddy explained, again checking over his shoulder. This time, the street was quiet. "Dates back to World War II, where they did high-end investigative work—top secret and above—stuff they didn't even trust to the Army intel folks. Oddly, the unit was supposedly disbanded after the Cold War."

"Yet here they are, doing an investigation big enough that it made Nola ignore the number-one military story in the country, just so she could come see it," Zig said as Roddy again made that *Mhmm* sound. He didn't have to say anything else. Whatever Nola was chasing all those years ago and whatever Mint was investigating—their paths crossed here, at a place called Grandma's Pantry, a military location whose real specialty so far seemed to be making high-end secrets disappear.

"What about Rashida and Elijah?" Zig said, referring to the other two soldiers in the painting. "Have you tried reaching out to them?"

Roddy offered a flat gaze, handing Zig the tablet. "Swipe left . . ."

Onscreen was a new photo, of a burned-out car—half of one,

really—the back seat and trunk completely missing, the blackened car sheared in half.

"This was yesterday, around midnight, down by SunCo," Roddy explained, referring to one of the many refineries near the Philadelphia airport.

Zig swiped left, to another angle on the car, this one slightly closer. Through the missing front windshield, there was a single figure—scorched from fire—slumped toward the steering wheel, her head dangling in that way that heads are never meant to dangle.

"Police report called it a suicide. Said the car rammed full speed through the refinery's metal fence, crashing into one of their big rinsing tanks. When you mix chemicals and combustion like that . . ."

Zig swiped to the next picture, a crime scene close-up of just the woman, her body burned so badly that she was nothing but a charred black crisp shaped like a human. One of her arms had somehow been spared, showing a patch of dark brown skin.

Rashida Robinson.

Fallen #2,548, Zig thought, catching himself. This wasn't his job anymore. He wasn't assigned to put this woman to rest. Still . . .

"It's hard to look at, yes?" Roddy asked.

Sadly, for Zig, it wasn't. During his decades at Dover, the very worst part of the job was that he got used to it. Death should be a stranger, not someone familiar—it's why he left Dover and its never-ending stream of young cadets sliced down in their prime, their families clinging to God and hating God all in the same breath. It's why Zig had sworn he'd never go back, and yet here he was, staring down at this woman's burnt body and blackened teeth.

With a few swipes to the right, Zig returned to the back of the painting and its three names.

ARCHIE MINT
RASHIDA ROBINSON
ELIJAH KING

Two days ago, Mint had been shot dead outside his home. Last night, Rashida Robinson was found dead, too. It was a hell of a coincidence. Or, Zig was starting to realize, not a coincidence at all. Whatever really went on all those years ago at Grandma's Pantry, someone seemed to be working their way down the list of the investigators who were stationed there.

"You understand now, yes?" Roddy asked. "That leaves Elijah . . ."

"And Nola," Zig whispered, the air going quiet. "She was just the painter, though. That doesn't mean anyone's coming for her."

"You sure about that?" Roddy asked, grabbing the tablet, his spidery fingers swiping to a new photo. He held it up for Zig. Onscreen was a muscular man in a suit, curled on the ground and holding his leg, clearly in pain.

"Staff Sergeant Buddy Adcock, one of the undercover agents stationed outside Mint's funeral. He's a meat eater," Roddy said. "Apparently, he surprised Nola as she headed toward the parking lot, tried to put cuffs on her."

"Oh, jeez. What'd she do?"

"Yanked a pen from his front pocket and jammed it into his kneecap, popping it like a bottle cap. He's currently being prepped for surgery to repair the dislocation."

Zig stared at the photo, at the pen protruding from the staff sergeant's knee, and at the man's oversized pistol, lying there on the sidewalk. An MP7. Submachine gun. Not a normal service weapon, which meant this guy Adcock was . . .

"Special Forces," Zig whispered.

"At a local funeral. In a small town," Roddy said. "That seem normal to you, Mr. Zigarowski?"

Zig stayed silent, and now he was the one checking over his own shoulder. Yesterday, the higher-ups at Dover had pulled him onto this case, clearly hoping to put their eyes on Nola. But if Special Forces was involved—pulling weapons like that—they weren't just trying to *talk* to Nola. They were hunting her.

Zig took another look at the young soldier, curled on the sidewalk, clenching his teeth in pain. This, Zig knew, was the moment he should walk away. *This has nothing to do with you.* For all he knew, Roddy was in on it, too, using Zig to flush her out.

"You look like I'm causing you pain, Mr. Zigarowski. You're worried I want to hurt her."

"Roddy, I just met you."

Roddy's face shifted. "I'm not a perfect person. I'm not proud of everything I've done in my life. But y'know why I'm a good cop? Because I don't care if people like me," he said, suddenly serious. "It's a bigger asset than you think. It lets me ask hard questions and get real answers. But if you think I'd hurt my sister—"

"I never said you'd hurt her. She just— When it comes to Nola, I'm not sure you understand what you're getting into. She's not gonna want your help, my help, anyone's help."

"That doesn't mean she doesn't need it."

Zig thought about that and once again, he could see twelve-year-old Nola at the Girl Scout campout, down on the ground, clutching her bloody ear after a can of orange soda exploded in the fire. *"Get her help . . . get her to the hospital!"* Zig's daughter was screaming. Yet what Zig remembered most was that when he reached down to scoop up Nola, she recoiled, scratching at him like a cornered cat. Half a second later, she caught herself, realizing Zig was just trying to help. No one else saw it, but Zig did. Even at twelve, Nola's instinct was to fight back.

"—garowski? Mr. Zigarowski? You okay?"

Zig looked up at Roddy. *No,* he wasn't okay. As he thought about it now, he hadn't been okay since the moment he walked into that funeral and saw Nola across the gym. For two years now, he'd been able to keep that part of his brain, his heart, in check—or at least tucked away—and then, at just the sight of her, it was as if someone had jammed a shovel into his chest and dug everything out—every old feeling, every wound, and every fear—about Nola, about his time at Dover, about his own failures, and of course about his daughter.

Waggs was right about that. It always went back to Maggie.

Before Zig left Dover, he'd spent over two decades working on the bodies of fallen soldiers. For Zig, being around the horrors of death meant that Maggie's loss was somehow . . . less. In the darkness of

Dover, he could escape the blackest caves of his own life. Of course, it was an illusion. As any mourner knows, when you bury someone you loved deep to your core, all it takes is a familiar smell, an old song, or even rusty high school lockers to bring back the pain.

"Mr. Zigarowski, I've been tracking Nola for two years. Even if you can point me to her friends—"

"She doesn't have friends." The words came so fast, it took Zig a moment to realize it was the most honest thing he'd said. Nola had no friends. She had no family. She had no one. Except, weirdly, Zig.

"I know you care about my sister," Roddy said, his long fingers again fidgeting with the tip of his tie. "This is your chance to finally help her. She could use that help right now."

Pure manipulation, Zig thought, looking back at the photo of the young soldier, in the fetal position, gripping his knee in agony. Waggs was right about that, too. The last time Zig had let Nola into his life, she didn't care who she hurt. She tore everything to shreds, shooting her own foster father in the head and wrecking his corrupt military unit, while Zig nearly died in the process.

Nola Brown is a gun. She's a weapon, someone had once told Zig, describing her time in the military. *You point her at something, and you'll get what you want—but just know it may come back in pieces.*

Zig looked up from the tablet, toward his house. For two years now, he'd been putting his own pieces back together. After Maggie's death and the divorce, he'd rebuilt his life, rebuilt his work at Dover. In fact, when he finally left Dover behind, he thought he'd turned a page, leaving the worst days behind him. The last thing he needed right now was to turn it all back into a jigsaw.

Walk away, Zig told himself. *Leave it be.* But as he played it through his head . . . Two people were already dead. Archie Mint and Rashida Robinson. He could see Mint's son, Huck, the boy sobbing with his mom in the hallway; his daughter, Violet, with the scabs on her knees and the vacant look in her eyes that would take a lifetime to fade.

These people—all of them—had hopes and dreams and lives. If Zig walked away now . . . if Nola was next on that list and she was killed, too . . . No. *Don't even think it,* he told himself. But that was all he could think. If he walked away and something happened to Nola, this would be on him. He already blamed himself for his daughter's death. He couldn't carry another.

"You're going to help me, aren't you, Mr. Zigarowski? You'll come?"

"Wha? Come where?"

"She won't listen to me—she runs every time I show up," Roddy said.

"I don't— Wait. You know where she is?"

"I got the call on the way here. We need to hurry. She has no idea what's coming, Mr. Zigarowski. Now do you want to help Nola or not?"

14

"Y'can't park there!" the valet called out.

Nola ignored him, shutting the car off and stuffing an iPhone into the glove compartment. The phone belonged to Buddy Adcock, the staff sergeant who'd pulled his gun and tried to handcuff her near the parking lot. While he was on the ground gripping his knee, she'd swiped it from his pocket.

"I'm looking for Richard Merante," Nola barked at the valet, flashing the badge she'd found in Buddy's wallet—from the same unit, *Semper Vigiles*—and using the name she'd found in one of his emails.

To protect against moments just like this, DISA—the Defense Information Systems Agency—was in charge of encrypting Army cell phones. But there was nothing DISA could do to stop Nola from pressing Buddy's thumb into the phone's fingerprint reader, adding her own thumbprint, and having access to everything Buddy and his unit had been looking at. Best of all, she'd pulled out the SIM card, so the government couldn't track her, but by holding on to the card, she could slide it back in for easy updates.

"Ma'am, you hear what I—?"

Nola shot him a razor-sharp dagger of a stare.

The valet stopped midstep. He wore a bright yellow rubber bracelet with the name of the local high school imprinted on it. In his hand, his phone screen was open to an Instagram model who was shaking her fake boobs in a way that only a high schooler might think was normal. *Just a kid,* Nola realized.

"If this is about . . . about the murder," the valet stuttered, "Mr. Merante is right in—"

She walked past him, toward the front door. *Slam.*

Inside, the restaurant looked like any other overpriced steak house—dark wood furniture, bright white tablecloths, bloodred walls, and the kind of low lighting that was supposed to be "sexy chic," whatever that meant.

Searching for her pencil and notepad, Nola reached into her pocket. Empty. Left it in the car, she realized, cursing herself for yet another rookie mistake. *What the hell is wrong with you? Pull it together.*

Too late for that. Between Mint's death . . . Roddy's arrival . . . plus everything she was working on before this happened . . . *Find your calm,* she told herself—or as Mint himself used to say, "Get emotional, and you get dead." It was good advice, given to her at Grandma's Pantry. But what Nola appreciated far more was the genuine concern that came with it—the way he'd looked her in the eye and grabbed her shoulder as he said it. He was concerned about her. For Nola, that was a rare thing. A new thing. One that wouldn't be forgotten.

It was that thought that actually worried Nola, who didn't like this feeling, of being worried, of the lack of control that came with it. In her pocket, she started doing that thing she used to do when she was little and Royall would bring over those friends who would stare at her a bit too long, using her nails to pinch the skin on her thigh, distracting herself with pain.

Today, in her pocket, she pinched herself even harder. This case . . . it was more than just a case . . . which, really, was the issue. From her first days as Artist-in-Residence, like any painter, Nola had been taught to remain objective. But considering her tie to Mint, she was anything but. No way could she ever repay him for what he did that day she needed him most.

At the back of the restaurant, a middle-aged man with thinning blond hair and trendy oversized eyeglasses was sitting alone at a private booth, clicking at his laptop. His sharp black suit made it look like he had money, but even from here, Nola spotted his shoes. Cheap. Scuffed. Worn. *Not a customer. An employee.*

"Richard Merante," Nola announced.

"Yup yup, gimme a sec," Merante said, still clicking at his computer, an ancient IBM ThinkPad with a University of Michigan sticker and one that read, *I'm not superstitious, but I am a little stitious.* There was an iPad right next to it. At the middle of his nose were two red indentations—from when he'd lower his eyeglasses to read. *Needs bifocals. Too stubborn to get them.*

Nola slapped the laptop shut.

"Hey!"

She pulled out her stolen badge, nearly ramming it into his face. "I need you to answer some questions."

He didn't look surprised. "Another detective? I assume this is about Wojo?" he asked, referring to the valet who'd been killed two nights ago.

"Actually," Nola said, no longer pinching herself as she slid in across from him in the booth, "it's about a bit more than that."

In the corner, by the bar, a waitress with a hacking cough was restocking martini and shot glasses. Nola shot her a look that sent her back to the kitchen. Nola took a final scan of the room. All clear.

Yet what she couldn't see was the valet out front. The high school kid with the yellow rubber bracelet was no longer staring at Instagram models. He was dialing a number he'd memorized.

It rang twice before someone picked up.

"Yeah . . . um . . . you said to call if— That you'd pay for—" The kid cut himself off, keeping his voice to a whisper. "I saw her," he said into the phone. "The girl you showed me . . . with the white hair . . . she's here. I saw her."

The young valet went silent, listening closely to the instructions on the other end. "Yeah, no. Don't worry. She's not going anywhere."

15

"You've been here before?" Roddy asked.

"Years ago," Zig said, tugging the steering wheel, his car creeping past the valet stand and the low cobblestone wall that lined the curved driveway of Barron's Steakhouse.

"With your wife? Back when you were married?"

Zig didn't answer.

"That place where you live now, that's not far from your old neighborhood, is it?" Roddy added. "And Nola's old neighborhood, too, when she was little."

For the entire forty-minute ride here, this was what their trip was like: Roddy shouting out everything that came to his brain, peppering Zig with question after question. But as Zig steered into a nearby parking spot, he had to admit, Roddy wasn't wrong. He might be a bit of a social misfit, but his cop instincts were solid. His conclusions were solid. His concern for his sister seemed solid—authentic. But still, for Zig, there was something about Roddy . . . like an itch in Zig's head, something that just set off his primal radar. *Heart or no heart?* Zig still wasn't sure.

"Can I ask you a question?" Zig interrupted.

"You do that a lot, Mr. Zigarowski. You ask a question before you ask the question."

Zig took a breath, put the car in park. "Finding my address isn't hard, but to be waiting for me at my house—how'd you know that's where I was going?"

For once, Roddy was silent.

"You tracked my phone, didn't you?"

"That would be illegal," Roddy said, sitting there in the passenger seat, staring straight ahead. Taking a breath, he finally said, "I followed you from the funeral."

Zig replayed his ride home. He'd checked over his own shoulder half a dozen times. Apparently, Roddy was there—right behind him—the entire way.

"I'd like to go inside, Mr. Zigarowski," Roddy added, reaching for his holster and pulling his gun, a tactical-looking .45. Yet what unnerved Zig far more was when he noticed that the pistol had a threaded barrel—the kind you screw a silencer onto. Definitely not department issue.

"Roddy, wait . . . !"

Too late. He was already gone, darting toward the open back entrance of the restaurant.

Zig was two steps behind him, reaching for the knife in his pocket, and praying this wasn't a mistake.

16

Nola was gone, of course.

"But you saw her?" Roddy asked the manager of the steak house. In one hand, Roddy held his police badge, in the other, a photo of Nola, from her old military ID.

"Yup, yup. That's her, though the pic doesn't do her justice," the manager, Merante, replied, flicking the photo with his middle finger. "She's hotter in real life. Angrier, too."

"Did you talk to her?" Zig asked.

"I told her what I told the others."

"Others?"

Merante took a long sip of his coffee, his eyes filled with a forced, cocky smirk that showed how much he liked being in charge. "Last year, one of my busboys got arrested for buying Sudafed in bulk, then grinding it up and selling it to meth heads. Cops came out once, maybe twice to ask me questions. But in the past two days? The entire law enforcement carnival came to town." From his jacket, Merante pulled out a short stack of business cards, fanning them across the table, each with a different government logo. "State police, Military Intelligence, Army criminal investigators, two FBI guys that were actually wearing black suits, and this one local detective, a Muslim girl, in full burqa—"

"It's not a burqa," Roddy said.

"Whatever they call it."

"Headscarf," Roddy insisted, flipping through the business cards, not making eye contact. "The preferred term is 'headscarf.'"

"Whatever," Merante said, making a face and taking another sip of coffee. Roddy pulled out his phone and took a photo of each of the business cards. *Ka-klik.* "Did you know that your valet was using your customers' cars to break into their houses?"

"Y'sure I can't offer you some coffee?" Merante asked Zig. "It's something special. We put cinnamon in it."

"Mr. Merante, I asked you a ques—"

"Wojo was thirty-two years old and still parking cars. So every few months did I get a complaint that sunglasses or an iPhone charger might be missing from a BMW? That goes with the job. But did I think he was driving to people's homes and treating it like some *Ocean's Eleven* sequel?"

"Dover Air Force Base," Roddy interrupted, holding up a business card for Zig to see. Zig didn't recognize the name, but it was clearly one of Dover's newest homicide investigators, hired by Colonel O. J. Whatley. The man who, according to Wil, specifically asked for Zig to be put on this case.

"Sir, what else did Nola ask you about?" Zig said as Roddy took a photo of the card. *Ka-klik.*

"Nola, huh?" Merante replied. "She told me her name was Kamille."

"I meant . . . She's actually—"

"I'm not offended, but do me a favor and spare me the bullshit, okay? I don't care what her name is. I don't care what she's up to. In this job, the majority of my clients are polished people: businessmen, judges. I know what polished looks like. Your girl's the opposite of that. She's not even really a cop, is she?"

"Mr. Merante . . ."

"You don't trust her, do you? I don't blame you. From the moment she walked in, she asked a few questions, but kept her head down, drawing the entire time."

Roddy looked up from the business cards.

"Did she draw anything in particular?" Zig asked.

"She asked for my pen, but she's not exactly a sharer. From what I could tell, it kinda looked like the restaurant. Like she was drawing the whole place. Otherwise, all she cared about was the Army guy, Mr. Mint."

"*Colonel* Mint," Zig corrected, though again, he wasn't surprised. Half a decade ago, Nola and Mint met each other on the same assignment, or at least in the same location, a place code-named Grandma's Pantry. Now, someone seemed to be tracking, and killing, the few other people who served with them.

"Oh, she also wanted our security footage," Merante added.

"I didn't see any cameras out front," Roddy said.

"There aren't any. The owners are cheap. Only places they record are the safe in back and our wine cellar. I gave both tapes to the Army investigators."

"You think she wanted to see Mint's interaction with your valet?" Zig asked.

"Actually, she was asking about interior cams—like she wanted to know who Mint was meeting."

Zig looked back at Roddy. It was a good question, one that Zig was already kicking himself for not asking. According to the police reports, once the valet took off, Colonel Mint jumped in a cab and followed him to Mint's house. But in all the back-and-forth over the deaths, they'd forgotten a key detail: people don't come to fancy steak houses to eat alone.

"Mr. Merante, is it possible to take a look at your reservation book?" Zig asked.

"Yeah, sure, of course," Merante said, putting his coffee down with enough speed that it was clear none of the other investigators had asked about it. "I got it right . . ." He reached to his left, but nothing was there. Confused, he lifted a nearby stack of menus, then his laptop, then started rummaging through his briefcase.

"It was just here. I had it when—" He cut himself off. "That bitch stole my iPad!"

17

The first thing Nola did was turn off the iPad's tracking.

Sure, she could've asked the steak house manager for a look at the reservation book, but if her hunch was right, the last thing she needed was for him to share it with others.

For the rest of the forty-minute ride, Nola did what she always did during drives or long runs—composed layouts in her head, in this case, a mental drawing of Mint that she'd been working on since the funeral.

Years ago, when she first drew him back at Grandma's Pantry, she'd focused on the obvious: his stubborn lips, absurd jaw, and buzzed blond hair, so crisp it looked like it was cut every hour. Same with his military uniform. When you wash camouflage too much, the shades of green take on a faded, whitish tinge. Not Mint. The moment he stepped into a room, you knew he was the commander, though Nola quickly realized it had nothing to do with his clothing or jawline. It came from the hardest thing to render, the charisma and energy that radiated off him.

That very first night at Grandma's Pantry, things ran so late, Nola popped into a nearby supermarket to pick up a cheap dinner. At the checkout was one of the young privates—some junior-level kid assigned to do coffee runs—who was doing the same. As the kid went to pay, the prices were clearly more than he'd calculated, so he started putting things back to lower his bill. What the kid didn't realize was that Archie Mint was in that same line.

To put a finer point on it, Mint wasn't one of those pushovers who took a recruiting command to avoid the field. He'd served in the Tenth

Mountain Division up at Fort Drum—a hard outfit that always deployed. But on that night in the supermarket, Mint pulled out his wallet and paid the bill. The kid was embarrassed, saying *thank you* over and over. Mint wouldn't have it. Told him it was just between them.

More important, when they got back to the office, Mint never said a word to anyone, never took credit. Nola wouldn't have even known about it if she hadn't been lurking in one of the aisles. In the military, so many commanders divided the world into Os and Es—Officers and Enlisted. Mint inspired loyalty because he knew there were things more important than those distinctions.

The mental picture disappeared as Nola's car bucked to a stop at a black metal security gate. She entered a four-digit code into a keypad, and the gate unclenched with a loud *ka-klunk*. The road ahead was unpaved. She hit the gas, knowing where she was going.

Finally. Home.

For nearly a mile, the road twisted and turned, tornadoes of dust cartwheeling behind her. Then, at the very back of the park, Nola made a sharp right into an empty service lot. Straight ahead was a dirt footpath that wove into the woods. She checked it for footprints. Two sets, just as she knew there would be.

"Psst, psst . . ." Nola called out, leaving the car behind. No answer, no surprise. As she started up the path, a mass of trees and brush swallowed her, hiding her from view.

Back in the early 1900s, this park—over one thousand acres—had been a private estate that held multimillionaire Pierre du Pont's summer home. Today, thirty-eight minutes from Mint's house, with greenhouses a mile and a half long, it was known as Longwood Gardens, the largest private botanical garden in the world, attracting over a million tourists a year. Here, though, at the back of the park, on the outskirts of the eighty-six-acre meadow garden, it was abandoned.

"Psst, psst . . . Sarah . . . *food!*" Nola called again. Still no response.

Nola glanced around, noting the silence. She rechecked the path. Still two sets of footprints.

Up ahead, the path ended at a dilapidated white milk barn that had been abandoned decades ago and was now used for holding the park's discarded tractors, ladders, and other random equipment. On her left was her real destination: the rusted silver Airstream trailer—a 1993 twenty-five-foot Excella—with a bent awning arm that made the entire blue canopy sag like a winking eye. As always, a single Tupperware bin sat on the cinder block steps: Nola's in-box.

"Psst . . . psst . . . Sarah, you there?" Nola called again, eyeing the way the Tupperware sat askew on the top step, like someone had moved it. She rechecked the dirt. Two sets of footprints. Nothing out of place.

Nola grabbed the Tupperware but didn't open it. Inside were three Polaroids—each one of a different plant, its name handwritten across the bottom. *Ficus benjamina,* aka the Dutch Treat. *Davallia tyermanii,* the bear's-foot fern. And *Sansevieria,* a rare snake plant with pristine white striping in the leaves. They were this week's assignments from Darryl, the head of Longwood's botanical library. For six months now, Nola had been painting their collection in return for room and board—though the best benefit was the solitude of living out here, in what had become her private art studio.

"Sarah, if you're hiding just to piss me off . . ." Nola warned, carefully pulling open the door to the trailer and—

On the floor, a dead toad was lying stomach up, its belly torn open.

Sssssss! came a low hiss from below the kitchen table, where an angry Russian blue cat with bald patches and forehead scars sat.

"Sarah Connor, did you mess up my floor?" Nola asked.

Ssssssss! the cat hissed again.

Nola rolled her eyes and picked up the toad, which was really all Sarah Connor wanted. Every few days, the cat would sneak out through the hole in the window screen and bring back a new gift: toads, mice, giant dragonflies . . . whatever she could find.

"You're a horrible cat," Nola said, tossing the toad outside.

Sssss, the cat hissed, satisfied, narrowing her white milky eye that had been scratched by a fox. Three months ago, Nola had found the cat bleeding, its paw broken and bent in a chain-link fence that it was trying to scale. No collar, no home, and clearly running from something. God, did Nola understand that.

The local veterinarian said to give up on her, that the cat would be dead in a week anyway. Nola brought her back here, where Sarah Connor refused to eat for four days, until Nola found her weakness:

buttered corn on the cob. The damn cat would do anything for that.

Sss . . . the cat hissed again, scratching at the peeling linoleum floor for no reason.

Nola barely noticed, pulling off her shirt to get a better look at her collarbone. Back at the funeral, when she took out the staff sergeant who tried to handcuff her, he'd stabbed one of the cuffs into her neck. Kid was quicker than he looked.

Good for him. Right instinct. Trained well, Nola thought, pulling aside the strap of her black bra, trying to get a close-up look in the bathroom mirror. There was a little blood, but she'd be fine.

Turning her attention to the iPad, she hit the power button.

Onscreen, the logo for Barron's Steakhouse bloomed into view, along with two buttons.

SCHEDULES   RESERVATIONS

Nola didn't hesitate. *Reservations.*

A calendar appeared. Today's date, then four columns.

HOUR   NAME   PHONE   NOTES

Tonight was a weeknight. The earliest reservation was at 5:30 P.M., party of three under the name *A. Epstein,* with a note that read, *Celebrating 75th B.*

Another half dozen reservations were listed below that.

Nola swiped back to Saturday, the night of Mint's death.

"Whattya think, Sarah Connor? A middle-aged man going to a fancy steak house by himself?"

The cat stayed silent.

"Yeah, me neither," Nola said, scrolling down and doing everything in her power to not reach into her pocket and pinch the skin on her thigh.

Time to see who Colonel Mint was meeting the night he died.

18

Nola scrolled through the iPad, scanning the reservation list for parties of two.

According to his death certificate, Lieutenant Colonel Archie Mint died at 7:46 P.M. That meant he probably pulled up to the steak house somewhere between 7:15 and 7:30 P.M.

Parties of two, Nola thought as she continued to scroll. *7:00 P.M. 7:30. 8:00. 8:30.* No one named *Archie,* no one named *Mint.*

She started again, expanding the search to bigger parties. There were plenty of names, each in its own digital column. *Bendis. Gaydos. Mack. Maleev.* But no *Mint* or anything close to it.

At the top of the screen, she noticed a Search box and quickly typed the name *Archie.*

No records found.

She typed the name *Mint.*

1 record found. Two years ago. October 15. Mint's birthday.

That meant he liked this place. Or used to like it. Either way, he hadn't been back—or at least made a reservation—until two nights ago, when he decided he needed some steak. Most likely, he didn't plan to eat alone.

Staring down at the iPad, Nola paced the length of the narrow trailer, whose walls were covered with hundreds of random pages, like a bulletin board in a student union—postcards, magazine photos, old album covers, and sketches from her notepad: of Nola's cat, of the milk barn, of the trailer, of every animal she'd spotted on the property, and of course of Longwood's open fields and native plants.

There were no drawings of people, except for one sketch of DeShawn from the metal shop, and naturally, a postcard of Bob Ross painting happy little trees.

Along the front wall were six finished canvases, leaning one against another, like dominos in midfall.

Rrrrrr, Sarah Connor purred, sniffing the spot where she'd left the dead toad.

It has to be in here. Check again, Nola told herself.

She scrolled back to the top of the reservation list, rescanning them one by one. That's when she saw it.

Spear.

That name—she knew it, from years ago. That was Mint's old code name: *Spearmint,* that was it, based on his favorite military saying, that the best units and best leaders lived *on the tip of the spear.*

Such macho awfulness.

But if that's you, sir . . . She scrolled to the right, checking the details.

Spear. 7:30 P.M. Party of 2.

Email contact was Ragdog1216@hotmail.com.

Ragdog? Nola didn't know what it meant. Maybe a nickname from his Tenth Mountain days? Mint's official email followed the usual format, name.mil@mail.com. He had a personal one on Gmail. But if he was also using Hotmail?

You cheating on your wife, sir? Nola asked, surprised by how much the thought riled her. Mint was a decorated soldier, a good father, a loyal investigator who once risked his life for— *No. Don't think it.*

But she had to. When it came to Archie Mint, it's all she thought. For years now.

"Hey, Sarah Connor, how're your password-guessing abilities?"

The cat turned away, sniffing the floor and licking it twice.

Nola pulled out her phone and opened a browser. Hotmail.com. She had his username. *Ragdog1216.*

Password?

She tried a few. Each had the same result. *Your password is incorrect.*

Eventually, a warning appeared: *You have (1) try remaining before we lock your account.*

Something opened in Nola's chest, a sharp, aching twist. She didn't know if it was anger or pain, but right there, she wanted to put her fist into the phone's screen. Turning back to the iPad, Nola reread the entry in the reservation book.

Spear. 7:30 P.M. Party of 2.

It was him. Had to be him. Replaying it again, she told herself it was probably just a work dinner. But who schedules work at 7:30 P.M. on a Saturday? More important, whoever Mint was scheduled to eat with, why didn't he or she step forward once Mint was found dead?

She studied the name. *Spear. 7:30 P.M. Party of—*

Huh.

Nola pulled the iPad closer. She'd missed it at first. In the far-right column . . . under NOTES . . . Mint's entry looked like it was blank, but it wasn't. At the very bottom of the cell, there was tiny, light blue type, like fine print. A few other entries had it, too. She expanded the image to see it better.

Most of the entries had the words *OpenTable,* the reservation app. Two others listed *Resy,* also a reservation app. But Mint's entry had this:

Black House

Confused, Nola clicked on it. Had to be a referral. If you made your reservation through OpenTable, the steak house's system listed *OpenTable* in your entry. Same with Resy. But as she clicked on the words *Black House* . . .

A pop-up window appeared. *Open in App Store?*

Yes, Nola clicked.

Another window opened. The words *Black House* appeared in a stenciled military font.

Nola's eyes narrowed. Her stomach churned. *Sir, what the hell were you doing here?*

19

Zig was thinking about the pencils.

"Can I see the photo again?" he asked, steering the car off the highway and blowing past the wooden sign for Wonderly Square. *Where Nature Smiles for Five Miles.*

Roddy turned the tablet toward Zig, the glow lighting his face in the dark car.

The photo was from outside the funeral this morning—of young, beefy Staff Sergeant Buddy Adcock, curled on the ground in agony, a pen protruding from his knee.

During the entire ride home, Zig had been thinking about this photo. When he first saw it, he couldn't help but stare at Buddy's face contorted in pain . . . at his mouth wide open in midscream, a spiderweb of spit forming a tightrope between his top and bottom teeth. At Buddy's knee, there was an unmistakable Rorschach blob of blood soaking through his slacks. But right now, Zig was focused on the bottom corner of the photo: the half dozen colored pencils littered across the asphalt.

Naturally, they were Nola's. She took her pencils everywhere. So for them to be scattered in such disarray . . . Buddy had hit her fast, caught her off guard, most likely as she was coming out of the building. It was a bad sign.

As the Army's Artist-in-Residence, Nola had spent years racing into war zones—Libya, Iraq, even that massacre when ISIS beheaded those three Marines outside of Raqqa in Syria. She stayed alive because she *wasn't* easily surprised. She didn't get caught off guard. And yet . . .

In the photo, a stray chocolate-brown pencil had bounced off the concrete path, sitting askew in the grass. A yellow pencil was right beside it. To leave her tools behind . . . Nola must have raced out of there at full speed, like she was scared of what else was coming. Zig had never seen her scared before, never seen her panic or make mistakes before. To anyone else, those pencils were just pencils. For Nola, who processed everything through her art, they were a lifeline.

"This isn't just another case for her, is it?" Roddy asked. "There's something personal she's chasing."

Or something personal that's chasing her, Zig thought, tugging the steering wheel and trying to think of the last time Nola ran from anything. And then this thought as he stared at Roddy: that nothing was more personal than family.

"Today seems like a day that if you painted it, it'd be dark red," Roddy said, taking a look out the window as they turned onto Zig's block. "Y'ever have that, where a day seems like it's red, or blue, or some other color?"

Okay, Roddy was obviously weird. But it was more than just being weird. Even if you put aside his awkward stare, the way he overshared, and of course the way he said every damn thing that came into his brain, there was still something . . . Zig didn't have a word for it yet, but he could feel it, lurking there, like Roddy had another layer that he kept hidden. Was Zig being paranoid? Of course he was. But right now, if he wanted to keep Nola safe, his best bet was to keep Roddy close and keep an eye on him.

"Mr. Zigarowski, do you know that woman?" Roddy added.

"What woman?" Zig asked, again glancing down at the photo.

"Not there. *There,*" Roddy said, pointing through the windshield, up the block, toward Zig's house.

Zig squinted through the dark, assuming Roddy had misidentified Mr. Munoz, whose wife died last year, and who often lingered outside people's homes, hoping to make chitchat while he was walking his dog.

Zig couldn't have been more wrong.

Sitting there on his front porch was a thin brunette, studying her phone like she was being quizzed on it. At just the sight of her—he hadn't seen her in a year, maybe longer—something needled at his throat. His rib cage clenched like a fist around his heart. *Not her. Can't be.*

"Stop the car," Zig blurted, forgetting that he was the one driving. He hit the brakes and the car bucked.

"Mr. Zigarowski, is that—?"

Zig wasn't listening. He was already out the door, moving in a blur, but never taking his eyes off her.

Charmaine. His ex-wife.

"Char . . . are you . . . is this . . . ? Is everything okay?" he asked. It wasn't.

20

It was a game, a first-person shooting game, Nola realized as she studied the screen, like Fortnite or Call of Duty, though unlike in those games, the graphics here were uncanny, the digital characters looking like real people in real uniforms.

Is this VR—some sort of virtual reality training program? Nola wondered, the screen buzzing with action as digital Rangers, Marines, even a group of SEALs ran through an Iraqi town, their uniforms rendered with every minute detail, from the most up-to-date camo pattern to the shoulder patches that list your blood type.

Welcome back.
Enter username or email.

Ragdog1216@hotmail.com, Nola typed.

A little hand grenade appeared, spinning round and round, then . . .

Password?
TipOfTheSpear.

Incorrect password. Please enter password.
TipOfTheSpear1216.

Incorrect password. Please enter password.
Spear1216.

Incorrect password. Please enter password.
Spear.
Incorrect password. Please enter password.

She thought about it a moment, then typed: *Spearmint.*

Incorrect password. Please enter password.
ScrewYouYouShitComputer.
Incorrect password. Please enter password.

She took a breath. Closed her eyes. Then typed . . .

HuckViolet.

Mint's kids.

Incorrect password. Please enter password.
HuckViolet1216.

The hand grenade appeared again.

Welcome back, Spearmint.
Resume session?

Nola grinned.
Yes.

21

On Nola's screen, the tiny grenade was still spinning.

Nola took a seat on her bed, its blue sheets unmade. Fuzzy cat toys sat up by the pillows, two of them shaped like mice, one of them shaped like broccoli for some reason.

A pop-up window finally appeared onscreen in the online game known as Black House.

Returning character already in use.
Play as new character?

Confused, Nola clicked *yes*.

The screen blinked. Bright yellow letters appeared:

Lt. Colonel Mint04 reporting for duty.

The screen blinked again, revealing a white room with walls that looked like they were made from ancient marble. Onscreen, Nola had a first-person view of whatever this new character—Lt. Colonel Mint04—was seeing.

The room looked exotic, something Persian or Indian—a church or a mosque—with peaked arch windows and sandstone carvings. The most disorienting part was the 360-degree view that kicked in as Nola turned and tilted the iPad, which she was gripping with both hands like it was a steering wheel. She stood up to get a better view.

At the center of the room, a black-draped pedestal held an ancient marble coffin.

This wasn't a church—it was a tomb.

Nola turned the iPad again. She knew this place. She'd been here before, during that trip to Afghanistan when she flipped her motorcycle racing the Army chaplain whose eyes were always red like a chili. After her surgery, Nola came here, where so many soldiers had no choice but to sightsee as they waited for flights back to the States. It was called *the most beautiful place in Kabul*—the Gardens of Babur, with the famous Tomb of—

"What're you doing?" a voice barked.

Nola spun around. It took a half second to realize it was coming from the iPad.

"Answer me!" the voice shouted again.

Already off balance, Nola kept turning. Onscreen, something moved. Someone. Headed right for her. She saw his legs first. Beige, pale green, and brown camouflage—the old Army desert combat uniform from Iraq.

She lifted the iPad, finally getting a good look.

Her mouth went dry, like someone was reaching down her throat, pulling her lungs out.

Th- That's not possible . . .

But there he was, onscreen. The buzzed blond hair. The lantern jaw. Even the pale blue eyes . . . He was supposed to be dead.

"What in fuck's name are you doing here!?" Lieutenant Colonel Archie Mint barked, plowing straight at Nola.

22

This was Roddy when he was eleven.

He was raging, his lips curling away from his teeth as he stormed upstairs. "Anne Marie! I know you have it! Gimme my Game Boy!" Roddy shouted, referring to the handheld Nintendo he'd spent six months saving for, mowing lawns, washing cars, even going door to door to sell off the old baseball cards he'd stolen from other kids.

"Roddy, please don't pick a fight," his younger brother, Darren, pleaded, trailing behind him as they reached the second floor, storming toward the door with a red-and-white metal sign that read:

DANGER!

TEENAGER INSIDE!
PROCEED WITH CAUTION!

The sign was right.

"Give me the damn Game Boy, you skank, or I'll—"

Roddy threw open the door, surprised to find . . .

Laughter.

On the bed, his older sister, Anne Marie, was lying on her stomach, feet in the air, twirling her left ankle like a satellite dish. She stared at the Game Boy, giggling.

She wasn't the only one.

On Roddy's left, in a pink beanbag chair, was a ninth-grade girl with crystal-blue eyes, her blond hair up in the same French braid she'd worn since elementary school. Missy Totino. Anne Marie's best friend—and the girl Roddy had had a crush on since that sleepover last year when Roddy walked in while Missy was on the toilet.

"See, he's embarrassed. Told you he loved you!" Anne Marie said to Missy.

"A.M.!" Roddy scolded. "She's joking," he insisted.

"So now you *don't* think she's pretty?" Anne Marie challenged.

"No, that's not—"

"Would you kiss her?"

"A.M.!" Roddy pleaded, the anger gone from his voice. He was begging now, trying to limit the damage. "Can I please just have my Game Boy?"

"Sure." Anne Marie grinned. "For a trade."

Roddy took a half step back, his younger brother already gone, too smart to be part of the collateral damage.

Back when Anne Marie had first started offering trades, they were small—she'd want an extra dessert or to get out of walking the dog. Last year, though, she'd found Roddy's wallet in the back seat of the car and upped the ante, offering to trade it back only if he did her week's chores. From there, Anne Marie did what the oldest child always does: took advantage of her younger siblings. Today, however, was the first time she'd use it for something sinister.

"I'll do your work-wheel for two weeks."

"You called me a skank. For that alone—"

"Three weeks," Roddy countered.

"For a *Game Boy*?"

"A month, okay? That's my—"

"Anne Marie, just give him the stupid game," Missy interrupted.

Roddy turned. So did Anne Marie.

"What'd you say?" Anne Marie challenged.

"A.M., please," Roddy pleaded, "just tell me what you want."

For the rest of his life, Roddy would never forget the look on his sister's face, a thin slit that looked like a grin, but carried no joy in it. "Take your shirt off."

"Wha?"

"You think I don't see you doing push-ups before bed? Show Missy your new body. Your shirt. Take it off."

"Anne Marie, that's not funny," Missy insisted.

"You said he was cute. Here's your chance to see him."

For a moment, it looked like Missy might argue. But in ninth grade, especially among teenage girls, there's a fine line between out-rage and self-preservation. Missy sat there in the beanbag, staring at Roddy.

"We're waiting," Anne Marie said, waving the Game Boy.

Roddy stood there, his skinny body barely filling his Shrek T-shirt, which was now damp with sweat. In front of him were Anne Marie and Missy. Behind him, his younger siblings, Darren and now Pau-lette, were back in the hallway. On any playground, when some-thing bad goes down, no one wants to miss it.

"I'm counting to three," Anne Marie said, reaching toward her nightstand for an open can of Diet Coke. She held the can over the Game Boy, ready to pour. "One . . ."

"Don't!" Roddy begged. "Please . . ."

"Two . . ." She tipped the can more.

Roddy could feel his fists tightening, could feel the Bad Roddy poking through, telling him to go for her throat. He'd done it before—on Mother's Day, when Anne Marie was teasing him for not having a real mom—but all he got was a black eye. Anne Marie was in high school, four years older. He'd be bigger than her soon enough. But not yet.

"Two and three-quarters . . ." Anne Marie counted.

"I-I'll— I'm doing it!" Roddy said, grabbing the hem of his Shrek T-shirt and giving it a tug.

He shut his eyes to make it go faster. All it did was turn the world into slow motion. The air felt frozen as he exposed his stomach. The very worst part was the burn of everyone's stares, slicing him at every angle, cutting deeper as he continued to lift his shirt, revealing his belly button. Anne Marie whistled with a catcall. Someone else let out a laugh.

At eleven years old, it was the first time in his life that Roddy wished he were dead. It wouldn't be the last.

"Eww, does he have a hard-on?" Anne Marie asked.

He didn't. Not that it mattered. Humiliation complete.

"It's enough, Anne Marie. Leave him alone," Missy said.

"Suddenly you're feeling bad?" Anne Marie challenged.

"Anne Marie, you're a shit," Missy added, hopping up from the beanbag and heading for the door. As she blew past Roddy, she crashed into him, sending him bumping into the wall. In the hall-way, his siblings scattered.

"Does that—? Can I have my Game Boy now?" shirtless Roddy asked.

Anne Marie rolled her eyes and with a flick of her wrist, chucked the Game Boy toward his feet.

"*No . . . don't . . . !*"

It crashed in that way that electronics aren't meant to crash, the screen shattering.

"*I'll kill you,*" Roddy muttered, dropping his shirt and running toward her. "I mean it, I'll—"

"No. You won't." Anne Marie shoved him hard in the chest, send-ing him tripping over a wastebasket and tumbling to the ground.

"Now get the hell out of my room." She kicked his shirt like a soccer ball. "And take your wuss shirt with you."

Down on his knees, Roddy picked up his Game Boy, which now wouldn't turn on.

Don't cry, don't cry, don't fucking cry, he told himself, already fail-ing miserably.

On this day, Roddy knew better than to fight back.

Soon enough, that would change.

23

"A-Are you—? You look . . ." Zig caught himself. Stopped. Started again, staring at his ex-wife. "Charmaine, is everything okay?"

"Ziggy, we should do this inside."

He knew that tone. He knew all her tones.

She got married. That was Zig's first thought. She wouldn't take a half hour drive unless it was big. Zig was tempted to ask her right there, but knew it would look desperate. They used to speak a few times a year—some texts during birthdays, then by voice on the anniversary of Maggie's death. That had stopped years ago, Charmaine saying it was "too much," whatever that meant.

"Mr. Zigarowski, you want me to wait?" Roddy called out from his police cruiser.

Zig waved him off, shoving open the front door and motioning for Charmaine to enter first.

As she brushed past him, he got a better look at her. She looked good. She always looked good, with porcelain skin and pale green eyes the color of palm trees. More important, he took in her smell, a mix of lavender and worn leather. Instantly, a rush of endorphins lit his brain, the kaleidoscope starting to swirl with old memories, all out of order. Their last meal at Patton's . . . an old Sting concert . . . the taste of her kiss . . . that night in the bathtub after her brother's wedding . . . that night in their car when they were first dating . . . the red lights of an ambulance . . . Charmaine screaming in rage, screaming in loss, screaming in agony—

"You had a funeral today?" Charmaine said, though it wasn't a question.

Zig looked down at his suit. It wasn't his clothing that gave him away. It was the smell. Charmaine hated the stench of embalming fluid. Back at Mint's funeral, he'd scrubbed thoroughly, dousing himself in cologne, but some things can't be masked.

"It's not— It was a Dover thing."

"I thought you were done with Dover," she countered, no judgment in her voice. "Never met a fallen soldier you didn't want to help, huh?"

"This one's different."

She made a face, that one she always made when she didn't want to get into it. "I take it this is your handiwork?" Charmaine said, setting her purse down on the antique tiger oak bench, complete with a lift seat that Zig had rebuilt from scratch. Next to it was an English pine coatrack made with five vintage railroad spikes that he'd personally pulled from the ground. "You're getting fancy in your old age."

Zig smiled, pretending the compliment didn't matter. But everything with an ex matters. He looked over his handiwork with a fresh eye, imagining how the pieces looked to her. Each project had taken months. He'd built the dining room table from barn wood, reupholstered the arts-and-crafts-style sofa, and personally sandblasted the porcelain on the antique barbershop chair that he'd pulled from a junkyard and made the centerpiece of his living room. He'd even sculpted the three soapstone hummingbirds anchored to the wall above the sofa. Zig was always moving, filling his home with project after homemade project. But at this moment, with Charmaine at the center of it, his house felt emptier than ever.

"Restroom this way?" she asked, heading toward the kitchen without hesitation, like she owned the place.

"What's the bad news?" Zig called out.

"Just relax," she replied, doing that thing where she twisted her wrists, jangling her yoga bracelets, which were made of shells, beads, and pale aquamarine crystals. Heading down the hallway, she forced a smile before disappearing into the bathroom.

It fooled most people. But it didn't fool Zig. And he didn't fool her.

She definitely got married, Zig thought, racing toward the kitchen, practically smashing his shins into the pinewood bench as he grabbed his laptop from the farm table. With a few clicks, he navigated to Facebook, the browser populating with the only profile he ever visited.

Charmaine Clarke.

Status: In a relationship.

Like most things on Facebook, it was a half-truth. Charmaine had gotten engaged months ago. No wedding date set, at least based on the few replies he'd seen on the subject.

He double-checked her feed. Her most recent post was a photo that a friend took after a recent car crash, airbag deployed, all the windows shattered, with a message from Charmaine: "Be thankful for what you have."

"SO TRUE!" someone replied.

"Love your posts!!!" wrote another, outdoing the caps with triple exclamation points.

For years after Maggie's death, Zig would check Facebook every day, eyeing Charmaine's relationship status. He swore it off years ago, on that night that he decided to leave Dover and his old life behind. New house, new town, new start.

Yet in two minutes, Zig already felt that familiar pit in his stomach, that cocktail of thrill and shame that only comes from being around an old flame.

"Sorry to ambush you. It's just—hoo boy," Charmaine called out behind him, her voice hoarse, like she'd been yelling. Or crying.

Zig slapped shut his laptop and spun around, getting a better view of her in the light of the kitchen. She still looked great, but she also looked tired. Her crow's-feet were deeper than he remembered, same with her *elevens,* which was what she called the two vertical wrinkles between her eyebrows—but her brown hair was long again, the way she used to wear it. *She's beautiful,* Zig thought, the emotional kaleidoscope spinning faster, anxiety colliding with excitement. *She looks better than last time. She hates me.* And of course, that steadfast nugget that always arrived as old memories mixed with old smells mixed with an entire lifetime that they'd shared and then discarded: *She still loves me.* Yet as Zig motioned for her to sit across from him, it was clear that when it came to old love, nothing got discarded, at least not completely.

"You and Warren okay?"

A small smile lit Charmaine's face—a real one. Back when they were married, Charmaine had taught linguistics at Drexel University, where she'd greet students with her favorite joke: *The past, the present, and the future walked into a bar. It was tense.* After Maggie's death, though, working with kids . . . Charmaine couldn't do it. Like most parents who bury a child, she couldn't do much of anything. What saved her was, of all things, yoga. Eventually, she opened Blue Yoga-maya, a small wellness center, determined to be on the *giving* side of helping others, rather than the *receiving*. The universe heard her loud and clear. A week after the opening, she met Warren. "He's great. Warren's great," she said, a true calm settling her voice, her elevens disappearing.

"Is this where you tell me you got married?" Zig asked.

"You say that like it's a bad thing."

Zig froze. "N-No . . . not at all . . . I just meant—"

"Joke. I was joking, Ziggy. We're engaged, you know that. No wedding date yet."

He nodded, trying to laugh it off.

"I didn't know you moved," Charmaine said. "I had to look this place up to find you. The house is nice."

"It's smaller—but y'know, we can't all live in model homes."

Charmaine flashed a grin, another real one. Her fiancé was a general contractor, specializing in model homes in preplanned communities. "Make fun all you want, I know you like Warren."

He hated to admit it was true. On the night they first met, bumping into each other at an airport, of all places—Charmaine and Warren were heading to Hawaii, Zig to Ohio for a mortician's conference—Zig was ready to put his carry-on bag through Warren's teeth. Instead, a snow delay in Philly gave them four hours in an airport bar, screaming at the Eagles game and bonding over who had the best mustache in Philly sports history. *Dave "The Hammer" Schultz! The Enforcer!,* who still held the NHL record for most penalty minutes in a season.

That night in the airport, as they hugged goodbye, Zig whispered two words into Charmaine's ear: *"Keep him."*

He meant it. Sure, it crushed Zig to see his ex so happy. But the only thing that crushed him more was to see her sad. Warren was decent, he was good to his older daughters, and his model homes were better designed than Zig would've expected. After everything Charmaine had been through, everything she'd lost, she deserved a model home of her own.

"So if you're not married, why'd you come all this way?"

Charmaine reached into her handbag. Her hand shot out, slapping a black rectangle the size of a brick against the table. An old videotape.

Zig grinned. "That's not from that night we—"

"I need you to look at something," she explained.

She didn't have to say another word. Like any long-married couple, they could have entire conversations with nothing more than a glance. He knew that look. This was about their daughter, Maggie.

"Why would—?"

"Just watch," Charmaine said, handing him her phone, her elevens firmly back in place.

Onscreen was a gray circle with a black triangle in it, a video. She'd used her phone's camera to record whatever was on the videotape.

"You need to see it for yourself," she added.

Zig hit Play. Then his whole world unraveled.

24

"What is this?" Zig asked.

"Just watch," Charmaine said as the video on her phone began to play.

Onscreen was another screen—an outdated television with a familiar silver border. "Is that our old—?"

"With the built-in VCR," she said. Zig recognized their old TV, the one that used to be in their basement, where Maggie, at barely a year old, held on to the coffee table, eating Cheerios and bouncing to the maddening theme of *Thomas the Tank Engine*. "It's the only VCR I could find."

Zig leaned on both elbows, down toward the phone. The video was grainy, showing a teenage girl—not Maggie, someone else—maybe fifteen or sixteen, with jet-black hair and shiny lip gloss. She was sitting on a couch, facing the camera, like she was being interviewed.

"Is that . . . what's-her-face . . . she had that dog who bit everyone . . . ?"

"Alexis Mayer. Lived around the corner. Babysat for Maggie."

". . . but what I really love are Broadway plays, especially musicals . . ." Alexis said onscreen, tucking her hair behind her ear. *"And choreography! I love excellent choreography . . . !"*

"Why do we care about this?" Zig asked, noticing the sign just above Alexis's head. It was in an eighties *Miami Vice* font, aquamarine and pink. *SuperStars,* Zig read, old synapses firing as he remembered . . . "SuperStars Modeling?" he blurted.

"That's the one. It was two towns over. The owner's daughter got booked on a commercial for Sunny Delight or something stupid like that. Back when the girls were little, half of Maggie's friends did tryouts at SuperStars with one of these videos."

"Please tell me you didn't let Maggie—"

"C'mon," Charmaine said, pointing him back to the screen, where young Alexis was adamant that *Newsies* changed her life.

Zig was trying to watch, but what he couldn't unsee was his old TV, its familiar plastic paneling playing tricks with his brain, like he was watching his past, spending a lazy Sunday in bed, back when he and Charmaine were first married, binge-watching VH1's *Behind the Music* long before they called it binge-watching, the two of them betting whether it was the guitarist or drummer who would have the drug problem.

"God, I remember buying that TV . . ."

"Circuit City," Charmaine said, still focused on the screen. "What matters is, SuperStars shut down years ago, once they realized that charging kids $49.99 for headshots that don't work . . . well, that's just not a long-term business model. Apparently, the owner of the place died six months back, leaving everything to her daughter, someone named Dianne Cash. Two weeks back, Dianne finally started going through her mom's stuff, at which point, she found boxes and boxes of . . ."

". . . old videotapes," Zig said.

"Exactly. At first, she uploaded a few to Facebook, everyone getting a laugh at how they used to look in their *Star Search* days. And then, as she was going through one of the tapes, Dianne saw *this* and reached out to me."

Zig studied the screen. As the girl in the video stood up to say goodbye, the video blurred, the screen filling with horizontal lines that got wider, then smaller, hiccupping with static.

". . . waaaaaaaant tooooooooo thaaaaaaaaaaaaaaaank . . ." young Alexis said, her voice warping, everything going black and silver. A thick band of static appeared, then disappeared, revealing a new image, something buried underneath. To make the Alexis video, someone had taped over an older video.

Now, that older video was playing.

"I-Is that—?"

Zig knew who it was, even through the static.

His dead daughter, Maggie. She was there, onscreen.

And she was sobbing.

25

It's him, Nola thought.

"Talk to me!" Colonel Mint roared, immediately barking orders, his voice a robotic roar. *"Who are you!? How'd you get here?"*

Nola stumbled backward, crashing into the foldout desk. Back when she first moved into the trailer, it took months to adjust to the small space, her body eventually gaining the muscle memory to avoid bumping into everything. Now, she hit the desk hard, knocking over a canvas as pencils and paintbrushes rained down. The cat jumped at the sound, scurrying out of sight.

Onscreen, Mint's face, his expressions . . . the digital image was perfect, right down to the small scar above his eyebrow, as if they'd scanned him in. They even had the gold medallion on his chest—the Soldier's Medal—awarded for heroism outside of enemy combat, Nola now mentally replaying the story they forced Mint to tell her: of him leaving work and hearing screaming from an elevator.

With his bare hands, Mint pried the doors open, finding the elevator trapped between floors. Sliding down through the small gap, he helped rescue the screamer, a severely overweight man who was clearly suffering from a panic attack. Mint shoved him up and out, all three hundred pounds of him, though it wasn't until the paramedics arrived that he realized Mr. Panic Attack was the CFO of Huntington Ingalls, one of the country's top federal defense contractors. As Mint used to tease, that's the only reason he got the medal—to make the CFO feel good.

"Did you hack this account?" he demanded through the iPad.

Nola opened her mouth, but nothing came out. *This isn't— Mint is dead. This can't be him.*

"We should go!" someone shouted. It took a moment to realize it wasn't Mint.

Nola turned the iPad again. Someone else was there. Another soldier, with darker skin. Hispanic. Close-set eyes. His fatigues were also beige, green, and brown, but the darker camouflage was the modern Scorpion pattern—the current ones you get in basic training.

"MOVE! NOW!" the Hispanic man shouted. Above his head, a beam of blue light shone down. His character began glowing, his body now pixelated, small digital squares of him disappearing, like he was being beamed up on *Star Trek.*

Plink.

The Hispanic man was gone.

A second blue beam appeared above Mint.

"Sir, don't . . . !" Nola shouted.

Too late. His body started pixelating.

"Sir!" she roared. *"Archie! Look at me! That's not you, is it?"*

Colonel Mint turned and locked eyes with her.

Was it him? It couldn't be. She went to say something else—

Plink.

Mint disappeared, leaving Nola standing there—alone in her trailer—staring at a digitized tomb in Afghanistan.

Mrrrrr? the cat trilled, trying to decide whether to approach or not. She stayed under the table.

Nola was too busy staring at the screen—was it a video game? An online hangout? She eyed the photo-realistic rendering of the tomb, the Afghan locale now making her wonder if Black House was something created by the military.

Did she believe Colonel Mint was suddenly alive? No—she'd seen the crime scene photos. There was no faking that. But whoever was just logged in there with her clearly knew that Mint used this space for something . . . and it wasn't just for making dinner reservations.

Nola turned the iPad slightly, watching the view of the darkened tomb turn with her. Whatever was really going on in this app—in this place called Black House—Archie Mint had an account here, and from the looks of it, was communicating with others here. If that was the case, with the right tools and the right person, whatever Mint was doing could be tracked.

Fortunately for Nola, she knew the perfect person for that.

26

Zion Lopez lost his temper too quickly. It would be his downfall.

"I mean it—stay back!" Zion yelled, swinging an empty vodka bottle like a sword. *"Stay back!"*

Across from him, in Zion's small but surprisingly well-decorated Japanese living room, complete with a shoji screen, a redheaded woman with different-colored eyes—one green, one blue—stepped toward him. She had a buoyant walk and wore a blue leather coat (it was faux leather, actually, since she was vegan), but she was the kind of person who made you feel uncomfortable, who you'd somehow know to walk away from. The kind of person you can feel watching you across a room, even when you're not looking their way.

"Reagan, you're not listening!" Zion yelled, holding the bottle by the neck.

He was wrong. Reagan heard every word. It's why, when she first walked into the town house, she was so impressed. Young street guys like Zion usually panic and run. A few wet their pants. Zion, a charismatic Dominican kid with a shaved head and trendy chin stubble, invited her inside, offering some sparkling water and a charming lopsided grin.

On his coffee table was a stack of Simon Sinek business books. Zion was a pro, quickly trying to make a deal: "Maybe there's something I can help *you* with." There wasn't. But how could she not admire ambition like that? Reagan was a professional, first and foremost. She took pride in her work. Whatever the job, do it best. Like her father taught her.

"Reagan, step the hell back! It wasn't me!" Zion shouted with another swing of the vodka bottle as he backed up toward the kitchen. *"Ask anyone! I wasn't there, Reagan!"* he insisted, thinking he was smart to call her by her first name. Keep it personal.

If he were really smart, he'd have known that the only reason Reagan used her real name was because she had no intention of Zion ever speaking to anyone again.

"I heard you met Mr. Vess when you were twelve," Reagan said, moving slowly, unafraid, her hands shifting in her pockets, like she was knitting with invisible needles.

On the dining room table, she spotted a butter-colored wooden bowl that was the exact same shade of yellow as an old 1960 guitar— a Les Paul Special—that she'd tried to bid on a few months back. According to the auction house, it supposedly belonged to reggae legend Peter Tosh. His name was engraved on the truss cover. A solid 8 out of 10. She shouldn't have let it get away.

"Reagan, I swear on my mother's life, I would never—!"

"They told me you used to play on one of Mr. Vess's youth basketball teams. That's real history," Reagan pointed out, still thinking about the guitar. "So you can imagine how upset he was to find out you were the one who—"

"It wasn't me! For the ninety-fifth time!" Zion screamed, spit flying, his fuse fully lit. He started to turn toward the kitchen.

"Zion, if you run . . ."

Too late. He was gone, the vodka bottle still in hand as he bolted through the kitchen, heading for the back door.

Reagan rolled her eyes.

Zion tore open the door and darted outside . . .

. . . where he collided with the chest of the massive man in a black windbreaker who was waiting for him.

The man held up a plastic Walmart bag that he'd fished out of Zion's trash. In the bag was a receipt and a box for a latex Oscar the Grouch mask.

"Today's show is sponsored by the letter M—for *moron*," Reagan said as her partner shoved Zion inside. "I see you met Seabass. Sebastian, meet Zion."

Zion looked up, noticing Sebastian's sad blue eyes and heart-shaped face. He was . . . *vast* was the only word to describe him, his chest wide like an iceberg. Up top, he had bright red—

Zion froze. *She and he . . . they both . . . red hair.* Now it made sense.

Professionally, they were called *the Reds.*

Reagan was an auburn redhead with alabaster skin; Sebastian was freckled and ruddy, pure Irish.

According to some, they were husband and wife. Others said brother and sister. Neither was true, though the rumors only intensified when people noticed that Sebastian didn't speak.

Some said he was mute. Others that it was from a Humvee accident in Yemen—he was an Army Ranger, and a shard of metal sliced into his throat. The most absurd theory was also the most popular: that he'd done it to himself in some sacred vow of silence.

The truth was, Seabass was simply quiet, a natural observer who preferred letting his thoughts marinate. Besides, Reagan talked enough for both of them. All the other rumors were nonsense—or as Reagan called it, *marketing*. It was the same with their name: *The Reds.* Short. Catchy. Easy to remember. Even in a business like theirs, marketing mattered. As for why they worked as a team, why does anyone work as a team? They were better together, at it for so long now, they moved as one.

"Get back!" Zion yelled, raising the vodka bottle like a bat. He never had a chance.

With a hand like a manhole cover, Seabass rammed his palm into Zion's nose, breaking it with a crack. Blood splattered like juice from a popped cherry.

Zion stumbled, wobbling, letting go of the vodka bottle, which smashed at his feet, glass scattering across the kitchen.

"I need him conscious," Reagan announced.

Seabass made a face. *Like we've never done this before?*

Wrapping his tree-trunk arms around Zion, Seabass bear-hugged the kid, pulling him against his chest and squeezing the air from his lungs. Unable to breathe, Zion raised his chin, his neck now exposed.

That was all Reagan needed.

From her pocket, she pulled out what looked like piano wire, though it was really a thin chain with tiny metal teeth—a camping tool from Reagan's favorite days, when she was little, back before her dad's arrest, when he used to take her on hunting trips.

With a metal ring at each end, the mini saw was perfect for slicing branches and firewood. Too thin for bone or taking off a ram's horn. But, boy, did it tear through flesh.

In one quick movement, like she was doing cat's cradle, Reagan looped the saw around Zion's exposed neck, pulling it tight against his skin.

"Zion, we know you're the one who shot Archie Mint. In a dumb rage, you also shot a valet named Anthony Wojowicz. So choose your next words very carefully," Reagan explained, tugging harder on the thin saw, letting it dig into Zion's Adam's apple. "I need to know who hired you."

27

The globus was back.

That was the doctor's word for it—the lump in Zig's throat, like a stuck pill, that Zig had for a full year after Maggie's death. It made it hard to breathe, even harder to sleep. Someone called it a "grief lump," affecting those who have been through wrenching despair. Whatever it was, one day, Zig woke up and it was gone.

Now, at just the sight of this video . . . of Maggie at twelve years old, right before she died . . . the globus was back, wedged in his windpipe. His head was buzzing, like he'd lost a minute of time. He looked around. He was somehow standing in his kitchen, one leg propped on the bench, though he had no memory of getting up.

"Wh-Why is she crying?" he asked, already crying himself.

Across from him, still sitting, Charmaine shook her head, tears in her own eyes. She had no idea.

The phone screen went black with a final burst of static.

The End.

"That's it?" Zig asked. "Where's the rest?"

Charmaine shook her head again. She looked gutted, her shoulders sagging.

Grabbing the phone and swiping his finger, Zig rewound the video, back to where Maggie first appeared. There was a loud, warped sound—loads of static—and then . . . there she was.

"Magpie," Zig whispered, not even realizing he'd said it.

Onscreen, Maggie's head was down, her hands clutching her face, like she was trying to hide. Even as a kid, Maggie wasn't a crier. At three years old, while spinning in circles outside the local ice cream shop, she'd tripped and landed on her wrist. She went quiet—dead silent—but never shed a tear. A woman who saw it happen said she'd probably just sprained it, but Zig suspected otherwise. To test his theory, he held up Maggie's favorite lovey, a plush purple monkey named Banana, directly in front of her. When Maggie refused to reach for it, he knew something was wrong. Sure enough, Maggie had broken her wrist in three places. "She's tough," the nurse in the emergency room said. "A little bag of nails."

In the years after her death, Zig carried that around with him. *Little bag of nails.*

Tonight, though, every detail that he carried was gone, like it'd been ripped away.

"I-I'm sorry . . . so sorry . . ." his young daughter whispered onscreen, her body convulsing, shaking.

At just the sight of her, the globus expanded in Zig's throat.

On the right-hand side of the screen, someone's hand appeared in shadow, giving her a tissue.

Maggie took it, wiped her eyes. *"You don't have t— They don't even know—"* She blew her nose, never looking up. *"I should've— I'm sorry to drag you into—"*

The static swallowed her whole. That was it. The End.

Zig scrolled the video back again.

"I'm sorry to drag you into—"

"Into *what?*" Zig asked. "Who's she talking to?"

Charmaine sat there, silent. Zig replayed it again.

"I'm sorry to drag you into—"

Zig put two fingers on the screen, expanding the image. As Maggie wiped her eyes with the back of her hand, he spotted a smudge of mascara on her knuckle. This was after she started wearing makeup. Twelve years old for sure, right before she died.

"I'm sorry to drag you into—"

He played it again. And again.

"I'm sorry to drag you into—"

"She sounds like— You think she was—? Was someone hurting

her?" Zig asked, the words tumbling from his lips, everything moving hyper fast and hyper slow at the same time.

Charmaine was crying now, head down, picking at the leather
strap on one of her bracelets. "The talent agency . . . the daughter of
the owner . . . I asked her, begged her . . . This was all she could find,"
Charmaine muttered. "Sh-She said there were no records of Maggie
ever being a client."

Zig rewound the video and played it again. Then again. Seventeen
seconds of his dead daughter sobbing—the hitch in her voice, the pain
. . . An old swirling hole opened in Zig's stomach, the one that took
him back to the old funeral home, to Maggie, her tiny gray corpse lying
there in the mortuary, Zig determined to prep her body, to wash her
hair and put her in her best dress, to take care of her one last time . . .
and then crumpling to his knees, unable to stand, unable to breathe,
unable even to cry, his entire body collapsing in on itself, a river of snot
running down his nose as he realized that when it came to prepping his
own daughter's body, he couldn't.

"Ziggy, please say something," Charmaine pleaded.

He was still staring at the screen. "Why would—? The way
she's— Who's she even talking to, anyway?"

"And why go to them instead of us?"

"Did she think we wouldn't listen, or is it—?" Zig squinted at the
screen. "This person . . . he looks like a man."

"It's *definitely* a man."

He looked up at his ex, the rage in her eyes catching him off
guard. "You do realize, Char, this is much easier when you're the calm
one, and I'm the one in the mad rage?"

"Ziggy, whatever's going on in that video . . . This is our girl,"
she said, the words stinging Zig's chest. "You can call Waggs. You
can call Dover. Hell, you can call every damn government operative
you've met in the last two decades who owes you a favor. Someone
should be able to find tax records for this rinky-dink SuperStars talent agency, and if there're tax records, there'll be an employee list. I
need to know who was speaking to our daughter. Even if this was
just her being a twelve-year-old girl, mad that . . . that . . . that some

friend didn't invite her for a sleepover or whatever the hell it was, I want to know who she was talking to. So go do what you do best and be a pain in the ass."

Zig sat up straight. *"Pain in the ass?"*

"I was saying it with love. Make it happen and I pretend buy you the *Back to the Future* car."

Charmaine froze as she said the words. She physically touched her own lips, like she was trying to put the sentence back in her mouth. Years ago, when she and Zig had first gotten married and money was tight, they'd make pretend purchases for each other. "I pretend buy you tickets to the Phillies World Series." In no time, it became their inside joke: "I pretend buy you these fourteen Yorkie puppies in this pet store window." It escalated from there: "I pretend buy you doormats with obscenities on them that we would never display in public." "Only if I can pretend buy you that historic house we saw in Missouri with the jail on the back of it." Needless to say, after the divorce, the pretend buying stopped—until this exact moment, when Charmaine accidentally let one slip out. "Just do me a favor, Ziggy, and find out what the hell's going on."

He nodded and grabbed the videotape, then his phone, already dialing. Even with records this old, there's always a trail to follow.

Fortunately for Zig, he knew the perfect person for that.

28

Amy Waggs was well aware she'd be late.

"I know, please don't give me guilt," she said into her phone, speed-walking through the FBI's nearly empty parking garage, her short brown hair bobbing with each step. "I'm on my way."

From the moment her office phone rang—7:00 P.M. on a weeknight, for Chrissakes—there was no avoiding it. In the FBI's Biometric Lab, late calls meant emergencies from time zones where the sun was just coming up. Picking up those calls was part of the job.

The truth of it was, Waggs got a charge from those calls, talking to a partner agency when a bomb went off in a Libyan church, helping them pull prints off a dead body so they could figure out if any of the victims might've been in on the attack. It wasn't an easy task. To print the dead, you need the right skin conditions as well as skin temperature. But again, phone calls like that were worth it.

What wasn't worth it? When the call came from a kid, some nineteen-year-old bomb technician in Kuwait who's so new on the job, he forgot to put ink in his print kit, and sorry, ma'am, but . . . um . . . what do I do now?

This is why no one likes children, Waggs thought, picking up speed in the garage, still annoyed at how long it took to teach young

Ahmad how to pull prints using adhesives like name-tag labels or even Con-Tact paper.

"Mikel, I swear I'm already in the car," she lied to her boyfriend, looking around, her only focus being where she'd parked. She'd regret that soon enough.

Her heels clicked across the concrete. On her wrist was a pale yellow corsage. Every few steps, she'd extend her arm to admire it, its elastic strap perfectly covering the small clock tattoo on the inside of her wrist, with the exact time her mother died. A few years back, Waggs became convinced that she'd most likely share a similar fate, eventually dying alone. It felt good to think she might be wrong.

"So, twenty minutes?" Mikel asked, sounding skeptical.

"Twenty for sure. Twenty-two at the most," Waggs insisted, knowing that at this time of night, with the traffic on 95, she probably wouldn't be there until—

"You know I can hear your voice echoing in the garage? You're not even in the car yet, are you?" he teased. "You're lucky you're so cute."

"Actually, you're the lucky one since . . . hurr . . . wow . . . no matter how I end this sentence, it's gonna sound either super self-congratulatory or like a deliciously plump middle-aged woman trying far too hard to flirt."

"Don't undersell middle-aged flirts. Not all heroes wear capes."

Waggs laughed at that, her round face lighting up, now thinking it was totally worth the humiliation of going into Victoria's Secret and asking that skinny chopstick of a salesgirl to help her pick out the new underwear she bought just for tonight.

Turning the corner and spotting her forest-green Subaru, Waggs popped the locks, opened the door, and slid into the front seat.

"Amy Waggs," a voice called out behind her.

"What in the f—!"

Waggs spun around, her phone dropping from her hand. In the back seat was a young woman with brutal black eyes, pointy features, and silvery hair with a dyed black streak.

Waggs had never met her face-to-face but recognized her instantly.

"Nola?"

"You're the one Mr. Zigarowski calls. The one who's good with computers." Nola turned on her iPad, its glow lighting the dark car. "I need to know about this place called Black House."

29

This was Nola when she was thirteen.

They had moved two towns over because Royall couldn't afford rent, which explained why he was teaching her how to cheat.

"Anybody thirsty?" Royall asked, pointing to the folding table covered in beer cans and liquor bottles.

"I am, I am," said Francis, a middle-aged blond man with a dimpled chin who loved saying things twice for emphasis.

A few of Royall's other poker buddies nodded, Nola quickly pouring six glasses of Johnnie Walker. The good stuff. Blue Label. Not that cheap Black Label crap that they mark down at Kmart.

Royall and Nola had spent the morning using a plastic funnel to fill the Blue Label bottle with an off-brand scotch that was so cheap, it came in a can.

Won't they know? Nola was tempted to ask. Just like she was tempted to ask, *Why do I need to dress up?* when he told her to wear "the tight jeans." But after six years of living with Royall, she knew better than to ask stupid questions.

"Here you go, *sir*," she said, leaning hard on the word *sir*.

Royall looked up. *Sir* was the signal. Nola was only supposed to say it when she was standing behind the person with the best cards.

"Y'understand?" Royall had asked her earlier, talking with a closed fist as he always did, happy or sad. "When you do refills, that's when you can peek at people's cards. Make sense?"

It made sense.

Since the moment the game started, her stomach had been bothering her. She was struggling to remember whether a straight flush beat four of a kind, or was it the other way around?

It only got worse as players began arriving, especially those she knew to avoid, like Hartley Spencer, who she could swear leaned in to smell her every time she poured him a drink.

For the first hour of the game, terrified of being caught, Nola kept her head down, trying to be invisible as she refilled bowls of tortilla chips, took away dirty ashtrays, and spied on cards while Royall's friends argued about the vital intellectual issues of the day, like which Dixie Chick was the biggest pain in the ass.

Eventually, Nola noticed that Repeating Francis—who recently had sold Royall nearly a hundred odd-lot water heaters that Royall was able to flip for a quick profit—scratched at a birthmark on the inside of his forearm, like he was slitting his wrist, every time he had a good hand.

She also noticed that Acne Steve with bad pimples and great teeth—who managed the local roller rink (and sold bootleg DVDs there)—would put his cards down and rub his hands together like a kid getting a toy, whenever his hand was a bust.

But what Nola noticed most of all was the wiry and extremely pale sixteen-year-old—Acne Steve's son—sulking on the sofa, elbows on his knees, lost in his brand-new Nintendo DS Lite. Nola had seen him before, dragged here on alternating weekends as the divorce required. Steve III, though everyone called him Trey.

"You guys got soda?" Trey had asked a few weeks back. Nola brought him an RC Cola, and as she handed it over, Trey thanked her with a quick smile that Nola missed—though Royall didn't.

"Stay away from him—older boys only want one thing," Royall had warned that night.

Today, Nola still didn't know what the *one thing* was, but the fact that Royall didn't like Trey made him—with his spiky, bleached-blond hair, a black concert tee with the word *Obey* across the front, and shockingly white Nike Air Force Ones—instantly more interesting.

Circling the poker table to refill the pretzel bowls, Nola stole a glance at Trey. He didn't notice, though truthfully, she didn't much care. Even with the churn in her stomach, as the game heated up, as the bets got bigger, Nola was, for the first time in a while, actually having fun.

That should've been her warning.

"Let me get that for you, *sir*," she said, pouring a refill of scotch for Royall.

Royall shot her a thin grin. On most days, he was armed with devil smiles. This was an angel one, like a joke between just the two of them. It actually made her feel good. Great, even. Like they were on the same team.

For Nola, it was a new concept. Back before Royall took her in, she'd thought that she and her old family—the LaPointes—were on the same team. But they'd tossed her aside, deciding to rehome her by listing her on an adoption website called Brand New Chance. Royall chose her the first night her photo was posted. The site was perfect for people like Royall, who would never make it through the adoption screening process. But it turned Nola into a *thing* . . . something cast to the curb. *Like garbage,* Royall used to tell her. Would real teammates do that?

It made Nola think of her real mom, who, truthfully, she barely remembered. When Nola was six, a caseworker said that her mom had been murdered. Nola didn't believe it. Surely you'd *feel* something like that. Which left her with her only original teammate—the one who scared her, but who was still forever tied to her, like a horrible magnet—her brother, her twin. Roddy.

For those first years after Royall took her in, Nola wrote Roddy letter after letter: How're things going? How're you doing? How tall are you? How tall is everyone else? And then, over time: Why didn't you write me back?

He was a horror, built with a cruelty that came naturally. Nola knew that, even at thirteen. Yet she'd still write him at least once a year, usually on their birthday, too young to understand that her dedication was really desperation. And yes, there'd be moments—usually when *Full House* was on—when she'd wonder if Roddy still thought of her, if he even remembered her. But right now, the only thing Nola was focused on was that angel smile on Royall's face.

For years, Nola assumed Royall took her in so she could cook and clean. That was certainly what he screamed loudest about, most recently when he pinned her to the wall by her throat because a stray red sock ruined the nice white shirt that he'd bought at *full damn price*. But maybe she had it wrong.

Indeed, as Nola stood at the edge of the poker table, her small hands gripping the scotch bottle, Royall's angel smile felt like the glow of a thousand suns. Could that be why she was here? To be part of *his* team?

"Okay, donkeys, just to make you feel better, I'm limiting my bet to one, two, three . . ." Royall tossed four orange chips—two hundred dollars—into what was easily the largest pot of the night.

"There's nothing sadder than a bad bluff," Acne Steve said.

"With a name like Royall, you really think he'd bluff?" Repeating Francis challenged.

"We'll see. I call," Acne Steve said, fanning his cards onto the table, trying to catch his son's attention. Trey stayed locked on his video game. "I flopped a set of jacks," Steve said. Three of a kind.

"Well, lookie there," Royall said. "Lucky for me, I got that seven on the river—straight to the jack," he explained, revealing his own cards. A 7-8-9-10-jack straight. Winner, winner, chicken dinner. "Pleasure doing business with you, donkey."

Acne Steve rolled his eyes. "Couldn't happen to a bigger asshole."

As Royall raked the pile of chips toward his chest, he shot a quick thank-you at Nola.

It pierced her chest like an arrow, expanding, filling her completely. God, it felt great to do something right.

Nola's stomach again started to churn. She ignored it, determined to live in the moment—to focus on just this joy—which felt like it would never end.

That should've been her second warning.

"New round, new round," Repeating Francis said, already dealing new cards.

Nola darted toward the bathroom to deal with her stomach. Royall shot her a look. *Don't leave. See what they have.*

Picking up the waste bin, Nola made her way back to the table.
"Here," she said, leaning past Acne Steve to grab a stray beer bottle,
"let me help you with th—"

A hand shot out, locking onto her wrist. *"Don't,"* warned a man
with butterscotch breath and narrow eyes the color of pennies. Hartley Spencer. The one who took a sniff of her when he first came in.
Hartley held firm to her wrist, refusing to let go.

Nola's instinct was to take the beer bottle and stuff it in his teeth.

Across the room, young Trey looked up.

"Hartley, she's just trying to clean up," Acne Steve said.

Hartley's grip stayed tight on her wrist. So did Nola's grip on the
bottle.

When it comes to your dad's friends, it's hard to know who's
dumb and who's smart. But even when you're thirteen years old, it's
easy to know who shouldn't be messed with.

Hartley leaned in, so close that now *she* could smell *him.* Cigarettes and wood chips. "I'm not done with my beer yet . . . *ma'am,"*
Hartley whispered in a tone that perfectly matched the way Nola had
been calling everyone *sir.*

Nola froze.

Hartley cocked a knowing eyebrow.

Royall and Nola's code. Somehow . . . Did Hartley know?

Panicking, Nola let go of the bottle and took off, racing for the
kitchen.

"Hartley, what the hell'd you say to her?" Royall challenged.

"CrapCrapCrapCrapCrap," Nola muttered, pacing in the kitchen,
the swinging door shutting behind her. As panic set in, a sharp pain
pierced her stomach. Did Hartley know? It sounded like he knew.
More important, if he told the others they were cheating, Royall
would blame—

"Nola!" Royall shouted from the other room, his voice a bullhorn.

She wanted to run. The kitchen started to spin. Grabbing the
counter to steady herself, Nola took a deep breath. Her stomach was
on fire—

"What the hell's going on?" Royall asked, shoving open the kitchen door.

"Hartley knows. He knows," she whispered, bent over, breathing heavy.

Right there, Royall started to laugh. "Hartley? The guy who keeps smelling you?"

Nola looked up, confused.

"The man's a moron," Royall explained. "He doesn't know squat. C'mon, get up. I'll prove it."

Royall reached for her hand, but Nola was still hunched, holding her stomach.

"I said get up. *C'mon,*" Royall repeated, gripping her by the armpit.

With a tug, Nola stood up straight.

Royall's face went white.

"Um, Nola," he said, pointing to the stain at the crotch of her jeans. "Why're you bleeding?"

"I . . . I think I just got my period."

30

Zion told them everything.

He told them how he was contacted, how much he was paid, and admitted that, yes, two nights ago, in Colonel Mint's driveway, he was the one who pulled the trigger on Mint and the valet. With tears and snot running down his face, he even told them about Black House.

"O-On my phone. Look at my phone!" Zion pleaded. "The pass code is my name! First name!"

With the camping saw digging into his throat, the metal teeth biting at his skin, Zion didn't have much choice.

"Who else knows? Siblings? A girlfriend? Who'd you confide in?" Reagan asked, pulling the saw tighter.

"N-No one!" Zion insisted, still up on his tiptoes, Seabass's grip unrelenting.

"I get very frustrated around liars, Zion."

"No one! I wouldn't do that to Mr. Vess! I-I swear on my mother . . . my father, too," Zion pleaded. *"You believe me, right?"*

Reagan shot a look at Seabass.

Seabass nodded.

With a sharp tug, Reagan pulled hard with her left hand, then her right, the camping saw slicing a thin line into Zion's throat. Wind-pipes are usually hard to penetrate, since they're protected by carti-lage and fibrous tissue. The camping saw tore through it all with ease.

Zion gasped, trying to scream, which was impossible with a severed trachea. Frothy yellow bile came up from his lungs.

Despite what Hollywood might make you think, there was no gruesome spray of blood. A thin red waterfall ran down his neck, pulsing with each heartbeat.

As the color ran from his face, Zion tried to fight, tried to grab at his own throat, thrashing wildly.

Seabass held tight until Zion's head slumped sideways, then forward. Nothing but dead weight.

"His phone," Reagan called out, pointing Seabass toward the living room, to a coffee table that held a new Samsung. Seabass made a face. *Who carries a Samsung?*

Following behind him, Reagan took out her own phone and dialed the number Mr. Vess had given her. It rang once . . . twice . . .

"Ellis Jewelers," a man with an unforgiving Boston accent answered.

"Hey there. I'm looking for Darcy," Reagan said.

"Sorry, Darcy's at lunch. Can I take a message?"

Reagan paused. "Tell her A.D. called." *A.D. All *d*one.*

Message sent.

"You got it. Have a glorious day now," the man replied. With a click, he was gone.

Reagan turned back to Seabass, who held up Zion's Samsung.

Onscreen was a logo in a stenciled military font. "Black House," Reagan read from the screen. Whattyaknow. The kid was telling the truth.

"Seabass, answer this," she said, heading back toward the kitchen. "You think that guy who bought the Peter Tosh guitar would sell it to me so soon after the auction?"

Seabass rolled his eyes.

"I know," she said, pulling out a Clorox wipe and running it down the length of her bloody camping saw. "I wouldn't, either."

It took half a dozen strokes to get the blade clean, then one last pinch at a stubborn spot of blood. *Take care of your tools, and they'll take care of you,* her father used to say. It was still true.

We should get going, Seabass said with a glance.

Reagan nodded, rolling up the saw and stuffing it in her pocket. As she followed him out of the town house and through the back-yard, they didn't realize they were trampling over Zion's small tomato garden. "So where to next?" she asked. "Black House, or this guy Zigarowski?"

Seabass shot her a look. It wasn't even a question.

31

"You do realize," Waggs began, "whatever you tell me, I'm taking it straight to Zig."

"I assumed you would," Nola said from the back seat. "So. Black House. Do you know it or not, Ms. Waggs?"

Ms. Waggs? Waggs turned in her seat, staring at Nola, whose face was lit by the glow of the iPad. It was the first time Waggs realized just how young Nola was. Sure, she had knives in her eyes like she'd lived three lifetimes. But she was still in her twenties. A child, scribbling at a notepad in her lap.

"Are you *coloring*?" Waggs asked.

"Nice corsage."

Waggs pulled the corsage off her wrist. "*This,* I'll have you know, is an ironic and spectacular tenth-level inside joke that you can't possibly—"

"I ruined your date. That wasn't my goal. I came about Black House."

"No. I need to say my speech. I've been practicing it in my head. And it starts with me telling you—I don't like you, Nola. And y'know why I don't like you? Because I've seen what you do to my friend. You're like the number thirteen—or a lightning rod: you attract bad things," Waggs explained. "For me, it's like going to the chiropractor. I sit all day so I give them my money twice a week. Anyway, a few years back, my chiropractor taught me about trigger points.

"Mine is at B48—this little spot at the center of the gluteal muscles in my buttocks. A literal pain in my ass," Waggs said. "I can be having a good day, one of those ones that starts with the security guy with the Travolta cleft chin smiling my way—but if you pushed my B48, electric bolts would shoot up my spine and right there, my whole day would turn into a river of shit," Waggs explained. "My B48, Nola. That's what you are to Ziggy. A lightning rod. A trigger point."

"Are you done?"

"I'm not. I want to make sure you fully appreciate the true intricacies of my B48 metaphor. Ziggy spent the past two years rebuilding his life, moving on from your last visit. And he actually did it . . . new house, new job . . . even put up new-agey wind chimes on his front porch, which is the middle-age equivalent of Buddhist enlightenment. Then you show up and—" She pantomimed tearing a sheet of paper in half, then tearing it again, to shreds. "I'm not letting you do it, Nola. You don't get to ruin his—" Waggs cut herself off. "Are you bleeding?"

Nola didn't answer, using her shirt to hide the wound that had opened by her collarbone. Some blood had seeped through the bandage.

"Cat scratch," Nola replied. "Tell me about Black House, and I'll—"

"I've never even heard of Black House!"

"Now you're lying," Nola said flatly, her head down, again drawing on her notepad. "I found your account, Ms. Waggs. On the Black House app."

Waggs went silent, glancing out the back window. Across the garage, a lone security guard was making his rounds. It made Waggs think: *Do we have actual guards in the garage? I thought it was just security cams?*

"I put in every email I could think of," Nola explained from the back seat. "Same response every time: 'User ID not recognized.' On a hunch, I put in your email—"

"How'd you get my email?"

"I put in your email. New words appeared. 'Enter password.'"

For a moment, Waggs sat there, looking at the rearview mirror and studying this young woman curled like a fist in the back seat. For years now, Waggs had heard stories about Nola—about her child-hood, her father, her temper. But to finally see her in person, Waggs was struck by her sheer intensity. It radiated off her, like plutonium.

"Black House," Nola said, never raising her voice.

Waggs cleared her throat, glancing again at the security guard in the distance. "Y'know what, Nola? I've changed my mind. I've decided I want to help you, because once I do—"

"I won't bother you anymore."

"No. You'll continue to bother me. But. I need you to stop both-ering Zig. That's my offer. We talk—I'll tell you what Black House is—but after that, you leave him alone."

"You talk about him like he's a child."

"Can you please—?"

"I didn't ask for Mr. Zigarowski's help."

"That's irrelevant! *Help* is his specialty. You were friends with his daughter . . . You saved her life. Do you have any idea what that does to him? When you stir up all that emotion? It's like having a long-lost family member show up out of nowhere."

Nola stopped drawing, her head still down. In her lap, her note-pad was tilted just enough so that Waggs couldn't see it. But Nola's sudden pause at the mention of a *long-lost family member* confirmed exactly what Waggs was looking for: whatever was going on, Nola's brother was definitely mixed up in it.

"Hand me your phone," Waggs said.

Nola stared at Waggs skeptically.

"I'm not pulling this up on mine. Now do you want to know what Black House is or not?"

Nola handed over her phone, shooting Waggs a look.

"The proper response is 'thank you,'" Waggs said, grabbing the phone. "As for Black House, it's a military term—a government site that dates back to, well . . . Y'ever heard of Richard Nixon?"

32

Two hours later, Zig was sitting in his backyard, in his favorite rusty lawn chair. He had a beer in one hand, his phone in the other.

Onscreen was Facebook—his ex-wife's profile.

In a relationship.

"Don't judge," Zig warned his favorite girls.

Mmmmmmmmmm, his hive sang back, hundreds of bees swirling and crawling around a white wooden box as big as a two-drawer file cabinet. Zig had built the box himself, complete with dovetail joints. Up on concrete blocks, it was the *only* piece of furniture Zig had kept from his old house, and the house before that—his and Charmaine's house.

"Oh, c'mon," Zig challenged. "No one's cool when their ex is around. Even Brad and Angelina crumbled."

Mmmmmmm, twenty-five thousand bees replied.

"I know," he said, refreshing Facebook again—*In a relationship*—not even sure what he was looking for. He could make a few more calls about his daughter and the videotape—that's what he'd done right after Charmaine left. He called Waggs (who must still be out on her date), he called an old CIA connection from Dover, and of course he texted back and forth with half a dozen people from their old hometown whose daughters used to do Girl Scouts with Maggie. There were still a few more calls he could make. But as he sat there nursing his third beer, staring at Facebook, and trying to lose himself in the hum of the bees, he knew that nothing good came from picking at old scabs.

Whatever had made his daughter so upset that day in the model-ing agency, could this possibly lead anywhere good? Of course not. If it was something harmless—a petty fight with a friend—it just need-lessly opened old wounds. And if it was something truly bad—the kind of nightmare every parent prays their daughter never faces—then those same wounds get opened, and there's a new horror to layer on top.

Still, the truth matters. Zig knew it did. So he should keep call-ing around, trying to track down old employees from SuperStars Modeling. But instead, Zig swiped back to his phone's home screen and clicked on *Recent Calls*. He redialed one of the numbers.

The phone rang once, then twice . . .

"Barron's Steakhouse. How can we help you tonight?" a man asked.

"Richard, it's Zig, from— I was in earlier."

"Looking for the iPad . . . sure," the manager said, the restau-rant bustling in the background. "Unfortunately, I don't have a better answer. We got the program for the reservation book open, but no one knows how to get in the email account to change the password. I think our weekend hostess knows it. I'll call you when I get it. I haven't forgotten."

With a click, the manager was gone, leaving Zig sitting there, wondering if it was bad to spend more time worrying about Nola's current safety, rather than his own daughter's decade-old videotape.

Mmmmm, the bees hummed as Zig flipped back to the photo Roddy got from the funeral, of the soldier who tried to jump Nola early this morning. He was clutching his knee in agony, Nola's col-ored pencils scattered everywhere.

C'mon, Nola, you never get spooked . . . so why the hell's this one getting to you?

Mmmm, the hive continued to murmur, lower than ever, despite the fact that Zig had just given them a snack, a new water-and-sugar mix that a friend called bee whiskey.

The party didn't last long.

Mmm, the bees added, already back to their baseline. When Zig got his first beehive in college, his professor had taught him that every hive would have its own personality. Once, Zig had a hive that was so chill, he called them *stoner bees*.

But this hive here? It used to be forty thousand strong. Now, they were down to almost half. Bad sign. Zig had checked for mites or beetles, but for weeks now, deep down, he knew the cause.

The queen.

"Diana-27, do *not* give up on me," Zig said, using the name he'd given every queen since Diana-1 and Diana-2. It was a tip of the crown to Princess Diana. Zig always wished she'd gotten her shot at queen.

"You're a fighter, Diana-27. It's like *Rocky III*—the best one! Get up off the mat! *There is no tomorrow!*"

Mmmmm, the hive replied sluggishly.

Typically, the queen was replaced every two years, but Diana-27 had lasted twice that long. Mystified, Zig called expert after expert, until a Chinese blogger from a site called Honey, Bee Careful told Zig that in 5 percent of hives, there can be *two* queens—a mother and daughter—who work side by side.

Right there, Diana-27 became Zig's favorite queen. Today, though, with this attrition, he could see that trouble was coming. Left to its own devices, his hive would die—unless he "squished the queen," meaning he'd have to manually grab Diana-27 and leave Diana-28 in charge. It was the only way the hive would live. Focus on the future, not the past.

Swiping back to the video of his daughter, Zig watched his Magpie sobbing into the camera, a stranger's hand on her shoulder.

With another swipe, Zig flipped back to the present, back to Mint's funeral and Nola's scattered pencils.

For decades, people had assumed Zig was a mortician because he liked taking care of the dead. They always had it wrong. From his first days at Dover, Zig's best reward was helping the *living*—the families of fallen soldiers. He brought them peace, kept their best memories alive, and gave them closure—the one thing he never got himself.

Again, he swiped back on his phone, to the video of his daughter. But again, he felt this thing he couldn't quite see, this uncontrollable pull, this *need*—that was the only way to describe it—a need to swipe back to Nola, to the present.

It was time to admit that for these past two years at the funeral home, Zig was no longer serving the living. His time had been spent with the dead, with clients like ninety-three-year-old Mrs. Paoli. It was time to come back to those who actually needed him.

The bees were still faintly humming as Zig dialed the number he knew by heart.

"Yeah, it's me," Zig said into the phone. "I got a favor. How hard would it be to get me another look at Colonel Mint's body?"

33

"What about Watergate? Ever hear of that?" Waggs asked.

"I'm not a moron," Nola warned.

"Don't take it so personal. A few months back, I asked an intern about Watergate and he said he'd seen the movie—starring Tootsie and some blond guy—though he probably deserved half credit for at least knowing Tootsie."

In the back seat of Waggs's car, Nola just glared.

"Anyway, Black House." Out the back window, the security guard was gone, but Waggs barely noticed. "Back during Nixon's Watergate days, he secretly taped his conversations in the Oval Office, never thinking they'd be used against him. Of course, they were—and once those tapes came out, Nixon's staff started wondering what other White House rooms had ears in them. Taking no chances, his top military officials started holding meetings in the White House bowling alley, dubbing it the Black House."

"For real?"

"If you worked for Nixon, would you hold your conversations in the great wide open?"

Nola didn't answer.

"Exactly. But what really matters is this: with each successive President, from Reagan and Bush to Obama and beyond, the Black House kept moving. During the Clinton years, George Stephanopoulos supposedly used the White House gym to hold off-the-record meetings. During W.'s time, it was Dick Cheney's office, with its man-sized safe. Era by era, whether it was senior staff talking in

Washington, D.C., or two generals meeting at a hot dog stand outside the Pentagon, 'Black House' became the nickname for that secret spot where you could speak freely and no one else would be listening."

"So now Black House is online?"

"Everything's online," Waggs said, holding up Nola's phone. "The world moves too fast for us to dead-drop a note under a park bench and then wait two hours for someone to find it and write back. For a while, we started using fake email accounts. When those got cracked, we switched to encryption, then to even better encryption. But guess what happened?"

"It all gets hacked."

"It all gets hacked," Waggs agreed. "A few years back, our friends at the CIA thought they found a true solution: Rather than actually sending emails, they'd open a Gmail account, write an email, and just save it in the Drafts folder. Then they'd give the password for that account to whoever the recipient was. That recipient would then open the draft email, reply in there, and save it as a new draft. Two people could communicate without ever sending anything into cyberspace."

"Why does that story sound familiar?"

"Because that's exactly how former CIA director General David Petraeus was communicating with his mistress before he got hacked. Petraeus was *the head of the CIA*! Back in 2016, the Russian hack of the DNC proved it even more. Today, the moment you type something on a keyboard, every telecom company, ISP, social media site, and cell phone manufacturer can put eyes on it, making everything vulnerable and traceable. So what's the solution?"

"Don't type."

"That's part one. It's definitely safer to chat verbally online. Some use FaceTime, though that runs through your phone, so it's like making a phone call. Others use the encryption on Signal or WhatsApp—or even video games that let you meet up in cyberspace, like Second Life, Minecraft, and Fortnite, since people often overlook games. But even those get run through your ISP."

"Which means?"

"It means that when you're sitting in your living room and shooting PlayStation pals in Call of Duty, the folks at Xfinity, AT&T, or any other ISP can always do a little eavesdropping. And since those of us in the military and intelligence community don't like it when people are eavesdropping, our tech folks came up with part two—exploiting one of the few digital loopholes that're currently left—the one thing that's on everyone's phone . . ."

"An app."

"An app," Waggs said with a nod, tapping the one labeled *Black House*. Onscreen, its digital logo appeared. "Even though they load on your phone, every app has its own proprietary protocols to communicate. That means it's actually more secure than your computer."

"So instead of using an existing video game . . ."

"Uncle Sam made its own." She clicked the screen, revealing her own avatar, which looked exactly like a taller, thinner version of herself.

"That's *you*?"

"Don't be the ruiner of all things," Waggs warned as, out the back window, the security guard appeared again in the distance. "They even let you pick your favorite weapon," Waggs said, pointing onscreen to a high-tech gun that looked more sci-fi than military.

"Ripley's pulse rifle," Nola said, recognizing Sigourney Weaver's gun from *Aliens*.

Waggs tilted the phone, and onscreen, digital Waggs followed the tilt, looking around and revealing an empty alley. Graffiti on the walls was in Arabic. "To anyone else, Black House is another mindless first-person shooter game, but when you scratch the surface, with modules for Iraq, Afghanistan—they even built some of the neighborhoods where our safe houses are in Qatar—you're looking at the safest online place for senior military leaders and secret squirrels to have real-time, untraceable conversations."

"Tell me how it—" Nola cut herself off. "It also interacts with other apps. Why would the military allow that?"

"It may look like a game, but the intelligence community doesn't play games when it comes to security. When Black House first started, it was a closed system, meaning you could only talk to other Black House users. The problem was, for many missions, you need to do more than talk. When we caught bin Laden, y'know how many informants had to be paid? Or how many had to be flown to other countries for their own safety? To do the job, Black House had to interact with the real world. So now, once you enter its virtual universe, you can book flights on it, send money through it . . ."

"Or make a dinner reservation."

"In the training module, they even teach you how to pay your informants by shipping them tanzanite, which apparently is now the jewel of choice for scumbags in the Middle East," Waggs explained. "Even Tiffany's started carrying it."

"So if someone tries to trace you . . ."

"It'll take them back to the black hole—back to Black House itself, which is far safer than risking your life and revealing your location on some hackable airline app. All you need is . . ." Waggs reached into her purse, rummaging for a moment, but quickly pulling out her own phone and holding it next to Nola's. "Install the app. Pick a meeting place. Black House connects us and takes care of the rest."

For a few moments, Nola sat in the back seat, staring intensely toward Waggs, but looking through her, like she was working through permutations.

"Nola, when I spoke to Zig, he said you were at Colonel Mint's funeral. I take it this is about him?" Waggs asked. "Was Mint a friend?"

Nola stayed silent.

"You found a Black House account for Mint, didn't you?" Waggs added.

Still silent.

Waggs sighed. It was like dealing with her son—Nola was about the same age. Midtwenties, utterly frustrating and completely self-absorbed. But still . . . just a kid.

Lord, why am I such a sucker? Waggs thought to herself.

"Nola, if you need help, I can—"

"Someone's using Mint's account. I saw them online," Nola blurted.

"Online where? On Black House?"

"If you sign in and someone's already logged into that account, it assigns you a new avatar. I saw them. Two men. One in Mint's account, plus someone else. They logged out and took off the moment they saw me." The words tumbled from Nola's lips, like even she was surprised she was saying them.

"Maybe it was one of our forensic guys checking his account?"

Considering that, Nola looked away. She was done making eye contact.

"Nola, I know working alone is emotionally safer, but we have people here who can—"

"I need my phone," Nola said, her hand snapping out like a cobra, snatching her phone from Waggs's hand. She kicked open the car door.

"Nola, wait—!"

"You don't have to worry, Ms. Waggs. I'll stay away from Mr. Zigarowski."

"Nola—!"

The door slammed with a boom.

For a split second, Waggs thought about giving chase, but there was no need. Reaching for her purse, Waggs pulled out a portable phone charger with five different cords running down from it. *The Octopus,* the Bureau called it, though Waggs had started seeing them in airports and even in the back of Ubers. People think they're plugging in for a charge—which they get—though what they also receive is some homemade computer code courtesy, in this case, of the FBI.

That's why you don't hand your phone to strangers, Waggs thought, replaying the moment a few minutes ago when she pretended to rummage through her purse while she plugged Nola's phone into the Octopus.

With a few clicks on her own phone, Waggs opened a map. At the center was a small orange square: Nola's phone. But to Waggs's surprise, the orange square wasn't moving.

It should be moving.

Waggs glanced outside the car, first left, then right. The lot was dark. Nola was gone.

It made no sense. Unless . . .

Waggs turned toward the back seat. Sure enough, Nola's phone was sitting there, discarded, tucked into the little groove by the seat belt.

"Okay, girl—bump, set, spike. Round one to you," Waggs whispered, her fingers again clicking at her phone, opening a new screen, this one labeled *History*.

By dumping her phone, Nola ensured that no one could see where she was going. But thanks to the passive location settings on every cell phone—ones that even Nola couldn't shut off—Waggs could at least see where Nola had been.

"Bump, set, even better spike," Waggs whispered, scrolling through Nola's history. "Round two to me."

She considered calling Zig, though quickly thought better of it. *Don't rile him up. Not until you know what's really going—*

Her phone rang in her hand. *Oh jeez,* she thought as caller ID kicked in. Her boyfriend, Mikel. "Hey, honey . . ."

"You're not even on your way, are you?"

"Mikel, can I just spare you the lame excuse and instead admit that I officially owe you one?"

"I appreciate the honesty. So let me be equally honest and tell you that in retaliation, I plan on eating this entire spinach artichoke dip appetizer by myself." He forced a laugh, but Waggs could hear the annoyance in his voice.

"Mikel, you really are th—"

Click. He was gone.

There was a knock on the passenger window. *"Everything okay?"* a voice asked.

Waggs jumped at the sound, but it was just the security guard.

"Y'okay there?" he asked.

"Yeah. I'm great," Waggs replied, eyeing her corsage, which was starting to wilt in the passenger seat.

You owe me for that one, too, Nola.

34

Charmaine hadn't bought cigarettes in a decade. She promised herself she'd smoke just one, but here she was, at nearly midnight, sneaking away in her own backyard, pacing around her patio furniture and puffing away, the pack already half-empty.

She hated to admit it, but she'd forgotten how much she liked the quick buzz—and the physical act of hiding, the smoke swirling through the darkness, a little treat for herself in the midst of so much heartache.

The taste of tobacco was an instant time machine, taking her back to a night in college when cheap beer and an overdose of Drakkar Noir got her to do things with a senior named Neil that she barely did with her current fiancé, except maybe on his birthday.

Dear Lord, am I really that cliché, reliving a wild night with an old flame? Undoubtedly. *And proud of it,* she decided, though like the cigarette, the buzz only lasted so long.

"C'mon, Ziggy, where are you?" she muttered, fingers swiping from email to texts and back again to voice mail.

No updates. She shouldn't be surprised. It'd only been a few hours since she showed Zig the old videotape, asking him to find out why Maggie was crying at the modeling agency. Did she really think he'd have answers this quick?

The sad truth was, she did. Her ex could be a pain in the ass, but as she'd learned during divorce proceedings, once Zig had your scent, he wouldn't sleep until he found what he was looking for.

Her phone buzzed. A text from her sister Deena. How'd it go?

Fine, Charmaine texted back.

Deena responded with the emoji face that looked upward, thumb and pointer finger on its chin.

Charmaine laughed. Her sister's marriage had ended two years back, when she left her husband after realizing that he wanted a mother more than a wife. Charmaine knew what Deena was really asking: *How'd he look?*

Good. He looks good, Charmaine texted back, though that was a lie. Zig looked great—fantastic even, with his five-o'clock shadow and that little scar that always undid her.

He got hotter, huh?

Please. Stop, Charmaine texted.

Says the girl who went to see him face-to-face when a phone call would've been fine. You're smoking, aren't you?

Charmaine took a deep drag on her cigarette, hating herself for making the trip in person. And hating herself even more for how great it had felt to see him again.

You tell Warren? her sister texted.

Charmaine didn't answer, which, to any sister, was enough of an answer.

When's your next session? Deena added.

Tomorrow, Charmaine wrote, glancing over her shoulder at their model home, at the flickering light upstairs in the guest room, where Warren was watching a late baseball game—and where he'd been sleeping for nearly three weeks now. I figure we need something good to talk about in therapy.

Three gray bubbles appeared onscreen—her sister writing her back that she shouldn't be playing with fire, that Warren was a good man, and that the therapist would help them work it out.

Gotta run, Charmaine texted, shutting her phone and agreeing wholeheartedly. The only reason she reached out to Zig was the videotape. How could she not bring it to him? The last thing she wanted was to let this affect her and Warren.

Headed back toward the house, Charmaine made one last loop through her email, voice mail, and texts. Still no word from Zig, which made her start wondering if Zig was in a similar spot, sitting in his backyard, talking to his bees.

Just the thought of it annoyed her. They'd been divorced for over a decade; surely they weren't this predictable. Though at the thought of that, a mental switch flipped.

Why was she waiting on Zig when she could figure this out herself?

With one hand, Charmaine swiped back to her texts. With the other, she put out her cigarette in a nearby terra-cotta planter—one that they'd bought to grow basil and other herbs, though the seeds were still inside, unplanted.

Helena, you up? she wrote to a number she hadn't texted in years.

Everything OK? Helena Coplon—one of the den mothers of Maggie's Girl Scout troop—quickly texted back.

Depends, Charmaine thought, hitting Helena's phone number.

"Charmaine, you're scaring me," Helena said, picking up immediately. "I haven't heard from you in . . . I can't think of when," she added, pronouncing the word *when* like *win.*

Pin/pen merger, Charmaine thought, the linguist's term for when someone takes words ending with *-en* or *-em* and turns them into *-in* or *-im*—most often found in southern states. Out here in the Pennsylvania suburbs, Helena knew the value of sounding like everyone else—but sometimes, when your guard's down, you can't always hide your Texas roots.

"Sorry it's so late. I'll be quick," Charmaine began. "Remember that modeling place in the shopping plaza—?"

"SuperStars. Of course. Dara loved it there," Helena said, referring to her daughter.

Charmaine wasn't surprised. Dara was a pretty girl, with the kind of mom who'd care about something as useless as headshots for a teenager.

"Why do you ask?" Helena added.

"I'm just wondering . . . can you send me Dara's current phone number? Something came up I'd love to ask her about."

35

"Ring it again," the redhead insisted.

Seabass shot her a look. He'd already pushed it twice.

"Just ring it again," Reagan called from the driver's seat, where she was parked out front, car still running, just in case it got ugly fast. It was barely 8:00 the following morning. Early, even for the Reds, but Vess wanted this done fast.

Standing on Zig's front porch, under a set of wind chimes, Seabass shoved his fat thumb against the doorbell. Tucked under his arm was the empty FedEx box they always kept in their trunk. If you're holding a FedEx, no one looks twice at you. Most important, when the person inside sees it, they'll open their door, making it far easier for Seabass to catch Zig off guard.

"Maybe he's in the shower," Reagan said, one hand on the camping saw in her pocket.

Seabass motioned to the empty driveway. *He's not in the shower. His car's already gone.*

She nodded, glancing down and scrolling through the M. L. Anderson auction site on her phone—looking at their newest listings of vintage guitars, plus 25 percent buyer's fees. *Markup like that is legitimate crime,* she thought as Seabass craned his neck, trying to look through Zig's window. If all was clear, he'd pick the lock. *We're clearly in the wrong business.*

"Need some help?" a voice called out.

Both the Reds turned, spotting an elderly man with saggy jowls who was walking a similarly saggy basset hound.

"Got a package for Zig?" the man added with a bit too much pep for this early in the morning. "I don't mind grabbing it for him if you want."

Seabass looked down, nearly forgetting he was holding the FedEx box.

"It's signature only," Reagan announced from the car.

"Idontmind," the man said as if it were one word. "We sign for each other all the time."

"*His* signature," Reagan clarified, shooting Mr. Jowls an icy stare that stopped him in his tracks. "Must be something expensive," she added, trying to sound friendly, but not really.

On Zig's front lawn, the saggy dog was sniffing around.

"We'll make a note for the next driver," Reagan added. "You happen to know when he'll be back?"

"You actually just missed him." The man gave a tug to his basset hound, to keep away from some fresh dog crap on the lawn. "He was so excited to get out this morning—to see his old friends at Dover."

Reagan and Seabass exchanged a glance. Dover Air Force Base. They'd been there before. It wasn't far.

Storming down the porch steps, Seabass headed to the car.

For a few seconds, Mr. Jowls stood there, staring, as if he was noticing for the first time that Seabass didn't have a uniform, or that he and Reagan were in a regular car rather than a FedEx truck. The man's mouth shifted slightly, like he was about to ask them their names, or what company they worked for. He even reached for his phone, his fingertips on the edge of his pants pocket, like he was about to snap a photo—but then, relying on centuries of evolution, self-preservation, and other primordial instincts he couldn't quite verbalize, his hand stayed where it was and he wisely stayed silent, narrowly avoiding a regrettable turn of events.

The old man was still standing there as the Reds sped up the block.

36

It'd been two years since Zig had been here.

At first glance, it looked the same—same long road, same brown-and-white welcome sign, same single-file line of cars, all waiting to get in. At the very front were the same armed guards in the same triangular-roofed building that looked like a tollbooth. Zig wasn't surprised. The military didn't like change, which was what he was counting on.

"To the left!" called one of the guards out in the street, directing traffic.

Zig took a breath and tugged his steering wheel to the left, following the line of cars around the one new addition—half a dozen concrete barriers that made the traffic zigzag from lane to lane, apparently to make sure no one could get to full speed and ram the front gate. Or at the very least to give the guards a better look at who was coming.

"Keep moving! Next!" the guard announced, waving the line forward.

In front of Zig was a Ford pickup, an extra-wide F-450, that blocked his view. It also kept him from being seen, which, really, was far more valuable.

"Next!" the guard called again.

Zig took a glance in his rearview. Still no one behind him. Then he pumped the gas, getting a better look at the guard up ahead, who was carrying an MP5 assault weapon.

At most stateside military bases, the guards carried M9s. Hand-guns. If they've got MP5s, they're on alert, or expecting a VIP . . . or keeping an eye out for someone. Zig again glanced at the rearview.

"To the left!" the guard called again as Zig pulled past him, telling himself not to be so paranoid. Especially here.

In front of him, the pickup pulled into the tollbooth. A minute went by, then another. Usually, it was quick. Zig craned his neck, but the truck in front of him was too big.

Behind him, the guard was still lingering in his rearview. No other cars in sight.

Zig took another breath, feeling a bead of sweat roll down from his armpit.

"Let's go—*next,*" called the tollbooth guard, a Black man in full camo, MP5 at the ready. The guard was a kid, barely twenty years old. "Welcome to Dover Air Force Base. Who you here to see?"

"I have an appointment," Zig said, handing over the pass he'd gotten from the visitors center. "At the mortuary."

37

It came down to cell towers.

Last night, for the first hour or so, Waggs picked apart Nola's cell herself. No voice mail. No email. And a browser history that had clearly been scrubbed. There were no texts, in or out—and the only recent phone calls were to Barron's Steakhouse, which Nola had called three different times. No question, Nola was smart. In today's world, it took work to keep a phone this clean.

Fortunately, in today's world, even the cleanest phone could still tell you plenty.

"Say ahhhh," Waggs whispered, clicking on a file named Babel-Street.com.

In Hollywood movies, the FBI and CIA have access to every cell phone in the world, able to track bad guys on high-tech screens with even higher-tech digital effects.

In truth, the U.S. government can barely handle a snow day, much less a state-of-the-art geospatial tracking system. So where does the intelligence community get its data? They license it—for a monthly fee—from private companies like Babel Street, which has a name that evokes the most powerful tower since biblical times: the cell tower.

Every day, through their towers, AT&T, Verizon, and other cell service providers collect zettabytes of information, which they license to Babel Street, which then licenses it to the CIA, FBI, Secret Service, and anyone else who can pay for it.

Clean your cache, dump your cookies, use all the encryption you want. The moment you turn on your phone, the nearest cell tower gets a ping. Put those pings together, and you can see exactly where someone's going—or where they've been. For a few extra dollars, Babel Street will even throw in a mapping overlay onto the data, so you can read it as easily as Google Maps.

"So this is her home base?" Waggs said to herself, leaning on her adjustable-height desk and eyeing the map onscreen, where a bright red dot marked Pennsylvania's largest botanical garden. According to the cell towers, it's where Nola spent the most time. "Then you go here," she said, following lines to other red dots—each one representing a place where Nola spent more than a half hour: a nearby grocery store, a pawnshop, a bar, even a local church. Church of the Grace. Methodist.

Maybe an AA meeting? Waggs wondered, thinking Nola didn't seem religious. Either way, what caught Waggs's eye was what wasn't there: she'd asked Babel Street to run a separate report where they'd show if there were any other people whose cell phone tower patterns pinged in the same order as Nola's, in hopes of seeing who else might be meeting her. By looking at speed and direction, you'd be able to tell if she were walking, running, or just in a car with someone else. Day after day, it was always the same: Nola's signal had its own solitary path. No friends. No work lunches. Always alone.

Picking up her own phone, Waggs checked her home screen. She'd texted Mikel early this morning to again apologize for standing him up last night. Still no response.

She swiped to her texts, staring down and trying to physically conjure the three little dots that indicated Mikel was writing back.

The dots never appeared. Waggs turned away from her desk and did that stupid stretch the chiropractor said she should be doing every hour. It didn't help.

Maybe she should text Mikel again.

No. Don't be desperate.

Usually, this was when she'd call Zig and he'd make some lame joke that would lift her mood. Right now, though, Zig had his hands full. She wasn't bothering him until she had real answers.

Turning back to her laptop, Waggs studied the various red dots—

focusing on the places Nola had been over the past few days. The high school where they held Mint's funeral. Barron's Steakhouse. Even last night at the Bureau's parking lot, which, Christ Almighty, shouldn't even be viewable on these reports, at least not since a few months back, when a CIA agent was tracked via cell towers from the Langley parking garage to his home in Maryland, thereby blowing his cover.

There was also a short block of time—right after the shooting— when Nola was near Mint's house. Same time the ambulances, police, and neighborhood rubberneckers were there. *Were you checking out the crime scene—or looking for something more specific?*

Either way, when Mint got shot, Nola came running. Fast.

Still staring at the screen, Waggs couldn't help but notice the small circle of red dots in Nola's town. On a typical day, Nola stayed within a few miles of where she lived. Then, once Mint was shot, she took a forty-minute ride at the drop of a hat.

On a hunch, Waggs clicked the dropdown menu, selecting a tab for *Past 30 Days*.

Onscreen, thousands of red dots appeared, all of them mottled together in a tight red blob. All in the same area, in Nola's town. But there were also three lines arcing upward like rising fireworks.

Nola, you sneak. You went for a ride, didn't you?

Waggs widened the map, revealing three brand-new red dots. In the past month, up until the moment Mint died, these were the only three places where Nola took an actual trip.

Waggs leaned toward the screen, examining each destination. One was a residential address, but the others . . .

Abingdon Medical.

St. Anthony's.

Huh.

Both hospitals.

Nola, why were you going to a doctor?

There was an easy way to find out.

Waggs reached for her keys and her badge. Abingdon Medical was barely an hour away.

38

The smell hit him first—cinnamon potpourri, lemon Pledge, and of course, a heavy dose of bleach—the military's way to hide death. It was a horrid smell, and the worst part was, Zig realized he missed it.

Pulling open the front door and getting just a whiff, he was sucked back in time, to his first days in the office.

It was no different with the décor. As he entered the main lobby of the Dover Port Mortuary, old memories flushed forward—his fortieth birthday, when everyone hid behind these sofas to surprise him after lunch, his commendation from General Sienkiewicz, dozens of goodbye parties, and naturally, all the send-offs as hearses pulled up to the front of the building to collect flag-covered coffins.

To Zig's surprise, he'd forgotten how nice the lobby was, more like a hotel's, with an arched glass atrium, indoor trees, marble planters, and the soothing sound of running water from a circular stone wishing well at the center of the lobby.

Over the years, as families limped inside, waiting to see the bodies of their fallen sons and daughters, Zig had watched hundreds of mothers, fathers, and children throw pennies into the fountain. None of them got what they wished for. Indeed, as the tinkling water mixed with the potpourri smell, all it did was bring Zig back to the height of the wars in Iraq and Afghanistan, when there were so many fallen soldiers coming through the building, they'd sometimes run out of caskets.

"Welcome home," Zig muttered, keeping his head down as he headed for the very first door on his left.

OFFICE OF THE CHAPLAIN

One of the few in the building where he knew there were no cameras.

Zig took a final glance over his shoulder. The lobby was empty. So was the lot outside, though that wouldn't last. Too bad for Zig, he had no idea who was coming. Without knocking, he threw open the door and closed it quickly behind him.

"You do know we're going to jail for this," a man with a Tennessee twang called out.

"Please tell me you got the file—and that you know when Chaplain Pete is coming back," Zig said to the fortysomething Navy chief in full camo who was sitting on the edge of the desk.

"Wait, this is the chaplain's office?" the man teased, holding up a thumb drive. "Forget jail. For this, we're going to hell."

39

"I-I'm a reasonable man," De'Veon pleaded. "I can . . . I'm reasonable."

He wasn't. If he was, he wouldn't be tied to a chair in his kitchen, begging for his life.

Twenty minutes ago, De'Veon woke up from a video game nap on his sofa, surprised to find Nola standing over him. She flashed her stolen badge. Better to start by playing nice.

"Tell me what you know about Colonel Archie Mint," she'd asked.

"*Who?*" De'Veon replied.

In a blur, she jammed her elbow into De'Veon's Adam's apple, knocking him unconscious.

Two minutes ago, De'Veon blinked himself awake, his shirt yanked over his head, his pants pulled down to his ankles. The shirt was to limit his sight. The pants were an old Army interrogation technique: take a man's pants, and he'll panic that you'll cut off his penis.

"I-Is this about money? I can get you money," De'Veon pleaded.

Nola believed it. She'd already picked through his three-bedroom apartment. Stainless steel appliances, but the ones you buy at Sears. Modern white sofa and a bronze African drum coffee table that Nola pegged as Pier 1. De'Veon was an assistant manager at the local Hyundai dealership. He was making money, but just starting.

"Wh-What's that smell?" he asked.

"Brylcreem. And chlorine," Nola said, opening her thermos, which held clear chlorine, like you'd find in a swimming pool. "Any idea what happens when you mix them together?"

Pulling out a heavy manila envelope, she squeezed the Brylcreem in one end, poured a splash of chlorine in the other, then turned the envelope so the chlorine was at the top. It started to slowly run down. Standing behind him, she slapped the envelope against De'Veon's sweaty bare chest, where it stuck in place.

"It smells like . . . What in the . . . ! Is that burning!?" De'Veon asked, twisting his body to no avail.

"In Afghanistan, we'd put these in underground tunnels. After about a hundred and twenty seconds, the chemical reaction would start a fire, and any bad guys hiding inside would come running without us having to waste a single bullet," Nola explained, still standing behind him. "I figure that leaves you about a hundred seconds. So. Again. Tell me what you know about Colonel Mint."

"I told you—I ain't hearda him!"

Another lie. Mint's neighborhood was nice, with a fancy homeowners association that made sure everyone power-washed their roofs and maintained their landscaping. On a hunch, Nola thought that a posh neighborhood like that would also have a security camera at its entrance so everyone felt nice and safe. Sure enough, once Nola tracked down the head of said association and flashed her stolen badge, he was more than happy to share the security footage.

"De'Veon, I need you to be smart for once. Three nights ago, Colonel Mint and a parking valet were shot in the head in Mint's driveway. Whoever pulled that trigger seemed to be hiding in Mint's house, or at the very least, waiting for him there. Interestingly, Mint's car was the only one parked outside, which means our shooter either walked all the way to Mint's house . . . or had someone drop him off."

"My chest . . . ! *You crazy . . . ! You smell that!?*" De'Veon was squirming now, trying to tip over his chair and knock the envelope from his chest. Standing behind him, Nola pressed down on the chair back, pinning him in place. "It's starting to . . . *It's burning, you crazy bitch!*"

Nola didn't budge. A few hours ago, when she checked the neighborhood's security footage, she counted thirty-three different cars that entered Mint's neighborhood on the night of the shooting. It wasn't hard to find out which of those cars was registered to someone with a criminal record.

"You dropped off someone in Mint's neighborhood. Then you came back and picked him up," Nola whispered into De'Veon's ear. "I want to know who."

"Get it off! Please! My skin!" De'Veon screamed, twisting and squirming, wisps of smoke now rising from the envelope on his chest.

Nola shrugged, though he couldn't see her. She glanced at her watch. Thirty seconds until the flame was at full—

"On my life . . . on my grandmother's life . . . I don't know shit!"

Nola turned to leave. The smoke was thick now, a rich black twirl. It smelled of burnt hair.

"Wait! My cousin! It was my fucking cousin, okay!?" De'Veon yelled. *"I didn't know what he was doing! He just asked me to drop him off!"*

Nola turned. "Name?" she asked.

"Zion. Zion Lopez. He's a moron."

Nola tore the envelope from De'Veon's chest and tossed it in the sink. Without a word, she headed for the door.

"Wait, what abou— My arms! They're still—! Untie me, you bitch!"

Nola kept walking, already typing the name into the browser on the burner phone she'd bought at a nearby gas station.

Zion Lopez.

40

They couldn't figure out how to shut off the music.

"Check behind the bookcase," Zig said.

"You think I didn't?" John "Casper" Williams asked, staring up at the speaker in the ceiling, then searching the walls for a dial or off switch.

The music was classical, something with a piano. It was one of the two constants when you came to see Chaplain Pete: he always played music, and he always had candy on his desk. Today was fruit-flavored Tootsie Rolls, though only the yellows and pinks were left.

"Maybe it's playing straight from God," Casper said, his Tennessee accent saying the word *God* like it was two syllables. The youngest of seven siblings, Casper had a plump nose, hair the color of smoke, and just enough of a devilish twinkle in his green eyes to make him the go-to guy when it came to throwing all five of his brothers' bachelor parties.

Those same talents had been put to use two years back, for Zig's going-away dinner, where Casper ordered a massive sheet cake with light blue frosting that read: *Goodbye Quitter!* At Dover, the Navy required a three-year rotation. Many request early transfers—the heartbreak becoming too much. Casper got a special exemption that allowed him to serve for nearly a decade, the third-longest-serving employee since Zig left. *Heart or no heart?*

Heart to the tenth power.

"Casp, it's fine—forget the music," Zig said, glancing out the window, making sure no one was coming. All clear, though he couldn't shake the feeling a storm was on its way.

"You expecting someone?" Casper asked.

Zig shook it off like it was nothing. He was wrong about that.

Zig took a seat across from the chaplain's desk and clicked at the laptop Casper had brought. Onscreen was a Dover Autopsy Report.

Name of Deceased: Mint, Archibald
Cause of Death: Gunshot wound of the head and neck
Manner of Death: Homicide

Zig had read the report yesterday. When you're the mortician, they give you a copy, along with a few ID pics stapled in the corner, so you'll have a guide as you rebuild the victim's face. Flicking his finger, Zig scrolled past the report, down to what he was really after. The file labeled: *Photos.*

"You take these?" Zig asked.

"Does Dolly Parton sleep on her back?"

Zig shot him a look. "Do not mess with Dolly Parton. That woman is a saint."

"Am I from Tennessee? You should be thanking my state just for birthing her."

Zig knew he meant it. After three years of running the Navy's newspaper on the USS *George H. W. Bush,* Casper had wanted one thing: to get off the ship. The first job opening that came up was Dover photographer, where he took photos when top Pentagon brass came to tour the main base so they could pose with the fighter jets.

Soon after, he got transferred to the mortuary, taking photos of the flag-covered coffins as they were carried off the cargo planes. But what really made him rise through the ranks was his ability—no matter how intimate the setting, even when the President of the United States came years ago to pay his respects after the passing of astronaut John Glenn—to disappear into the background. *Like a ghost,* someone said, earning Casper his nickname.

"Casp, you sure this is everything?" Zig asked with a finger swipe to the left, scrolling through a cascade of photos, every moment since

Mint's body arrived at Dover. The first shots were always the same: a closed transfer case with Mint's ID tags, then the canvas body bag with handles on the side, when its steel zipper was first opened. Priority number one was making sure you had the right fallen soldier.

From there, as the fallen soldier's body was placed on a conveyor belt and x-rayed to make sure there was no unexploded ordnance or other booby traps hidden inside, Casper took photos of all of Mint's personal effects—wedding ring, cell phone, crumpled receipts in his pockets, plus every item in his wallet, from his driver's license to gas cards, gym membership, school pictures of his kids that were clearly a few years old, and an old laminated fortune from a fortune cookie that Mint kept: *Your dearest wish will come true.*

Casper even took photos in the autopsy suite, where there were ten-foot ladders, like someone was painting the ceiling. Casper had installed the ladders years ago, so he could climb high enough for a shot of the entire body. As the autopsy progressed, he'd add shots of each wound at every point of impact—from bullet wounds in the skin to punctured livers or hearts—as well as every scar, tattoo, and beauty mark . . . details that a family needs before they'll accept that their son or daughter is dead.

In the photo Zig was looking at, Mint was on one of the autopsy tables, naked, his clothes cut away, his bare arms and legs bent awkwardly in that way that only a corpse bends. He had two small tattoos, both on his right shoulder: baby handprints with cursive script underneath—one labeled *Huck,* the other *Violet*—his kids. Zig swallowed hard, taking a quick glance outside, like he was checking to see if Chaplain Pete was coming. But right now, he wasn't thinking about Chaplain Pete.

"Another couple inches and the bullet would've blown out his whole face," Casper said.

Zig nodded, turning back to the screen. Yesterday at the funeral, Colonel Mint was dressed in full dress uniform, looking serene, the repair work all done. In this picture, taken just before the autopsy began, his buzzed blond hair was a mess of blood and sweat, his mouth sagging open. There was a tidy black hole in Mint's left cheek, then a bigger hole where the bullet exited, diagonally down the right side of his neck, bits of burnt skin shredded like black crepe paper.

According to the medical examiner, the bullet missed his skull, hitting only soft tissue. What actually killed him was when it pierced the carotid artery in his neck.

"Is it me, or does his coloring look off?" Zig asked, flipping to the next pic, one of just the top half of the body, enlarging Mint's face.

"Gray is gray. That's his skin," Casper replied, standing over Zig's shoulder, reaching for the chaplain's candy dish and unwrapping a pink Tootsie Roll.

"Not his pigmentation. His . . ." Zig pulled in even closer, to Mint's right cheek—the one without the bullet hole. "Here. Does it look like something got smudged or wiped away?"

Casper leaned down, squinting at the screen. "Mayyyyybe?" he said, eyeing the slightly darker sheen just below Mint's eye. When Dover photos are taken, the photographers are supposed to clean things up, so the focus can be just on the wound. "I honestly forget. Swipe back to the beginning," Casper said. "Sometimes, when you pull someone out of the body bag, blood smudges across their face."

With a hard swipe, Zig scrolled back to the very first pics, but even there, Mint's right cheek looked a bit darker.

"Ziggy, you searching for something in particular?"

"Just a hunch."

Casper made a face, rolling his tongue inside his cheek to pick out the Tootsie Roll from his back teeth. "How about the truth this time? Tell me what you're really doing here."

"Casp, I told you—"

"No. Don't say this is just some random hunch. I know that look, Ziggy. I see the way you keep eyeing the window. Like someone's hot on your tail even though you're in a secure military facility. You came here for a reason. Tell me what's got you so anxious."

Zig again glanced out the front window, that photo of Mint's belongings still fresh in his head—gas cards, a gym membership, a few receipts—the crap we leave behind. *Your dearest wish will come true.*

Onscreen, Zig swiped to the end of the file—to the autopsy—where there was a blue sheet with a round hole in it that offered a close-up of Mint's face. The sheet was there to block out everything in the background—so that in each photograph, you could focus just on the fallen soldier, not the nearby rolling carts with the scalpels, rib cutter, or bone chisel.

In the photo, one of Mint's eyes was open, staring straight up, his pupil cloudy and dark purple, like a scab.

"Here. It's *here*," Zig said, flipping back to the full-body shot of Mint's naked body flat on the table. Zig shifted the photo onscreen, pulling in tight on Mint's right hand, where there were three red marks—the same ones Zig noticed during the funeral when he readjusted Mint's hands.

"Scratch marks?" Casper asked. "What about 'em?"

"Whoever shot Mint, they did it from the driver's side of the car. Mint was in the back seat; in front of him was the valet, who was behind the wheel. Both of them took bullets on the left side of their heads, through the driver's-side glass. So who made these marks on Mint's *right* hand?"

Casper shook his head. "Maybe those scratches were from a different night."

"Look at the photos. That's not old blood."

Casper leaned in closer, flipping forward a few photos. As photographer, he took close-ups of every wound. Sure enough, he had a close-up of the scratches. He squinted at the screen. The wounds were fresh. "What if the valet scratched him—y'know, when Mint grabbed him from behind?"

"Another good theory. Except I called the local MEs who did the valet's autopsy. There was no skin tissue under his fingernails."

"Okay, Ziggy, I get it—you're doing the full Quincy. But for all you know, Mint scratched himself," Casper explained. "Remember that pilot who popped out his own eye when his Chinook got shot and crashed? You've seen what happens on impact."

"Casp, that was a helicopter crash from one thousand feet. This is a man sitting in his own back seat. Supposedly by himself."

Casper's eyes narrowed. "Back up. Time out. You think Mint was with someone else in the back seat?"

"That's a hell of a theory," Zig said, a thin grin spreading across his face. "One I bet we can check."

They both sat there a moment, classical piano still playing from above.

"One last file, Casper. That's all I need."

41

Most people hate hospitals. Waggs loved them. They reminded her of giving birth, and those very first days when her son, Vincent, was a little pink marshmallow, lying there on the nursing pillow as she'd gently tickle his toes to make sure he stayed awake during feedings. So much had gone wrong in Waggs's life—what happened with her mom, plus her marriage, which, even then, was already sinking—but when that baby arrived, healthy, with no complications . . . for Waggs, it was the only thing that had ever gone exactly right. God, it'd been a lifetime since she felt like that.

"Welcome to Abingdon. Who you here to see?" asked the security guard, a seventy-year-old man with a cauliflower nose, skeptical hazel eyes, and 1950s horn-rimmed glasses that were so old, they'd come back in style. His name tag read *Stan the Man*.

"It ain't a hard question, ma'am," he added in a heavy Philly accent, already annoyed. "You here to see someone? Only two choices: doctor or patient?"

"I'm actually looking for . . ." Waggs pulled out Nola's military ID photo. "Her name's Nola Brown. She look familiar?"

"She looks miserable."

"That's her smile."

Stan the Man laughed, warming up. On the corner of his desk

was one of those day-by-day dog breed calendars. "You sound like a cop," he told Waggs.

"Let me guess," she replied, "you used to be one."

"Thirty years in South Philly. In the bag," Stan the Man added proudly, meaning he didn't ride a desk. He was in uniform, on patrol, working the radio. "Dealing with actual *people*."

Waggs smiled. Thirty years on patrol meant no promotion, which probably meant he was a wild one back in his youth. Sure enough, among the liver spots that dotted the old man's knuckles were a fair share of old scars.

"Here's some cheap advice: don't leave. The real world sucks," Stan the Man said. "Anyways, tell me who you're on the job for. Because you smell like a fed."

"You still got it, Stan the Man," Waggs said, flashing her FBI badge.

"Now that's a nice photo. You got a good smile."

"I tell people that. No one believes me."

"Oooh, a charmer, too? That's my weakness. You got a boyfriend?"

Waggs hesitated for half a second.

"I'm joking," he teased. "Tell me about Nola Brown . . . what'd she do?"

"Unclear. Apparently, she was here three weeks ago. I'm trying to figure who she was seeing. If she signed in, I assume that's in your system?"

"Is this the twenty-first century? I used to have to knock on ten doors to get all we got in here. Let's take a look . . ." he said, pecking slowly at his keyboard. Eventually, he hit Enter, squinting at the screen. "Yeah, I got her right here."

42

"Ziggy, if I get fired for this, you're taking over my house payments, my car payments. My Netflix, too. And Disney Plus."

"You're not getting fired. You're doing your job," Zig said, sitting there at the chaplain's desk, the background classical music suddenly familiar, something that'd been in an American Express ad a few years back. He was locked on the laptop screen, no longer glancing out the window. If he had been, he might've spotted the car that was just pulling into the parking lot.

"Almost there," Zig told Casper, adding check marks to various digital boxes, like he was placing an online restaurant order and picking toppings.

At the top of the screen were the words *Hounsfield Units,* the measurements used to describe the radiodensity of a CT scan. On-screen, a grayscale image appeared showing a full 3-D rendering of Colonel Mint's body.

In the Dover mortuary, CT scans were still a new thing—instituted back in 2006, when the military decided that every fallen service member from Iraq and Afghanistan required one. It wasn't out of kindness. The 3-D record was a way to learn how bullets and shrapnel tore through a body. After seeing wound after wound in the same spot on soldiers' necks, the Army realized that their body armor needed to be redesigned to better cover their necklines.

It'd been a constant for centuries: with every death, governments learn how to make better war.

"These scans are gonna put me outta business one day, aren't they?" Casper asked, squinting at the laptop.

Onscreen, the CT showed Mint's organs—lungs, kidneys, heart—in muted gray tones, with precise details, right down to the mazelike squiggles on his brain.

"Are those spots—?"

"Blood," Zig said, pointing to what looked like gray leopard spots in Mint's neck, trailing down toward his lungs. "When the bullet pierced his throat, he started inhaling, and— Those final breaths filled his lungs with blood."

Casper nodded while his hands twisted the wrapper from the Tootsie Roll into a tight braid.

Of course, what jumped out most was the actual wound: bright white spots—tiny supernovas—running from Mint's cheek diagonally across his neck, leaving a spray of scattered gray gravel in their wake.

"The gray spots are bone and tissue, but these bright white dots are metal—fragments of the bullet," Zig explained, tapping the tiny supernovas onscreen. Back in his Dover days, Zig used these CT scan images when he was rebuilding a fallen service member's face—so he'd know where the roughest patches of shrapnel would be.

"Is this supposed to tell us something about the scratches on his hand?" Casper asked.

"Depends who did the scratching," Zig explained, scrolling up to Colonel Mint's skull. "According to the Dover medical examiner, the valet was in the front seat, and Colonel Mint was in the back. But with the magic of technology . . ."

Zig clicked on a dropdown menu labeled *Imaging* and deselected the boxes marked:

☐ Blood
☐ Soft tissue
☐ Muscle

With each click, the CT scan blinked. The leopard spots showing Mint's blood disappeared. His lungs and the rest of his organs disappeared. Then his musculature disappeared, eventually leaving only one box unchecked, the sole thing Zig wanted to see: bone.

Onscreen, Mint's chest became a rib cage, his face now a pale gray Halloween skull, though his empty eye sockets and nose were faded because the CT allowed you to see a full 3-D image that ran all the way through to the back of the head. As before, where the bullet first hit, there were bits of stray bone floating inside Mint's skull, fragments of Mint's mandible that got embedded in the soft tissue of his throat. Since the bright white bullet fragments were no longer visible, what jumped out now was . . .

"Ziggy . . ."

"I see it," he said, eyeing a brand-new set of speckled white dots, like gravel, that were embedded in the side of Mint's skull. Not on the left side, where the bullet hit. On the right side, just above his ear.

"Are those—? Is that bullet shrapnel?"

"Not bullet," Zig said, pointing to the checked box. "It's bone shrapnel."

Zig hit another button, zooming in close, the tiny white fragments looking like a dozen broken pencil points, all embedded deep in Mint's skull. "We couldn't see it in your regular photos—it was hidden under his hair."

"Ziggy, I still don't— Mint got shot on the *left* side of his face. So how did bits of his own bone— How'd they get on the right side of his face, much less that high in his hair?"

"Because of this right here . . ." Zig scrolled in closer, the pencil points now looking like snowy mountaintops. "That's not *his* bone."

Casper nodded as it started making sense. He'd photographed it plenty of times before. With bombs and bullet wounds, fragments of one victim get lodged in the other. "Okay, so if those bones aren't Mint's— You're saying they're the valet's?"

"Not at that angle. The valet was in the front seat. This hit Mint squarely on the side—some of it behind his ear, which means . . ."

"Ziggy, you're giving me these dramatic pauses like I'm supposed to be reading your mind. Just say it."

"*Here . . .*" Zig pointed to his own skull. "If I'm Mint, and the valet's in the front seat, when the valet gets shot, bone shrapnel will most likely hit Mint here," he said, pointing to his own forehead and his temple area. "But for fragments to hit me here," he said, pointing diagonally above his ear on his right side, "at this angle—"

"—you think Mint wasn't the only one in the back seat. That someone else was next to him?"

"You got a better explanation?"

Casper gave the twisted Tootsie Roll wrapper one last twirl as it finally tore from the tension. He was still staring at the CT scan of Mint's grayscale skeleton. "Is that who you think scratched those marks into Mint's hand? The shooter put a bullet in Mint, then a bullet into the valet, then they crossed around to the passenger side and— *Scratch.*" Casper paused. "Ziggy, if you're right—"

"I'm right."

"I'm not arguing. I'm just saying—" He pointed his torn Tootsie Roll wrapper toward the screen. "For those bone fragments to be jumping out like that, well . . . How'd our own Dover medical examiners miss it?"

"Who said they missed it?" Zig challenged.

Casper sat up. The classical music was still playing, though both of them barely heard it. "Time out. You think someone here—"

"All I'm saying is, three days ago, Mint's body should've gone to Pennsylvania's *local* medical examiner—he's a civilian. Instead, for reasons we still can't explain, it came here. To make that happen, they said Mint used to work at Dover, but we now know that's a lie. Then they brought me in as the mortician, telling me they needed my rebuilding skills, which was their second lie, since near as I can tell, they brought me in because of my link to Nola. The point is, whatever really happened with Mint's death, far too many people are putting in far too much work to make sure no one finds out what the hell is really going on."

Casper nodded, standing from his seat and tossing the Tootsie Roll wrapper in the trash. On a short filing cabinet in the corner were neat stacks of dozens of Bibles, each stack a different denomination, for families of the fallen. "Maybe you should . . . I don't know, go to the top. Talk to Colonel Whatley," he said, referring to his boss, the head of Dover.

"Whatley's the one who put me on the case!"

"Whatley was? You're sure about that?"

"Casper, whoever did this helped alter Mint's medical examiner report, and his death certificate. On top of that, the way they sped him through Dover—you know how cases move, it can take up to two weeks—but Mint was in the ground within three days, which also keeps law enforcement and everyone else from getting a good look at the body. You really think they could pull all that off if they didn't have permission from every higher-up in here?"

Casper stared at the Bibles, well aware of the answer. "Ziggy, maybe this isn't the best fight for you to be picking right now."

"So I'm supposed to just turn away and ignore it all?"

"No, you're supposed to stay out of trouble, which I guarantee won't happen if you keep digging into military secrets. For all you know, Mint's a secret squirrel, and they're just trying to keep his mission quiet."

"You really believe that?"

Casper stayed silent. He'd been through enough secret squirrel cases to know their vibe. "Fine, I hear you—this one reeks. But if you're not careful . . . Y'know how many cameras you passed coming in here? You need an actual plan."

"I have a plan," Zig insisted, rapping his knuckles against the screen. "I find out who these bones belong to, and once I have that—"

The office door swung open, revealing a petite woman. She had chestnut-colored hair and military posture. Zig knew her, though not from here.

"Sorry . . . oh, jeez . . . I'm interrupting, aren't I?" she asked. "I'm Archie's— I'm Colonel Mint's— I'm his wife," Tessa explained, holding up a manila envelope. "I'm looking for the chaplain. They said he was— Am I even in the right office?"

Zig froze, but not for long. "C'mon in," he said, closing the laptop and motioning her inside. "This is absolutely the right place. Please. Take a seat. Welcome to the chaplain's office."

43

"Wait, I *know* you," Mint's wife blurted.

Zig started to speak but never got the words out.

"From the funeral," Tessa insisted, stepping toward him, shutting the door behind herself. "You're the guy. You worked on Archie . . . on his body. The mortician."

"Zig," he said, extending a handshake, which she gripped like a lifeline.

"You fixed his smile. I appreciate that." She searched for more small talk, but that was all she had in her. Her eyes were puffy, her bottom lip showing signs of an emerging cold sore. At the funeral, she wore her public face—stoic and composed—but there's only so long you can hold that in place. The façade was fraying.

"Mrs. Mint," Casper interrupted, "if there's anything you need . . ."

"Archie used to say you should never trust anyone who doesn't have family photos up in their office," she said, forcing a laugh and looking around at the pale yellow walls, which, in addition to a Navy poster, held a simple crucifix as well as a framed Navy flag that looked like it was from Vietnam. "But I guess in here, you don't want to—"

She didn't finish the thought. She didn't have to. When you bury a family member and come to the chaplain's office, the last thing you want to see is someone else's smiling family.

"I got this letter," Tessa added, holding up her manila envelope.

Zig knew what it was. When someone in the military dies, their family gets a packet notifying them of every available procedure and benefit, from how many honor guard will fold the flag at the funeral to how to get the autopsy report, which must be requested. On average, 85 to 90 percent ask for the autopsy, which came in the exact type of manila envelope Tessa was now holding. Inside was a cover letter that read in bold letters, "It is STRONGLY RECOMMENDED that you read this in the presence of people that can provide you with emotional support." Families can also request the photographs that were taken of their loved one's body. Only 10 percent ask for those.

Tessa was one of them.

"I'm gonna regret this, aren't I?" she asked, pulling the report and a stack of about eighty photos from the envelope, the military still printing them out like it was the pre-digital age.

"Mrs. Mint," Casper interrupted. Now he was the one staring out the window, though Zig didn't know it. "If you wait, the pastor will be back in a—"

"My neighbor offered to come sit with me," she said, not hearing a word. "But the thought of doing this in my house, with the kids . . ." Her voice trailed off, her eyes locked on the first photo, showing Mint's metal transfer case with his ID tags on top. "So is this . . . ? They took these right when he arrived, huh?" she asked, flipping to the next photo, of her husband's gray face peeking through the open body bag.

"Ma'am, you don't have to do this now," Zig said.

But she did.

In the past twenty-four hours, Tessa had seen the body, hosted the funeral, and held her shaking kids as the casket was lowered into the ground. But like so many military families, it's not until she examined the raw photos, with their mundane, dreamlike images of his lifeless head and bloodied wounds, that it finally hit her—that her husband was never coming home.

For two minutes, Tessa sat there silently, flipping through the photos like an old record collection, her perfect posture just starting to crack. Grief at a funeral is communal. Here, it felt like just her and Archie. She was gutted. Undone.

"Y'know, I met him in the Army," she said, flipping to a new photo. "At Fort Drum. I thought I wanted to be a combat medic. Archie was so pushy, he signed up for a new shift, to drive a bus on one of the routes I took every day. That kinda guy," Tessa said as Zig stepped closer, putting a hand on her shoulder.

"Didja know they tell everyone not to touch us?" she asked, Zig not sure whether he should keep his hand there or pull away. "It's part of the training—for the team that comes to tell you that your spouse is dead: no hugging, no touching . . . just deliver the news and leave."

Casper shot a look at Zig—they shouldn't be here; this wasn't their job—but Zig wasn't leaving her.

"When we got married, Archie stayed in the Army—he wanted to deploy—but I left. Figured dental school was safer." She laughed, flipping to a new photo, a close-up of Mint in profile, the small black bullet hole in his cheek. "As a military spouse, you don't want to imagine the worst, but you do—especially when a friend told me to count how many people they send. If one person shows up at your door, your loved one is wounded. If two show up, he's dead."

"Mrs. Mint—"

"I know it sounds bananas, but for all those years he was deployed, that's how I thought it'd happen. I'd come home and see two soldiers in my driveway, and I'd just know. But instead"—she flipped to the next photo, the close-up of the exit wound in Mint's neck—"my phone lit up with a text. That's it. I'm sitting at Violet's nightly baseball game, yelling *Good job* for every kid who strikes out, and this text pops up from Jerri, my neighbor. *You need to get home.* By the time I did, there were sirens up and down the block," Tessa said, flipping faster through the pics, barely looking at them, until—

She stopped at one of the last ones. It wasn't of Mint. It was a photo of his open wallet.

"Personal effects," Zig explained, though it was clear that Tessa knew what she was looking at.

She flipped to the next photo, also of Mint's wallet, though here it was empty, all the money, every dollar—three singles, two fives, and four twenties—spread out on a wooden table, close enough that you could read the serial numbers.

When a fallen soldier returned home, these bills became totems, final gifts passed down from parent to child. As a result, Dover was meticulous in making sure that each and every dollar, even the stray coins found in a victim's pocket, were the exact same ones they arrived with.

"God, look at him here—he's a child," Tessa said, flipping to the next photo, which showed Mint's driver's license, military ID, and the rest of his credit cards.

In both ID photos, Mint had the same look—chin up, chest out, the full at-attention stare, his ice-blue eyes fixated on something distant.

"Did I tell you he didn't know how to smile?" Tessa asked, flipping to a photo with a AAA card, his Costco membership, and a random assortment of—

Tessa made a noise—an actual gasp—at the one she should've seen coming: half a dozen school photos of their kids. They were all out of date, scuffed by bits of wallet crud and laid out one next to the other, like crooked teeth. In the first one, their son, Huck, was wearing a wide smile, prepuberty, showing off braces. His blond hair was a sweaty mess, his face red and damp, since that was the year the photo was taken right after gym class. Next to it was a photo from their daughter's Little League—a fake baseball card, with Violet in batting stance, holding a pink metal bat like a murderer.

"You have kids?" Tessa asked without looking up.

Zig's usual answer was no. When you bury a child, the last thing you want is to answer the standard follow-ups: *How old? Are you close? What do they do now?* Better to say no and keep things easy. But for reasons he wouldn't understand until he was lying in bed later that night, Zig said . . .

"Yeah. A daughter."

Casper shot another look at Zig. *Do not engage.*

"How old?" Tessa asked.

"Twelve."

She turned around. "Same as Violet," Tessa said, her voice straining, her eyes pleading.

Zig knew that tone—and that look. He'd seen the same look on his ex-wife . . . and on himself. It always came after the funeral, when mourners sit in solitude and grasp at those thoughts that are too hard to think about but can no longer be avoided. When you recognize your new reality and it dawns on you how much you don't want to live in it.

"They're going to be okay," Zig told her, motioning to the photos of her kids.

"*She* will be," Tessa said, tapping her daughter's baseball card. "Violet's afraid of nothing—like her dad. But Huck . . . he's who I'm worried about. My idealist," she said, flipping to the next photo. "I fear we've cracked his faith in the u—"

She cut herself off, spotting something in the next photograph.

In Zig's pocket, his phone started vibrating. Caller ID said Roddy. Zig hit Dismiss.

"Are these—? Is this right?" Tessa asked, Zig craning his neck and now seeing what she was looking at: a photo of Mint's dog tags, cell phone, and wedding ring.

Zig's phone vibrated again. A text appeared. Also from Roddy. Pick up. Emergency. I'm serious.

"Who took these?" Tessa asked.

"The photos? Those were— That was me, ma'am," Casper called out from the corner. "Is everyth—?"

Zig's phone buzzed again. This time, he picked up, stepping away from Tessa. "Make it quick," he whispered.

"I found him," Roddy blurted.

"Found who?"

"Mrs. Mint, are you okay?" Casper asked.

"I-I'm just—" Tessa pulled the photo close to her, pointing to the iPhone in the picture. "His phone . . ."

"Did you not get it back?" Casper asked. "They should've given his phone to you. At the funeral."

"They did. In the bag. They gave me his ring, his wallet . . . and his phone. His iPhone," she said. "But here . . . Look. There are *two* phones here." She pointed to the bottom corner of the photo: Mint's iPhone, but also an outdated flip phone.

Zig turned, no longer listening to Roddy.

"Why'd my husband have a second phone?" Tessa asked.

It was a good question, but not nearly as important as the one already twirling through Zig's brain. *Where was that phone right now?*

44

Nola started at the town house's back door. To her surprise, it was ajar.

She shook her head. Bad sign.

Sure enough, as she used her elbow to open the door, she found the kitchen floor caked in blood.

From her pocket, she pulled out two blue plastic foot covers, tugged them over her shoes, and stepped inside. The neighborhood was on the edge of the hood, but nice enough that cops would come running. Last thing she needed was her footprints being part of whatever had happened here.

On her left, toward the sink, was a young Dominican man, twenty-five years old: Zion Lopez.

Nola let out a sharp breath through her nose, more annoyed than anything else.

She squatted down for a better look. Zion's throat was slit, a clean, deep slice. Single incision, no big swipes or slashes, which meant no struggle or fight. More important, no hesitation wounds. Whoever did it, they did it fast, precise. Definitely a pro. Someone who knew their way around a body. Like a soldier, or doctor. Even a cop.

Was this Roddy's work? Too soon to tell.

Next to Zion's body was a shattered vodka bottle, its stem still intact. *Caught off guard. Or maybe using it as a weapon.* At the foot of the body was a Walmart bag with a box for an Oscar the Grouch mask. A final message.

This was the guy who'd pulled the trigger on Colonel Mint.

She could feel it, though it wasn't bringing her the resolution she'd thought. Instead, it just added more questions, more anger, and another dead body.

It reminded her of one of her first missions as Artist-in-Residence, painting Navy SEALs who were tracking a Taliban leader to the small Afghan village of Sabray. To keep Nola safe, they put her in back, with the command and control element, so she'd be the farthest from the action. Yet as they approached the town, they were ambushed from behind—by thirty attackers from an entirely different village. The old back became the new front. Nola fought hard that day. They all did. But what stuck with her was something the SEAL commander said when the medics came: In every mission, the one thing to always worry about is *what you don't know*. The unknown unknown. Especially when it's coming for those you care about.

At that, her brain flipped to Mint's wife, Tessa, and the kids, Huck and Violet, wondering what their night was like. And then she was thinking of Mint himself, and that very first evening in Grandma's Pantry, when Mint came back from a short dinner break and surprised everyone by bringing chicken sandwiches for the whole team, including Nola. *He must want something,* she instinctively thought back then as she pulled the tomatoes and lettuce off the sandwich. She was wrong—though even then, she didn't realize how much. Two days later, Mint again brought sandwiches, giving Nola one with no tomato or lettuce, handing it to her as if she'd been on the team for years.

Such a stupid story, Nola realized, though she'd now thought about it three times in the past twenty-four hours.

With her foot, Nola nudged Zion's head to the side to get a better look at his wound. As she knew, slit throats usually started high on one side of the neck and finished lower. Higher on the left side meant the killer was right-handed, slicing left to right. Higher on the right side meant left-handed. Oddly, Zion was sliced dead center.

Nola made a mental note. Piano wire. Fishing string. Even a thin metal saw. Once, she'd heard of Iraqis who used glass-laced kite string to take off the head of a kidnapped journalist.

Leaning down, she went through Zion's pockets—wallet, keys, but no phone. She made a note of that, too. But what was niggling at Nola more than anything else was the unknown unknown. Zion killed Mint. Tracking him here, finding Zion . . . that should've been the end. Instead, it led to another beginning, a new front. Someone else had gotten here first and murdered Zion. A new player. And by the looks of it, a far more dangerous one.

Glancing over her shoulder into the sun-drenched backyard, Nola noticed two different paths through the tomato garden—multiple footprints, like a team.

Nola pulled out her pad and pencils. For the next few minutes, she stood there by the sink, sketching the body, the kitchen, then the rest of the house, trying to see what she missed.

A quick sweep of the bedrooms revealed a stash of synthetic marijuana, Adderall, and Molly—all hidden in a fireproof toolbox in Zion's closet—plus nearly four thousand dollars in cash literally tucked under his mattress.

Drug dealer. That's what it looked like—or was supposed to look like. *Small time. Trying to work his way up.* So was that what this was about? Some petty deal that went wrong? Nola stared at her notepad, at her drawing of Zion's stash of pot and Molly. It didn't seem right. Colonel Mint was pure polish. He didn't drink coffee, much less buy drugs from some twentysomething scrub. More important, whoever killed Zion, they left the stash behind—plus the cash. When they came here, their mission was clear: take down Zion. So was this punishment for Zion killing Mint—or just a way to keep him quiet?

Still rolling through the permutations, Nola made her way back to the living room, where she sketched the pale green shoji screen, the bamboo bench, and all the other overpriced accessories that looked like they were from West Elm's Japanese collection.

Every other room in the town house was bland, practically bare. Upstairs, Zion's bed didn't even have a headboard, much less all this Japanese décor.

Zion was entertaining down here, doing business. *Trying to make an impression,* Nola thought as her pencil skittered across the page, giving shape to the black lacquered bookcase with upturned shelves that resembled the flying eaves of an Asian rooftop. More Chinese than Japanese, Nola thought.

Item by item, she filled in the shelves of the bookcase, drawing quick renditions of a narrow Japanese bud vase, a paper lantern, some old books, a jade tea set, and . . .

On the page, Nola sketched a bright yellow doll—a stuffed animal. It was a Minion, actually, from *Despicable Me,* with one big eye and overalls that—

Nola looked up from the page, at the bookshelf. Then back toward the living area.

Every single item in the room—the couch, the lamp, the shoji screen, the tea set, every knickknack on the bookcase—it was all Japanese.

Except this yellow Minion.

Cocking an eyebrow, Nola headed for the shelf. The Minion's overalls had a little black dot at the center, like a belly button, but as she got closer, the way it shone . . .

Nanny cam.

Of course Zion had a nanny cam. He was doing business here. Even drug dealers need an insurance policy in case something goes sideways.

Two minutes later, Nola was sitting at Zion's laptop, a USB cord running from the computer to the port underneath the Minion's foot.

Waiting for the camera to connect with the desktop, she also noticed—onscreen—an icon for Black House. Zion apparently had an account—or at the very least, was watching someone else's.

Right there, Nola's brain flashed back to the scene . . . when she'd first logged into Black House and saw Mint's digital avatar, or whoever was using his avatar . . . There was another soldier there. A Hispanic one, with close-set eyes. That was Zion. No doubt about it, Nola realized, looking back at the body in the kitchen. Yet as she re-played it in her head, it begged the question: Who was Zion meeting with in Black House? Someone who was a friend, or was that who killed him?

The question would have to wait. On the desktop, there was a ping as the icon for the nanny cam appeared.

Wasting no time, Nola hit Play.

Onscreen, the last few minutes of Zion's life bloomed into view.

45

"I knew it!" Tessa barked, storming out of the chaplain's office. *"Those lying motherf—!"*

"Mrs. Mint, please!" Zig pleaded, chasing after her. "This area— You can't—!"

"I know you hear me! You think I wouldn't find it!?" she shouted, waving the manila envelope, her tight ponytail pumping behind her as she plowed down the carpeted first-floor hallway that contained Dover's senior staff offices. The Carpet Canyon, everyone called it, a not-so-subtle jab. Every other floor in the mortuary was concrete or industrial tile, surfaces built to withstand blood and body parts.

"Ma'am, I need you to stop," a male secretary called out, rising from his seat. He wasn't nearly fast enough.

With a sharp right, Tessa stormed into the one office that every staffer knew was off-limits. Inside, a Black man with a side part shaved into his Afro looked up from his desk. He had a wide face, like a billboard. Late forties. Retro gold wire-framed glasses and wearing a drab olive Air Force flight suit. Zig knew who he was, even without the name tag on his chest—Colonel O. J. Whatley—Dover's wing commander, the second Black man to ever hold the top job.

Zig had never met him before, but c'mon, his outfit alone . . . Most heads of Dover wear formal uniforms—military dress, shirt and tie. Their flying days are mostly done. So for Whatley to still be sporting a flight suit like he's about to take off in *Top Gun* mode . . . *Heart or no heart?* Outlook not good.

"O.J.," Tessa said in a tone that would leave a bruise.

"Tessie," he replied, trying to make nice.

Zig was still in the hallway, determined to stay out of sight. "Casper?" he whispered to his friend. But as Zig turned, the photographer was long gone. Soon enough, Zig would realize he should've taken off, too.

"Mr. Zigarowski?" a voice called out. O.J.'s secretary.

"Arturo?" Zig asked, recognizing the kid with the squatty fingers who used to work in Dover's laundry, ironing fresh sheets for the fallen. "What're you doing here?"

"Promotion. You? Because, um . . . it kinda looks like you're eavesdropping."

"I'm actually with a client. Recent widow," Zig said, pointing toward Tessa, who was still unleashing on Colonel Whatley.

Arturo nodded. He'd seen it before. "Y'know, one night, I was delivering laundry at like two in the morning. Everyone was gone. But you were here, Mr. Zigarowski, working on this young female naval aviator whose F-14 went down. Two A.M. And that wasn't the only night I saw you here," he added, heading up the hallway and waving goodbye. "I need coffee. Enjoy your eavesdropping, Mr. Zigarowski."

"Tessie, please, take a seat," O.J. said, still standing behind his desk as he motioned her to a chair. With his pointer finger, he pushed the bridge of his gold-rimmed glasses up on his nose, Zig wondering if it was O.J.'s way of buying a moment. "With all you've been through . . ."

"I want his phone, Oren."

"If you just sit down . . ."

"I WANT HIS PHONE! I SAW THE PHOTOS!" she roared, waving the manila folder so hard, a few of the pictures rocketed to the floor. She caught her breath, locking eyes with O.J. Whatever was going on, these two knew each other. "Two phones, O.J. My husband clearly had an extra one. I know you have it."

"It's my job to have it. We're still investigating—"

"That's another lie. It's like your helmets," she said, pointing to his credenza, the I-Love-Me section of his office, which held half a dozen flight helmets. "Y'know, Archie once told me that most of those aren't even yours, they're your dad's—but you thought keeping them on display would help you make full bird. And look at that, here you are, *Colonel.*"

"Tessie, I know you're in pain—"

"Spare me your pathetic TED Talk! He was with *her,* wasn't he? That's who the phone was for."

For the first time, O.J. didn't respond.

"You think I'm an idiot? I know him twenty-five years," Tessa said, her voice finally slowing down. "You have any idea how much Rashida cost us in marriage therapy?"

Rashida. Zig knew that name, from the back of Nola's canvas. One of her first military paintings—from Grandma's Pantry.

Archie Mint
Rashida Robinson
Elijah King

It reminded Zig of— Wait. He just saw— There. Right in front of him, on the assistant's desk, was an old-school logbook for incoming and outgoing calls. Every wing commander's assistant used one, to make sure there was a written record for when a fallen soldier's family member insisted, *I called ten times and no one called me back!*

At the top of the logbook were two entries. Outgoing calls—one last night and one this morning—to Elijah King. The third name on the list.

Comments: Left message. Still no reply.

"I'm getting warmer now, aren't I, Oren?" Tessa said, still focused on Rashida. "Maybe it's better if I call her myself," she added, pulling out an imaginary phone. "Hey, Rashida—remember all those years ago when you were fucking my—"

"She's dead," O.J. said.

"What?"

"Rashida's dead. We found her body two nights ago. Out by the airport, burned to a crisp. Cops tagged it as suicide, but . . . Let's just say we're looking into it."

Some spouses would've burst into tears. Military wives? They were built different.

Sure enough, Tessa stood at the center of the office, planted like a telephone pole. She stared down at the folder of photos, her brain still working through the details.

"Archie told me—" Her voice wavered, but not for long. "He said he was going to the steak house—that it was a work thing, but—" She shook her head. "Is that who he was with—? Were he and Rashida still—"

"She met him at the steak house—we know that for sure," O.J. said. "What we don't know is— When the shots were— We think she might've been in the back seat with Archie when he got shot."

She was. Zig knew she was. He'd seen it on the CT scan . . . from the bone shrapnel that he'd found in the side of Mint's face. When Zig first saw it, he didn't know who the bones belonged to, but to hear this—that Rashida and Mint were meeting at the restaurant, and that their history was more than just work related . . .

Zig glanced around the empty hallway, putting together his own pieces. Could O.J. and the Dover medical examiners have missed it on the CT scan? Maybe at first—especially since it now seemed clear that someone had pulled Rashida's body from the back seat. But from what O.J. just said, he knew that Mint wasn't alone when he got shot. On top of that, he knew that Mint and Rashida were together that night. And if that was the case . . .

"How could you not tell me?" Tessa asked O.J.

"Tell you *what*? That we're as concerned and lost as you are?"

"This is from that night—it goes back to the Pantry, doesn't it?"

"That's a theory."

"It's more than a damn theory! It's why you took this case!"

"It *is* why I took the case. But Tessie, I swear to you, it wasn't until we actually brought him in that we found the second phone, which by the way, forensics is still digging through. Call me old fashioned, but I prefer not to dredge up my friend's worst mistakes until I know what the hell actually happened, which I'm glad I did, considering we're now chasing a second body."

"So you think . . ." Tessa swallowed hard, trying to steady her breath. "The fact they're both dead . . . You don't think they were still—?"

"Tessie, if you're asking me why they were meeting in a steak restaurant, I can't possibly give you a definitive answer. Years ago, with Rashida, Archie made a mistake that I know he forever regretted. And I realize how it looks. But now, for them to *both* turn up dead . . . plus all the extra work that someone put in to make sure none of this seems connected . . . I know it's emotional, but objectively speaking, at least to me . . ." O.J. again pushed his glasses up on his nose. "This seems less like something intimate, and more like something work related."

It was a perfect explanation, presented with perfect logic, but as Zig stood there in the hallway, it still didn't explain one key detail: If everything the colonel just said was true, who the hell moved Rashida's body?

In truth, Zig had seen it before. When two of our spies were killed on a top secret mission, to protect their identities, the government would sometimes move one of the bodies so no one would know they were working together. Could that be the case here—that it was done before O.J. and the Dover folks got there? It was as good an explanation as any. But to pull it off took manpower—paperwork had to be filed, supervisors had to approve—and most important, the right undercover team had to swoop in fast enough t—

Mothertrucker. Zig missed it at first, but there it was, on O.J.'s credenza: the flight helmets. These days, the Air Force had stopped letting pilots decorate their helmets like Maverick himself—but since the colonel was older, his helmets had printed call signs above the front visor. There were a few from the Cold War era that clearly belonged to his dad. The newer ones had the word "Poptop" along the top visor—those were O.J.'s—along with various wing and squadron emblems along the sides. The very last one also had a familiar unit logo, a hand grabbing two bright yellow lightning bolts: *Semper Vigiles.*

Zig felt the blood rush from his face. Of course—

Archie Mint
Rashida Robinson
Elijah King
And now, Colonel O. J. Whatley

All of them in the same unit, a unit that clearly had a deeply personal stake in whatever happened all those years ago at Grandma's Pantry.

"So at the steak place— You don't think they were—" Tessa let out a huff, her eyes welling with tears—good tears—as a wave of relief rolled over her.

"Tessie, he loved you . . . You were his— *C'mere*," O.J. insisted, crossing around his desk, arms extended for a hug.

Tessa stepped toward him, arms flat at her sides, her head sagging back, crumpling desperately, thankfully, into his embrace. As a mortician, Zig had spent decades seeing people at their best and worst. Yet there's always that moment when a mourner reaches their physical limits and finally realizes that no matter how strong they're pretending to be, death always sees you for who you really are, and always gets what it's after. Fight all you want. At some point, there's nothing to do but surrender.

"This doesn't mean I'm forgetting about his phone," Tessa whispered.

The colonel laughed, tightening his embrace. "You'll get it. I swear. I'll bring it tonight, maybe for dinner? You still have to eat, right?"

"What about Elijah? Have you heard from him?" she asked.

"We're trying. No response. Let's get you home," the colonel added, ushering her to the door—both of them now headed toward Zig.

Zig tried to run, but there wasn't time. Sliding into a nearby rolling chair, he kept his back to the colonel, quickly skating toward the assistant's desk, which had the same Captain America mouse pad used by nearly half of today's young troops.

"Anything else you need . . ." O.J. began, their voices fading up the hallway. For two seconds, Zig sat there, frozen.

In the distance, a door clicked. All clear. They were gone.

Wasting no time, Zig took off at full speed, rounding the corner as—

"C'mon now, Mr. Zigarowski," Colonel Whatley said, pushing his glasses up on his face. "Did you really think I wouldn't see you sitting there?"

46

"Mrs. Silvestri? Mrs. Silvestri, you awake?"

No response.

"Mrs. Silvestri, can you hear me?" Waggs asked, standing in the threshold of room 404. According to hospital records, it was the same room Nola came to visit three weeks ago, to see this particular patient: Mrs. Thelma Silvestri.

Inside, the lights were off, though on the far right, two big windows framed the morning sun as it bathed the room in a golden glow. From what Waggs could tell, Mrs. Silvestri was asleep, her head turned away, toward the sun, as various machines beeped and whirred in their usual chorus.

"Ma'am, are you—*ahem* . . ." Waggs added, faking a cough loud enough to wake even the deepest sleeper.

Mrs. Silvestri still didn't respond.

"She's not gonna answer," a male voice called out.

Waggs quickly turned, spotting a barrel-chested African American orderly with hangdog eyes and an outrageously contagious smile. He was pushing a rolling cart filled with old paperback books. Name tag read *Rolly*.

"What's wrong with her?" Waggs asked.

"You a cop?"

"How does everyone know that?"

"Stan the Man. Walkie-talkie," he explained, pointing to his belt. "For some reason, he likes you. He doesn't like most people."

Waggs forced a laugh, hoping to keep him talking. "You were saying about Mrs. Silvestri . . . ?"

"Listen, with HIPAA—I got three kids—I need this job, so can't get into details, but look around. You see what floor you're on?" Rolly asked, pointing to a sign by the nurse's station: *Neurology.* "Apparently, as Mrs. Silvestri was driving down the highway, some kid on an overpass thought it'd be funny to drop a ski pole on a passing car. It hit her, *fttttttt.*" Rolly made a noise like a dart hitting cork as he pointed to the center of his own forehead. "Traumatic brain injury. Right through her frontal lobe. Can you imagine?"

Waggs could. For the better part of a decade, she'd seen firsthand what homemade bombs do to victims around the world. Taking another step into the room, she got a good look at Mrs. Silvestri's face for the first time. Her mouth was open in an upside-down crescent moon, frozen midscream. She was probably only forty, but was so gaunt—her hair ragged, her skin practically translucent—she looked twice that. There were tubes in her nose, throat, and stomach. Ventilator, tracheotomy, feeding tube.

"So she doesn't speak?" Waggs asked.

"Not until a few weeks ago. Didn't you—? I figured that's why you were here. It was all over the news," the orderly said. Reading Waggs's confused look, he added, "Mrs. Silvestri's accident happened nearly two years ago. She couldn't speak—minimal brain activity—complete vegetative state. Then, three weeks ago, out of nowhere, she wakes up, asking for two things: chocolate pudding and her husband, who died a decade ago."

"I saw this story."

"Everyone did. The local news went wild, demanding interviews. It was a total madhouse. It didn't last long, though. Four days later, her eyes rolled back into her head and she returns to this." He motioned toward the patient. *"Isn't that right, Mrs. Silvestri!?"*

No response.

"Let me ask you," Waggs said, "those few days she was awake . . . was one of those June nineteenth?"

Rolly squinted upward, at the room's popcorn ceiling. "Yeah, I . . . that sounds right. Why do you—?"

"What about this woman?" Waggs asked, pulling out Nola's photo. "Ever seen her before?"

"That's a terrible picture. Girl can't smile. But yeah, I seen her."

"Describe 'seen her.'"

The orderly went silent.

"Please don't make me use the badge," Waggs pleaded.

"She gave me fifty bucks, okay?"

Waggs cocked an eyebrow, confused. "Why would Nola give you fifty bucks?"

"I told you, the news crews—they all wanted access. One of the nurses took two hundred dollars to get a photo of Mrs. Silvestri finally eating her pudding . . . and it wasn't even the chocolate one."

"So Nola paid you—?"

"To paint. Draw. I don't know, I figured she was one of those artists who paints pictures in courtrooms. She asked for ten minutes; I gave her ten minutes."

"Was that when Mrs. Silvestri went back into—?" She pointed toward the bed.

"*What?* No! She went back into her coma *after*. It had to be after." He thought about it a moment. *"Right?"*

Waggs pulled out her phone, quickly doing the math. According to hospital records, Nola had been here on June 19, two days after Mrs. Silvestri woke up from her coma. From the online news report, she went back into her coma the following day, on the twentieth. "Do we know why she lost consciousness?" Waggs asked.

"Wait. You think your artist friend—?"

Waggs didn't know what to think. It could've been Nola. Or someone who visited *after* Nola. Hell, it could've been any of the ten thousand things that usually go wrong when someone has a traumatic brain injury. No way to know for sure.

Still staring at her phone, Waggs swiped back to the map with the other locations that Nola made special trips to over the past few weeks. Three places in total.

One down. Two to go.

47

"Does being back feel like a time machine, Mr. Zigarowski? Someone told me this was your old office."

"It wasn't," Zig shot back. "Mine was down the hall, closer to Embalming. And the actual fallen. Where the real work gets done."

Colonel Whatley stayed all smiles, sitting at his immaculate desk, which was made of glass. Through the top, Zig could see O.J.'s legs, his chair, and his right hand, which held a staple remover that he was clicking like a tiny shark—chomp, chomp, chomp.

Like his predecessor, O.J. dedicated the left wall of his office to freestanding flags: American flag, Air Force flag, POW/MIA flag, and of course flags for Dover's 436th and 512th Airlift Wings, each on its own flag stand, lined up like a firing squad. The only thing that had changed in the office was the ceiling.

Zig couldn't see it until he got inside: above the desk, O.J. had removed two of the industrial ceiling tiles and replaced them with translucent ones that held a big full-color photo of what looked like a Hawaiian paradise, complete with crystal-blue water, palm trees, and an empty lounge chair with a coconut cocktail on one armrest and a purple orchid lei draped over the back. Zig had seen something similar in his dentist's office. The hygienist said the ocean view helped people find calm. A simple trick so you don't focus on the coming assault.

"You know, I've been to your funeral home," the colonel said, his grin perfectly in place. "Must've been four, five years back—I don't think you were working there yet. A friend of my grandfather—

ninety-two years old, full life. Though all I really remember is everyone saying it used to be a Dairy Queen. I mean, a funeral home in an
ice cream shop? What's crazier?"

"A politician in a flight suit?"

O.J. laughed out loud, like that was the plan all along. Chomp,
chomp, chomp. "Mr. Zigarowski, despite what you think, I'm not
the enemy."

"I know you hired me," Zig blurted. "For Mint's funeral. You're
the one who pulled me into this."

"Our office only hires the best morticians."

"You could've called any local mortician. You brought me in because you knew my connection to her—you thought it would help
you keep Nola off balance."

"And if I did?"

"You could've just asked me!"

"That's good advice, Mr. Zigarowski. I think I'll take you up on
that," the colonel said matter-of-factly, his hands now resting on top
of his desk, still holding the staple remover.

Zig shifted in his chair, glancing up at the Hawaii photo glowing
in the ceiling. "I don't understand."

"Do you really think I just want to talk about your old job, Mr.
Zigarowski? What I really need is a favor."

48

This was Nola when she was thirteen.

It was four days before Christmas, which, for Nola, didn't mean much. Since he first took her in, Royall had told her that good Catholics knew Christmas wasn't about decorating or gift giving, which just promoted excess. Yet for some reason, in this small house that they'd moved to, where there was a plastic bucket on top of the refrigerator to catch the two leaks whenever it rained, Royall was suddenly pointing out cobwebs in the ceiling corners and having Nola vacuum with Carpet Fresh (or rather, with some knockoff called CarpetRenew). Most important, he was buying stuff. Real stuff.

For years, Royall hadn't purchased stockings, a tree, or even presents, except for that year he got her a cinnamon candle because he said she was starting to smell.

First thing this morning, though, Royall went full Christmas Spirit. Stockings. Lights. An actual gingerbread house. Even a big fake silver tinsel tree that most people bought for kitsch value, but Royall bought because he thought it looked expensive—plus he didn't want craploads of pine needles all over his CarpetRenewed carpet.

"Who's coming?" Nola asked. Had to be a client.

It was. Elias Avery Jr., who ran a chain of motels from Pennsylvania to New Jersey, was a potential buyer for the two hundred odd-lot

fax machines that Royall bought at auction last week. Most important, he loved Christmas nearly as much as Jesus himself.

"Make it look good, girl," Royall warned on his way out.

That was two hours ago. So when the house phone rang twice,
then went silent, Nola knew the signal. Royall and Mr. Avery were
on their way home from their fancy seafood dinner. Make sure the
house is perfect.

Scrambling and rearranging the last few ornaments, she brought
as much as she could to the front, thinking it didn't look perfect, but
definitely better than before. It reminded her of her last (and only)
Christmas with her old family, the LaPointes, and how all the kids
were encouraged to decorate, but as they did, Mrs. LaPointe would
circle the tree behind them, subtly redoing everyone's work, moving
tinsel and ornaments higher and lower, none of the other kids noticing that they had nearly nothing to do with the breathtaking final
product. Nola tried to remember what she got that Christmas, but all
she remembered was that Roddy kept asking for one of those magic
tricks where you pretend to cut off your finger.

Hearing a car in the driveway, Nola scooped up the packaging
for the ornaments, darted for the kitchen, and stuffed it all under the
sink—so Royall could return everything when this was done.

Ding-dong.

Coming! she started to yell, then caught herself, remembering
how Royall told her to say it. "On my way!"

As she sprinted back to the door, she reached under her skirt and
pulled down her blouse to straighten it, a trick she'd seen that bitch
Leslie Cushman do in the girls' bathroom.

With a twist, she opened the door and smiled.

"Ms. Konnikova?"

"Nola, how are you, dearie?" asked a heavyset woman with brown
hair in a tidy ponytail. Lydia Konnikova, the troop mom from Nola's
old Girl Scout troop who used to run carpool and drive everyone
from school, which really was the only reason Royall signed her up
for Scouts in the first place. Nola hadn't seen her in at least a year.

"Is it too late? It's too late," Ms. Konnikova said, Nola remembering that she always answered her own questions. "I know it's been

a while, but when you moved away, no one knew how to find you—Joyce Gluck said she heard you were living on a houseboat, which is actually a dream of mine . . ."

"Ms. Konnikova—"

"All I'm saying is, I'm not usually such a snoop, but last week, I saw you and your stepdad pulling out of the gas station by Robbie's Grill, and, well, I know technically you're now zoned for the troop in this county, but, well, we miss you, so . . . Tah-dah!" she announced, holding up a dry-cleaning bag with a lime-green Scout uniform inside.

"It's great, isn't it? So great!" Ms. Konnikova added, stepping inside even though Nola didn't invite her. "We want you back. Say yes. Oh, and if it doesn't fit, I can hem."

"Ms. Konnikova, I'm not supposed to let anyone—"

"Huh . . ." Ms. Konnikova said, her wide hips shifting as she scanned the dingy living room, with its cracked black leather sofa and outdated glass coffee table that held a neat stack of *Sports Illustrated*s. There were no pictures on the walls, no curtains on the windows—but all Ms. Konnikova was staring at was the sparkling silver Christmas tree that stood in the corner like a stripper pole.

Years later, Nola would have the right word to describe the look on her former Scout mom's face. She thought it was confusion, or disappointment. But it was pity.

"What're you doing?" a sharp male voice called from outside.

Nola turned, her stomach folding in on itself.

"You hear me?" Royall demanded. As he burst through the doorway, Nola searched for the familiar rage in his eyes. But for once, there wasn't any.

"Nola, you okay?" Royall asked, sounding concerned.

Nola cocked her head. It was a tone she rarely heard.

"Looks like a party," another voice called out behind Royall, a balding man with a cul-de-sac of silver hair. Royall's client, Elias Avery Jr. That's why Royall was on good behavior.

In barely two minutes, the entire interaction was finished.

Ms. Konnikova thanked everyone for letting her interrupt—*please, Nola, think about it, we'd love to have you back*—then headed home. Royall and Elias were on their way to the den, excited for the fake-labeled drink that Royall would be serving from the bar. And Nola? She was right where they left her, standing by the silver Christmas tree, still clutching the hanger with the brand-new Girl Scout uniform. No question, there'd be a price to pay tomorrow for letting a stranger in the house. She saw it as Royall turned the corner, glancing over his shoulder with his devil smile, that look she knew so well. *We're not done, girl.*

Right now, though, the far more brutal wound was the *other* look—that one she wouldn't be able to shake for weeks—the sadness and sorrow on Ms. Konnikova's face when she got a look at Nola's life.

49

"It wasn't me! For the ninety-fifth time!" Zion screamed onscreen, stumbling through the living room.

Nola leaned toward the screen of Zion's laptop. The video from the Minion nanny cam was crisp and in color—4K, she realized. Ultrahigh-def.

As Zion raced toward the kitchen, a woman with pale skin and a blue leather coat strolled behind him. She moved gracefully, almost joyfully, like she was relishing it. No question, a pro. Her head was turned, so Nola couldn't get a good look. But her hair—a redhead.

"Zion, if you run . . ."

He ran—scrambling forward—out of the camera's eye, disappearing into the kitchen.

From there, the rest of the video was an empty living room with far too many Japanese accessories. Once Zion and the woman reached the kitchen, the audio was muddy. Nola couldn't hear a word. Someone yelling, then silence.

A few minutes later, a towering boulder of a man—also with red hair (though he looked more Irish)—lumbered into the frame. Entering the living room, he headed straight for the coffee table, his meaty paw grabbing the one item that Nola hadn't noticed at first: a phone.

Now it made sense.

These redheads, two of them. They killed Zion, they took his phone, and clearly, they had a head start.

Not for long.

50

"I don't like being manipulated, Colonel."

"I'm inviting you to join the team. You should be excited," O.J. said, standing and crossing around to the opposite side of the desk, toward Zig.

"Y'know who you're reminding me of right now? In *Karate Kid*—the guy who runs the evil dojo? Sweep the leg?"

"Cobra Kai."

"You've got his subtlety."

"They made a Netflix series where he comes back. As the hero of the story," the colonel said. "I'm giving you an opportunity to actually be helpful."

"Can I just make one last point? The Netflix series is about Johnny, the student, not the sensei, who's still a doucheface. Anyway . . . you were saying, you need a favor?"

"It's about Roddy."

Zig was listening.

"I know he reached out to you, Mr. Zigarowski."

Zig sat there, not moving. Was O.J. bluffing? Didn't sound like it, which meant that the colonel had either been watching at the funeral or listening in on Zig's phone. Zig made a mental note, eyeing the big Hawaii photo on the ceiling.

"He's not your friend, Mr. Zigarowski," the colonel said, Zig now realizing that O.J. was one of those people who says your name over and over, hoping to create familiarity. An old military interrogation technique.

"I barely know Roddy. He's a stranger," Zig said.

"To us, too. We'd like to change that. Hence my offer: next time you hear from him, we'd like to know. That's all we're asking, Mr. Zigarowski."

Zig stayed silent, flushed with that feeling he'd get when a family member would say that their dead relative was "a real character." They were trying to keep things nice, but there was clearly so much more they weren't saying. "And this'll help you track down Nola?" Zig asked.

"This has nothing to do w—"

"I'm not a fool, sir. I know you're looking for her. I know that when you tried to bring her in, one of your crew got a pen jabbed into his kneecap. And don't tell me he's not part of your crew, because it's not hard to recognize hands grabbing lightning bolts," Zig said, motioning over to the colonel's credenza and the row of flight helmets. "Semper Vigiles, Colonel. Latin for *why don't you stop bullshitting me and tell me the truth?*"

Leaning on the front corner of his desk, Colonel Whatley stared down at his staple remover, closing it in slow motion. "Mr. Zigarowski—"

"Call me Zig."

"Mr. Zigarowski, do you really even know Nola Brown?"

"Why do I feel like you're about to make a speech?"

"She grew up in your hometown, didn't she? I also saw she was in the same Girl Scout troop as your daughter—that's some real history you share."

"She saved my life."

"I read about that. But back when Nola first joined the military, do you truly know what she was like? Or to put it more succinctly, when no one's looking, do you know what she's capable of?"

"I know about Grandma's Pantry."

"No. You don't. If you did, you wouldn't be here sniffing around."

"Then tell me about it," Zig demanded.

"You keep acting like this is a negotiation. You have no idea what—"

"In World War II, your unit did specialized investigations. Is that what this's about? Some old investigation that Nola found out about?"

O.J. rolled his eyes, his thumb rubbing at a wedding band that was no longer there. "Lord Almighty, do you even realize what a pain in the rear you are, Mr. Zigarowski? Stop thinking you're in a position to make demands."

"Then stop thinking you're getting my help. Because last I checked, *you're* the one who needs the favor from *me*," Zig said, standing from his seat and heading for the door.

"Where're you going?" O.J. asked.

Zig kept walking, picking up speed.

"Mr. Zigarowski, if you don't sit down—"

"You keep acting like this is a negotiation. Have fun solving this yourself," he said as he was about to leave.

"It's for the end of the world," O.J. said.

"The *what*?" Zig asked, stopping at the threshold.

"Grandma's Pantry. That's what it was designed for," O.J. said, stealing a glance at the ceiling tile, at the calming photo of the Hawaiian ocean palms, the purple lei, and the coconut drink. "It's where the government prepares for the end of the world."

51

"Ohhh, Mrs. Z, it's been . . . How *are* you!?"

"Well. Really well," Charmaine replied, saying it twice as if that'd help her believe it. Her phone was flat on her kitchen table, on speaker so she could nurse her morning coffee. Outside, she eyed the bird feeder that Warren put in all his model homes, filled with safflower seeds, since squirrels tended to hate them. Yet there was a squirrel, feasting on them anyway.

"When my mom said you'd call—" Dara stopped herself, overcome with excitement. "Ohhh, Mrs. Z—"

"Charmaine. You can call me Charmaine."

"I can't . . . I'd never . . . How long's it *been*?" Dara asked, her intonation rising at the end of her sentences. Uptalk. Older generations label it as flakiness or an insecurity, but as Charmaine knew, language is *supposed* to change. It's no different than fashion: Why do people wear skinny jeans? It signals you're part of a group. Kids don't listen to the same music as their parents, or wear their hair the same way. Like it or not, it's a good sign—proof that, as a culture, we're moving forward. And as people, we're getting older.

"Your mom said you're starting your last year of law school. That's wonderful," Charmaine added, feeling a twist in her belly that reminded her of those first years after Maggie died, when she'd go to supermarkets two towns over to avoid seeing anyone she knew.

"Insane, right? First semester ends right before my due date."

Charmaine froze, nearly spilling her coffee. There was no breath left in her body.

"Mom didn't tell you?" Dara asked. "Mrs. Z, I'm sorry—I didn't—"

"It's fine. I'm thrilled for you."

"You know I'd never—"

"Dara, please. We're good. That's a blessing—it should be celebrated," Charmaine said, blinking over and over, kicking herself for not seeing it coming. Like any parent who's buried a child, Charmaine had become a connoisseur at avoiding subjects she knew would slice her in the underbelly. Staring out at the squirrel who was still munching away, she felt the knife continue to twist.

"I appreciate you saying that, Mrs. Z. You and Mr. Z, you were always— Anyhoo, tell me how I can help. Something with Super-Stars, my mom said. That place was therapy fuel for my entire adolescence."

It didn't take long to explain the rest: the old video of Maggie crying, and that from the looks of the tape, she was clearly crying to someone who couldn't be seen onscreen. "Dara, if you know who that might be—if you have any ideas, I'd owe you forever."

There was a pause, but not a long one. "I'm sorry, Mrs. Z, I really am," Dara said. "But the honest truth is, if Maggie was crying in the studio . . . or even her being at the studio . . . I've got no memory of it."

52

"When you say 'end of the world' . . . ?"

"I mean the *actual* end of the world. Or at least the end when it came to the Cold War," O.J. began, still sitting on the front edge of his desk, motioning Zig to take a seat.

Zig waved him off, preferring to stand.

If it annoyed the colonel, he wasn't showing it. He was too busy glancing to his left, at his window.

Zig followed his gaze outside, realizing O.J.'s office overlooked the small lot on the side of the building that Dover used as a side entrance to help the families of victims who needed a bit more privacy. O.J.'s glance lingered a second too long, and now Zig couldn't tell if the colonel was trying to make sure they were alone, or looking for someone who was coming.

"You were saying about the Cold War?" Zig asked.

"I was saying this was back in the 1950s, when, well . . ." He turned back to Zig. "Guess what America was building faster than anyone back then?"

"Why do you keep asking questions I can't possibly know the answer to?"

"Humor me, Mr. Zigarowski. It's 1954. President Eisenhower is at the top of his game—and is rightfully convinced that Russia is building an arsenal of missiles that they're determined to bomb us with. So what do we start building in return?"

"More missiles to bomb them."

"Correct. But here's the rub: Eisenhower's a military man. He knows we need a good offense, but he's also savvy enough to know we need—"

"A good defense. That's a wonderful history lesson, but what's this have to do with Nola or Grandma's Pan—?"

"This is the context," O.J. said, stealing another quick glance outside. Side entrance still clear. "In 1949, six years after the Pentagon first opened, they realized that a surprise Russian attack could easily take out all of Washington, D.C.—so military higher-ups decided that their top priority was to build a backup command center somewhere *outside* D.C. in case they needed to keep the government running.

"It started in Adams County, just over the Pennsylvania line from Maryland, where Uncle Sam quietly started buying land like they were Walt Disney himself. From there, they started digging. And on June 30, 1953, seven months after Eisenhower was elected, the government opened—"

"I know about Raven Rock . . . and Mount Weather," Zig said, referring to the government's two most secret military bunkers—one underground, one in a mountaintop—that were still in use today, including on 9/11 when Dick Cheney and other top officials were evacuated there. "I've buried fallen from both."

"Then you also know that both bunkers are solely for government honchos and military employees. That's a fraction of the picture. What happens to everyone else—the millions of U.S. citizens around the country? When the bombs fall, who takes care of them?"

Swaying there a moment, Zig stayed quiet, noticing a gray Buick pull into the parking lot.

"It's a potent question," O.J. added, both of them now eyeing the Buick as its door swung open and a middle-aged woman with hip cat-eye glasses got out. Edna from Veterans Affairs. No one to worry about, though the way O.J. was turned toward the window, Zig noticed a small sweat stain in the armpit of his flight suit. Whoever he was waiting for, this wasn't a friendly visit. "In 1954, to find the answer," O.J. explained, "the organization that specialized in keeping civilians safe, the FCDA—Federal Civil Defense Administration—was moved out of Washington and into an old sanitarium in Battle Creek, Michigan . . ."

"And this is real?"

"Look it up. The goal of the FCDA was crystal clear—civilian defense during an atomic disaster, which they quickly narrowed to three possibilities: dispersal, evacuation, or shelter—or as they put it, 'dig, die, or get out,' and c'mon, you really think anyone wants to die?" O.J. asked, turning back to Zig and pushing his glasses up on his nose.

"I still don't see what this has to do with Grandma's P—"

"This is where it was born. Mount Weather was code-named High Point. This Michigan sanitarium was called Low Point, a place where the government would consider every different invention and scenario to protect civilians if a hydrogen bomb hit: two-hundred-bed pop-up hospitals that could fit inside a tractor trailer and be driven to a radiated area within four hours of an attack, collection teams that would mobilize to ID all the bodies . . . They even came up with an emergency plan to move the dead: seven thousand Post Office trucks that, instead of carrying mail, would carry corpses."

"Upbeat place to work."

"You do realize we're now standing in a mortuary?" O.J. asked, still locked on Zig. "The point," he continued, "was that by 1955, the best ideas were turned into actual exhibits, sent to tour around the country and to state fairs."

"And people enjoyed that?"

"In 1955? People loved it. Atomic fever and bunker building were in full swing, especially when it came to one of the most popular campaigns, named . . ." O.J. paused.

"Is this where you want me to say 'Grandma's Pantry'?"

"Grandma's Pantry," O.J. said. "A campaign that urged families to stockpile enough food and water to last seven days. Even had its own slogan: 'Grandma was always ready for an emergency.'"

"Catchy."

"You have no idea. It became so popular, Sears started putting

Grandma's Pantry displays in stores around the country, encouraging people to buy supplies and food to save their families. As the Cold War escalated, billions were poured into civilian shelters, massive stockpiles were built, and the Continuity of Government movement was born—focusing around every doomsday scenario imaginable, especially as the FCDA evolved to FEMA, then got folded into Homeland Security. But at the heart of it all was this simple truth . . ."

"None of it would work."

"None of it," O.J. agreed, stealing another glance outside. "If a war began and a nuclear bomb really hit U.S. soil, top officials might make it to a shelter, but the rest of us would be leveled."

"So that was the end of Grandma's Pantry?"

"It was. Until the late 1990s, when a government employee named Steven Bice wrote a paper recommending that a new stockpile be started—a new Grandma's Pantry, so to speak. But his theory was that instead of focusing on canned goods, this one should focus on pharmaceuticals. According to Bice's paper, the threat to America had changed. Nuclear missiles weren't the threat anymore. Bioterrorism was."

"He's right," Zig said, still remembering the antibiotics and chemical bath he was forced to take when the body of a thirty-two-year-old female State Department employee came through Dover, and they realized she was killed in a ricin attack.

"He was absolutely right," O.J. agreed. "And the amazing part is, for *once,* the government actually listened. Embracing Bice's idea, Uncle Sam opened a vaccine and bioterror stockpile in 1999."

"Grandma's Pantry 2.0," Zig said, quickly doing the math. "Just in time for—"

"A year and a half later, 9/11 happens. Then come the anthrax attacks. For both, the newly named Strategic National Stockpile—the SNS—was ready, shipping Push Packages with anthrax vaccines that saved potentially hundreds of thousands of lives. And in the aftermath of 9/11 . . . ?"

"It set off the biggest spending spree for national defense since the days of Eisenhower himself," Zig said, well aware that that's when the

Dover mortuary was upgraded, moving into its current multimillion-dollar building. With new threats and new wars in Afghanistan and Iraq, Uncle Sam needed new facilities to handle the dead.

"Mr. Zigarowski, I know words like 'secret government warehouse' sound like something from the end of *Indiana Jones,* but it's real. Today, there are eleven undisclosed warehouses carefully hidden across the country," O.J. said, with a new tone in his voice, one Zig had never heard before. "Each one is filled with vaccines for smallpox, SARS, hantavirus, you name it. That's who handled Ebola in 2014. And Zika in 2016. And who would've been storing all the COVID-19 vaccines had they existed before the pandemic. Whatever health disaster hits—toxic attacks, viral attacks, chemical weapons—they've got antidotes, antivirals, surgical equipment, sedatives. Where do you think half the COVID ventilators came from? Hell, they store cobra venom for whatever the hell that does, and I'm not even making it up.

"Thanks to Mr. Bice's paper, they can get you the meds you need within an hour for well-populated areas, a maximum of five hours for the most rural locations," O.J. said, glancing up for a half second at the Hawaiian paradise in the ceiling. From its angle diagonally above O.J.'s desk, it made Zig wonder if instead of being there to calm visitors, the Hawaiian ceiling tiles were actually there for O.J.'s benefit.

"I appreciate the context, Colonel. But can we please get to the part you're obviously leaving out."

"Pardon?"

"I worked here on 9/11," Zig said. "When those first anthrax victims were sent our way, I still remember the plastic smell inside the oxygen suits they trained us in. And y'know who did that training? The CDC. The Centers for Disease Con—"

"I know the acronym."

"Then you should also know they trained us for Ebola, SARS, smallpox, and even that nerve agent that killed one of our spies in Saudi Arabia a few years back. It was always the CDC, working with Homeland Security, FBI, CIA, even the DIA. But never once did they call in a top secret Army unit whose specialty was clandestine investigations."

For the first time since Zig stepped into the office, O.J. didn't say a word.

"It goes back to that night, doesn't it, Colonel? Five years ago, your crew got the call to go to one of those secret Grandma's Pantry warehouses. Something happened there, didn't it? Something more than just some missing Post-it notes from the supply closet."

"There was a break-in," O.J. said.

"What?"

"A break-in. Five years ago. That's what started all this. We had a break-in at Grandma's Pantry."

53

"So, like a *robbery*?"

"That's not what I said," O.J. replied.

Zig knew that tone. He replayed the facts. All those vaccines in one place . . . the smallpox alone. If a terrorist got their hands on that . . . "What'd they get?"

"They didn't get anything."

"So you stopped them? Or did someone—?" Zig caught himself, almost forgetting the real reason he was here. Nola. "This goes back to Nola, doesn't it? She was there that night, too."

"Mr. Zigarowski . . ."

"Can you please stop repeating my damn name!?"

"Then can you please shut your mouth and listen for once!? Nola's job—as Artist-in-Residence—do you even know what it was?"

"She did paintings for the Army."

"No," O.J. said, using the word like a blade. "She did paintings of *disasters*. That's why Nola came to Grandma's Pantry. To bear witness. To see up close the shitstorm Mint and his crew were dealing with."

His crew. Zig made a mental note. From the sound of it, O.J. wasn't there that night.

"What matters is, when the break-in happened, Mint was the one who got the call," O.J. explained. "His team was first on scene. Nola came a few hours after, but you can imagine what she was walking into—everyone scrambling, people yelling at each other. And that's the thing about stressful situations—they'll make you do things you'd never do otherwise," O.J. said, letting the statement hang in the air.

"Colonel, I know you're amping up the drama to impress me, but I have no idea what you're getting at. I thought you said the thieves didn't get anything."

"No. I said the people who *broke in* didn't get anything. But someone did."

"And that's—? You're saying *Nola* stole something that night?"

O.J. didn't answer.

"One of the bioterror samples, or—?"

"Mr. Zigarowski, you asked me what happened. I told you. Five years ago, on a night everyone would rather forget, we had a break-in at Grandma's Pantry. The thieves were caught. Yet what they were targeting still somehow walked away."

"But to blame Nola . . . Can you even prove—?"

"*Prove?* Here's what I *know:* Mint was there that night, and he's dead. Rashida was there, and she's dead. And when it all went down five years ago, well . . . considering that Artists-in-Residence get to choose the different disasters they want to paint, it seemed pretty damn convenient that of all the places Nola could've painted that night, she picked Grandma's Pantry. So asking her to now come in for a sit-down seems like a pretty reasonable request—even if it's just to understand the sudden reappearance of her brother."

Zig froze.

"I told you, we know you've been talking to Roddy," O.J. added. "I'd like to know what he said."

"He's looking for Nola. I'm doing the same."

"So this is all just coincidence? Roddy shows up, and suddenly Nola's past is back to haunt her? Mr. Zigarowski, I asked your former coworkers here about you. They said you were a stubborn man . . . a loyal man . . . and definitely a lonely man. But not a naïve one."

Zig rolled his eyes. "Do you even realize how much bad dialogue you stole from *Law & Order?* You're the one who brought *me* in— you asked for *my* help. So until you have proof that Roddy found this old secret about his sister—"

"You keep acting like this is your investigation. It's not," O.J. insisted. "My old unit . . . our specialty was the problems that Uncle Sam preferred to keep off the front page—and making sure that every loose end got properly buried. But it's the one truth every mortician knows. Just because you bury something doesn't mean it goes away."

"Listen—"

"No. You listen: I have two soldiers who were murdered, one of whom I knew so long, I wouldn't be sitting here today without him. I owe his wife, I owe his children, and I intend to repay that debt, Mr. Zigarowski. I'm telling you how to help me, so if you hear from Nola—"

"You keep saying it's her, but for all you know, Mint and Rashida were the ones who took your stolen item. Maybe that's why they were killed: someone finally figured out it was them."

A swell of rage took O.J.'s face, his clenched jaw about to open. It reminded Zig of the way his father used to yell, exploding with a roar. To Zig's surprise, though, as quick as the wave of rage hit, it disappeared, O.J. staring straight up and taking another long visual drink of the Hawaiian ocean palms, the coconut cocktail, and the purple lei. "Mr. Zigarowski, in the military, do you know what the single best skill is to rise in the ranks?"

"I'd take a guess, but you're about to tell me."

"The ability to tell the difference between what you can change versus what's inevitable," O.J. said, his chin in the air, still focused intently on the Hawaiian palms. "It's where you're currently failing."

Now Zig was staring up at the Hawaiian photo.

"You think she'll come around, but she won't, Mr. Zigarowski. That's how Nola is. It's how she always is. You can give her all your attention . . . you can take a bullet to keep her safe . . . you can find the truth, catch Mint's killers, exonerate her in every way. But you'll still never be part of her life."

"That's not why I'm doing this."

"Keep telling yourself that," O.J. shot back. "We all need what we need. I know her a long time. Every Nola story has the same ending. When the smoke clears and the blood's being mopped from the floor, you're gonna put your hand up for that high five—and she's gonna slip out a side door and get as far away from you as humanly possible. It's what she does. *Inevitable*."

Outside in the parking lot, a black Chevy Suburban pulled in near the side entrance. Zig didn't notice. He was still eyeing the ceiling's Hawaiian paradise, wondering what photo he'd choose if he needed to bring himself some calm. Nothing came to mind.

"Mr. Zigarowski, if Nola or Roddy contact you again—"

Zig's phone started ringing. Caller ID told him the rest.

"Tell me that's Nola, and I'll believe the universe is fair," O.J. said.

"It's not. But I need you to know, I'm not working against you, Colonel. If I hear from either of them, I'll let you know."

"I have your word on that?"

The phone rang again. Zig headed for the door. "Sorry, Colonel, I really need to take this."

O.J. yelled something else, but Zig was already racing up the main hallway, toward the wishing well, still trying to think of a photo that brought him calm.

"Ziggy, you there?" a familiar voice announced in his ear. It was his assistant at the funeral home, Puerto Rican Andy. "I made the calls," Andy said as Zig ran out the front door, into the main lot. "You need to get back here. I spoke to SuperStars, the modeling place— She gave me a name—"

"Andy, how about putting together a complete sentence?"

"You need to see this. I found someone, an old employee. It's bad, Ziggy. He knew your daughter."

54

"So you remember her?"

"With hair like that?" asked a very pregnant nurse named Sandie as she pointed at the photo of Nola. "She wasn't exactly a talker." Sandie had a square face, long fingernails with tiny rhinestones, and a necklace with a gold charm for each of her three children, all boys. "Plus, we don't get many visitors around here," Sandie explained as they walked down the hallway and she motioned to the other rooms they passed.

Waggs nodded, eyeing the patients through the open doors, every one frozen in bed, their mouths agape, their hands clenched, their legs curled in ways that legs weren't meant to curl. In the previous hospital, Mrs. Silvestri looked bad. These patients looked worse.

"You get used to it," Nurse Sandie said, reading Waggs's mind.

From her years at Dover, Waggs knew it was true. It was the best and worst feature of the human brain—you can normalize anything.

"So when Nola showed up here . . . ?"

"She said she was a friend of Mr. Soule—asked for him by name . . . did a little painting of him . . . I thought it was sweet," Nurse Sandie explained as Waggs made a mental note. If Nola was painting him, she was looking for something.

"And you didn't think it was odd having someone just show up?"

"Like I said, it was sweet. No one had visited him in fourteen years."

"Fourteen?"

"Our specialty is long-term care, emphasis on the 'long.' We've got one patient, she's been here nearly thirty years. Truth is, we were just happy Mr. Soule had some company. When it comes to the coma ward, people aren't exactly banging down th—"

"*Coma?* Another brain injury?"

"I'm not sure what you mean by 'another,' but you do realize that's our specialty here . . . traumatic brain injuries."

Waggs nodded, glancing around. That's why the hall was so silent. "Do you happen to know how Mr. Soule got injured?" Waggs asked, her voice picking up speed.

"Not that I— He's been here so long, I actually don't."

"What about Nola? When she came to visit, any idea what she was looking for?"

"You should ask him," Sandie said.

"Excuse me?"

The nurse pointed to room 141, the open door on their left. "I thought that's why you were here," she explained. "Mr. Soule . . . he's been awake for a few weeks now. You can ask him yourself."

55

In ten minutes, the blood would be everywhere. But for now, the sun was in Zig's eyes as he gripped the phone in his fist.

"C'mon," Zig muttered, "pick up the damn—"

"It's me," Waggs's recorded voice said. "No one answers their phone anymore. Send me a text if it's important."

Beeeep.

Zig hung up with one hand, holding the steering wheel with the other. The ride from Dover wasn't long—a quick half hour—and he'd tried Waggs half a dozen times. Sent texts, too. No response. It wasn't a shock. At the Bureau, Waggs was always getting called onto other cases.

Still, every few minutes, Zig glanced down at his texts. *Not funny, Waggs—where are you?* He wanted to talk things through, and after his visit with the head of Dover, he needed her tech help, too.

According to Colonel Whatley, all those years ago at Grandma's Pantry, something bad went down—a break-in, a *disaster,* he called it—which is why Nola came to paint it in the first place. From what O.J. said, the people who broke in didn't get anything. But someone did.

Okay, Nola, what would make you steal something? Zig wondered, thinking of Nola's history of disagreements with her superiors. *Something that pissed you off? Or maybe something illegal that you saw someone else stealing?* To Zig, it didn't make sense. Nola wasn't a thief. Though on that night, someone clearly was.

So what's worth stealing? That was the question, he realized, replaying O.J.'s description of the Grandma's Pantry warehouses. Anti-dotes, vaccines . . . all the germ warfare vials would be worth millions on the black market. O.J. also mentioned sedatives, which five years ago . . . That was the height of the opioid crisis. Grandma's Pantry would've had enough doses to cover a city. If someone tried stealing that . . .

Zig rolled it again through his brain. As theories go, both made sense, but the one loose thread that kept sticking out from the sweater . . . was O.J. himself. Dover's wing commander wasn't just a passive bystander. He used to be in the same investigative unit as both victims—Mint and Rashida. A unit like that would have tons of resources to call on. So would Dover. But instead of calling in those resources, O.J. brought in Zig.

Was O.J. being smart . . . or just desperate? Either way, he was breaking protocol. Zig wasn't sure what it meant, but he did know this: for O.J., something about this case was touching a nerve. The colonel was rattled, this whole thing somehow personal.

On top of that, according to Mint's wife, it seemed pretty clear that Mint and Rashida had had an affair. Did Nola know that back when they were at Grandma's Pantry? And far more important, what was Mint doing with a second, apparently secret, phone?

It made Zig think of the third name on the back of Nola's paint-ing. Elijah King. According to the logbook, O.J. was trying to track him down. *No response*. Time for Zig to reach out as well.

Following the curve of Route 1 past the fire station, Zig again glanced down at his own phone in the car's cup holder. Still no word from Waggs, who was the only person with enough security clearance to get a look at whatever old files might still exist from Grandma's Pantr—

Zig's phone vibrated with a shudder. A text, from Puerto Rican Andy.

You far? Andy asked.

Two minutes, Zig typed back, trying to refocus. Earlier, Andy had tracked down someone at SuperStars Modeling, someone who knew Zig's daughter. It's bad, Ziggy. Get back here. Now.

Zig bit the skin on the inside of his lip. With a tug of the steering wheel, he skidded into the parking lot of Calta's Funeral Home. But as he parked in his usual spot on the side of the building, something caught his eye.

The red light. A single bulb, above the employee entrance.

Decades ago, during a private viewing, one of the flower delivery guys had barged through the side entrance, practically crashing into an elderly mother saying goodbye to her middle-aged son. The next day, the red lightbulb was installed—an unsubtle signal that, when lit, meant *Stop. Client inside. Come around front.*

Zig got out of the car and headed for the front door, already confused. Mrs. Paoli was buried two days ago. Did someone new come in? If they did, Andy would usually say something. Yet as Zig turned the corner and reached the front parking lot . . .

Dead empty, not a single car in sight. He looked around the side. Puerto Rican Andy's white van was where it always was, next to Zig's car. No other vehicles. So whoever was inside . . . they *walked* here?

Zig glanced at Route 1, where a scattering of cars blew past, quickly disappearing. This was a commercial district. No one walked here.

Zig looked back at the funeral home, at the red light. His arms felt heavy, his skin like a fraying rag. Sometimes in life, there seemed to be an invisible rope pulling you toward something—and other times, it seemed abundantly clear you're supposed to stay away.

Was Zig being paranoid? Maybe. Yet as he headed for the front door of what used to be a Dairy Queen, he reached into his pocket and gripped his knife, a SOG Trident Elite. It was a gift from the spouse of a fallen Navy SEAL, who modified the blade with a deep groove at the top so it could be opened as it was pulled out. The groove also did extra damage, adding a puncture to every slice.

There was a soft, almost imperceptible magnetic *click* as Zig opened the door—the funeral home's notification system, which sent an entry alert to both Zig's office and the embalming room in back.

"Who's hungry for Munchkins!?" Zig sang out, using Puerto Rican Andy's favorite line from his daily Dunkin' Donuts run.

No answer.

On his right was a dark wood podium that usually held the

sign-in book. Beyond that was a closed door—to the room that displayed the different types of coffins. In nearly every funeral home in America, the biggest coffin manufacturers will sell to you only if you display the cheapest coffins in front, the most expensive in back, so that by the time a family sees the good stuff, they'll be cornered and easier to close. When Zig took over, he told those companies that their services would no longer be needed.

"What about quidditch—anyone want to play quidditch?" Zig added, trying to get a response.

Still nothing.

Zig looked up at the in-ceiling speakers. On days when there wasn't a funeral, they played soft piano music. Currently, the music was off.

"Andy, you okay?"

No response.

Zig's skin felt brittle, like it was starting to tear. Regripping the knife in his pocket, he headed slowly, carefully, toward the main viewing area.

"Andy, I'm dialing 911 right now!" Zig shouted, entering a wide room with rows of empty pews and dark burgundy carpet. "So if this is like that time when you were pretending to be Voldemort in the final movie, well . . . fifty points from Gryffind—"

"Mr. Zigarowski, I'm trying to save you from an awful day. So I'm asking this once. Your knife. Put it where I can see it. Please," a female voice announced.

Zig spun toward the front corner of the room, toward an open door that led to a foyer for private family viewing.

"Ziggy, I . . . I'm sorry," Puerto Rican Andy whimpered, his lip bleeding, his right eye swollen shut. "S-She asked if you were carrying— If I didn't tell them . . . or say that stuff about Maggie—*Hkkk.*" Andy coughed, like he was choking.

Behind Andy, a redheaded woman with piercing, different-colored eyes pulled a string she held to Andy's throat. No, not a string. A thin metal saw.

"The knife, Mr. Zigarowski. I know it's in your pocket," Reagan said.

56

The woman was tall, nearly as tall as Puerto Rican Andy, which was saying something.

"Let him go," Zig demanded.

"I don't think you're hearing me, Mr. Zigarowski," Reagan said. "The knife . . ."

"I don't think you're hearing *me*," Zig said, hand still in his pocket. "Let him—"

"I'm slitting his throat now," Reagan said, starting to tug.

"*WaitWaitWait!* No . . . my knife. Here . . . *here* . . ." Zig said, pulling out his knife and tossing it on the floor, where it cartwheeled across the carpet.

That was all they needed.

In a blur, something moved behind Zig—someone who was hiding by the old ice cream drive-through window that had been reframed into an alcove with a hanging American flag.

Before Zig knew what hit him, a tree-trunk-sized arm wrapped around his neck, squeezing him in a brutal choke hold.

Stupid old man, Zig thought, cursing himself for not seeing it coming. The attack on Andy—it was just a distraction.

Zig tried to turn, tried to fight. He didn't have a chance. His attacker was massive, a huge Irish redhead as big as a building—moving with a speed his size shouldn't allow. He hit Zig like a tornado, hooking his arm around Zig's throat and pinching Zig's neck in the crook of his elbow.

Zig gasped for air. Nothing came. He was choking, his face bright red, barely able to breathe.

"Let's try this again, Mr. Zigarowski. I'm trying to save you from an awful day," the redheaded woman repeated. "It's a rather simple question. Tell us what you know about Black House."

57

Zig's head was about to pop. Blood flushed his face. He was fighting for air, trying to say something.

"Seabass, I think we all get the point," the redheaded woman called out.

The big man—Seabass—rolled his eyes. *Really? Like I'm some kinda novice?* He eased up on his choke hold. Zig gasped, starting to cough.

"I don't like funeral homes, Mr. Zigarowski. They bring back a bad memory for me about my sister," the woman added. "So whatever you know about Black House—"

"I-I never . . ." Zig was still coughing, Seabass's forearm still at his throat. "I don't know Black House . . . never heard of it."

The woman's gaze slid sideways to Puerto Rican Andy. She gritted her teeth, tugging on the saw at his neck.

"Ziggy, please . . ." Andy begged. Snot, tears, and blood poured from his nose and lips.

"Wait . . . that place . . . Black House," Zig said, hoping to buy time. "I can help you. Maybe I know it by another name. Tell me more about it."

"You're trying to stall," Reagan said.

She was smart. Posture like a flagpole. Military for sure. The most unnerving part was her voice. As Zig had learned from years of reading Dover casualty reports, when a soldier panics or is about to do something desperate, they usually take *suicide breaths,* quick huffs to psych themselves up. Reagan was a flatline. If anything, she had a twinkle of larceny in her eyes.

"Andy, you okay?" Zig asked, purposely saying his name. *Keep him human and you'll keep him alive.*

Andy nodded, the thin saw a black line across his larynx.

"Ma'am, I know you don't know me, but I'm a man of my word," Zig said. He was up on his tiptoes, still in a choke hold, his chin raised like he was standing in the deep end of a pool and trying to keep his mouth above water. "What I said about Black House . . . Let me help you. At the very least, trade me for him. Let him go. I can help you."

The woman didn't answer. She turned toward her partner. "Seabass?" she asked.

It was a bad sign. If she was using Seabass's name, she'd already made her decision. Zig—and Andy—weren't walking out of here.

"Ziggy, my kid . . ." Andy called out.

"You're gonna be fine. I got what they want," Zig insisted. "Ma'am, listen to me," he added, locking on Reagan. "This place . . . Black House—it's obviously a code name, yes?"

The two redheads exchanged another glance, then another, having an entire conversation in silence, like an old married couple . . . or brother and sister. Seabass shook his head. *Don't fall for his crap. He doesn't know shit.*

"Okay, so if it's a code name . . . Talk to me about it," Zig added. "Maybe I know it through someone else."

Seabass shot another look at Reagan. *Don't let him fool you.*

"It's a location. Online," Reagan said as Seabass rolled his eyes again.

"Like a website?" Zig asked.

"Like a place where people want to talk. Privately."

Zig glanced around at the empty pews, mentally running through the details from his Dover visit w— *Oh crap.* "Colonel Mint. That's who was talking privately, wasn't it?"

Reagan stayed silent, the knuckles on her middle fingers now white from gripping the camping saw at Andy's neck. "Make your point, Mr. Zigarowski."

"When I was at Dover— There's another phone. Mint's wife . . ." Zig took a breath. "He had a second cell phone . . . From what I can tell, they're still going through it."

Reagan stared at Zig. "Anything else?" she asked.

"I'm trying to help you get what you want. If someone was having a private talk with Colonel Mint—or trying to meet up with him, I don't know . . . maybe this Black House place . . . You sure it's not part of Grandma's Pantry?"

Reagan cocked her head, confused. "What's *Grandma's Pan*—?"

Ftttt. Ftttt.

The blood hit Zig first, a hot spray across the back of his neck.

The world slowed to a halt as Seabass started to turn. His choke hold loosened, though just slightly.

Zig was still focused on the back of his own neck, thinking someone had spit at him.

Seabass continued to turn— No, not turn. He was off balance, falling. He smacked himself in the face, like he was swatting a mosquito on his cheek.

There was no mosquito. Just a small dark hole at the center of his cheek, charred at the edges. Instinctively, Seabass stuck his fingertip inside it, looking mad . . . annoyed even . . . the pain still not registering. Then he tasted the blood. It was nowhere, then everywhere, pouring from Seabass's mouth. He tipped sideways, like a drunk who'd lost his battle with gravity.

Zig was still in midturn as Seabass began to tumble.

To Zig, it made no sense. *All that blood. And the hole.* Then it hit him like a fist. *Shot. Someone shot Seabass in the face.*

"Zig! At your nine! Get low!" someone yelled.

Zig turned to his left, still barely registering the words. He knew that voice.

A shadow turned the corner. Roddy.

58

Roddy ran straight at Zig, raising his gun.

"Get low! Get low!" Roddy shouted, aiming his pistol. It was the tactical .45, with the silencer.

Ftttt. Ftttt.

Two more shots. Zig was still in midturn, his first thought simply that, as Roddy turned the corner, it looked comical—the way he was perfectly framed by the old ice cream drive-through window behind him.

Seabass was bent over, holding his cheek, spitting blood and teeth. He'd been shot in the face. "You crazy motherf—"

Like an NFL lineman, Roddy plowed into Seabass, both of them tumbling toward the pews, crashing to the carpet.

Roddy was half his size, but momentum was on his side. So was his police training. They hit the carpet with a thud, Roddy using his forearm like a nightstick, pinning it to Seabass's throat, squeezing the air out of him.

Roddy saved me, Zig thought, still wobbling as he tried to find his footing. Barely five seconds had passed since Roddy raced into the room. Zig was still trying to process how these . . . how these redheads surprised him and—

No. Not just him.

"Ziggy, run . . . !" Puerto Rican Andy screamed.

Oh, God. He almost forgot. The metal saw . . . Andy!

"DON'T!" Zig yelled, spinning toward his friend.

Too late.

With a ruthless tug, Reagan yanked the thin metal camping saw at Andy's neck. Andy tried to grab it. He didn't have a chance.

"ANDY!" Zig screamed.

A thin red line appeared across Andy's throat, like a crimson smile. His hands bled, too, his palms facing out, the saw digging into them.

Zig was already running down the center aisle of the sanctuary, plowing straight at them, straight at her. He didn't have a plan. Just get there, get to him—

"Let him go!" Zig yelled.

To his surprise, Reagan did exactly that. She wasn't letting Zig tackle them. Like any pro, her first priority was self-preservation.

Lifting her foot to Andy's back, Reagan kicked him straight at Zig. Her left hand let go of the saw, but her right one held tight to it—so as Andy flew forward, momentum took care of the rest, spinning him like a top. The saw bit into his throat, slicing even deeper.

"Hkkkkk!" Andy gasped, stumbling, his legs buckling.

"I got you! I'm here!" Zig insisted, catching him midfall.

Andy was dead weight. He hit like a boulder, blood waterfalling down his neck, down his shirt . . . it was everywhere.

No. Nonono.

Zig dropped to his knees, lowering Andy to the floor.

Out of the corner of his eye, Zig spotted Reagan running up the far-right aisle, toward the back of the sanctuary. Zig could catch her or save Andy.

It wasn't a choice.

"Hkkkkkkkk!" Andy wheezed, gasping for air. Nothing came out. His eyes were wide, dancing back and forth, pleading for help. Already in shock.

"The good news is, she missed Fawkes," Zig said, staring down at the phoenix tattoo on Andy's neck. "You're gonna be okay," he added, though he knew it was a lie.

Tiny air bubbles gurgled from Andy's throat. Bad sign. She'd sliced his trachea.

"Roddy, I need you!" Zig shouted, clamping his hands on Andy's throat to stop the bleeding.

Past the last pew, Roddy sat on Seabass's chest, burying a punch into the big redhead's face. Seabass tried fighting back, raising his arm. Roddy hit him again, then again, Seabass finally going limp, unconscious.

It didn't slow Roddy down. He unloaded with another punch, then another, the ferocity catching Zig off guard. Spit flew from Roddy's lips, then a strand of drool dangled down. A plump vein swelled at his temple, his punches getting faster.

"Roddy, get over here! He's gonna bleed out!"

Roddy was just a blur now, slamming his fist into Seabass's face, then winding up and doing it over and over, pile driver after pile driver, each impact a sickening wet crunch of meat and bone. With each hit, Roddy let out the kind of grunt you'd hear during sex.

Hff. Hff. Hff.

Zig called his name again, begging for help. Still no response.

As Roddy cocked his fist back for another hit, there was blood on his knuckles—Zig now realizing that with each punch, Roddy had been targeting the bullet wound in Seabass's cheek. Just like Nola, feasting on the weak spots.

As Roddy unleashed another vicious punch, a stray spatter of blood bit his cheek. If Roddy felt it, he didn't care, his plump vein swelling thicker than ever.

"RODDY, GET OFF HIM! MY FRIEND'S GONNA FUCKING DIE!"

Roddy turned at the outburst.

"C'mon! He's about to pass out!" Zig added as Roddy started to run, sliding next to him, down on his knees, eyes wide with concern, specks of blood on his face.

Andy's eyes were glazed, his skin starting to turn gray. He was losing too much blood, his breathing barely audible.

"Roddy, I need you t—" Zig didn't have to finish.

Zig let go of Andy's throat, and Roddy clamped his hands in place. Basic triage. Cover the windpipe, but don't crush it. Most important, stop the bleeding.

The problem was, the blood was still flowing, seeping between Roddy's fingers. "Mr. Zig, if she nicked his trachea—"

"Don't say it! You don't know that!" Zig shouted, reaching to his left and grabbing a pew cushion from the front row. Something absorbent. Frantically tearing open the cushion, he pulled out its foam stuffing, tossing it to Roddy.

Roddy stuffed the foam into place, but the blood was still coming. Andy's eyes rolled sideways. Red air bubbles seeped from the wound. Blood was in his airway.

On his phone, Zig dialed 911.

"His wound—it looks terrible," Roddy said in his usual flat tone. "They won't make it in time."

"Use the foam!"

"You're not listening. Blood is filling his lungs—"

"Use the damn foam!" Zig yelled, darting to the front of the sanctuary, toward the open door in the corner. As he ran, he told the 911 operator to send an ambulance to Calta's Funeral Home. But Roddy was right—they wouldn't make it in time.

Zig picked up his pace, ramming the door with his shoulder and plowing down a narrow hallway to a room at the back of the building.

DANGER—HAZARDOUS MATERIALS

The smell was proof of that. As Zig burst inside, on his left, up on a dolly, was a Rubbermaid trash can filled with powdered formaldehyde. He could taste it on his tongue—the pungent ammonia scent that reminded him of his mother's cancer.

On his right, a medical cabinet with extra scalpel blades, autopsy saws, and a handheld bone-dust vacuum stood next to a garment rack filled with mothballed suits and sequined dresses—clothes he stored for his elderly customers who already knew what they wanted to be buried in.

Zig beelined for the back wall, to an old oak desk covered nearly to the ceiling with cardboard boxes. Overflow storage for cremation urns that came in every size and shape, including football urns, Harley-Davidson motorcycle engine urns, and even old leather book urns, complete with an engravable spine for your loved one's name.

"C'mon, where the hell are you?" Zig muttered, feverishly pulling open all the drawers of the desk, until . . .

Gotcha. From the top right drawer, Zig pulled out what looked like a clear straw with a miniature spoon at the end of it—the mortician tool for transferring a loved one's ashes into small containers, like jewelry or lockets. The tube was made of industrial plastic, but since it functioned as a funnel . . .

"Roddy, pull the gauze!" Zig shouted, grabbing one more item from the drawer and racing back to the sanctuary.

Turning the corner, Zig scanned the room. The redheads . . . Seabass and the woman . . . in the chaos . . . both were gone. In the back of the sanctuary, there was a thick trail of blood across the carpet. *She must've dragged Seabass out of here.* Roddy had done a number on him, and he was too big to carry. Zig was relieved. One less disaster to deal with.

At the front of the sanctuary, Roddy was hunched over Andy. In the back of Roddy's waistband, his pistol peeked out under his shirt—the .45 with the silencer. Zig barely noticed. He was too busy staring at Andy, who wasn't moving.

"Mr. Zig, it's bad. He's not—"

"Stop talking!" Zig shouted, dropping to his knees. From Andy's neck, Zig peeled away the layers of blood-drenched foam himself, revealing . . .

Oh, God. Andy's face was gray, his breathing down to a ragged gasp. The worst part was his throat—a slit shaped like a gruesome smile. Red air bubbles gurgled from the wound, rising and falling with each shallow breath. Zig had been around enough bodies to know what came next.

"The bubbles . . ." Roddy began. "It means blood's pouring into his lungs. If you don't stop that—" He didn't have to finish the sentence.

In overdone TV movies, scrambling EMTs stab makeshift tracheostomy tubes made from hollowed-out pen barrels into a patient's throat to kick-start breathing. The reality wasn't nearly as easy. To get to the actual trachea . . .

"Have you ever done this before, Mr. Zig?"

Zig shot him a look. He didn't have a choice.

Poking his thumb and pointer finger into the wound, Zig spread his fingers like he was enlarging a photo. The slit in Andy's throat widened like an open mouth. It was the only way to find . . . There. The whiteness of the windpipe itself.

Feeling around with his fingers, Zig spread aside the muscles and fatty tissue to get to the windpipe. It was stiff to the touch, covered in ridges. From there, he simply followed the tiny red bubbles to a small notch. That's what he was looking for. The cut in the trachea.

With his other hand, Zig slid the plastic cremation funnel into the slit of Andy's neck. It took Zig a moment to realize he was still holding his own breath. Over the years, he'd removed hundreds of stents from the windpipes of fallen soldiers. This was just the opposite of that, he told himself, almost believing it.

The bubbles were his guide. Zig slid the tip of the funnel along Andy's windpipe, carefully aiming the tiny spoon until . . . He held his breath again as it notched into the actual cut. That's the spot. The tip of the funnel was at the right entry point. Now came the hard part. Getting it in.

Zig tightened his grip on the funnel, trying to ignore the beads of sweat that he could taste on his top lip.

"Mr. Zig, if you push too hard you can rupture his—"

"Roddy, I will physically take your head off your body if you utter another syllable."

Roddy went silent.

Zig took another breath, licking the sweat from his lip.

Gripping the plastic funnel like a screwdriver, he notched the funnel into the windpipe. With a quick twist, Zig gave it a quarter turn clockwise, then twisted it back again—twist and twist it back, over and over, carefully trying to wedge it in just—

There was a muted burst of air, like Andy belched, followed by a hiss. Drops of condensation appeared inside the plastic funnel. Air. Andy was getting air.

"That's—! Mr. Zig, he's breathing!"

Determined to keep it that way, Zig let go of the windpipe with one hand, then reached into his pocket and pulled out the one other item he'd taken from the desk.

Every mortician's secret weapon. A tube of skin glue.

Grabbing a flap of skin at Andy's throat, Zig squeezed it around the neck of the funnel and slathered it with skin glue. The glue turned pink from all the blood. But so far, it was staying shut. Now to deal with the wound itself . . .

Feverishly working left to right like he was sealing a Ziploc bag, Zig pinched Andy's skin shut and added more glue, then another pinch of skin, then another gob of glue. Inch by inch, he worked his way across Andy's throat, squeezing it so tight and adding so much glue that a few times, his own fingers were stuck together. In the end, it left a bubbly pink scab across Andy's throat, the plastic tube sticking up like a flagpole—but the bleeding . . .

Zig gave it a moment, watching the skin stretch and pucker with the rise and fall of Andy's chest. He waited for more blood to seep through, but instead . . .

Done. Stopped. Andy's eyes blinked awake. He looked around, panicking, still in shock, but the color was already back in his face.

"I gotta be honest, Mr. Zig—I didn't think it would work," Roddy said, "but you—"

"Did you know they would be here, Roddy?"

Roddy turned, confused. Zig was still on his knees, breathing heavily, trying to catch his breath. There was so much blood caked along his fingers, Zig scratched an itch on his nose with his forearm. "Did you know?" Zig repeated, refusing to look at him.

"I don't understand."

"The redheads—Seabass and his sister-wife, or whatever the hell she is," Zig said, his voice low, simmering with anger, as he motioned to the back of the empty sanctuary. In the distance was the faint wail of a siren. An ambulance, still a few blocks away. "We would've been dead—they would've killed us—but for you swooping in and saving our asses. The timing was remarkable," Zig explained. "So answer my question, Roddy. Did you know those redheads would be here?"

Roddy cocked his head, like Zig was speaking Chinese. "How could I possibly know that?"

Zig turned, finally making eye contact, the siren growing louder. "Then why'd you come here, Roddy?"

"The guy. I found the guy. From the back of the painting," Roddy explained. "Elijah King—the third guy from Mint and Nola's original mission. I spoke to him and he said . . . he said he's willing to talk to us."

59

Zig needed this shower—and not just to get rid of the blood.

He needed the quiet, the few minutes of solitude that came with standing naked, swallowed by the steam, in the small bathroom just off the funeral home's embalming area.

The water was too hot—tiny needles on his skin—but he didn't adjust it. Better to feel something, to feel anything. Zig lifted his chin, letting the spray hit him in the face.

Most of the blood came off easily, antiseptic soap sending reddish-pink suds coiling like snakes down his arms and legs. The smell was the harder part. In the corner of the shower, Zig picked up a gallon jug of Clorox. Pouring the bleach onto his hand, he used a nailbrush to scrub away the stubborn blood under each fingernail. Same as cleaning a corpse.

According to the cops and the EMTs, Zig's makeshift tracheostomy had saved Andy's life. It didn't make Zig feel any better. What happened today . . . what they did to Andy . . . Zig closed his eyes, unable to stop seeing it. The redhead with the saw . . . *she slit Andy's throat!* And for what? Something called Black House, whatever the hell that was.

According to the redhead, it was a location online. *"A place where people want to talk. Privately."* Zig thought about that. If Mint was one of the people using Black House . . . Who was he talking to? And what were they talking about?

Zig was still scrubbing so hard with the nailbrush, he didn't even realize he'd opened a hairline cut underneath his own thumbnail. It burned from the bleach. Zig barely flinched, thinking he deserved it.

Half an hour ago, when the EMTs first arrived at the funeral home, Roddy flashed his badge. Zig knew it was a good thing, a way to stay in control—but it was time to admit, since the moment this started, Zig hadn't been in control. That needed to change, especially wi—

Tap tap. A knock on the bathroom door.

"Roddy, I'll be out in a sec!" Zig called.

The door opened with a click.

"Roddy, I swear, if you're standing there with a knife like *Psycho*—!"

A hard yank sent the shower curtain sliding sideways.

Zig spun around, naked, surprised to see a woman. She had silver hair with a black streak, and dark eyes with flecks of gold, just like her brother.

"Nola . . ." He bent forward, trying to cover himself with his hands.

Nola grabbed a nearby towel, tossing it at Zig. He was so focused on her, it hit him in the chest and fell to the floor.

"Sorry, lemme just . . ." Zig reached down, picked up the towel, and quickly covered his waist. "What the hell're y—"

"The Reds, Mr. Zigarowski. Tell me what you know about the Reds."

60

"What're you doing here?" Zig challenged.

Nola held a finger to her lips. Be quiet.

She'd been hoping to avoid this moment, but she didn't have a choice.

To her surprise, as Zig stood there in the silence, he was calm, scrambling just slightly as he wrapped the towel around his waist.

Zig saw himself as a tough man. The kind of guy who asked hard questions and could deal with hard situations. For decades, that was his job. When the families of fallen soldiers came to Dover, he'd grant them his strength, giving them his last reserves so they could lean on him in that moment when they felt abandoned by every belief they once thought would never leave them. As Nola knew, that's where Zig found his self-worth—it's how he felt less alone, and less guilty for his role in his daughter's death—by giving to others the one thing he'd never have. Closure.

Yet right now, as Zig stood there with a towel at his waist in the still-running shower, Nola couldn't help but notice that even with the confusion on his face, there was also—

A nervous grin.

Of course there was. Nola shook her head. It's what Zig always did when he saw her, seizing on some decade-old familiarity and acting as if she and he were friends, or even acquaintances.

"It's good to see you," Zig finally whispered, going to shut off the shower.

"Keep it on," Nola warned. She locked the door. They needed privacy.

"I take it the cops are still outside? You avoiding them or your brother?" Zig asked, his voice still low.

Nola didn't answer, glancing around the small 1980s bathroom, complete with a salmon-colored backsplash and a teal toilet. There were cracks in both the backsplash and floor tiles. *Easily repairable, but ignored.* It was the same with this Dairy Queen turned funeral home—and really, she realized, the same with Zig—once something happy, but now, over time, hollowed out from spending so much time around death.

"You look tired," Zig added.

He looked worse. The lines in his face were deeper than Nola remembered, his skin papery. As he stood there on the small ledge of the still-running shower, what stuck out most was the way his eyebrows now dominated his face—they were overgrown, as was a clump of hairs along his ears. No one to pluck them for—or to do it for him. Nola's first thought was that he'd aged in the past two years, but that was quickly replaced by what felt like a rift in her brain: that she was still remembering Zig from when she was twelve years old, back in Girl Scouts. *Don't let him take you back there . . .*

Mongol . . . Faber . . . Staedtler . . . Ticonderoga . . .

Opposite the sink, she pushed aside a set of ratty curtains, revealing a four-pane window. Bigger than she thought. Crusted paint chips along the far ends of the sill. Good. Not painted shut. Anyone comes, that's the way out.

"Nola, if you need to sit down . . ." He pointed to the closed toilet, a pinwheel of steam twirling in the wake of his motion.

"I'm fine," she insisted, hating that concern in his voice, even as she caught herself in the slowly fogging mirror. Zig was right. She *did* look tired—exhausted, even—dark bags under her eyes. Her hair was greasy, stray strands pointing at different angles. From her earliest Army days, Nola was a street fighter put into a uniform. They taught her to be focused and in control. Now, the way she stood there, swaying slightly, she felt harried, off balance. She didn't like it.

"Tell me about the Reds," Nola insisted.

"The *who*?"

"The ones who attacked you. The redheads. They call themselves the Reds."

"That's a terrible name," Zig said, opening the window on his left as the steam was quickly sucked toward the crack. "The big one—the guy—I think his name was . . ." He paused, Nola watching to see if his tongue touched his incisor, which Zig did when he was lying. "She called him Seabass. I'm guessing Sebastian."

True.

"The woman is Reagan," Nola replied. "Both were discharged years ago, for selling stolen military gear on eBay. I need to know what they said, Mr. Zigarowski. Anything that they might've—"

"Black House. They wanted to know what I knew about Black House."

"And?"

"Truthfully, I was just trying to stall—or at least fish for info. She said Black House . . . She called it an online meeting place."

Nola made a face. "She only told you because she was planning to kill you."

"I know that. You think I'm a moron?"

"Mr. Zigarowski, you don't want to know what I think."

"*Then tell me,*" he growled with a look she'd never seen before. "Because even when I put aside the fact that two sociopath redheads probably still want me dead—and that's a hard thing to put aside—your insults and the whole lone-wolf act are starting to wear thin. You obviously came here for a reason, Nola. I'd like to hear it."

In truth, she was surprised to see him this pissed. She didn't think he had it in him. But as Nola knew since she was little, everyone has it in them. "You've obviously had a hard day."

"No, this is way beyond *hard day*! My friend . . . Andy . . . he . . . he . . . he . . . Right now, he's in the back of an ambulance, racing to the hospital! That's his blood—*look* . . ." Reaching inside the shower, he grabbed the soap, which was streaked with dark red stripes. "*That's his blood!*"

"Mr. Zigarowski, if you don't lower your voice—"

"Then what? You'll treat me like you already treat me? I get that you don't like me, Nola—and I know it physically kills you when someone actually offers you help—but let me give you one unarguable fact: the only reason you're standing in this tiny bathroom is because there's someone out there right now who is scaring the *shit* out of you. Maybe it's the cops, or the Reds, or—oh, let's just be honest for once, we know it's your brother."

"You know nothing about him."

"I don't need to. The facts are obvious. Someone put a bullet in the head of your friend Archie Mint—and because you and Mint had a relationship—"

"We didn't have a relationship."

"Because he was your commander . . . because you feel like you owe him something . . . because back in the day, he bought you a paint set that you used to write 'Rosebud' on your sled . . . Whatever the damn reason is, Nola, you've been frantically searching for his killer. But in your usual scorched-earth approach, the only person in this entire damn mess who you *absolutely know* is on your side . . . is *me*."

"I know why you're trying to help, Mr. Zigarowski—and it has nothing to do with concern for me."

"What're you talking about?"

Nola stood there, watching him grip the shower curtain, nearly pulling the rod down with it.

"Maggie. You think this is just about Maggie," Zig challenged, referring to his daughter. "That I've put my life on the line—me digging into this case—that it's just about the fact you two were in Girl Scouts? And you think *I'm* the narcissist here? At Mint's funeral, did you . . . did you even see his wife? What about his kids, whose lives are now in ruin—the son who couldn't stop sobbing, and his daughter—"

"Her name is Violet."

"I know her damn name—I put her baseball glove in her father's coffin!"

"*Lower your voice.*"

"Then open your ears," he whispered. "I wouldn't be on this case if it weren't for you, but *they're* the ones who deserve our attention.

Their father was murdered—people are still being murdered—and as far as I can tell, your name is on that same target list."

Nola started to turn. Behind her, outside the bathroom, there was a noise. Someone was—

"Mr. Zig, we should get going!" Roddy called, hitting the door with a loud knock.

Nola froze. So did Zig. A swirl of steam twirled between them from the still-running shower.

"Almost done, Roddy! Sounds great!" Zig called back, his tongue touching his incisor. Definitely a lie.

"I'm out front when you're ready!" Roddy replied.

Seconds later, a door slammed, then another, Roddy leaving the embalming room and heading back to the main sanctuary.

Taking no chances, Nola reached into the shower and turned on an old Sharper Image radio that hung from the shower nozzle and once seemed like it was from the future. Prince started singing about calling up a shrink in Beverly Hills—Dr. Everything'll-Be-All-Right . . .

"Nola, if you'd just accept some help—"

"Stop talking," she said. "I found his account. On Black House," she explained. "I know who killed Colonel Mint."

61

"Who the hell is *Zion Lopez*?" Zig asked.

"Drug dealer. Small time," Nola explained, quickly telling Zig about her visit to Zion's cousin, the Oscar the Grouch mask, and what she found on the Minion cam.

As the shower continued to run and Prince continued to sing about an elevator bringing us down, Zig stepped out, put on a shirt, and took a seat on the closed toilet. "I assume you don't think this is about some petty drug deal?" he asked.

"Mint didn't smoke, much less do drugs. More important, Zion was a runt," Nola explained. "Kid like that doesn't give orders; he takes them—from someone bigger, or at least smarter."

"And you think that was the Reds?"

Nola shook her head. "The Reds show because someone pays them to show. They're hired guns—specialty is cleanup."

Zig thought about that. "At Grandma's Pantry . . . all those sedatives and opioids . . . Could Zion—or his boss—be the one who—?"

"Who told you about Grandma's Pantry?"

"Colonel Whatley."

"Whatley's a toolbag."

"I'm sure he'd be thrilled to hear your assessment. Anyway, the opioids—"

"This isn't about opioids. Stay with the Reds."

"I told you. She kept asking me about Black House. Is that where Mint—? You said you found his account?"

"When I logged in, two people were already there," she said, mentally replaying the avatar of the Hispanic soldier with close-set eyes. "I think one might've been Zion."

"And the other was the Reds?"

Nola made a face. She didn't think so. But that was the question—and the reason she came here. "Whoever was in Mint's account, they were using his avatar. The voice was robotic, impossible to ID."

"So that second person . . . Either they were having their own private meeting with Zion—"

"Or they were doing exactly what I was: hacking into Mint's account, trying to figure out what's really going on."

"Well, if it makes you feel better, it wasn't me," Zig insisted. No tongue to his incisor. Truth.

"That wasn't my concern."

Zig looked up, his eyes narrowing. "You think it was your brother."

She forgot how quick he was.

Nola stood there, the Prince song giving way to the Spin Doctors singing about a pocket full of kryptonite.

"Nola, we're hiding in a bathroom and playing old eighties songs just to avoid him. If you think Roddy was the other person in Mint's account—"

"How did the Reds know to come here?" she asked.

"Excuse me?"

"Last night, they went to Zion's house and slit his throat. Today, they showed up here, gunning for you. How'd they know you were working the case?"

"Maybe they saw me at the funeral. Or someone from Dover told them."

"Maybe. Though what about the timing of their attack? They were about to kill you and your employee . . ."

"Andy."

"They were about to kill you and Andy. Then Roddy got here just in time. Saved you all. What a hero."

"I thought the same. When I asked Roddy, he seemed shocked by the accusation. And I hate to say it, but I believe him."

"That's a mistake."

"So you think Roddy . . . you think he's playing puppet master? That he found Mint's Black House account, then set this whole thing up . . . and then *what*? That he brought in the Reds and sent them after me, somehow hoping it would flush you out of hiding? No offense, but when Roddy burst into the funeral home . . . *He's* the one who shot Sebastian."

"Did he kill him?"

"He shot him in the face!"

"I'm not saying he's some criminal mastermind or that I have the full picture yet, Mr. Zigarowski—but I guarantee you, you don't know who he is at his core."

"Then let me tell you what I *do* know: your friend Colonel Mint, on the night he was killed—he wasn't eating alone at that steak house, was he? He was having a private sit-down with another old friend of yours from Grandma's Pantry—Rashida Robinson. In my experience, Nola, people don't have secret dinners behind their wife's back unless they have something that's worth keeping secret."

"Colonel Mint was a good man."

"He also cheated on his wife."

"And was a decorated soldier who tried his best to act with honor. Something rare these days."

"I'm not judging him. I'm just trying to save your life," Zig insisted, careful to keep his voice lower than the music. "At Dover, I saw Mint's files—his medical examiner report, his death certificate—both were altered. Colonel Whatley's been fighting to keep things quiet."

"I told you, Whatley's a toolbag."

"I'm not disagreeing. But here's the thing he's right about: years ago, there was a break-in at Grandma's Pantry. Alarms went off, investigative teams arrived, and as Artist-in-Residence, you raced in to do a painting. But something went wrong, didn't it? The bad guys got nabbed, yet someone still swiped something from the government's secret warehouse."

"If we knew who it was, we would've had them arrested."

"I'm sure you would've. But right now, for some reason, people are showing up dead—and in case you haven't noticed, whoever's behind this seems pretty damn focused on your old Grandma's Pantry crew: You. Mint. Rashida. Some guy named Elijah King. It's not a long list, Nola—and you're right at the top of it."

"Mr. Zig, we really have to go!" Roddy shouted from the main sanctuary.

At the sound of her brother's voice, Nola turned, her wrist bone smashing into the sink. A shock of pain ran up her arm. She cursed herself, hoping Zig didn't see it.

"Be right there! Getting out right now!" Zig called to Roddy as the Spin Doctors gave way to a radio ad where someone was trying to sell cars by talking at light speed. Staying focused on Nola, he whispered, "You're worried it's him, aren't you? That Roddy . . . that your brother has a hand in this?"

Nola stood there, waiting for Zig to say something else, or ask the same question in a different way, which he always did when faced with silence. But for once, he just sat there on the toilet, elbows on his knees, waiting for her answer.

"Mr. Zigarowski, you ever had your past come back and surprise you in the exact moment when you wished it wouldn't?"

Zig took a deep breath through his nose, elbows still on his knees. "Every damn day."

For a few seconds, the two of them stared down at the cracks in the tile floor, one of them a zigzagging hairline that ran from below the sink, across the floor, all the way toward the window. Nola knew, when cracks were that long, there was no slip sheet installed on the concrete. Evidence of a deeper problem.

"Nola, what you just said about your past coming back . . . Were you talking about Roddy or Colonel Mint?"

Nola thought about that, remembering what an Army therapist wrote in her psych profile after she was reprimanded in Afghanistan for hitting her captain in the jaw with a plastic cafeteria tray. *Suffers from RAD—reactive attachment disorder—seen in children who go through early neglect. Incapable of forming attachments or loving relationships.*

"Nola, you were close with Colonel Mint, weren't you?"

Mongol . . . Faber . . . Staedtler . . . Ticonderoga . . .

"I didn't sleep with Mint," Nola blurted.

"Whoa. No. That's not what I was—"

Thump thump thump.

"Mr. Zig, we really need to go!" Roddy called out, pounding on the door.

Nola closed her eyes. It'd been two decades since she'd heard her brother's voice. It sounded so different—and perfectly the same.

"Seriously, Mr. Zig—Elijah said he's only around for another hour or so!" Roddy added, referring to Elijah King, the last name from the back of Nola's painting. And the only person not accounted for from that night at Grandma's Pantry.

"You should come with us. To meet Elijah," Zig whispered to Nola, getting up from his seat on the toilet.

"Mr. Zig, who're you talking to?" Roddy asked, fighting with the doorknob. He banged harder, the door now starting to shake.

Nola darted for the slightly open window. Time to go.

"Roddy, give me a damn minute! I'm on a call with my wife! My ex!" Zig insisted.

As Nola reached for the window, Zig put a hand on her shoulder.

In a blur, Nola spun, slapping his hand out of the way. Pure instinct. But what caught her off guard . . . She felt bad, which pissed her off even more.

Undeterred, she pried her hands into the crack of the open window and gave it a sharp tug. There was a shriek. The window opened a bit more, then got stuck. *Shit.* She couldn't leave.

"Mr. Zig!" Roddy shouted, banging harder, the door about to burst.

Zig slid next to her, both of them grabbing the window's lower sash. *On three,* Zig said with a glance. Later tonight, when the bodies were being carted away, Nola would think back to this moment and wish she'd said *thank you* to Zig. But right now, with Roddy pounding on the door, she had only one thought. *Get out, get out, get out.*

With a violent tug, the window opened its mouth, fresh air licking their faces.

Nola raised her leg, straddling the windowsill. Halfway in, halfway out.

"You don't have to do everything alone," Zig offered.

He was wrong about that.

The doorknob clicked with a new sound. Roddy picking the lock.

"They didn't take anything out," Nola said.

"They wha—?" Zig asked.

"Grandma's Pantry. The break-in. Whoever did it, they weren't trying to take something *out* of the warehouse," she said as she ducked down and slid outside. "They were trying to put something *in*."

62

"MR. SOULE!? IS THAT YOUR WIFE!?"

"No, do it louder," Nurse Sandie said. *"MR. SOULE!? IS THAT YOUR WIFE!?"*

"Hmhmm," Robert Soule said, nodding in slow motion, his head barely bobbing, as though his chin were so heavy, it was hard to lift his head.

Like many men in their nineties, Soule had a face that puckered toward his lips, his blue eyes cloudy with cataracts and his jowls sagging like a hound dog's. After sixteen years in a coma, muscle atrophy took the hardest toll. Still, there was a sweetness to him, reminding Waggs of an interview where Anjelica Huston said that when you get older, you get the face you deserve.

"Th-that's my wife, Rochelle," Soule said, his hand shaking as he pointed to the picture frame next to his bed. "We got married in . . . in . . . in . . . in . . ."

"IN TORONTO!" Waggs said.

"In Toronto," Soule said. It was the fourth time he'd been asked about the black-and-white photo, which showed him and his wife in their early twenties, both of them holding Cincinnati Reds pennants. As the nurse explained, talking about Soule's wife was the surest way to give him a kick start.

"My pretty bird," Soule said, smiling and revealing just a few bottom teeth that were left. "Big baseball fan. Kept her own box score."

"THE REDS WERE HER TEAM?!" Waggs asked, also for the fourth time.

"Hm-hmm. Mad for 'em."

"Okay, try now," Nurse Sandie whispered to Waggs.

"WHAT ABOUT THIS GIRL?" Waggs asked, holding up a photo of Nola. Again, for the fourth time.

Soule's chin was still down by his chest. He looked up with just his eyes. "Pretty bird, too," Soule said, clearly excited.

"HER NAME IS NOLA BROWN. DO YOU REMEMBER NOLA COMING TO SEE YOU?"

Soule stared at the photo, his eyes slowly drifting sideways. Four times now, this was where he petered out, never able to verbalize an answer. Waggs eyed the scar on his left temple. According to Soule's file, he had what they called a "penetrating injury"—a pointy branch had stabbed him through his frontal lobe, on his left side, which explained why his language was so impaired. For the first time, though, his smile was still on his face.

"DO YOU REMEMBER HER COMING TO SEE YOU!?" Waggs repeated.

"He's really trying," Nurse Sandie said. "It's just hard for him t—"

"I-I saw her," Soule blurted.

"You did? That's wonderful," Waggs said.

"THAT'S WONDERFUL, MR. SOULE!" the nurse corrected.

"DO YOU REMEMBER ANYTHING SHE SAID?" Waggs added.

"Hm-hmm," he said, nodding.

"GREAT! THAT'S GREAT!"

"Hm-hmmm," he repeated, his hands starting to tremble, then his chin. His head was now trembling, too.

"PLEASE, MR. SOULE . . . IF YOU KNOW WHAT NOLA SAID . . ."

He nodded, excited to help, though the trembling was getting worse. He stopped looking at Waggs—his gaze sliding diagonally down, unable to hold eye contact—but he was still fighting to get the words out.

"You sure he's okay?" Waggs whispered, again eyeing his scar. "He doesn't look so good."

Nurse Sandie took Soule's hand in her own. She'd been at this long enough to know what he needed.

"M-m-mmmm," Soule stuttered, looking pained and frustrated, like the words were stapled inside his lips.

Sandie held his hand tighter, rubbing a small circle into his wrist. He reacted immediately, looking her way, blinking, pleading. Just as quickly, he was gone, staring into the distance, his eyes empty like no one was home.

"He needs a break," Sandie said, still rubbing his wrist. "Maybe you can come back tomorrow or later in the week."

For Waggs, it should've been a relief. She'd been traveling all day; time to get back to her life. She did have a life, she told herself. And a boyfriend. If she was smart, she'd call him right now and make peace for standing him up last night, but as she took out her phone . . . No. She'd texted him twice this morning, plus left a cute voice mail. Mikel still hadn't bothered to reply. No way would she grovel.

Still, as she thanked Nurse Sandie and headed out into the fluorescent-lit hallway, Waggs wondered if she was doing that thing she was always scolding Zig for: spending time on someone else's life rather than her own. How many times had they had that fight, Waggs yelling that Zig should stop surrounding himself with the dead, with ghosts from the past . . . and instead focus on the living? And yet here she was, picking at those same puzzle pieces Nola had left behind.

Was *that* the reason she and Zig had stayed so close all these years? It was a question worth asking. Maybe, after the ass-kicking that life had given them, they were both finding safety in the same place. You don't have to think of your own problems when you're trying to solve someone else's.

Or maybe that was all just psychobabble manure, and it was time to face the harsher reality: that the real reason Waggs had spent the better part of the morning running hospital to hospital—

or had the Bureau install a secure line in her house so at any hour she could help agents around the world find the one thing no one else could find—was simply because . . . she loved it. Was that her real truth? That she loved it and was good at it?

Shoving open the double doors at the front of the building and feeling a blast of summer heat toast her neck, Waggs again checked her phone. A few messages from Zig. Still nothing from Mikel.

Just call him, she told herself.

Instead, she swiped back to the Babel Street map with Nola's first two stops. Two patients. Two paintings. Two victims of brain injuries. A simple pattern. But still a puzzle.

Luckily, Waggs knew how to find more pieces.

"We're getting warmer now, aren't we, Nola?" Waggs whispered, spreading her fingers onscreen and pulling in toward the next stop on the map.

Landenberg, Pennsylvania.

Private residence, not a hospital.

Why'd Nola go there?

It was a question worth asking.

63

It was dumb to be mad at Zig. A waste of energy, Nola decided.

Yet as she darted through the gravel pit along the back of the funeral home and finally reached the corner of the building, she was still mad, still annoyed, still kicking herself for letting Zig worm his way back into her—

"Nola . . . ?" a familiar voice asked. Behind her, from the back door.

Nola froze. She knew that voice.

"Wh-When did you—? Why're you—? What're you doing here?" Roddy asked.

Run, she told herself. Only a fool wouldn't run—though before she realized what she was doing, she was turning, following the sound.

"You look scared," Roddy said, his hands in the air. A show of trust. At his waist, his gun was still holstered. Same with his police baton. He was trying to prove he wasn't a threat. But as he turned his hands slightly, Nola spotted his knuckles, purple and swollen. No doubt, her brother was always a threat.

"Nola . . . I— Your hair looks different. Straighter."

He looked old, shorter than she expected, his face pointier, his ears bigger, everything the wrong size, like going back to your childhood room and having to redo the math to make the proportions make sense. The only things that hadn't changed were his black eyes, mirrors to her own, though they were sunk deeper in his head than she remembered. Weary.

Do I look that tired, too? she wondered, and then she was hit with a forgotten memory of when they were kids, in the LaPointes' house, a group of them sliding down the stairs as Roddy stepped on her fingers, digging in with his heel, pinning her in place and trying to make her cry. Instead, with her free hand, she dug her nails into his ankle, drawing tiny semicircles of blood.

There was blood here as well—though he'd clearly tried to scrub it clean from the chest of his uniform. On his sleeve, she spotted service stripes. Five years, which is usually when you see a cop's gear start to look worn. Instead, Roddy's uniform looked sharp. Pressed pants. Center-line crease still crisp, no worn spots at the pockets or where the gun and holster rub. To top it off, his badge was shined. He'd even polished and oiled his leather belt. Rare for a cop. Working hard to make detective, or did someone teach him right? She couldn't tell, which unnerved her even more.

Don't let him sucker you. Get out of here, she told herself, pivoting her foot in the gravel.

"Nola, please . . . don't run."

Just the sight of him stopped her. It stopped him, too. He had a stillness about him, a wounded stiffness in his voice. Something moved between them, brother and sister. A cobweb brushed away.

"You know why I'm here," Roddy said.

Nola turned, refusing to answer.

"I wouldn't bother you," he added, "but this . . . it's about *her* . . ."

Nola still wouldn't face him. From her spot at the corner of the building, she had a clear view of the side lot, of her car, a gray Dodge. Twenty feet away. Not far at all.

"I know this is hard," Roddy added.

The gravel shifted, like quicksand. She stayed locked on her car.

"I don't blame you, Nola. With everything going on, I know you don't want to trust me, but . . . but . . . but . . . I'm not who I was before."

"Neither am I," she shot back, stabbing him with a glare.

That's it. That's all she was giving him.

Fuck you, Roddy.

"Nola, *don't!*"

She began to run. Tearing open the door to her car and sliding inside, she started the engine and hit the gas. As the tires spun, kicking gravel in a pinwheel, she pulled away, Roddy chasing behind her, smacking the trunk of her car and running to his own car at the front of the building.

She didn't have much of a head start. Roddy was still police. Once he flipped the lights on his cruiser, she'd have no choice but to—

"What in the f—!" Roddy shouted.

Reaching the front lot, Roddy screeched to a halt, finally getting a look at his police cruiser. And its two flat tires.

The puncture holes were clean. Back when Nola first arrived . . . she took a knife to them. Just in case.

On Roddy's right, there was a rev of an engine and a loud screech. Following the sound, he turned just as Nola's car swerved out of the lot and onto Route 1.

64

Tessa started with their credit cards.

They were easy to check. Mint was the one who paid their bills—a detail that she, like many new widows, was suddenly ashamed of—but the payments were online, and her husband's password wasn't hard to guess.

HuckViolet1216.

Same one he used everywhere.

Six minutes of clicking and scrolling revealed what she already knew—that Mint might've been dumb and reckless enough to once again be sleeping with Rashida, but he wasn't stupid enough to use his own credit card to pay for the one item that Tessa was now hunting for. Mint's second phone. The one O.J. had found—and that his Dover forensic folks were now digging through.

Back when Tessa first entered dental school, one of her professors told her, "If you don't know what's causing the problem, you can't fix it."

There were answers on that phone. Details about her husband. Yet during the hour-long drive home from Dover, Tessa couldn't help but wonder, would O.J. share those answers with her?

O.J. and Mint had started their careers together, served together, and buried their fathers within three months of each other. Over a decade ago, O.J. was one of the people they nearly asked to be Violet's godfather, though they eventually went with Tessa's flaky but wealthy brother. Family over friends, Tessa had insisted over Mint's protests.

So would O.J. tell her the truth about the second phone? Depends what was on it.

Feeling her rage start to swell, Tessa slapped the laptop shut, plowed toward her husband's closet, and rifled through the sock drawer where he hid his watches and cuff links.

That's where she found the plug—an old micro USB, like the one used by their Kindle back in the day. This plug was new, though. As she suspected, from a burner phone. *You made a mistake keeping it here, Archie, which means you probably made more.*

It didn't take long for Tessa to pull apart the rest of his drawers, or the mini safe where they kept their passports and birth certificates, as well as, at the very back, the plaster imprints of the kids' handprints from when they were born. The plaster was wrapped in pink and blue tissue paper, and as old memories flooded back, she hated her husband for ruining something that used to bring her so much joy.

"Couldn't help yourself, could you?" Tessa muttered, gripping the charger and storming out into the hallway, toward Mint's other favorite hiding spot—his home office. She was gritting her teeth so hard, a high-pitched note filled her ears.

As she threw open the door to the office, the smell hit her first, a mix of old leather furniture and coconut oil from the fancy bodywash she bought him for Christmas last—

"Fuuuh!" Tessa shouted as the high-back chair swiveled and moved. She wasn't alone. Someone was already here.

Her first reaction was to raise a fist, to attack—but as she got closer . . .

"Huck?" she started to ask, though the word didn't leave her lips.

He was slouched in his seat, his teenage body curled like a magic lamp. In his lap was Mint's iPad, Huck swiping left, then swiping again, slowly, obliviously, as if he hadn't heard her come in, or didn't care.

Onscreen was a childhood photo from Halloween—Huck at seven years old, dressed as Darth Vader. He'd dressed as Darth Vader three Halloweens in a row, loved wearing that massive plastic helmet everywhere: riding his bike, in his car seat, or even in the waiting room at the pediatrician's office ("for protection," he used to say). To complete the Halloween outfit, Mint had dressed as Obi-Wan those same three years in a row, complete with Jedi robe and glue-on gray beard, though this photo was just of Huck, open hand pointed at the camera, pretending (and believing) that he was using the Force. If only life were that simple.

"Old photos. Really going for the full melancholy, huh?" Tessa asked, kneeling down and wrapping her arms around the chair and her son, embracing them both in a massive hug.

In the last year, Huck had gotten so big—he had his driver's license, had already been through his first and second girlfriends, and had even been grounded for drinking White Claws at Chris Weiss's house—but as Tessa knew all too well, when a parent dies, we all become kids again.

Huck again swiped left, revealing a photo of him and his dad—Vader and Obi-Wan—lightsabers crossed in midfight.

"Luke would've been the funnier costume," Tessa added.

Huck nodded, his head shaky, fighting back both laughter and tears. "Y'know why he picked Obi-Wan?"

"Because you asked him to?"

Huck shook his head. "I asked him to be the Emperor. He liked Obi-Wan because Obi-Wan never loses. In the movies, he's the only Jedi—the only one—who never gets beaten."

"Doesn't Vader beat him?"

"That's Obi-Wan's choice. He shuts off his lightsaber to help Luke. Same with Dooku, when he stupidly gives his lightsaber away because . . . don't ask me to explain the prequels. But Darth Maul, Grievous, Vader, the Vader rematch . . . Obi-Wan rules them all."

Tessa cocked her head, staring at the digital photo of her dead husband in his fake beard. "That sounds like something your dad would like."

Huck swiped through a few more photos, stopping on one of Violet dressed as a baby Princess Leia (which was quickly replaced by the Phillies baseball players she'd dressed as nearly every year since), then a close-up of Mint, his smile so wide, the stickum beard was starting to peel away from his face.

"I remember that beard shedding all over our sofa," Tessa said.

"You were so mad at him," Huck replied with a laugh.

Tessa nodded, fighting back tears of sadness and rage that were mixing as one. "C'mon, let's find you something less depressing," she said, plucking the iPad from Huck's hands and sliding it next to the laptop. With a loving push, she edged Huck toward the door. "Take your sister outside. Violet hasn't been out all day, which means she'll take it out on us tonight."

Yet as Huck headed toward the kitchen, he didn't notice that right behind him, Tessa had tucked Mint's iPad—and his laptop—under her arm, waiting for a quiet moment when she'd be examining far more than her husband's old photos.

65

"You have my number. Call me if anything changes," Roddy said into the phone, "especially if he stops breathing."

He hung up.

"That was the charge nurse," Roddy explained from the passenger seat. With his tires still flat, they took Zig's car instead. "She calls him Puerto Rican Andy, too—says she knows him from the pickups he does when someone dies in the—"

"Just tell me what she said," Zig interrupted, holding tight to the steering wheel, staring straight ahead as the highway blurred in front of them.

"He's still in intensive care, but his color's improving. She said it's a good sign."

"Unless of course he stops breathing," Zig replied.

Roddy blinked twice. "Oh. You're making a joke about my comment. To help yourself feel better."

Zig glanced up at the rearview. Nearly two hours ago, they'd left the funeral home, following the narrow two lanes of Route 322 onto I-95. The entire time, Zig had been searching the highway for who else might be following. No doubt, the Reds were still out there. So was whoever hired them. And so was Nola.

"Roddy, can I ask you a question? Why're you really doing this?"

"You mean going on this ride?"

"Not just the ride. The fighting . . . the investigation . . . I know you're a cop—"

"Police."

"Police. Sorry."

"I don't take offense, Mr.—"

"Can you please stop talking and just listen for once? I get that Nola's your sister, but even still . . . until today, back at the funeral home, you hadn't seen her since you were seven years old. You grew up, you built a life, you became a— You became police. From what you said, the way she took off—"

"She came to the funeral home for a reason."

"For all we know, she heard the police report and that's what brought her here," Zig said, still keeping her visit in the shower to himself. "So the real question is, after all these years, why the sudden interest in her? Why now?"

Roddy sat there silent, which he did a lot. "Do you know who you are, Mr. Zig?"

"You mean a mortician?"

"That's your job. I don't care what you do for a living, or where you're from. I mean at your *core*. I was a bad kid growing up. I worked hard to turn that around—or I like to think I turned that around. But other days, especially on hard days . . . Don't you want to know, Mr. Zig? At your core, *who are you?*"

"And you think connecting with your sister will tell you that? Like some magic answer?"

Roddy stared straight ahead, reaching to adjust the small A/C vent, though it wouldn't quite open. Pressing his thumb into the plastic, he popped it back in place. Good as new. "At the funeral home, your friend Andy . . . Why'd you offer to die for him?"

"Excuse me?"

"Back in the sanctuary, I saw what you did. When the redheaded woman, Reagan—"

"How'd you know her name was Reagan?"

"You said it earlier," Roddy insisted, though Zig could swear he'd kept that to himself. "It's just, when Reagan was about to slit Andy's throat . . . You said you would trade your life for his. Those were your words, Mr. Zig. That she should let Andy go. That if someone had to die, she should kill you instead."

Up ahead, an ugly metal structure rose in the distance—the

arched Turnpike Toll Bridge, separating Pennsylvania from their destination in New Jersey. Zig didn't like bridges. He'd buried too many soldiers who'd jumped from them.

"Mr. Zig, I can't name a single person who'd do something like that for me."

The car's tires began to hum as they crossed the bridge. In Zig's head, he couldn't help but start his own list, though it felt just as empty. He thought of his ex-wife, his daughter, and of course, the person who saved his life two years ago . . . Nola.

Glancing back at the rearview, Zig knew she had to be close. No way would she let them get to Elijah without trying to listen in and—

"Check the glove box," Zig blurted.

"*What?* Why?"

"Check the glove box," Zig repeated, feeling his pants pockets, shirt pockets, then the crevices of the seat. He knew Nola's tricks.

"You think the Reds . . . You think they bugged us?"

"Unclear," Zig said, though it was just as fair a point.

For the next few minutes, they combed through the car: the center console, the sun visors, the dome light, and, yes, the glove box. He even pulled over, searching the outside and underneath. Nothing. All clean.

Picking up speed, Zig checked the rearview again. There were only a few cars on the road.

It made no sense. Back when Nola cornered Zig in the shower, she was clearly still working the case, still asking questions, still trying to figure out the truth behind Black House, the Reds, and whoever had hired Zion to pull the trigger on Rashida and Mint. Yet the more he thought about it, this case was working her. The speed that she ran out of there . . . Her hands were shaking as she tugged open the window, like her life depended on it. Roddy said the same—that she ran without even talking to him. For Nola, Mint's death was more than just a normal case. It was one that cut to something deeper, something from her past. Something she'd rather keep there.

Zig glanced over at Roddy, who sat calmly, his posture a perfect

L-square. There were damp spots across the chest and arms of his uniform, where he'd scrubbed away the blood, but his shoes were still a mess. So were his knuckles, which were bruised and swollen, covered in a dozen red-and-purple cuts—each a tiny screaming mouth.

Zig could still picture Roddy sitting on the big redhead's chest, pounding Seabass in the face, pile driver after pile driver, with a savagery and ruthlessness that came far too naturally.

From the moment Roddy first showed up, Zig thought his best bet was to keep him close. But what if that was wrong? The way Roddy exploded on Seabass was like a grenade. And only a fool keeps a grenade close. Nola's words echoed in his brain. *You don't know who he is at his core.*

"What'd she say?" Roddy asked.

Zig turned. "I-I'm not sure what you're—"

"Your ex-wife. In the bathroom. When I was banging on the door, you said you were on the phone with her. What'd she say?"

"Ex-wife stuff. Nothing really."

"It must've been important if you took the call in the shower."

Zig's eyes again slid toward Roddy, who was still staring straight ahead, palms down on his thighs, like he was sitting in church. "It was about our daughter," Zig replied.

"The one who died."

Zig didn't answer.

"I'm not trying to pry, Mr. Zig. When we first met, I looked it up. The old newspapers . . . the obituary . . . none of it listed a cause of death."

This was the point where most people stopped talking.

"I found the old police report," Roddy added. "It said your daughter was run over. That you and your wife were having an argument—and that your daughter ran outside and hid under your car."

Roddy had part of the story, the police never knowing that for Zig and Charmaine, it was more than an isolated argument. They were having marital problems, made even worse when Zig found out that Charmaine was cheating on him. That's why Maggie ran out that night. To avoid the screaming, she hid under the car and eventually fell asleep.

"The report said when you realized she was gone, you jumped in your car to go find her," Roddy added. "But as you backed up in the driveway, you accidentally—"

"Listen . . ."

"I'm just saying. I'm sorry it happened. That must've been—" Roddy couldn't find the right words to finish the sentence.

"In one mile, take the exit for Route 130 on your right," a robotic Google Maps voice said from Zig's phone.

Zig hit the gas. They were close.

"Mr. Zig, if today were a color, I'm thinking it has to be black. Or midnight blue."

"Anything else, Roddy?"

He thought about it. "You think anyone's waiting for us at Elijah's?"

Zig tugged the steering wheel, heading for the exit. "We're about to find out."

66

Reagan did stupid things when she was angry. And she was due for another right now.

"I need you to think good thoughts. You got a good thought?" Reagan asked, frantically emptying a red-and-white Target bag, a few of the contents falling to the car's floor.

Crumpled in the passenger seat next to her, Seabass gave a quick nod like all was well, but there was no hiding the pain. She'd reclined his seat to keep him out of sight, and stretched a bloody beach towel across his chest. His mouth was a ground-up mess from where the bullet had pierced his cheek and kicked through his teeth. In dental terms, he had an Ellis III fracture, involving the enamel and running all the way down to the pulp layers. Even worse, since the nerve root was exposed, it absolutely *killed* when cool air hit it.

Like now.

"You're thinking of that woman in Peru, aren't you?" Reagan teased, though she couldn't mask the irritation in her voice. Diagonally across the Target parking lot, she glanced for the second time at a gray SUV near the front of the store. Reagan had parked in one of the very last spots, but even from here, she could see two young sisters—around four and nine years old, both of them with messy bird's nests of blond hair—arguing in a mini civil war.

"Clara, *sit . . . still!*" the older sister scolded as the younger one squirmed in her car seat like Houdini in a straitjacket. Just like Reagan's own sister used to. At the trunk of the SUV, their skinny, distracted mom was gabbing on her oversized cell phone, holding it away from her face like a teenager, which made Reagan want to storm across the parking lot and tear it from her hands.

Breathe, Seabass said with a glance, reaching over the car's center console and cupping his giant paw of a hand over her own. *You need a breath.*

It was his standard move. He'd used it last year in Montana, when that security guard at the freezer company shot up their car. And in Brazil, when Reagan got drunk and picked the wrong fight. And even back when they were junior enlisted, at Fort Leonard Wood, when that staff sergeant with the Arkansas twang put his hand on her ass and she reached for her gun.

"Will you stop!? I'm fine!" she insisted, slapping his hand away. Four hours from now, when Seabass went down, this was the moment she'd go back to, hating herself for her reaction.

Across the parking lot, the four-year-old sister started crying, kicking wildly in her car seat, and now, all Reagan could picture was her own sister all those years ago, and everything that went wrong on that night she'd never be able to take back. Reagan was stupid that night, too—though not nearly as stupid as—

Seabass again reached for her hand—not to calm her, but for help. He was sinking in his seat, about to pass out.

"Sebby, the girl from Peru . . . !" she shouted, tugging him upward to keep him from aspirating on the blood he was now coughing all over his own chest. His face was bone white, his eyes not focusing. She needed to be fast. Rule 1 in any ER: forget the pain; stop the bleeding.

"Sebby! *WAKE! UP!*" she exploded, rummaging through the shopping bag. "Look, I got you presents!" she explained, pulling out a football mouth guard and a pack of Crayola rainbow modeling clay. As she opened the clay, she got a whiff of her childhood.

Yanking off a hunk of yellow clay, Reagan stuffed it into the mouth guard. Ideally, she'd use dental cement to create a tamponade at the bleeding area and apply some pressure, like packing gauze into a knife wound. It'd also hold his teeth in place. But with no cement? Modeling clay would do.

"Sebby . . . c'mon," she pleaded. She pinched his wrist to wake him up. "On two, okay?"

He nodded, still groggy.

"One . . ."

She lifted the mouth guard, filled with clay. He opened his mouth.

"Two."

With the heel of her palm, Reagan stuffed the mouth guard between his lips. Seabass curled forward, twisting, squirming, electrified by pain. She grabbed his chin and his forehead, shoving his head backward, into the headrest. As she forced him to bite down, bloodied yellow clay oozed between his lips like a human piping bag.

Pressing his skull into the headrest, Seabass did everything he could not to yell, howl, or scream. He clenched his jaw tighter than ever, breathing hard through his nose with frantic huffs like he was in labor. *Fffff . . . ffffff . . . ffffff . . .*

For nearly thirty seconds, he swallowed the pain, pretending it wasn't there, leaning backward and biting down. He focused on an old memory, back when he first arrived at Fort Leonard Wood. He could do this . . . he had it, he told himself, his huffing getting softer and softer, until . . . like a leaky balloon, he let out a high-pitched indistinct wail that brought matching tears to both his and Reagan's eyes.

"I can make more jokes about the Peruvian girl," Reagan said. "That's who you were thinking of, right?"

He nodded over and over, his sad blue eyes staring straight up, like he was trying to will himself out of his body, out of existence, out of sight from the only woman he ever honestly thought about— Reagan.

"Sebby, if the pain's too much, I can take you to a hospit—"

He shook his head, pointing to the other bloody mess, the bullet wound in his cheek. The swollen black slit was barely a centimeter long, but still stinging from all of Roddy's punches. It definitely needed closing.

Just finish, he said with a glance, Reagan quickly shaking the last items from the shopping bag: a pack of sewing needles and a spool of silk thread.

In the movies, homemade stitches were made with fishing line, but as her dad taught her, fishing line unravels. If you want the knots to grab, you need texture.

"Okay, in that fantasy with Ms. Peru, here's where she takes her top off," Reagan finally said, lowering the threaded needle to his cheek. "On two. One . . ."

Seabass grabbed the center console with one hand, the car door with the other. *Talk to me,* he told her with his eyes.

"Have we worn out the Peru bit, or should I just tell you the fifteen different ways I'm gonna murder Zig and that runt cop who did this to you?"

Seabass nodded, holding a pretend phone to his face. She knew what he meant. Their handheld GPS. Back when they ran out of the funeral home, Reagan put a tracker on Zig's car. *Where are they?*

"Jersey," she said, pushing the needle into his cheek and looping it into a quick mattress stitch. "At a bar, of all places."

For the next two minutes, Seabass sat there, eyes shut, as Reagan made another few loops and pulled the thread tight. That's all it took. Compared to the mouth guard, the stitches were the easy part.

Fighting to sit up in his seat, he lowered the sun visor, checking her work in the mirror. His face was bloated and swollen, but at least the bleeding stopped.

He pointed to the GPS. *How far?*

A small grin lit Reagan's face. She did stupid things when she was angry. But so did Seabass. "Not far at all, Sebby." She started the car. "We'll be there in no time."

67

Nola wanted to draw, though now wasn't the time.

Hitting the gas and weaving through the afternoon traffic, she blew past a fortysomething dad in a minivan, no kids in back, blaring nineties hip-hop as he bounced to the beat. She was trying to put as much distance as she could between herself and Zig's funeral home. But that didn't stop her from drawing in her head.

It was her brother Roddy who she mentally started to sketch, still kicking herself for letting him get so close. Careless. Another damn mistake. It was happening over and over, like she was a noob grunt again. Yet as she replayed the sound of Roddy banging on the door— just hearing his voice again . . . and then to be standing there face-to-face, to finally see him . . . the deep-set eyes, the polished uniform, worn like a costume to make him look helpful and good.

You know why I'm here. Those were his words. The words of someone who wants something. She replayed it again. Roddy said this was about *her*. There was only one her. *A trick. Had to be a trick.* No way did Roddy know what Mint did for her all those years ago, the real reason she was so attached to this case—and then, to her own surprise, her mental drawing quickly shifted to Zig.

Their little meeting in the funeral home bathroom—she didn't want to say it was *good*. She'd never give him that. But she had to admit, his concern . . . the panic in his lonely eyes . . . his hands were shaking as he tried to open the window so she could sneak out.

She wanted to say there was something nice about not being in this alone, but she wasn't convinced of that. Maybe it was just that she knew, she absolutely knew, that even here, in a case that was making her far too emotional, Zig wouldn't screw her over—and she couldn't say that about most people.

Turning off the main drag and down a narrow side street, Nola wove her way toward the back entrance of a long-dead strip mall that held the corpse of a hollowed-out Blockbuster Video, that became a twenty-four-hour gym, that became a Spirit Halloween store, that finally became a place where—to judge from the scattering of beer cans and Red Bulls—local high school kids came to drink at night.

Good sign. Kids know where there are no surveillance cameras.

Pulling out her iPad, Nola opened the app for Black House and entered Zion's phone number. A digital hourglass appeared onscreen, along with a single word:

Locating . . .

That's how she'd tracked the Reds in the first place—from when they grabbed Zion's phone.

Back at Zion's house, after watching footage on the nanny cam, Nola had combed through his emails, home computer, and anything else she could find. It was there she noticed the Black House icon on his desktop, confirming her theory that back when she'd first logged into Black House, Zion was one of the two digital avatars she saw there. The question remained: Who was the other? For a while, Nola thought it might be O.J. or another investigator. But the more she thought about it—the way the two avatars logged off together—the more it seemed like it was someone Zion knew, like a friend. Or employer.

Hoping to find the answer, she'd tried logging into Zion's Black House account. But unlike with Mint, she had no chance of guessing Zion's password. Still, the fact they each had their own login . . .

Opening Mint's Black House account, Nola clicked the button labeled *Contacts,* and entered Zion's name.

Contact not found.

She entered his email.

Contact not found.

She entered his phone number.
A pop-up box appeared:

(1) Known Associate.
Connect? Y/N

She hit *Yes*. Onscreen, a new pop-up appeared:

Locating . . .

Lazy, Nola had thought, rolling her eyes. Most Black House users were probably smart enough to disable their location services. But again, Zion was a runt, a moron. And completely trackable—assuming the Reds still had his phone.

Across the Blockbuster/gym/Halloween store parking lot, a gust of wind rolled a stray beer can into a shopping cart turned on its side. Onscreen, the digital hourglass blinked. The word *Locating* disappeared, replaced by . . .

Signal Unavailable

Nola reentered the phone number, double-checking each digit.

Signal Unavailable

They know. Of course they know. The Reds weren't novices. Seabass got shot in the face. They either disabled tracking on the phone or tossed it.

Undeterred, Nola reached into her pocket and pulled out a folded sheet of paper that was covered with phone numbers. Like most people, Zion paid his bills online. A quick search of his browser history turned up a T-Mobile account, which revealed all of Zion's incoming and outgoing calls over the past two weeks.

There were nearly fifty in total, most of them late at night. *Customers,* Nola thought, remembering the stash of drugs in Zion's closet.

Starting at the top, she entered the first phone number into Mint's Black House account.

Contact not found.

Next number.

Contact not found.

It was the same, over and over.
Nothing.
Nothing.
Nothing.
Until . . .
Something.
Onscreen, a new pop-up box appeared, with a little red triangle that had an exclamation point inside.

Restricted Access for XXX-XXX-XXXX
Subject Flagged for Confidential Purposes
Contact DOJ's Special Identities Unit

Special Identities Unit. She'd seen it before. Whoever owned that phone number, she was supposed to stay away.

But that was always Nola's problem. She was never any good at doing what she was *supposed to.*

On the iPad, she opened a browser. It was the best part of finding a phone number—from there, it's not hard to get an address.

68

"Who you looking for?" a female voice challenged.

Zig turned, spotting a ninety-year-old African American woman with cannula tubes at her nose. They ran down off the edge of the bus bench she was sitting on, to a portable oxygen tank that was bedazzled with pink rhinestones. On her face, to block the fading sun, were oversized Jackie O sunglasses that made Zig think he was in the presence of royalty.

"Just trying to find a bite to eat," Zig told her.

Lady Rhinestone looked at him skeptically. It got even worse as she eyed Roddy's police uniform. Across the street was a food hall built into an old bus station, an artisanal ice cream shop, and a make-your-own-pottery place called Every Clay Is a New Clay. Each of them had a water dish for dogs out front. It was the same in cities from Seattle, to Washington, D.C., to right here in Jersey; the arrival of whites in minority communities led to gentrification and dog dishes for everyone. Of course, if you went down the wrong block, some of the neighborhood was still rough around the edges.

"Lemme guess, you're looking for Elijah," Lady Rhinestone said.

"How'd you know that?" Zig asked.

"You look the same as the other guy."

Zig raised an eyebrow. *Other guy?* "Ma'am, was there someone else looking for Elijah?"

Up the block, two twentysomethings on electric scooters were riding in circles. Lady Rhinestone took a huff of her cannula tube. "Last night. Handsome fellow. Looked like that young man who played Black Panther and Thurgood Marshall. He had a part in his hair, which, let's admit, is a crime for an Afro, but he made it work."

Zig and Roddy exchanged a glance. *Colonel O. J. Whatley.* He was here last night, though he never mentioned it when Zig was in his office.

"So you work here?" Zig asked, spotting the apron she was wearing, embroidered with *Every Clay Is a New Clay.*

"Sweetie, that's my shop. I'm the owner," she said coldly, lowering her chin just enough to give him the stink eye above the rim of her sunglasses.

"Yeah . . . no . . . that's what I meant."

"Forgive him. He's white," Roddy said. It made the woman laugh. "If I could ask one last question," he added. "The address we have— Elijah gave us his home address, but I think we might have it wrong."

"You passed it," she said, pointing behind them, toward the twentysomethings on the scooters. They were still riding in circles, though now a block closer, past a refurbished two-story redbrick building that looked like a trendy bar. No dog dish in front. "He sleeps upstairs," Lady Rhinestone explained. "Just be careful when you go inside. He's been known to shoot at white people."

Zig froze.

"I'm teasing. That's humor."

Roddy offered her a fist bump. She took him up on it.

Of course she did. When Zig first met Roddy, he wrote him off as a social misfit, but it was time to admit . . . from the funeral home, to finding Elijah, to tracking him here . . . over and over, Roddy's eyes never left the prize. Even if Zig didn't trust him, it was time to stop underestimating him. And to start using him.

Zig headed for Elijah's, the summer sun fading in the purple sky.

"She liked me better because I'm nicer," Roddy said, running to catch up. "You should laugh. That's a good joke."

Zig ignored it, eyeing the scooter guys, who were still making circles, winding their way closer. There were other people on the streets—nearly all of them young twenty- and thirtysomethings, all of them with a professional veneer. This was a neighborhood on the rise. And Elijah was part of it.

"I need your cop brain. Can we go back to Grandma's Pantry for a moment?" Zig asked.

"You mean the break-in?"

"I've been thinking about it. What if instead of taking something *out,* well . . . on that night five years ago, what if someone was actually trying to sneak something *in?*"

Roddy thought about that, the scooter guys now barely half a block away. "Why would someone bring something in?"

"That's the question, isn't it?"

"I'd bring something illegal," Roddy decided. "A warehouse with security like that—I'd bring drugs."

"Drugs are one possibility. Weapons, too," Zig acknowledged. "But thinking of all the antidotes they keep there—for smallpox, SARS, Ebola—what if someone brought in lesser versions of those, to dilute the real stuff during an actual catastrophe?"

"Or maybe just to create doubt so the government orders even more," Roddy said, nodding over and over like he was enjoying himself. "If you really want to be destructive, bring a bomb inside—blow up the warehouse itself."

"Or blackmail it," Zig agreed. "Gimme fifty million, or the whole place goes boom."

Zig stopped at the redbrick storefront.

Hopportunities, read the hand-painted sign on the front glass. In the bottom right-hand corner, in one of those trendy typographies that you instantly know is cool but also somehow reminds you of the font of an eye chart, were these words:

PROPRIETOR—ELIJAH KING

The fourth and final member of Mint's team.

69

Sabrina S. wasn't any help.

Neither was Gina Castronovo, or Sherri Goldman, or the twins, Rachel and Julia Cohen.

For hours now, Charmaine had been staked out at her kitchen table, using Facebook to track down cell numbers, making phone call after phone call to Maggie's childhood friends.

As expected, the hardest part was the small talk, hearing that Sabrina S. and Leah were both married with kids, Pamela had gone back to school to be a physician's assistant, Jodi was running for the local school board, and Melanie had started her own web marketing business—all of them in their late twenties, hopes and possibilities spread out in front of them, while Maggie was forever twelve, forever a Girl Scout.

It was no different with Katelynn Rose, who spent a solid five minutes explaining that she'd been teaching kindergarten and recently got engaged, though all Charmaine remembered about her was that her teeth always seemed too big for her mouth.

"I met him online, of all places," Katelynn added with a gaspy laugh. "He wants a destination wedding, but I'm trying to convince him that everyone hates those couples."

It was yet another cute story from yet another well-meaning young woman, but as Charmaine sat there, elbows on the table, hunched toward her speakerphone, there was actually something surprisingly satisfying, even reinvigorating, about hearing these updates and recaps.

At first, Charmaine chalked it up to the afterglow of nostalgia, to hearing the girls' voices all grown up and trying to plot the course between now and then. Or maybe it was just her own dismal expectations. But to sit here and take in the contours of their fledgling lives, to listen to their stories and all the emotion packed into them . . . just the act of tracking them down and wondering where they've been . . . it made her feel like a parent again. And that, for Charmaine, was something glorious.

"It's funny, y'know what always makes me think of Maggie?" Katelynn asked, actually saying Maggie's name, a detail most shied away from. "Convertibles."

"Y'mean *cars*?"

"She took me for my first ride in a convertible, or rather Mr. Z did after one of our Scout meetings. White car, maroon top."

"Ford Mustang, anniversary edition," Charmaine said, the smell of the leather interior—plus a musty scent from a leak—quickly flooding her senses.

"I was ten, maybe eleven. He pulled up and told us to hop in without opening the doors. When he hit the gas and our hair started whipping everywhere, I honestly thought the car had a rocket, and we might take off. He even used to do a countdown. *Three . . . two . . . one . . .*"

Blast-off, Charmaine thought, a heartfelt smile lifting her cheeks. Zig had saved years for that car—he'd wanted one since high school—then refused to buy it once Maggie was born. As a mortician, he'd seen too many overturned military jeeps and the closed caskets that came with them. It was Charmaine who pulled the trigger, sneaking off to the local Ford dealership and surprising him on his fortieth birthday.

"He really let you jump in the car without opening the doors?" Charmaine asked.

"In *and* out. Every time. He'd blast the Beastie Boys' 'Sabotage' and tell us to pretend we were seventies cops."

Charmaine laughed with a snort, a swell of tears seeping out behind her eyes. That sounded like Zig—back when life was so easy . . . or at least before everything got so hard.

"Who's on the phone?" a deep voice asked behind her.

She barely turned as Warren entered the kitchen, searching the fridge for a snack.

Nothing. Work call, she pantomimed, waving him away and taking the phone off speaker.

"Again, Mrs. Z, sorry I couldn't be more helpful about Maggie," Katelynn added. "My SuperStars days were limited to Sabrina's horrible birthday party where she told us we were all fat."

"If it makes you feel better, she just had a kid who's making her miserable by refusing to sleep through the night."

"I don't wish bad on anyone." For a half second, Katelynn paused. "Except maybe her." As Charmaine laughed, Katelynn added, "Back to SuperStars for a moment, have you tried calling the Ainsleys? Their beauty supply place was in the same plaza."

"Actually, GBS Beauty was one plaza over. SuperStars was with Kuba Thai, that pack-and-ship place, and that—" Charmaine stopped, sitting up straight.

"Mrs. Z, did I lose you?"

"Yeah . . . no . . . I'm here," she insisted. Yet as she remembered one last store in the SuperStars plaza, Charmaine had a brand-new idea.

70

It was a card store—Card Kingdom—dedicated to greeting cards, of all things.

Nola didn't need a sketch pad to know something smelled. Parked diagonally across the street, she eyed the storefront, which took up the ground floor of a two-story concrete thumb of a building sandwiched between a gas station and a skate park that was empty except for an elderly man sitting there with a little black dog on his lap. The neighborhood, just outside Philadelphia, wasn't bad; it just felt left behind.

As for Card Kingdom, the front window held a giant Hallmark logo sticker that bubbled against the glass, along with an oversized Christmas present filled with faded rolls of wrapping paper featuring Garfield and the Smurfs. If Card Kingdom was trying to attract business, they weren't trying hard.

Back during her early military training, they called it *sizing up the building*. Clear front entrance. Single access point. Standard locks. Most important, no cameras. If time were on her side, she'd do a full sweep, checking all the angles. But the way things were going, if someone beat her here . . .

Kicking open the car door, Nola plowed toward the storefront. An actual bell rang overhead as she stepped inside, the smell of old paper wafting over her and bringing, in the midst of this, an actual good memory—her teacher Ms. Sable taking her to the art supply store for the first time.

Inside, Card Kingdom was nicer than she expected. Its four aisles of yellow, seventies-era, faux-blond-wood display cases were old, but the greeting cards seemed new, or at least not picked over.

On her far right, the cash register was manned by a twentysomething guy—thin eyebrows and delicate features—wearing a plaid flannel shirt and one of those gray slouchy beanie hats that looked ridiculous in the heat of summer and instantly told Nola he was more fashion victim than threat. Scrolling on his phone, he barely looked up.

Hoping to be quick, Nola wove through the narrow aisles, passing sections for birthday cards, anniversaries, get well, and farewell . . . and even, as she turned the corner, a section labeled *Dirty for Him/Dirty for Her*.

Scattered along the walls were Formica shelves of snow globes, ceramic figurines, crystal animals, and every other useless knickknack that a store like this sells to stay in business, but what caught her eye . . .

"Any Father's Day cards?" Nola asked.

"Tomorrow," Beanie Hat said with a grunt, still phone-scrolling.

Nola made a note. Father's Day already passed. *Strike one.*

At the back of the store, a vertical sliver of light revealed a back door that overlooked a small parking lot behind the building. She squinted, spotting three cars—for a store with only one employee. *Strike two.*

Yet what caught Nola's eye more than anything else . . . There. Along the right-hand wall.

An elevator. Polished steel. High-tech call buttons. State of the art.

Like something you'd use for a fortress.

71

"A man walks into a bar . . ." Zig called out, easing the front door open.

Decades ago, Zig's father would make the same joke when ten-year-old Zig would enter their local pub, on his regular quest to "get your father's ass back here." As a kid, Zig laughed along with his dad's joke, even though he didn't quite get it. When he got older, he saw it for what it was: a great way to disarm, especially when trouble was coming.

"Mr. King? Elijah . . . ?" Roddy added, beer whiff rolling over them, but also another smell, a faint sour and sweet one that Zig couldn't quite place.

As Zig followed Roddy inside, he noticed that Roddy's hand wasn't on his gun. When a uniformed cop enters a bar, people look away and shut down. Roddy clearly wanted answers, not trouble.

Inside, the bar itself was a gorgeous rustic counter, the front of it made from brushed corrugated metal, like you find on posh farmhouses that no longer have real farms and that people rent for fancy weddings. A dozen industrial stools sat in front of it, purposefully mismatched in bronze, white, and gunmetal. But the real stars of the show were the taps—at least twenty of them, lined up one next to the other along the right-hand wall, like a self-serve yogurt place, but for craft beers with names like Liberty Ale, Hale to the Hop Thief, and AmiRite?

"You see him?" Zig asked, glancing around.

A dozen customers—all young, a mix of Black and white, some

with an educated polish, some looking more working class—were scattered throughout, drinking and eating jalapeño poppers and nachos.

"You're just a cop?" a man called out.

The door to the kitchen swung wide, revealing a bald African American man with thick caterpillar eyebrows. Slightly younger than Zig, though he looked older than he did in the painting.

Strolling behind the bar, he never took his eyes off Roddy's police uniform. Behind him, on the back wall, was a framed dollar where someone had written, "This was in a stripper's thong! Go, Elijah!" in thick black Magic Marker.

"You said you were a fed," Elijah added, calm as could be. He had an ease about him, pouring himself a glass of water, which he sipped like a scotch.

"I said I was investigating," Roddy countered, two of the higher-polished customers, both with bougie beards, already getting up to leave.

"He's also Nola Brown's brother," Zig added.

There was a pause.

"We're trying to keep her alive," Zig explained. "You as well. We know what happened to Colonel Mint and Rashida Robinson."

Elijah studied Roddy's face. "You got her eyes, alright," he said. "Now lemme guess—you wanna chat about Grandma's Pantry."

72

Nola spent the next hour around back, in the skate park.

From her angle, on a bench that was spray-painted with a Puerto Rican flag, she pretended to flip through a newspaper, her eyes never leaving the small Card Kingdom parking lot. Three cars in total.

Old light blue Kia.

Even older Honda Civic.

And the one Nola was watching: a sleek black Audi A8. Freshly waxed. A hundred-thousand-dollar car. Find the driver, and she'd find who'd paid for the elevator.

According to the sign in the front window, Card Kingdom closed at 5:00 P.M. Half hour to go. Just had to wait.

Sure enough, at 5:02, the back door swung open. Beanie Hat strolled out, lit a cigarette, and drove off in his old Civic, where a decal in the back window read: *The Empire Doesn't Care About Your Stick Figure Family* as Darth Vader sliced apart a bunch of stick figures.

Twenty minutes later, the back door opened again. This time, it was an older woman—Asian, midfifties, angry gait—who plowed toward the light blue Kia. As she pulled out of the lot, an old AC/DC song faded behind her.

Even before the Kia was out of sight, Nola jumped from her seat, quickly hopping the chain-link fence that separated the skate park from the parking lot.

From her back pocket, she pulled out a small leather case that held colored pencils, an X-Acto knife, and a few metal tools that looked like dental instruments—a torsion wrench and short hook among them. Lockpick kit.

With a careful push, she shoved the pick into the door's keyhole. Same cheap lock as the front door. Was smarter than it looked. In neighborhoods like this, expensive locks make people take notice.

For a moment, she jiggered the tools.

Click.

Glancing over her shoulder one last time, Nola tugged the door open and slipped inside. The card store was dark, lit by a faint red glow from a section of lava lamps. On her right was a bookshelf filled with half a dozen picture frames, all with the same stock photo: a graduation shot of a girl in cap and gown, her mom, dad, and brother embracing her in a group hug, like it was the greatest day of their lives.

For a few seconds, she spied the room, moving left to right, dividing it into more scannable sections. Military training told her that the last place you ever want to be is on an elevator. Tactically, it's like being on a submarine. Plus, around the store, there were no cameras.

She shook her head, knowing better. When things are this easy, it's always a trap. Whatever they were hiding upstairs, they didn't want any record of it.

But it wasn't like she had a choice. Nola continued looking around. If there were stairs, she couldn't find them.

Hesitantly, she headed for the elevator, spotting a keypad above the call buttons. *Crap.* She'd need a code. Yet before she could even hit the call button, to her surprise, it lit up.

There was a sound. A metal hiccup. The elevator doors slid open, revealing a bearded man with pale white skin and crooked teeth the color of margarine.

"Yeah, I see her," he said with a thick Philly accent into a high-tech walkie-talkie. He was big, with a trendy tribal-font tattoo that read *Big Sleeps* across his forearm.

Nola planted her feet. He had a stupidly oversized luxury watch on his right wrist and leaned forward as he moved. Left-handed. And used to being on the offensive.

"C'mon, girl," he warned, stepping toward Nola. "You really think we wouldn't see you coming?"

73

"Can I get you a drink?"

Zig was about to say no, but Elijah had a vibe like an old coach or mentor you didn't want to let down.

"You said it's Zig, right? Z-I-G?" Elijah asked, spelling it out. He'd been doing it for years—spelling people's names as a way to remember them. Comes in handy when you're tending bar. "And Roddy, yes? R-O-D-D-I-E?"

"With a Y," Roddy said.

"R-O-D-D-Y. Roddy," Elijah repeated, handing them two empty pilsner glasses and pointing them to the taps that lined the far-right wall. He even blinked slowly, like he was moving in an unhurried time. "If you got a sweet tooth, the ones on the end are ciders."

Zig liked cider. But c'mon. Not more than free craft beer.

"I got a room in back that's a bit more quiet," Elijah offered as Roddy headed for one of the taps.

"Here's fine," Roddy shot back.

You sure? Zig asked with a glance, confused. He scanned the bar. The biggest guy in sight—a heavyset man with a receding hairline and undone tie who was nursing a beer and scrolling through his phone—didn't look like much of a threat, except to his jalapeño poppers.

Roddy motioned to the far corner of the bar, to a slight gangly man with outdated rectangular eyeglasses. Hanging behind his chair was a nylon messenger bag embroidered with the words *PRP Consulting*. Certainly not a threat—that is, until Roddy pointed down low and Zig finally got a look at the man's ankle holster. Definitely carrying.

As before, Roddy didn't miss a detail. That explained why he'd rather be out here. Better to see what's coming—in a crowd and near an exit—than be trapped in back.

"It's not working," Roddy said, pulling a tap labeled *Hop Drop N Roll*.

"You need— *Here* . . ." Elijah said, yanking one of three red wristbands off his wrist and tossing it Roddy's way. When Roddy put it on, he reached again for the tap and—*beep beep*—it unlocked, filling his glass with fancy craft beer.

"There's a chip inside," Elijah explained, pointing to the red bracelets every customer was wearing. "You buy the wristband, open a tab, and pay by the pour."

"Nice gimmick—and even nicer neighborhood," Zig pointed out.

"Credit to my ex-brother-in-law," Elijah explained, grabbing a metal mixing bowl from behind the bar and heading for a quiet table in the corner. "Three years ago, he started working in the city commissioner's office. He's the one who gave me the heads-up that the town was putting up a minor league baseball stadium a few blocks down. That's what built this place. They tore down the old neighborhood and redid it all. I was first on the block. Took every last dollar I had. But on Saturdays now, people pour outta the stadium and walk right to me. We need extra wristbands those days," he said, straightening out a nearby chair before taking a seat, though he never took his eyes off Roddy. "Now tell me about Nola. How's she doing?"

"Fine." "Hanging in," Zig and Roddy said simultaneously, arriving at the table.

Elijah shot them a look. "You have no idea where she is, do you?"

"We do," Zig insisted, taking a seat.

Elijah nodded, tapping his thumbs on the metal bowl, which was filled to the top with loose Starburst candies. That was the sweet-and-sour smell Zig couldn't place. Elijah used them on trivia nights. "Processed sugar?" he asked, offering Zig some candy. Elijah was trying to play nice, but he wasn't a moron—and he certainly wasn't buying their story.

"I realize honesty is more valuable than free Starbursts," Elijah began, "but are either of you even assigned to this case, or you just personally invested since Nola is his sister?"

"Elijah, I know you don't know us," Zig said, trying to keep his voice down, "but I swear, I wouldn't be here if I didn't think Nola's life was in danger. Yours, too."

"You already said that. But y'know what I know first and fore-most about Nola? She doesn't need saving. And y'know what else I know? She only talks to the people she trusts—so if she's not talking to you—"

"You don't understand."

"I'm not a fool. And neither is she. If she wanted your help, she'd reach out. But that's not the case, is it? You haven't seen her, heard from her, haven't even spoken—"

"I have," Zig blurted.

Roddy turned, nearly spilling his beer.

"Back up. You lost me," Elijah said.

"Nola. She— I saw her, spoke to her— At the funeral home—"

"You *what*?" Roddy asked, leaning toward Zig, who was still locked on Elijah.

"You saw her, too," Zig insisted.

"She ran away from me! You never said— You *spoke* to her?"

"I didn't know she'd be there," Zig insisted. "She surprised me . . . in the shower . . . told me not to say anything."

"When?" Elijah asked.

"Hours ago. She's been tracking the Reds—"

"Who the hell are the Reds?" Elijah asked.

"My sister. *You spoke to my sister?*" Roddy asked with a strong tap to Zig's shoulder, trying to get his attention.

"Roddy, not now," Zig said, trying to wave him off. "Elijah, you know she—"

"*Why the hell didn't you tell me?*" Roddy roared, grabbing Zig's shoulder.

"Get *off*!" Zig said, trying to pull free. Roddy tightened his grip. Annoyed, Zig gripped Roddy's hand, tearing it away.

That was it. As Zig learned during his years at Dover, things don't go wrong in three minutes; they go wrong in three seconds. As Zig turned, still trying to pull free, Roddy's eyes went dark, like an internal switch had flipped. One fist gripped Zig's shoulder, the other held tight to the pilsner glass, holding it like a nightstick.

Zig froze. Elijah froze. The whole bar froze, customers turning, the crowd now staring at the sudden and violent shift in the bar's ecosystem.

Roddy blinked a few times, looking around, his grip slowly relaxing.

In the awkward silence, as adrenaline wore off, Roddy looked . . . *ashamed* was the only word for it. "Mr. Zig, I'm sorry . . . I shouldn't've—"

Don't, Zig scolded with a glare that hit like a punch.

"Everybody, relax! No blood here. They're just doing a mole check (for you precancerous middle-agers)!" Elijah called to the crowd. No one laughed, though the customers—including the consultant with the ankle holster—all quickly returned to their original equilibrium. Lowering his voice, Elijah turned back to the table. "Okay, now that we're all socially uncomfortable, can we get back to Nola? She really came to see you?"

"Trust me, I was just as surprised. But that's the thing about Mint's death—it's got your whole team scurrying," Zig said, carefully eyeing Elijah's reaction. "Nola comes to see me; O.J. comes to see you . . ."

Elijah froze. "Who told you Colonel Whatley was here?"

"The old woman with the rhinestoned oxygen tank. Owns the clay store."

Elijah sighed. "Miss Neicy. Lord, is she a pain in everyone's ass."

"That doesn't answer my question."

"You didn't ask one—all you did was come inside, throwing accusations. As for O.J., he's doing what he's always doing: looking out for O.J."

"I'm not a fan, either," Zig admitted, noticing the way Roddy had shrunk in his seat, like he was punishing himself.

"Tell me about Nola. What'd she say?" Elijah asked, picking up some loose Starbursts and resetting a stack of coasters that got knocked over on the table. He was trying to look casual, but his voice was clearly impatient.

"We talked about that night . . . about the robbery at Grandma's Pantry. Most important, I told her I was coming to see you," Zig explained. "She didn't object—which tells me, well . . . considering Nola hates everyone . . . somehow, someway, she thinks you might be one of the few people who's worthy of some trust."

Elijah gripped the stacked coasters, squaring them like a deck of just-shuffled cards, then squared them again for no good reason. "*Flattery?* You're playing the old Nola nostalgia card and using flattery on me?"

"Is it working?"

"I haven't decided."

"Then let me be clear: You've got two team members dead. I'm trying to prevent a third. Nola told me about the robbery—that something was snuck inside. If you know what it was . . . what they put into the warehouse—"

"Not 'what,'" Elijah interrupted.

"Excuse me?" Zig asked.

"That night at Grandma's Pantry . . . You said 'what' they put into the warehouse. It wasn't a *thing*," Elijah explained. "What they snuck inside . . . It was a person."

74

Five years ago

Chaz "Salty" Trebbiano always kept a two-dollar bill in his wallet. *For good luck,* his father used to say, though Salty never believed in such nonsense. Over the course of his sixty-two years, Salty had never been in a car accident, never broken a bone, never had a cavity . . . even still had a head of thick gray hair that matched his gunmetal eyes. Six months ago, however, Salty's luck ran out.

"This part of my punishment?" the old man complained from the back seat.

"Just for that, I'm turning it up," said the U.S. Marshal who was driving, a thin Asian woman who, two years back, had broken both ankles (but still caught the perp) when she jumped from the upper deck of a bridge to the lower deck. Her name was Piper Grace Lin, though everyone called her P.G. With a twist, she raised the volume on the radio.

"Don't take it so personally," Salty said. "I'm not an audiobook guy."

"It's Sherlock friggin' Holmes!" said Titus Huddleston, the other Marshal in the car, a beefy twenty-eight-year-old Mississippian who spent most of the ride thinking about his upcoming trials for the U.S. Olympic fifty-meter riflery team. He was sitting next to Salty in the back seat. "Who are you to not like Sherlock Holmes?"

Salty shrugged, a light jingle coming from his handcuffed wrists and the connected belly chain. Six months ago, he'd been arrested for a dozen murders that stemmed from the multimillion-dollar weapons supply route he ran, selling illegal guns to white nationalists from Virginia to Texas. Early this morning, Salty testified against his old buyers in exchange for some plastic surgery and a new name. In Marshals' parlance, he became a "client."

P.G. and Titus's job was to keep him alive during the six-hour ride from the Virginia courthouse to their destination: Otisville federal prison in upstate New York. When you enter witness protection, you don't just leave your trial and race to your new hometown. All across the country, certain prisons had private security wings that specialized in keeping witnesses safe until their new identities were ready.

"I'll give you five grand apiece to put on some music. Ten to play Sinatra," Salty teased.

P.G. rolled her eyes, making Sherlock Holmes even louder.

Annoyed, Salty stared out into the darkness, thinking of the old treadmill he always picked at the gym—to get the best view of the girl at the check-in desk with the lush eyelashes.

Ten minutes later, P.G. glanced at the car's digital clock. Nearly midnight—and it felt like it as they hit one of those stretches of highway where you can't quite remember the last few miles or what the hell you were just thinking. That is, until the bright lights of another car—an SUV from the height of it—appeared in the distance behind them.

P.G. noticed it first, squinting at the lights in the rearview. On the seat next to her was what they code-named a "WITSEC shotgun," meaning it had a cut-down barrel to move and aim easier in the close confines of a vehicle. Titus gave her a look, reminding her that his own gun was in the front glove box. If you ride in back with the prisoner, you're not allowed to be armed.

The SUV picked up speed, pulling neck and neck, then quickly blew past them. As the SUV disappeared into the darkness, Sherlock Holmes pointed out that life is infinitely stranger than anything the mind of man could invent.

"Okay, forget the stupid audiobook," Salty said. "Fifty grand if you can find us a Starbucks or a proper cup of—"

"Whoa. You feel that?" P.G. interrupted.

Titus nodded. "Flat tire."

Salty looked around, confused. "Feels good to me."

"It's not," P.G. insisted as she and Titus exchanged a glance. Didn't matter that the highway was empty—or that in front of them, the faint red taillights of the SUV were barely visible. When you have a client, you don't just pull over.

"We need a port," P.G. said—a place where Salty would be safe.

Titus was already scrolling on his phone, looking for the usuals: nearby police stations, firehouses, even a hospital if need be.

"Got one," Titus said. He pointed up ahead. "Here. Get off at this exit."

P.G. tugged the wheel as the car veered toward the exit ramp in industrial New Jersey.

In the back seat, Salty glanced around, still lost. "Doesn't feel like a flat."

"Definitely is," P.G. said, though both she and her partner knew that wasn't true. "Titus, how much farther?"

"A few miles. Not far." He was right about that. Fifteen minutes later, they were at Grandma's Pantry.

75

GRANDMA'S PANTRY
Five years ago

By the time they entered the warehouse, they'd told Salty the truth—or at least most of it.

"I gotta say, I thought both of yas was retards," Salty said with a laugh. "God, I love being wrong."

He was still in handcuffs and leg irons, shuffling down a wide aisle that looked like a meticulously clean Costco—though instead of being stocked with pallets of industrial-sized mayonnaise and six-pound cans of tomato sauce, this aisle was filled with tall, refrigerator-sized boxes. Salty was too excited to notice they were labeled *Ventilators,* each with a cord running out of the box to charge them once a month.

"What the hell is this place, anyway? Feels like a morgue," he said, looking around and realizing they were the only ones in the entire building. He glanced up at the massive American flag that hung from the wide back wall. "Or maybe that warehouse in *X-Files.*"

"What's *X-Files*?" P.G. asked.

"Like *CSI,* but with aliens and— Y'know what, forget it," Salty said, trying to throw his hands in the air, though his cuffs were still connected to the belly chain.

"Salty, how about you stop running your mouth and start moving your ass?" Titus asked, giving him a shove from behind.

In truth, Salty had thought this meeting was going to take place a few days ago at the courthouse, where it's usually done. When that didn't happen, he assumed they'd set it up at the prison. But leave it to the Marshals to fake a flat tire and bring him to the one place no one would ever think to look.

"Should be unlocked," P.G. said, pointing them to their destination, a metal door with a latch that looked like—

"A freezer?" Salty asked, his voice echoing through the cavernous room. "You made her wait in a walk-in freezer?"

"Relax, it's not even on—still being installed," Titus explained.

Salty nodded like it made perfect sense. In a warehouse this big, better to find a smaller space. But what P.G. and Titus didn't mention was that the freezer was one of the only places in the building with no cameras.

"My kinda place," Salty teased, pumping his shoulders with a little strut, like he was on the way to his own surprise party and already secretly knew everyone was gonna be there. In reality, Salty had no idea what was coming.

"How long's she been waiting?" Salty asked.

"Ask her yourself," P.G. said, grabbing the door's metal latch and giving it a tug.

When you enter the WITSEC program, the first rule is simple: no contact. No contact with your relatives, no contact with your former neighbors, no contact with your previous life. They'll tell you there's no way around it, but as with any gatekeeper, they'll make exceptions—for an elderly parent dying, a sick sibling, or, in the worst of all scenarios, if something happens to your child.

The freezer door swung outward, revealing a row of clear plastic slats that hung like vertical blinds. Salty squinted to make sure he was seeing it right. Through the slats, in an office rolling chair, was a scrawny woman—thirty-five years old, though she looked twice that, her pink floral leukemia scarf askew on her head. Her face was gaunt, her eyes sunken, her skin so pale and brittle, she was practically see-through.

"D-Dad . . . ?" she whispered.

"Pop-Tart," Salty said, his voice cracking, tears filling his eyes.

Salty started running toward her, not even realizing P.G. was unlocking his handcuffs.

Plowing through the plastic slats, he embraced his daughter, Melinda, pulling her close, one of the cuffs still hanging from his wrist. The impact knocked her scarf from her head, tumbling across her shoulder. Salty closed his eyes, hating to see her bald, but still thinking she was the most beautiful girl in the world. "Pop-Tart," he repeated, starting to sob. "I'm here, I'm here, I'm right—"

Click.

Salty heard it before he felt it. Something cold at his neck.

He started to turn. P.G. pushed harder, pressing the barrel of her gun into the back of Salty's head. There was another click as Titus did the same to Salty's daughter, pointing his gun at her pale bald skull.

Salty took a breath through his nose, slowly raising his hands in the air. He knew things had been going too well. "This is why everyone hates the feds," he said.

"Y'know, as a white nationalist piece of trash, you really shouldn't look so shocked that you bring out the worst in people," P.G. said. "Now step away from your daughter."

"Titus . . . both of you . . . Be smart. Whatever you want, I can pay. I've got money."

"We know you do, jackass. Just like we know what you two were planning for this little meeting—since it clearly wasn't just about her cancer. Now . . ." P.G. cocked her gun and gripped the trigger, pressing it even harder against Salty's head. "Titus and I have a proposition for you."

76

"So it was a lemon drop," Roddy said.

"Lemme say it like this," Elijah began, getting up from the table with his empty water glass and heading for the wall of taps. "Lemon drops always smell like lemon drops."

"I'm lost," Zig said, taking his own sip of beer. "What the hell's a *lemon drop*?"

"Special delivery—when you try to sneak something to someone, especially something sweet," Roddy explained, glancing out the front window, eyeing the twentysomethings up the block, who were still zipping on scooters up and down the street. "Looks like a normal meeting—two guys saying hi—but what you don't see is that as they go in for the bro hug, they pass a note, or a phone . . . In jail once, we caught a mom trying to pass her son a diamond stud earring that she was hiding in her mouth."

Elijah approached the tap on the far left, closest to their table, and there was a *beep beep* as he poured a cider named Suicider. "It was the same with Salty and his dying daughter."

"So the daughter really had cancer?"

Elijah finished his pour and didn't say a word until he returned to the table. "Stage four leukemia. I wouldn't wish it on my worst enemy," he finally explained, glancing over his own shoulder for a quick scan of the bar. Everyone was lost in their own conversations. "But that night at Grandma's Pantry, Salty didn't give two turds about his daughter's cancer. His real goal was his very own lemon drop. As he hugged her goodbye, he was going to secretly whisper in her ear the bank account number for the twenty-two million in arms profits he'd been hiding from the government."

"Son of a bitch," Zig said.

"Literally and figuratively. According to the warehouse's security cameras, at 11:43 P.M., all four of them met up inside the walk-in freezer. Six minutes after that, the freezer door opened. Salty and his daughter were both dead at the Marshals' hands. Multiple bullet wounds to the head and chest."

"So you're saying the Marshals—you think they killed Salty and his daughter to get their money?"

"That's why our unit got the call," Elijah explained, taking a sip of Suicider and grabbing an orange Starburst. "They needed an outside investigative team with no dog in the fight. Within an hour of the shooting, Colonel Mint's phone rang. Then he reached out to me and Rashida—"

"Why *you*?" Roddy interrupted.

Peeling open the orange Starburst, Elijah shot a look at Roddy. "Anyone ever teach him manners?" Elijah asked Zig.

"I looked up the jurisdiction," Roddy said. "Security for Grandma's Pantry is done by the Marshals Service, which explains why P.G. and Titus picked that as a meeting place. But if there's a break-in—or a murder—that's a federal building, meaning jurisdiction goes to the FBI. So why did a top secret military unit—Semper Vigiles—get the call?"

Zig stared at Elijah, who was now chewing on his Starburst, a fat round lump in his cheek. It was a good question.

"Military blood," Elijah finally said.

"Pardon?"

"The SNS storehouses were designed to keep civilians safe. But if you've got the right clearance, you know they also have an additional mission: DOD storage," Elijah explained, referring to the Department of Defense. "All the extra blood for our troops—Army, Navy, Air Force, Marines—plus all military force protection from Ebola, smallpox, and all the rest . . . the warehouses store all of it. So when those gunshots went off that night, Pentagon phones started ringing off the hook."

"They thought it was a foreign attack?" Zig asked.

"Lemme say it like this," Elijah said, pulling another Starburst—a yellow one—from the bowl. "Three thousand service members have been killed in Afghanistan—but you tamper with our spare blood or the vaccinations that're stored in these warehouses? We'd be burying our young men and women by the *battalions*."

It made Zig think of those days at Dover when U.S. troops were helping battle Ebola in Liberia. Contaminated bodies weren't allowed to be sent home. Instead, they were bagged and put in mass graves.

"Crack of dawn the following morning, Mint, Rashida, and I arrived at Grandma's Pantry. Nola showed up an hour or so later," Elijah explained, his voice slowing down as he tossed the yellow Starburst back in the bowl, unopened. All his ease was gone, like he was suddenly talking about his own funeral. "Truthfully, it was a pretty standard sweep—examining the blood spatter . . . collecting footage from security cams . . ."

"What did the Marshals—?"

"P.G. and Titus," Elijah corrected.

"Exactly—what did P.G. and Titus have to say?"

"That's the question, isn't it? Mint and the rest of us interrogated them for two hours. According to P.G. and Titus, they were simply doing their jobs—facilitating a final father-daughter visit in an SNS storehouse, one of the most secure facilities in the country. The location was a bit odd, but otherwise, it's standard procedure. But when they started questioning Salty about his missing twenty-two million dollars . . . they said that's when the old man lost his temper, charging straight at them and trying to grab their guns. In the close confines of the freezer, well . . . you know how these things go. *We were just trying to defend ourselves*."

"They were lying," Roddy said, his focus across the room, at the consultant with the ankle holster.

"Of course they were lying," Elijah said.

"So what'd they say when you confronted them?" Zig asked.

"It was actually kinda hard to tell, considering P.G. and Titus were both found dead later that same night—facedown in a gravel parking lot of what had to be one of the very last Bennigan's in the country. Single shots to the temple. Military kills," Elijah said, putting a finger gun to his own head and pulling the pretend trigger. "Oh, and Salty's twenty-two million? Right after our interrogation—*poof*—the twenty-two million suddenly magically disappeared as well."

"Oh, crap," Zig muttered, nearly knocking over his beer.

"*Oh, crap,* for sure. According to the time stamp on the wire transfer, the money went missing right after our interrogation. So when it came to making the suspect list, it went downhill from there."

77

"So they thought someone from your team stole the money."

"That's when the full hurricane hit," Elijah said, fidgeting with the bowl of Starbursts. "They started pointing fingers at me . . . at Mint and Rashida . . . at Nola . . . For all we knew, it could've been someone on the inside at the Marshals . . ."

". . . or the white nationalists, taking revenge for shooting their pal Salty," Zig pointed out.

"We told them the same. None of us knew what happened to the money, but in the military, when two of your suspects suddenly show up dead and twenty-two million dollars goes missing . . . They had to launch an internal inquiry—led by everyone's favorite uptight sphincter."

"Colonel O. J. Whatley."

"*Major* Whatley back then. He had a year on me, two years on Mint, but we'd all come up together," Elijah explained. "The fact they put him on the case showed he was pulling ahead, and to prove them all right, he dove right in. The first person he cleared was—surprise—everyone's favorite straight arrow, his pal Mint."

"How'd they know Mint was clean?" Roddy asked.

"They didn't. But at military bases, y'know those private side entrances that they have on buildings—the ones just for top commanders so they can feel important? Mint had access to those entrances . . . but he always walked through the regular door with the rest of us. No question, O.J. would clear him first. Then he cleared Rashida, despite the fact that everyone knew she and Mint sometimes did use those side entrances, since they were sleeping together for the better part of a year. And then . . . lemme say it like this—"

"He blamed it on you and Nola," Zig said.

Elijah started to laugh, a low rumble that sounded like it came from the earth's core. "O.J. couldn't point the finger at us without evidence, but in the right hands, there's an art to properly wrecking someone's military career. To make us pay, he issued a finding of *no fault*—nothing bad, nothing good—the death knell for an officer who needs good reports for promotions. Nola got sent back to her command—as Artist-in-Residence, it didn't change much for her. But for me, career-wise, it was enough of a stink that I was done. My next evaluation was, let's just say, below center mass. From there, I had a choice: get passed up for promotion, or leave Army life behind. For O.J., it was a hell of a chess move. Bloodless execution."

Roddy cocked his head. "Why'd he want to single you out?"

"Have you met O.J.? He's a proud Black man who was determined to make full-bird colonel, then general. At the time, I was a proud Black man also trying to make colonel, then general. Guess how many spots for proud Black generals he thought there were? I'll give you a hint: him and only him," Elijah said, raising his glass in a mock toast. "That first year, at nearly forty years old, the best job I could find was working alcohol concessions for the Trenton Tigers," he added, referring to the local minor league NHL team. "Though God bless it for showing me the power of beer. Three minority-owned-business loans later, I was able t—"

"Can we go back to last night?" Zig interrupted. "You said O.J. was here at the bar—asking questions. What was he—?"

"Nola," Elijah said. "That's the only thing he cared about. Wanted to know where she was. Had I seen her? Did I know who she was with?"

"Mhmm," Roddy whispered, more to himself than anyone else.

"What'd you tell him?" Zig asked.

"You're joking, right? That walking piece of excrement wrecked my life. You really think I'd tell him what I found?"

Zig's ears perked up. He shot Elijah a look.

Roddy did, too. "Mr. Elijah, what do you know about my sister?"

Elijah unwrapped another Starburst, a red one. An awkward silence hung in the air.

"Elijah, please, we're on your side here," Zig said. "You see what this case is doing to Nola—the way she's sneaking around, making mistakes she never makes. You should've seen the way her hands were shaking. She's clearly at the core of this . . . and you obviously have something you're not saying . . ."

Elijah sat there silently, popping the red candy in his mouth. Did he trust these two? Not really. But in the end, if they were here to help Nola, then by extension, maybe they could help him.

"If I had answers, you'd have them already," Elijah said. "All I've got is a theory, okay?"

"What kinda theory?" Zig challenged.

"When O.J. strolled in here last night, all smiles and charm, I almost— I'll just say it pissed me off, which I'm not proud of, but that's what it did. It's the only reason I even took a look."

"A look at what?" Zig asked.

"Employment records," Elijah said. "You have to understand . . . all those years ago, when everything went down at Grandma's Pantry, the government fired everyone who worked there—every staffer who was anywhere near the storehouse that night: the warehouse supervisor, the vaccine manager on call, the lift operator, all the security guys, of course . . . even the maintenance and janitorial staff. But last night, when O.J. left, I couldn't help myself. I called a buddy who does surveillance work for the Pentagon—he owes me for setting him up with his second wife. The point being, I asked him to pull the staff list for Grandma's Pantry. Accidentally, he sent me the *current* list rather than the old one."

"I'm not sure I follow," Zig said.

"You will. On the list was a guy named Axel Padilla."

Zig made a face. The name didn't ring a bell.

"He's a security guard at Grandma's Pantry," Elijah explained. "Low-level guy, one of the many hired by the Marshals."

"Back then or now?" Zig asked.

"That's the kicker. Axel is a pretty memorable name, which made me look twice at it—and then I saw it, glowing on my computer screen: Axel Padilla is on the *current* list of guards . . . but also on the *original* list from five years ago."

"I thought you said the Marshals fired everyone."

"That's what I thought. Except, apparently, for a guy named Axel. He's the one and only person who was there on the night when Salty was killed, the next day, when the twenty-two million went missing—and also, for reasons that defy all logic, still somehow has a job working security there today."

Zig sat there a moment, watching a few stray bubbles rise in his craft beer. "Think he's a whistleblower?"

"That was my thought—though he could be anything," Elijah said, knowing there were plenty of cases where a whistleblower was so helpful, the government brought them back to the job once the disaster passed.

"This guy Axel, where's he right now?" Zig asked.

"I have no clue. He was a night guy, so maybe . . . at work?"

"It's a good idea," Zig said, taking a final swig of beer and heading for the door.

"Where the hell're you going?" Elijah asked.

"You tell me: Do you know where Grandma's Pantry is?"

"Yeah, but—"

"Great," Zig said. "Show me."

78

His favorite part was picking the music.

Today, most elevators have stopped playing overhead music, but when you buy your own, you can choose to play whatever you want. According to a leading communications expert, music in an elevator is like "amniotic fluid that surrounds us. It never startles us, it is never too loud . . . it's always there." It's why the saleswoman at Atlas Elevators suggested soundtracks with names like *Easy Listening* and *Calm Pop*.

"You want to be in the *background,* not the *foreground,*" she'd told him.

But screw it. *Who the hell wants to live life in the background?* he'd decided, picking a soundtrack with Grandmaster Flash and a ton of Marvin Gaye.

Indeed, his office was so quiet, as the elevator made its way up, he could hear the faint beat of "Got to Give It Up."

Within seconds, the green digital indicator light lit up, but didn't ping. They'd turned the ping off months ago for being too annoying.

The elevator doors slid open as the man craned his neck, looking to see just how bad the rest of his day would be.

Sure enough, Nola stormed out of the elevator, pistol at the ready. She spotted the man instantly, in the open doorway of his office. He had a knife of a nose and a leprechaun smile.

Nola plowed toward him, her pistol aimed straight at his face. Her lower lip was split. At least Dominic got a lucky punch in.

"Relax, I'm not your enemy. Not even armed," he insisted, hands in the air, signaling his own surrender. "Friends, okay? *Friends?* Adrian Vess," he said, offering a handshake.

Nola stayed silent, her finger on the trigger. "I know you're the one who did this."

"I hate to break it to you, kid, but you don't know nothing," Mr. Vess said, hand still in the air. Heading for his office, he motioned for her to follow. "Now, c'mon—I got something you're gonna like," he added, his leprechaun smile widening. "I promise, I won't bite."

79

"Suck it, fartwizard!"

"Kevin!" Nana Dotty scolded, her grandson barely reacting. "Apologies, Ms. Waggs, he's just— Boys are animals."

"I have a son," Waggs agreed, sitting at a tiny faux-wood kitchen table that was built for two, but had three seats around it. From a mug that read "What Happens at Grandma's Stays at Grandma's," Waggs pretended to enjoy the instant coffee that had all the flavor of backwash. In the living room, two boys—Kevin and his brother—were frantically jumping on a sagging orange couch, playing an old Wii baseball video game like it was a cardio workout.

"Swallow *that*!" the shorter boy yelled, hitting what appeared to be a digital triple.

"Paul!" Nana Dotty shouted, wearing a sheen of exhaustion that only comes when you're eighty years old and your daughter's opioid habit leaves you raising two tween boys.

"You were saying about his accident," Waggs began.

"Actually, ma'am, I hadn't said anything," Nana Dotty replied, taking a long sip of coffee. "My daughter's been arrested five times, Ms. Waggs. So forgive me for being suspicious when someone with a badge knocks on my door."

Waggs took a breath, noticing that above the stove, above the fridge, above every single doorway including the bathroom, was a metal horseshoe, for good luck. Right about now, she needed it. "Can we go back to his brain injury?"

"You wouldn't even know from looking at him."

Waggs nodded, eyeing Paul—the younger of the two boys—swinging his Wii controller like a bat. He limped slightly, his movements jerky, like his left side wasn't wired quite right. But the way he kept shoving his older brother, Paul had real swagger, even at age nine.

"Ever been in a car accident, Ms. Waggs? On that night, they were two blocks away. Literally, two blocks," Nana said, her body shifting as she relived the moment. "It was late, and Paul—he'd just turned six and had fallen asleep, so Casey . . . my daughter . . . When she carried him to the car—it was two blocks—so she let him lay across the back seat. No seat belt. The other car . . . it was moving full speed and coming head-on . . ."

"Oh, no."

Nana didn't say anything else. She just shook her head, her thumbnail scratching at a nick in her coffee mug. "The way his skull split—Dr. Sandberg said we should prepare for the worst."

Waggs looked over at the two boys, who were still lost in their video game.

"Three months later," Nana explained, "he wakes up out of the coma, asking to watch *Sesame Street,* which I swear, he hadn't watched since he was little. A month after that, he's running around—with a limp, sure—but running around like nothing ever happened. Our pastor called it a miracle. That's the only word for it. Same word your friend used. The painter."

"Nola," Waggs and Nana said simultaneously.

Waggs nodded, though *miracle* didn't sound like a word that Nola ever used—that is, unless she was trying to get a grandmother's permission to paint young Paul.

"One last question," Waggs began. "Why'd you say yes?"

"Pardon?"

"With your grandsons . . . You seem quite protective—rightfully so. But if that's the case, why'd you let Nola into your house to do a painting?"

At first, Nana Dotty didn't answer.

"Ma'am, if Nola did something, or threatened you—"

"She paid me. A hundred bucks, okay? And before you give me a look, y'know what it takes to feed growing boys? And the physical therapy on top of that?" She pointed over to both boys standing on her couch, shouting at the TV. "You wanna pay me to paint my grandkid for an hour? You can come to my house every damn night."

Waggs nodded, glancing at Paul, then picturing the two senior citizens who she'd visited at the other two facilities earlier today. Three different patients. Three different incidents. Three different outcomes. The only thing they had in common? A traumatic brain injury. And a near impossible recovery.

At that, Waggs replayed Lieutenant Colonel Mint, three nights ago, sitting in the back seat of his car, a single bullet burrowing into his head. Was that what Nola was looking for? Did she know Mint's murder was coming—and she was trying to help him survive the attack? Or did she have a hand in it—was she the one who was supposed to pull the trigger—and she was trying to figure out how to do the least amount of damage?

It made Waggs think back to last night, to Nola curled down like a fist in Waggs's back seat. Whatever was really going on, Nola wasn't gunning for Colonel Mint. She was hurt by his death, reminding Waggs of what Zig said: that Roddy was asking his own questions. At first, Waggs had assumed Roddy was looking for Nola, but what if that was the part Waggs had wrong? What if *Nola* was the one looking for *him*? It was a fair question, especially considering everything Nola asked about Black House. What was it she said? That she saw someone in Mint's account—

Wait.

Mint's Black House account.

Pulling out her phone and excusing herself from the table, Waggs dialed a number she never liked dialing. It rang once . . . twice . . .

"What is it, my precious?" a man teased in a poor *Lord of the Rings* impression.

"Gary, I need you to not be weird for once. Just tell me: When someone logs into Black House . . . do we keep a record of where they're logging in from?"

80

"You're the one who hired the Reds," Nola said, her gun aimed at his face.

Mr. Vess rolled his eyes, which were brown and threaded with hints of orange. He was pear-shaped, with copper skin and a slicked-back expensive haircut that came to a perfect widow's peak. *New money or old money?* Nola eyed the intricate gold chain around his neck, made up of tiny male and female figures intertwined in a sexual 69 position. *New money.*

"You do realize you can lower the gun," Vess said without looking back as Nola followed him into his office.

He didn't seem upset. Emotional sweat—from stress, fear, or pain—is most evident on the palms, forehead, and some sweat patterns on the scalp. Mr. Vess had none of it. If anything, he seemed polished. Fancy tan loafers. Matching belt. And a fashionably untucked white shirt that was clearly altered to hide his girth. But no amount of money could hide the odd slant of his knuckles on his pinkie and ring fingers. *Boxer's break,* they called it. *From fighting bare-handed.* Nola made a note. *Plus the fact he led with his right.*

"Water? Seltzer?" Vess offered, pronouncing each word slowly, carefully, with true precision. *Former stutterer? Or just trying to impress wi—*

Nola never finished the thought. As she entered his office, she caught sight of his . . . *look at all the art.*

There was a canvas on each wall, plus a triptych behind his antique partners desk. She lowered her gun without even realizing.

Most corporate artwork is picked to match the color of the walls—or worse, modern trash that's expensive only because it came from an overpriced gallery. But these . . .

"You like the paintings," Mr. Vess said.

Nola did, though she'd never say it.

Each was an oil painting, though none of them felt stuffy or old. On the left wall was a woman in profile, her sundress bathed in light as she cupped and admired a pink rose, reminding Nola of a classic Waterhouse. Another—a steep cliffside with a tangerine sky in a thunderstorm—reminded her of a Delacroix. This was a curated collection.

For a moment, she told herself this was what she never wanted—art captured and locked away—but God, did she love being so close to something this good.

"Don't look so shocked that I've got taste," Vess said.

He also had Frogger, Nola noticed, eyeing the video game in the corner.

"You a fan? Want to play?" he asked, following her gaze to the machine.

He was sharp—more observant than she expected—and unafraid to use it to his advantage. He didn't get here just by those crooked knuckles.

"Your loss. I got first game," Vess said, heading for Frogger.

Nola raised her gun again. She had a commander who used to do this—act like he didn't have a care. But men in charge? They always have a care.

"Ask whatever you came to ask," Vess said, hitting the 2-UP button as the Frogger theme started to play.

"I know about Zion Lopez," Nola said, lowering her gun, though not by much. "I was at his house."

"I don't know who that is."

That was a lie. She knew it before he even touched his gold chain, running his fingertips along the length of the naked figures.

"Zion called you a few hours before he died," she explained. "He's a petty drug dealer. My theory is, you're his supplier. Maybe you brought him in for some odd jobs."

Vess tapped the joystick upward, eyes never leaving the screen. "Y'know why I love this game? You move the frog and go home. That's it. One simple objective. Don't you wish life was as clear as that?"

"Mr. Vess, I want to know about—"

"Archie Mint," Vess said.

Nola froze. There was a loud *plink* as Frogger leaped into one of his frog homes at the top of the screen. Vess was still in profile, his shoulders back, no fear at all.

"*Colonel* Mint," Nola corrected, feeling the gun in her hand, her finger sliding toward the trigger.

"Oh, c'mon—I knew that'd be your first question," Vess said, his fist tightening around the joystick. "I told you from the start, I'm on your side. Archie Mint may've loved playing the golden boy, but don't you wanna know what he was doing in private?"

81

"Lower the gun," Vess insisted. "I told you, I want the same thing you—"

Pulling back the slide and cocking the gun, Nola aimed it at Vess's foot and pulled the trigger.

A tiny black hole appeared near the big toe of Vess's shoe. A crimson puddle bubbled up, then disappeared, like a broken water fountain. It took half a second before he realized it was his blood and screamed out in pain. *"My toe! You shot my toe!"* he exploded, hopping backward and holding the Frogger machine for balance. *"Are you outta your fuckin—!?"*

She pointed the gun at his leg. "I'm gonna shoot you in the calf next, then work my way to your femur. I broke my femur before. You won't like it," she said. "Your pain is now in your hands. Tell me what you know about Colonel Mint."

"D'you understand what I'm gonna do to you for—?"

Nola aimed at his calf and pulled the trigger.

Vess felt a needle prick, a bite of electricity. Instinctively, he swatted at his calf, but was already off balance, falling sideways and crashing to the floor.

"GHAAAAH! What in the hell is—? Why would you do that!" He clenched his teeth, pulling off his leather belt to make a makeshift tourniquet. He'd been shot before, or saw a few too many war movies. *"Christ Almighty, that HURTS!"* he shouted, his face already going pale. *"Why would you—? I said I was on your side!"*

"I want to know about Colonel Mint."

"What do you think I was trying t—!?"

She pointed the gun at his thigh, her finger on the trigger.

"Stop! Stop! Just listen . . . Zion . . . He . . . he . . . he—"

"I know Zion pulled the trigger on Mint. I also know Zion worked for you—he sold drugs for you. You're a street boss, maybe a state boss if you're lucky. That's correct, yes? He was your employee?"

Vess nodded over and over, his eyes starting to flood with tears. Snot ran from his nose. His leprechaun smile was gone. "My leg . . . I need a doctor."

"Mr. Vess, look at me. Are you looking? I need you to think carefully about your next words. When Zion killed Mint—did you give Zion that order?"

"I swear on my life . . . on my daughter's life . . . Zion's a dreamer, all hustle. A little spic CEO. Sold Molly and K2 like they were Tickle Me Elmos on Christmas. That's why I brought him on . . . But with Mint . . . my hand to God, Zion was freelancing—and he knew, I don't stand for freelancing."

"So you called the Reds."

"You think I had a choice!? He killed a local military hero—that's like . . . it's like putting a bullet in the head of the mayor. Y'know how many eyes that brings toward Zion . . . toward my business? That's why I told you . . . I-I'm on your side . . . whoever hired Zion to kill Mint . . . I want to find them just as much as you do."

Another lie, or at least a partial one. Vess wasn't in this for justice—he wanted containment, to keep his drug enterprise from being exposed, which was all too likely when Zion suddenly brought it this much attention. Still, that explained why the Reds turned their attention to Zig . . . and presumably anyone else sniffing where they weren't supposed to. But it still didn't make sense.

The Reds were pros. When they went to see Zion, they wouldn't have left without asking the most vital question. "This is your femoral artery," Nola said, digging the barrel of her gun into his thigh. "If you bleed out, you're gonna ruin these nice floors. So tell me, Mr. Vess: Who hired Zion to kill Mint?"

82

Vess's hands were shaking, still struggling to knot the belt around his calf. As he fought to pull it tight, blood was already soaking the cuff of his pants. "Did you really have to shoot me?"

Nola started to squeeze the trigger.

"O-On my desk! There's photos! The iPad! That's what they sent me! Hand to God, that's what I was—that's what I wanted to show you!"

"Stop talking," Nola said, heading for his desk. As she grabbed the iPad, she couldn't help but steal another quick glance at his paintings.

"The pass code is all zeroes," Vess called out.

Nola rolled her eyes.

A few clicks later, she was staring at a text from a 215 number: Philadelphia. No written message, just two photos—the first of Mint and Rashida sitting at a table in what looked like a nice restaurant. This wasn't the steak house; it was somewhere else. It had a hidden-camera feel, both of them smiling and leaning toward each other in a way that former coworkers weren't supposed to lean toward each other.

From the crow's-feet at Mint's eyes, this wasn't an old photo. This was recent.

"You see it, right? Like a dog in heat. At Mint's funeral . . . they filled a gymnasium . . . *Pennsylvania's local hero and golden Boy Scout.* But he was just another cheater, sleeping around on his wife with some Black piece of—"

With a violent kick, Nola pounded her heel into Vess's wound.

"*FUUUUUH!*" he screamed, rolling sideways, hugging his knee toward his chin.

"Who sent these?" Nola asked, swiping to the iPad's next photo. It was a screenshot, literally—someone had held up their phone to snap a picture of a computer screen. The image was pixelated and harder to read, but it looked like an online bank statement.

On the far right were deposits—dozens of them, at least one a day—$8,500, $9,500, $9,200—always just below $10,000, the amount that Nola knew triggered banks to send a report to the IRS. Whoever this money belonged to, they were working hard not to be seen.

In the last month alone, total deposits were over $242,000.

Account Name: Mint, Archibald C.

A sharp pain stabbed Nola's throat, like she'd swallowed a needle that sliced her as it descended toward her stomach. Mint was in the reserves, making sixty thousand dollars a year. Where was he suddenly getting this cash?

"You said the Reds found these photos?" she asked.

"On Zion's phone," Vess explained, still clenching his leg in pain.

Nola closed her eyes, the iPad feeling like an anvil in her hand. *Mongol . . . Faber . . . Staedtler . . .*

"Salty Trebbiano," Nola announced. "Does that name mean anything to you?"

Vess glanced upward, clearly lost.

Nola swiped back to the first photo, of Mint and Rashida eating at the restaurant. Slowly . . . finally . . . the walls of the maze were starting to crumble.

Five years ago at Grandma's Pantry, arms dealer Salty Trebbiano was killed, and his twenty-two million went missing. After Mint and the rest of his Semper Vigiles team raced in to investigate, two dirty U.S. Marshals also showed up dead, turning every person there—Mint, Rashida, Elijah, and of course Nola herself—into instant suspects. In the weeks that followed, O.J. drove the internal review. To this day, Nola assumed one of Salty's white supremacist groups was behind it all, but in the end, the only truth was this: whoever took the money got away with it.

That is, Nola thought, until a few years passed, and maybe, they finally started spending it.

With another swipe at the iPad, Nola glanced down at Mint's bank account, now flush with nearly a quarter of a million in the last month alone. The needle in her throat expanded, thick as a nail, pushing out from inside her skin. Nola shook her head, praying she had it wrong. All these years . . . all the good Mint had done . . . all he'd done *for her*. *Sir, you're supposed to be better than this.*

Just the thought of it made her feel gutted, exposed . . . and so damn naïve. It also made her feel something else, like someone was yanking an ancient piece of armor from her chest, one that she didn't even realize she'd been wearing.

She replayed it all, reshuffling the details. From the photo, it looked like Mint was once again cheating on his wife with Rashida. That, she could deal with. Good men make dumb decisions every day. But did that mean that he was the one who killed two U.S. Marshals and took twenty-two million dollars that night at Grandma's Pantry? Maybe. Or maybe someone else took it, and Mint—or Rashida—somehow found out about it. Could that be where Mint's deposits were coming from—a hush payment, or Mint asking for his own cut? That actually made more sense, especially considering the one trapdoor at the center of the maze: that Mint and Rashida were dead. Someone ordered that hit—and from the sums in Mint's account . . . that money came from somewhere. Find the missing twenty-two million, and she'd find who was really behind this.

It wasn't a long suspect list. With a final swipe backward, Nola spread her fingers, enlarging the original photo of Mint and Rashida. With them gone, the only remaining team members from Grandma's Pantry were O.J. and—

"*Elijah,*" Nola blurted.

"The guy with the bar," Vess said, still clutching his leg on the floor.

Nola turned. "What'd you say?"

"*Elijah*. That's his name, right?" Vess said. "The Reds . . . they mentioned him . . . said he had a bar. Selling faggoty microbrews."

"Who told them that?"

"No idea. They said—"

Nola leaned closer, giving Vess a deep, long look at the fight he didn't realize he was picking. Later tonight, Vess would still be thinking about her stare. Her eyes were patient, like they knew something was coming. There weren't many people who knew about Elijah, much less that he had a bar. Zig was one, though he'd never share info with the Reds—which left . . . "Mr. Vess, how do you know my brother?" Nola asked.

"Your *brother*?"

"Roddy LaPointe. He's a cop in Jersey—and a general scumbag. You're a drug boss in Philly. Barely an hour and a half from each other. You're telling me that's just coincidence?"

Vess stopped, glancing up. He was still in pain, but his brow was furrowed. He looked lost, confused. "Roddy? That's an actual name? *Roddy?*"

Vess didn't know him. It made no sense. To track Vess here, Nola had relied on his listing in the Special Identities Unit. It was a watchdog list—the ultimate *Do Not Disturb*—usually for people the government had under surveillance. But one of the other biggest groups on that list? CIs. Confidential informants. Some were petty criminals, but some were bosses themselves—ratting out their fellow scumbags, hoping that the government, or even a local cop, might turn a blind eye or somehow take it easy on them.

"So you're not Roddy's informant?" Nola asked. "That's not how your paths first crossed?"

"If I'm gonna rat, you really think I'd pick a dink cop? At least bring in the feds," he stuttered, though it sounded like an insult.

She pointed her gun at Vess's head. "Mr. Vess, I want to know who told the Reds about Elijah."

"This guy Elijah— You think he's the one who did this?"

She grabbed the trigger and quickly pulled—

"*Ask them!* Ask the Reds! I-I don't know shit! I swear on my daughter!"

Nola stood there for half a second, pressing her gun into Vess's widow's peak. His face was white. Not from fear. He was losing blood. Fast. "Email or phone?" she asked.

"I don't underst—"

"When the Reds contacted you, email or . . . ?"

"Phone . . . in my . . . it's in my desk . . . top drawer . . ." Vess insisted.

Crossing to the other side of the desk, Nola pulled out an old Motorola flip phone that reminded her of a girl she used to hate in junior high. On the corner of the desk, next to the keyboard, she spotted a new iPhone. She grabbed that, too.

"*Yo, that's my phone!* You can't—I need that to call an ambulance!" Vess shouted.

Nola was already at the door, checking the pass code. All zeroes again. *Moron.*

"*I'm serious! If you leave and I pass out—!*"

Vess was still yelling as Nola stepped into the elevator and pulled out her own phone, dialing Zig's number. No answer. She glanced at the time. For sure, he would've reached Elijah's by now—or even Grandma's Pantry. Zig had no idea about the twenty-two million—or what he was walking into. Nola pounded the Door Close button with the heel of her hand.

"*You're never gonna get there in time!*" Vess shouted as the doors slid shut. "*Your friend the mortician . . . if he's headed there . . . he's already dead!*"

83

"If you need to go, go now."

None of them moved—Zig, Roddy, or Elijah—all three staying in the car, staring straight ahead at the Sunoco minimart, where four twentysomething guys walked out the front door.

"That's a lotta backwards hats," Zig said.

"Jersey," Elijah offered.

Zig nodded, turning back to his phone, where he was texting with Waggs.

You free??? she had asked with extra question marks. Zig knew what that meant.

You found something, didn't you? Zig texted. Tell me.

You still with Shaggy and Scooby?

Tell me what you found, Zig texted.

Voicemail from tech guy Gary. Was about to call him back. Thought you might want to join.

Zig's eyes slid sideways toward Elijah, who was on his own phone, Facebook-scrolling by the looks of it.

Can't. Lemme know what he says, Zig texted back. Waggs gave it a little thumbs-up.

Three gray dots appeared onscreen. Then finally: Any Nola sighting?

Zig checked the rearview, still convinced she couldn't be far.

"Actually, I do have to go. To the bathroom," Roddy added, opening the car door and sliding out. He took a few steps toward the minimart, then doubled back and knocked on Zig's window.

"Everything okay?" Zig asked, tucking his phone in his pocket.

"They have ice cream sandwiches," Roddy said, pointing to a sign in the window showing a Fat Boy ice cream sandwich propped up on a Chipwich. "Buy one get one free," he explained. "I can't resist an ice cream sandwich. Want me to grab one for you?"

"I'm good," Zig said.

"Mr. Elijah?"

"I'm fine, too," Elijah added from the passenger seat.

"I'll probably get an extra anyway. Y'know, buy-one-get-one," Roddy said, heading toward the minimart.

For a moment, Zig and Elijah sat there, watching through the windshield as the crowd of twentysomethings took a look at Roddy's police uniform and parted around him. Roddy disappeared inside without acknowledging any of them.

"His belt doesn't quite go through all the loops, does it?" Elijah asked.

"I like to think he's got the parachute, but he might be missing the rip cord."

Elijah started to laugh, but his face was serious. "You sure you trust him?"

"Who? *Roddy?* He's . . ." Zig paused. "It's complicated."

"It shouldn't be. I get that he's worried about his sister, but where we're going . . . this security guard Axel . . . if he's even there . . . if he knows something about the twenty-two million . . . You really think we should put Roddy in the center of that?"

There was a click from the gas pump—the tank was filled—then a loud knock at the window. Zig jumped at the sound of the attendant—a curly-haired kid wearing an *Elliot in the Morning* button on his surprisingly clean Sunoco shirt, and yet another backward cap—knocking on the window. "Thirty-seven twenty-seven," Curly Hair said.

Zig gave him two twenties, pantomiming to keep the change.

"At the bar, when you said you spoke to Nola, the way he jumped at you . . . exploding instantly," Elijah added. "When someone's got a fuse that short, you don't sit them next to the dynamite."

"I'm not saying he's not weird."

"Weird is fine. We're all weird, brother. Back in the day, his sister was weird, too. But Roddy and his little fuse? Lemme say it like this: When we're trying to talk our way inside Grandma's Pantry, you sure he won't detonate?"

It made Zig think back to Roddy gripping his shoulder—that empty look in Roddy's eyes, when a switch seemed to flip. Or when the Reds attacked, and Roddy savagely pummeled Seabass's face over and over and over. Was that normal behavior? Of course not—though the attack on Seabass probably saved Zig's life. That had to count for something, right?

Zig took a breath, eyeing Roddy in the minimart, heading for the freezer. From day one, Roddy had been working this case as hard as anyone. Their interests were aligned—and if Zig was being honest, without Roddy, they might've never gotten this far, much less found Elijah.

In the end, though, Zig kept coming back to what he always came back to: Nola. To see her at the funeral home, hiding in the bathroom, scrambling to open the window, practically smashing through the glass to get away from her brother . . . She was running from him. And Nola never ran from anyone.

"You don't know who he is at his core," Nola had warned.

It was an overdramatic thing to say, but the question remained: Who did Zig believe?

Inside the minimart, Roddy opened the freezer case, letting the cool air waft over him, his arms wide, like he'd just conquered Everest.

"Elijah, how much farther did you say Grandma's Pantry was?"

"Twenty minutes, tops," Elijah replied. "If it makes you feel better, we can call him an Uber or a—"

Zig pulled out his phone to send Waggs a text. Instead, he saw a text from his wife. Call me. I'm on M's case, Charmaine wrote, using the single initial they always used for their daughter.

It'd have to wait. Swiping back to Waggs's question—Any Nola sighting?—Zig sent a final text. She's gotta be close. He then started the car and put it in drive. Roddy was still in the minimart, grabbing his ice cream sandwiches.

"It's the right call," Elijah said as they pulled out of the gas station.

Picking up speed and veering toward the turnpike, Zig kept glancing in the rearview, the minimart shrinking behind them, a pinprick in the darkness.

He was already second-guessing himself—but he didn't slow down.

84

"They slowing down?" Reagan asked, glancing over at the handheld GPS that Seabass was clutching in the passenger seat. A half hour ago, onscreen, a small red triangle weaved down Shoemaker Boulevard, leaving Elijah's craft beer bar and heading for the turnpike. Zig and Roddy were on the move—but now, finally, they were pumping the brakes, pulling into a rest stop, by the looks of it.

"Gas break," Reagan realized.

Seabass agreed, studying the map. They weren't far. Time to close the gap.

Tugging the steering wheel and veering into the turnpike's right lane, Reagan punched the gas, blowing past a stubborn Mazda with a bumper sticker that read: *I was an Honor Student—I don't know what happened!*

They both read the sticker; they both glanced at each other. Seabass's eyes curled into a grin, the baseball-sized gauze shifting on his cheek.

"Sebby, don't laugh at dumb jokes like that. If you do, we get more of—"

A phone buzzed, both of them now eyeing the cheap silver flip phone vibrating in the cup holder. Caller ID showed a number they'd never seen before—but they knew who it was.

The first time he called, they ignored it. Second time, too. This was the third, all within a few minutes.

Seabass shot her a look. *Maybe he knows where they're headed.*
The phone rang again.

Reagan rolled her eyes. "Ellis Jewelers," she answered.

"I call you three times, and you don't pick up!?" Mr. Vess exploded. *"Are you forgetting who you work f—!?"*

Reagan hung up, tossing the phone back in the cup holder.

Is that really helpful? Seabass said with a head shake.

Vvvttttttt, the phone buzzed again. She let it ring once more. Just to teach Vess a lesson.

"Have you learned to speak like an adult?" she finally answered, putting him on speaker.

"Do not pick a fight with me," Vess warned. "This is for your benefit. You're about to have a problem."

"Not until you tell me about this number. Where're you calling from?"

"Elberton General."

"The hospital? Why would y—?"

"BECAUSE I GOT SHOT IN THE FUCKING LEG! *And my toe! I lost my . . . she shot off my toe!"*

"Slow down. Who's *she?"*

"You think she left a business card? Skinny bitch. Silver and black hair. Eyes deader than yours, Reagan. The way she was talking . . . she said you know her brother . . . some cop. Roddy something."

"Roddy LaPointe," Reagan said, now curious as Seabass turned her way. "What'd she say about him?"

"I'm in a hospital gown with my ass hanging out! I don't care about him, or the mortician, or every other damn rando who can't seem to stay away from this giant shitfest Zion sucked us into. The *only* thing I give two craps about right now is *her.* From here on in, *she's* the mission. There must be *consequences!"*

Vess was still ranting as Reagan tossed a look toward the passenger seat. The moment Seabass was shot in the face, they were done with the job, done taking orders, done protecting Vess's business, and certainly done with his current revenge fantasy. From here on in, their only priority was Roddy.

"If it helps, you can track her," Vess added. "She has my . . . she took my phone and iPad."

"You mean the phone you've been calling *us* on?" Reagan challenged.

Seabass cocked an eyebrow. Earlier, they'd tossed Zion's phone to keep anyone from following. Even if she was on their trail, it wouldn't be hard to lose her again. Snatching the flip phone, Seabass opened the window to toss it outsi—

"*Don't,*" Reagan warned, grabbing his arm. She took back the phone as a whirlwind of air twisted through the car. Turning back to Vess, she added, "When did she leave your office?"

"Half hour ago, tops."

Reagan nodded, doing the math. They'd still reach Zig and Roddy first.

"You're not even listening, are you?" Vess asked. "For thirty years, I've been dealing with vengeful pricks. This girl, though . . . She's different. You can see it in her eyes—she's got broken parts inside."

"She sounds unbearable," Reagan said as Seabass nodded. Neither of them was worried. Like her dad taught, if you wanna hit the cover off a curveball, you just have to know when it's coming.

Reagan glanced down at the GPS. *Fourteen minutes to destination.* Plenty of time to be ready.

85

Zig was confused—and he never liked that.

A few miles back, when he first spotted one of the big green high-way signs with a little airplane graphic at the bottom, he didn't think much of it. On the New Jersey Turnpike, everything connects with the airport sooner or later.

Even when Elijah told him, "Next exit," and Zig pulled off at 13A—labeled *Elizabeth,* along with a bigger airplane graphic— Zig focused on the former, assuming this was just the first step to a smaller, less-trafficked area better able to hide a secret government facility. God knows, between the ports, freight yards, and all the sur-rounding warehouses and refineries, Newark was full of nondescript areas to choose from. Hell, it was big enough to hold the first U.S. IKEA. Yet as the exit ramp looped them into a wider stretch with multiple lanes . . .

"Stay in the middle," Elijah said, pointing to the lane labeled *Airport Traffic Only.*

Zig glanced around, searching the distance. The road narrowed and twisted, then narrowed even more, eventually dead-ending at a single-lane service road. In front of them, turnpike shrubbery gave way to a chain-link fence and signs for *Terminals A, B, C.* Home of Newark International Airport.

"Are we flying somewhere?" Zig asked.

Elijah flashed a grin.

Today, there are eleven undisclosed Strategic National Stockpiles—eleven Grandma's Pantry warehouses—carefully hidden across
the country. In choosing locations, all eleven were logistically situated
to maximize their ability to send supplies to the closest neighboring
states. Naturally, secrecy was also key. A stockpile in the Northwest
was located on a horse-breeding ranch, in a long aluminum-sided
building designed to look like a slaughterhouse in satellite photos.
The one in the Midwest was hidden in an old jelly bean factory. But
all eleven had one thing in common:

They were all near an airport—although only one was located
in one.

On Zig's left, a United 737 buzzed low in the night sky, its engines roaring as it came in for a landing.

"Don't look so shocked," Elijah teased. "It's why people love big
cities—so you can hide in plain sight."

"Wait . . . so Grandma's Pantry," Zig said, still glancing around,
"you're telling me it's—"

"You were expecting a neon sign? Make a left," Elijah said, pointing with his chin. "We're almost there."

86

This was Nola when she was fourteen.

Acne Steve had brought cigars to poker night. Nola didn't mind the stench—it was actually better than what Royall's friends usually smelled like. But when they smoked, they drank more, which meant they made more of a mess, which meant, for Nola, there was more to clean.

"C'mon, dickface, use an ashtray," Royall shouted at Repeating Francis, who smoked cloves just to be a pain. "Nola . . ."

On it, she said with a glance, already rushing to the kitchen to grab an extra ashtray.

Royall started to say something else.

"And pretzels. I saw," Nola added, eyeing the empty pretzel bowl on the foldable side table.

Across the room, Steve's son, Trey, looked up from his newest device—a T-Mobile Sidekick, a high-tech phone with its own QWERTY keyboard—then glanced back down, going back to whomever he was texting.

"Possible to get some more ice, please?" said chubby Digger from the gas station, who'd started wearing a Bluetooth earpiece to remind everyone he was now Assistant Manager Digger from Tire Kingdom. Nola knew it made him look like a tool, but Digger was the only one who ever said *please.*

"And a blow job. Can you get us one of those, hon?" Hartley Spencer teased, his narrow penny-colored eyes locked on Nola's ass.

"Hartley, don't be a turd," Digger scolded.

Nola ignored the joke—she'd heard worse—though she did take the long way around so Hartley wouldn't have a chance to sniff her.

As she passed Trey on the couch, the sulky tenth grader looked up, shaking his head at the adults. It was a moment of solidarity, though Nola didn't know how to read it. She just liked his light brown eyes, the color of iced tea, and was mesmerized by the all-knowing maturity and general hostility that he was endlessly directing at his own dad. Nola understood that better than anyone.

As a new hand was dealt, Royall and his friends debated their usual topics, like whether the girl at the Vin's Groceries deli counter had real tits or falsies, which quickly devolved into tearing Acne Steve apart for using the word *falsies* in front of his son.

In the kitchen, as Nola refilled the pretzel bowl, even she laughed at that. In truth, she liked these nights—life was better, or at least easier, when there were friends to keep Royall busy. She even found herself rooting for a few of them, like Repeating Francis . . . and for Digger, who would probably do better if he ever figured out that he would clench his teeth behind his lips and start counting everyone's chips every time he bluffed.

"Okay, donkeys, out of pity, I'll keep this small . . . one, two," Royall counted, tossing two orange chips—a hundred dollars—into the pot.

"I'm gonna push—I need to get my kid home," Acne Steve said, raising with four chips, everyone knowing that whenever he sounded like he was in a rush to leave, that meant he had a fantastic hand.

Not as good as Hartley's, though. "Check," Hartley said, trying to play it cool.

In the kitchen, Nola had pulled an ice tray from the freezer, twisting it back and forth, then grabbing a nearby knife to pry out the stubborn cubes.

"C'mon . . ." she said, wiggling the knife, working the far side of the tray and putting her weight into it, the knife now facing her own belly.

In the living room, Royall and his friends were getting louder. She was too preoccupied to hear it. To keep suspicion low, Royall only had her spy when his cards were good. This was one of those hands, though neither of them knew it at the time.

Gripping the knife with both hands, Nola wedged it toward herself, working it back and forth, the plastic tray sounding like it was about to crack. She pushed harder, her knuckles going red, until . . .

Thwip.

Just like that, the final cube popped out, sliding across the counter. Nola scooped it up, tossed it in a bowl, and grabbed it along with the pretzels and the ashtray.

". . . and I'll repop you to three hundred," Acne Steve said, tossing his chips into what had quickly become the biggest pot of the night.

"Call," Royall said, betting the same and eyeing Nola as she reentered the living room. She knew that look. Time to go to work.

"I'll raise to whatever Royall's got left," Hartley teased as Nola placed the pretzels on the side table. She was smart, taking her time before approaching the main table with the ice and ashtray. "To be honest, I wish you had some more, since I love robbing you blind."

"How much more you wanna raise to, *Norm*?" Royall challenged, using the name his favorite TV private eye used when he wanted to give someone a verbal shove.

"More than you got in that piss pot," Hartley shot back as Nola slowly rounded the table.

"I'm out," Acne Steve said, tossing his cards, knowing the result when it got this personal.

"Me, too. Fold," Digger said, the blue light blinking on his headset.

"Pick a number, pick whatever you want," Royall said, reaching for his watch. "I'll put my damn Piaget in if I have to."

"You think we don't know that watch is fake? C'mon, *Norm*," Hartley shot back. "Steve tried to sell us the exact same piece of garbage. You wanna make shit interesting, why don't you bet . . . I dunno . . ." Hartley's eyes narrowed into thin slits as he flashed his own devil's smile. *"Her,"* he said, eyeing Nola. "How 'bout betting *her*?"

"You're a skeev," Royall said.

"I'm not talking sexual. Just y'know, like you got here . . . house-keeper stuff. A night of housekeeper stuff. An afternoon. That's it."

Nola froze midstep, an ashtray in one hand, a glass of ice in the other.

"Leave her alone," a voice called from the sofa.

They all turned toward Trey, the tenth grader, who had finally looked up from texting.

"What'd you say?" Trey's dad challenged.

"Steve-O, tell your boy to watch his mouth," Hartley warned.

"Get your ass in the car. Go!" Trey's dad bellowed, using a tone Nola had never heard him use before. *"Now!"*

With venom in his eyes, Trey stormed toward the door, stealing a beer from the side table as he left. At the moment, though, there were bigger issues to deal with.

"I ain't joking," Hartley said, everyone turning back to the poker table. "I need a good housekeeper. Just for an afternoon."

Nola stood there, the room so silent, she could hear the ice popping in the glass.

"C'mon, Royall—you're always talking that she's such a pain in the ass. Put your money where your fat mouth is. How good you feeling about those cards?"

87

Newark Airport was not a quiet place.

Last year, as the twelfth-busiest airport in the country, it served over forty-six million passengers. To pull it off requires pictorial and international signs, TSA officers who speak twenty-four different languages, and outdoor maps labeled with oversized arrows to make sure people won't get lost going from long-term parking to the main terminals.

Still, there's one street at Newark Airport that's always been a bit harder to find: Conrad Road.

Put it into Google Maps—where it crosses Brewster Road, the service road surrounding the airport, the street view simply stops.

Most people assume it's a glitch, or that it's because of what's on the corner, in Building 15—the small but elegant private-jet terminal known as Signature, which serves gourmet tea in a well-appointed lounge as you wait for your private charter. Certainly, the Signature clientele prefer the anonymity.

Still others—the Newark employees who have been here for decades—assume it's due to what's at the end of the block, the art deco historic site known as Building 1.

Built in 1935, with a semicircular canopy that resembles a South Beach hotel, Building 1 was Newark's *original* terminal, hosting aviation legends like Amelia Earhart and Charles Lindbergh. After World War II, as the airport expanded, Building 1 became too small. But to preserve its history, the entire concrete structure was cut into thirds and moved here—to Conrad Road—where it became the headquarters for the airport's own law enforcement, the Port Authority Police Department.

When 9/11 hit, it was the perfect excuse to get Conrad Road blurred on Google Maps. But that wasn't the real reason.

Nearly every day, some random tourist accidentally turns onto Conrad Road. Some are smart enough to ask directions in the private-jet terminal on their left. Others make it all the way to the end of the block, to the police station. Both are perfect distractions. People are so busy staring at the private planes or the crush of parked cop cars, they don't look twice at what's across the street: a fenced-in parking lot with a prefab guard booth, like you'd find at a gated community.

It was the same tonight. The shed looked old—by design—though the windows were bulletproof. Inside was a guard—a fit, middle-aged man with heavy-lidded eyes, chewing nicotine gum like it was his final meal. On late shifts like this, he knew to keep the lights in the booth off. Indeed, since his bosses jammed all cell signals for security and location purposes, his silhouette was lit only by the faint glow of his laptop, which he was using to watch a YouTube video counting down the best TV theme songs.

He was singing along with the theme to *Diff'rent Strokes* when a set of bright headlights appeared up the block.

"Whatchu talkin' 'bout, Willis?" he muttered, thinking of his mom, who used to hate the show because back in Providence, Rhode Island, Reverend Williams once incorrectly said there was an episode where they cussed, using the B-word, as she used to call it. Momma hated the B-word, telling her son that if you want to be a man, you speak like a gentleman. She wasn't wrong, he thought, eyeing the car up the block. It was slowing down, like every other lost tourist.

Typically, most cars headed for the police station across the street, but when the lights turned his way and the car pulled toward his booth, he didn't think much of it. Especially these days, some people won't trust cops.

"Lemme guess," the guard announced, opening the drive-through window and squinting toward the headlights. "You can't find the main terminal?"

"Actually, Axel . . . the only thing we're looking for is *you*."

The guard, Axel Padilla, took a half step back, not even hearing the *Miami Vice* theme playing from his laptop. "Son of a B."

Zig smiled from the driver's seat. Next to him, Elijah leaned closer for a better view.

"C'mon, Axel, this is your moment," Elijah offered, his caterpillar eyebrows knitting together. "Here's the part where you're supposed to say, *Welcome to Grandma's Pantry*."

88

"Newark Airport? You're sure?"

Seabass nodded.

"Think they got on a flight?" Reagan asked.

Seabass shook his head, pointing to the little red triangle on their GPS, then scrolling sideways on the map.

"A police station? Why would they park by a police station?"

That's the question, Seabass said with a glance. Flashing his plastic mouth guard, he was trying to look animated, but really just looked paler than ever. The gauze on his cheek was clean, the bleeding stopped. But the way he was clenching his jaw, the white in his eyes now yellow . . . He could lie to most people. But not to her.

"Sebby, I'm dropping you off," she said, tugging the steering wheel toward the next exit.

Don't, he pleaded, grabbing the wheel, the car swerving back into its lane. *I'm fine.*

"You look like death."

We do this together, he insisted, pointing to her, then back to himself. That was their rule, for years now. He tightened his glance. *That's how it's always done. Together.*

She nodded, knowing he was right, hoping he was right, adrenaline kicking in as her anger—at Zig, at Roddy, and especially at herself—swallowed her in a rage. "You sure you're okay?" she asked, glancing over.

Seabass forced a grin, quickly sitting up straight. He couldn't break his sweat. Coppery saliva slid down his throat—he was swallowing blood, and it was getting worse. On his left, he glanced over at Reagan, who was clenching the steering wheel, staring straight ahead with that inferno in her eyes. There was nothing more attractive than someone who knows what they want. How could he deny her that?

I'm fine, he told her, smiling excitedly with his eyes.

"You sure?" She reached out, putting a hand on his shoulder, to physically feel if he was telling the truth.

Reagan, I'm fine. I swear.

She nodded like she believed it. She had to believe it. "Just five minutes," she said, hitting the gas and steering toward the exit for Newark Airport. "That's all it'll take."

As the curve of the exit ramp sent him leaning against the car door, Seabass gave her a thumbs-up. Five minutes and they'd be done. Simple as that.

89

Zig was trying to ignore the light drizzle, trying to keep up with Elijah and the guard in the blue windbreaker, Axel, as they darted through the empty parking lot. Axel tried making an excuse about leaving his post, but he didn't have a choice.

Along the side of the building was a parked trailer. There was a refrigeration unit on top. They had trailers like these back at Dover— overflow freezers for when the bodies piled up. Here, they kept trailers like this to ship across the country, which is what they did when COVID first hit. Yet as Zig got closer, he caught a glimpse of a pair of eyes peeking out from below the trailer, reflecting through the darkness like tiny milky mirrors.

Initially, he thought it was a cat, but the snout . . . the pointy nose . . . plus that thick rope of a tail . . . A possum, fat and crouched like a ball, was nibbling furiously at something.

To Zig, who would never admit to being superstitious, just the sight of it felt like a bad omen, though the science side of his brain knew that was absurd. A hot drop of summer rain hit Zig at the center of his forehead, like a bull's-eye. He wiped it away almost frantically.

"You okay?" Axel called back, still chomping on his nicotine gum.

"Just get us inside," Zig insisted, which, really, was all Axel was trying to do.

Picking up speed and leaving the mobile mortuary behind, they followed the curve of the lot toward the front of a gray concrete warehouse that had all the charm of a prison. Similar buildings were scattered all across the airport perimeter, with mundane names like M&H International, Swisshaven USA, and Longport Logistics— featureless warehouses dedicated to shipping, exporting, and everything else that goes with the infrastructure of an airport. On a brown awning, the words *K&W Importers* were so faded, you could barely make them out from the street, which was the point.

"Marlon, I got two," Axel said into his walkie-talkie.

Zig thought about getting Waggs on the line. He pulled out his phone. *No signal.* Elijah had warned him as much. As they approached the doorway, Zig spotted two separate black dome security cameras, both with solid steel mounting plates and collars. Same as Dover, military level. But what he noticed most of all was how quiet Elijah suddenly was.

"You see something?" Zig whispered.

Elijah shook his head, glancing at the dents in the old door, the rips in the old awning, the cracks in the building, all of it . . . so many memories. Last time Elijah was here, on that night five years ago, he lost the life he'd had, or at least the life he'd planned for himself. If Zig understood anything, he understood that.

"If you're armed, there're gun lockers inside," Axel added.

There was a low buzz, then a magnetic *click* as the door popped open.

"I smell rain—it raining out there?" the receptionist, Marlon, called out in a Bronx bellow. Sitting at an L-shaped desk, he was older than Axel, with sandy blond hair, hands that moved like hummingbirds, and a lopsided grin. *Heart or no heart?* Zig didn't know why, but he liked him instantly.

"It's a good evening for a good evening," Marlon added as the three of them entered.

"This is— Wow, it's all the same. You didn't even change the old posters," Elijah said, glancing around, like some middle-aged alumnus walking into his old dorm. On the walls were faded oversized photos of the Gulf War parade in New York City, as well as one of President Biden placing the Medal of Honor around a soldier's neck.

On their right, a coffee table held a neat pile of *Army Times* newspapers. In the corner were two sets of gray metal lockers with at least fifty safe-deposit-sized doors, one set marked *Phones,* the other *Guns.*

"Marlon, thanks for buzzing us in," Axel said, not slowing down but adding a wave as he passed the desk. He was headed for the closed metal door dead ahead, and the metal detector protecting it— the true entrance to Grandma's Pantry. "I already cleared them both."

"On the V-log?" Marlon asked, sounding confused, turning to the visitor's log on his computer. His hummingbird hands danced across the keyboard. "I don't see anyone listed in—"

There was a *click.*

Zig turned at the sound. It was already too late.

Reaching into his jacket, Elijah had pulled out a gun—a bright nickel-plated and polished HK P7. He racked the slide and chambered a round. "I'm sorry, son, but this is on you," Elijah said, aiming the pistol at Marlon's face.

Marlon's head was still down, his eyes on the computer screen. He never saw it coming.

"Elijah, no!" Axel shouted.

"DON'T—!" Zig added.

There was a thunderclap. Bits of blood and bone hit the wall, causing a spiderweb crack in the framed photo from the Gulf War parade. The way Marlon's head was bent, the bullet hit a soft spot that fractured the top of his skull in a messy crater. Zig was still yelling as Marlon's head teetered and wobbled, then slowly sagged forward, momentum taking over, his forehead pounding the keyboard with a sickening thud.

"What're you—!? *Are you insane!?"* Axel exploded.

Elijah barely reacted, his gun still raised, finger still on the trigger.

"He was about to buzz us in!" Axel added.

"He was looking us up," Elijah said, calm as could be.

"So what if he—? He has *kids* . . . a daughter starting college! And now he—he—" Axel clenched both fists. "You said no one would get hurt!"

"No," Elijah said, rolling his eyes. "That doesn't sound like me at all." In one quick movement, Elijah turned his gun toward Axel and pulled the trigger.

Another thunderclap.

A black burn mark appeared in Axel's forehead, just above his left eyebrow. This hit was clean, instantly sending Axel backward, like a marionette with cut strings, crashing to the carpet.

A decade ago, Navy psychologists studied how humans react when faced with imminent death. According to action movies, everyone in the crowd runs and screams. In reality, however, your most likely reaction is simply doing nothing. Faced with fear, we freeze.

Zig reached for his knife. Elijah was faster, aiming his gun.

"Mr. Zigarowski, whatever you've got in your pocket, I suggest you leave it there."

Zig stopped, his fingertips still at his pocket. "So that story you told us back at the bar—about the reason O.J. fired you . . . He suspected you, but couldn't prove it."

"If it makes you feel better, he's a shitbag *and* he suspected me. Which is more than I can say for you." Raising his gun to Zig's face, Elijah slid his finger around the trigger. "Don't look so wounded, Mr. Zigarowski. This was the twist you should've seen coming."

"I actually did, asshole."

Click.

Elijah was still facing the welcome desk, so focused on Zig, he didn't hear the door to the parking lot open behind him. And he certainly didn't feel the barrel of the gun until it was pressing into the back of his own head.

"You really think he'd leave me at a janky rest stop?" Roddy asked a bit too loudly in Elijah's ear. "Oh, and by the by, that fancy beer in your bar sucked."

"C'mon, Elijah, don't look so wounded," Zig added. "This was the twist you should've seen coming."

90

This was Roddy when he was fourteen.

It was just a matter of the paperwork.

"Sit," the police officer said, shoving teenage Roddy—in hand-cuffs and an Eminem buzz cut—toward the metal chair.

Roddy knew he was in trouble the moment he entered the room. Two-way mirror. Desk bolted to the floor. This wasn't the juvenile area—this was an adult interrogation room.

"Bad day for you, dumbass," said Officer Barry Baltamacchia, though everyone in the station called him Bull for always breathing so hard through his nose. He was forty-three, but like so many over-weight cops, looked at least a decade older.

Bull was right, though—it was a bad day.

Two hours ago, Roddy had been prowling the Nordstrom park-ing lot, using a bolt cutter and screwdriver to clip hood ornaments from any Mercedes or Jaguars unlucky enough to be parked nearby. Vegas Larry at the body shop offered seventy-five dollars apiece for them. Roddy already had two Mercedes ornaments in his pocket. As he started working on a third—a gray S-Class that needed a wash—he got spotted.

"Hey!" shouted a fortysomething Black anesthesiologist who was ROTC in college and had seen a few too many Spider-Man movies.

Deciding he had great responsibility, the man headed toward Roddy. "What're you doing!?"

"Suck yourself," Roddy shot back.

That was his first mistake: picking the fight. His second was thinking he had a chance. Roddy was fourteen. The anesthesiologist had at least fifty pounds on him. As the man rushed forward, Roddy instinctively sliced the screwdriver through the air—in self-defense, really—slashing a deep scratch across the man's forearm. That was his final mistake.

Six seconds later, Roddy was facedown on the ground, screaming in pain, his shoulder dislocated, his arm pinned behind his back. When Officer Bull arrived on scene, his first reaction was laughter.

"You don't even realize what you did, do you, dumbass?" Bull asked as Roddy took a seat in the interrogation room.

Roddy didn't say a word, even as Bull placed an evidence bag, with the screwdriver, on the table in front of him.

"Moron, know what happens when you use a weapon?"

"That ain't a weapon—"

"You slashed his arm. It's a weapon, which means you just kicked this up from robbery to felony assault. Happy birthday, fool. No more juvie for you. Now you're all mi—"

"Bull, your wife's on line three. Again," announced a female voice through Bull's walkie-talkie.

Bull didn't move.

"She sounds upset," the female voice added.

With a huff of air through his nose, Bull undid Roddy's handcuffs and recuffed them to the thick metal bar bolted to the table. "Don't move," he warned, stuffing the screwdriver in his pocket and heading to the door. What he didn't say was that his wife was at a doctor's appointment this morning. They'd found a lump.

"Can you at least get me a snack? I heard you give snacks," Roddy called back as the officer reached the threshold.

Bull never made it.

Crumpling sideways, he hit the floor with an awkward thud.

At first, Roddy thought it was a joke—a pratfall—or that he'd

tripped on the plastic wastebasket. But as Roddy craned his neck . . .
"*Officer?* You okay?"

Bull was curled on his side, wheezing, his body convulsing, his
eyes rolled back in his head. Later, they'd say his blood sugar dropped,
causing a diabetic seizure. As with any emergency, the key was how
quickly they could react.

"*Officer . . . ?*"

A small puddle of blood expanded from Bull's forehead. He'd hit
his head when he fell.

Roddy's mouth went dry. He tried standing up, but his handcuffs
were chained to the table. He couldn't get up, much less get near him.
Roddy glanced around. He could still yell for help—get someone to
come.

Then a new thought hit Roddy.

Peeking out of Bull's pocket . . . there it was . . . the plastic bag. The
screwdriver. If Bull died here . . . if he didn't get help . . . No one would
know what happened.

All Roddy had to do was keep his mouth shut.

On the floor, the convulsing and wheezing stopped, replaced by a
stillness that Roddy had never seen before. Bull's head jerked slightly.
He was foaming at the mouth, frothy saliva making the puddle of
blood pink.

Just stay quiet, Roddy told himself. *It's your chance for a new start.*

Bull wasn't moving. At all.

Roddy stayed locked on the bright yellow handle of the screwdriver.

The room was so quiet, he could hear the crick of his own neck,
little bones shifting.

Just keep your damn mouth sh—

"Help! Someone . . . ! *He needs help!*" Roddy shouted, leaping to his
feet. When no one answered, he banged the table, screaming louder.
"Please! Someone help! This dude's dying!"

Two hours later, Roddy sat there, all alone, in the office of someone
named Detective Conaway. He was munching on a bag of Funyuns
from the vending machine, waiting in a wooden chair that looked like
it escaped from a 1960s schoolhouse.

"*Funyuns?* That's the best they could do?" a raspy voice called out.

Roddy didn't look up as Officer Bull hobbled into the office, plopping into the seat next to him. Once the EMTs had given him some apple juice, his blood sugar stabilized, which is really all they can do—though he was still moving with the grace of a land-bound walrus.

"They should at least give you the extra quarter for Cool Ranch Doritos," Officer Bull added.

Roddy stayed quiet, rubbing Funyun dust from his fingertips.

"You know they're calling you a hero," Bull said.

Roddy rolled his eyes. Even he thought it was absurd.

"Want to know what I think?" Bull asked. Before Roddy could answer, Bull pulled out the plastic bag with the screwdriver and slapped it against the desk.

Roddy stared, looking confused. "*Wha?* You're letting me go?"

"What're you, insane? Of course not. You vandalized multiple cars, stole hood ornaments, *and* slashed a doctor's forearm. He wants his pound of flesh for that. But since my wife got a good report, and I'm in a really grateful mood right now, instead of felony assault, I'm gonna ask for reduced charges. I'll also be testifying on your behalf in the juvenile court," Bull explained. "The judge'll probably have you do community service, but here's the catch . . ." Bull paused for a solid ten seconds. "That community service—a full year of it—is gonna be done right here . . . in police headquarters."

Roddy's eyebrows knit together. "I don't get it. This a punishment, or—?"

"What you did today . . . that was a good thing," Bull explained. "And yeah, with the screwdriver, you also did a bad thing. But no one's all one thing. That's how it is for all of us. Like my favorite detective taught me, it's not what you've done—it's what you do next that defines you. Does that make sense?"

"Not really."

"You're not a bad kid, Roddy. Y'hear me? You're not a bad kid. Today, when the crap hit the fan, you picked the right side. You gotta keep picking the good one."

Roddy shook his head, still confused. "Why're you doing this?"

Bull thought about it. "You'll see."

He was right. When Roddy's community service was done, they brought him on as an intern, where he worked until he got his GED. Eventually, when Roddy applied for the police academy, Bull wrote his recommendation: *Roddy was on the path to being a ringleader— but now he's a real leader.*

He was right about that, too.

91

Today

There was a bug in her car. A tiny larder beetle, black with mustard spots, crawling diagonally up the windshield. Waggs knew it on sight, from an incident a few years back when she learned larder beetles feast on dry pet food.

Assuming it was outside, Waggs hit the windshield wipers and the gas, hoping highway speeds and aerodynamics would clear it away.

The wipers never touched it. The beetle was inside.

"Does every damn creature on the planet need something from me today? *You* need something, too?" she asked.

Overhead, the car's hands-free speakerphone let out a throaty ring, Waggs still waiting for the person to pick up on the other line. In the pause between rings, she rolled down the passenger window a few inches, as if the small gap would affect the level of suction.

"I'm trying to free you!" Waggs shouted at the beetle, wind whipping through the car. It still didn't budge.

"Waggs, that you? You in a wind tunnel?" a male voice announced, picking up.

"Yeah, lemme just . . ." With the push of a button, Waggs closed the window, the beetle still in place.

"I called you twice—where you been?" Gary asked.

It was a bad sign. For nearly a decade, Gary's conversations led with small talk, usually about whatever obscure BBC detective show he was suddenly obsessed with, before he explained your IT problem. If he was diving into business . . .

"You found who was in Mint's Black House account?" Waggs asked.

"Actually, by design, all Black House accounts are binary, with seeded hash and the highest entropy keys, meaning they can't—"

"*Bored!* Speak English, not instruction manual," Waggs said, grabbing a notepad from the car's cup holder and leaning toward the passenger seat to swat the beetle from the windshield. Since she was still driving and holding the steering wheel, her arm wasn't long enough. Annoyed, she threw the pad at the beetle. Still didn't move.

"Waggs, do you know how the NSA catches bad guys?"

"If I say yes, can you get to your point?"

"It's a philosophy. The NSA knows that if every crook has encryption and there's no way to get the keys, there's only one choice: you wait for the bad guys to make a mistake. So here, when you're dealing with secure operating systems or Starlink satellites—"

"Gary, if you don't tell me who you found in Mint's account in the next three seconds, I'm gonna drive straight to the office and throw away every damn action figure on your desk, including that homemade Benedict Cumberbatch Sherlock Holmes Lego set."

Gary went silent for a full five seconds. "You can't tell anyone I told you this."

"Elementary, my dear Watson."

Gary took a breath and Waggs could picture him tugging his shirt away from his sweaty belly. "Waggs, you need to understand, by design, Black House accounts don't come with an exploit—though they do come with instructions . . . and paramount among them is that it's designed to be used on mobile."

"You download the app, and that's what gives you security."

"Exactly. The app is a closed system. But if you run it on desktop, now Black House is going through a browser, which means open identifiers—"

"Just give me the name, Gary."

"*Names*. Plural. There were two of them—though it doesn't give us actual IDs. We get IP addresses, which you can then use t—"

"You're speaking nerd again. Tell me the addresses."

"One of them traced to a residence. Owned by someone named Zion Lopez."

Waggs nodded. They already knew Zion was the one who'd pulled the trigger on Mint. The question was, who hired him—and why? According to Zig, it went back to the twenty-two million dollars that was stolen five years ago from Grandma's Pantry. So whoever was behind this, is that who was in Mint's Black House account? Did they think Mint stole the money and they were looking for it? Or was it the other way around—that Mint, and maybe Rashida, figured out who actually stole the money, and they were threatening to go public?

"Gary, I need the other person who was in Mint's account."

"Pull over. I'm texting you the address. Tell me if it looks familiar."

On her phone, Waggs swiped to texts. "I don't see it."

"Not until you pull over. For safety purposes, texting and driving isn't—"

"Gary, send the damn address!"

Her phone vibrated.

The words popped onscreen and her eyes went wide. *No. Nonono.*

Hanging up without a word, Waggs quickly dialed Zig's number. "C'mon, Ziggy, pick up . . ."

No answer. Of course. At Grandma's Pantry, they blocked all cells. Still, if Zig was already there . . . and if Nola was headed there, too . . .

Waggs hit the gas, and the car took off. Up on the windshield, the beetle hadn't moved.

Right in front of her the entire time.

92

Nola didn't like being back here.

Tugging the steering wheel hand over hand, she felt that familiar shift in her stomach—that same sense of dread from when she was little and would come home from school, grab a snack in the kitchen, and spot a newly emptied bottle of scotch in the trash.

Even at nine years old, it's not hard to know when trouble's coming.

Tonight, as her car rounded the corner, Nola rode the brakes, taking it slow. There were no other cars around, no one in sight. At 9:00 P.M., the block was quiet, but it looked darker than she remembered. There. On her left. A bulb out in one of the streetlights.

Mongol . . . Faber . . . She never got through it, never got to the names of the other pencils that her art teacher, Ms. Sable, had given her as a gift and that meant so much to her all those years ago. Just being here—being *back* here—this place was an echo, vibrating through her, vibrating through time, old memories tugging her down in their undertow.

Years ago, during her first visit, Nola came here to do good, to set things right. But like any decision you look back on through the lens of time, what you marvel at most is how *naïve* you were.

Halfway up the block, Nola parked on the street. Better to approach by foot, so no one would see her coming. For a moment, she just sat there, wrists resting on the steering wheel, the undertow still tugging. She hated that feeling of old wounds throbbing like new wounds—but what she hated most of all was that old version of herself, the one who allowed her to get hurt in the first place.

Kicking open the car door, she could see Mint on that first day, could still hear his corny speech that everyone said he gave at the start of every investigation. *Humans are born with two fears: falling and loud noises. Every other fear is learned.*

He was right—though that didn't make your fears any less real. Only way to do that was to tackle them head-on.

Speed-walking up the block, Nola stuck to the shadows. The cars out front told her who was already there—and who wasn't. At just the sight of her destination, the undertow was overwhelming.

It didn't slow her down.

At the front entrance, she took a final glance over her shoulder and gave the doorknob a twist. To her surprise, there was a *click*. Unlocked.

Never a good sign.

If she were still in the Army, this was when she was supposed to call the ops center for cover.

Instead, Nola reached into the back of her waistband and pulled her gun.

Without a word, she elbowed open the front door—and disappeared inside.

93

As Zig shoved a handcuffed Elijah into the warehouse, the first thing he noticed was the flag.

He saw it the moment he stepped inside, hanging from the vaulted ceiling. The warehouse itself was wider than a Costco and BJ's side by side. Throughout its nearly seventy aisles, the words *Grandma's Pantry* weren't written anywhere. Outside, there was no sign for *Strategic National Stockpile*. Yet as Zig stared up at the nearly football-field-sized American flag, there was no mistaking the message: this place belonged to Uncle Sam.

"Try there . . ." Zig said, moving quickly to get out of sight and pointing to what looked like a conference room on their right.

"It's gonna be locked," Elijah warned, his hands cuffed behind his back.

Roddy squeezed the cuffs, steering Elijah between stacks of short pallets that clogged the front of the warehouse—twelve-hour Push Packages, each loaded with fifty tons of antibiotics, antidotes, and medical supplies in case of a chemical or bioterror attack. On the left were industrial scales, on the right was a small parking lot of forklifts, all of it at the ready so that when the order was given, they'd race out onto Newark's runway and deliver salvation in twelve hours or less.

"Mr. Zig, it's locked," Roddy said, trying the door.

Elijah rolled his eyes. "Did I not just say that?"

"Roddy, he's a liar. Ask him what the code is."

"Are you both deaf?" Elijah asked. "There's no way in—these are senior staff offices—"

With a harder squeeze, Roddy pressed the cuff into Elijah's wrist. As Roddy learned during his first year on the job, handcuffs are their own art. A little pressure makes a tremendous impact.

"Gaaaaahh," Elijah screamed, his body twisting in pain.

"You do realize if Roddy breaks your wrists, someone will need to feed you for the next month?" Zig asked, taking a glance over his own shoulder. Back by the check-in desk, the guard—Axel—was facedown in his own blood. The receptionist was slumped forward on his desk. Two more needless deaths, Zig thought. Fallen #2,549 and #2,550.

"*U Sam!* That's the pass code. They never change it!" Elijah exclaimed as Roddy pressed Elijah's face into the door's keypad. "*U Sam!* L-Like *Uncle Sam.*"

Roddy quickly entered the pass code.

There was a magnetic *thunk*. The door opened.

Squeezing the cuffs even harder, Roddy steered Elijah toward the entrance. Behind them, Zig didn't follow.

"You coming?" Roddy asked.

Zig nodded, heading toward them and grabbing a final glance over his own shoulder.

"You're looking for Nola, aren't you?" Roddy asked. "You think she's coming."

"Roddy, can you please just get Elijah inside so we can—?"

"You're not answering my question. If you know Nola's on her way—"

"You think she'd tell me anything? That's not how she operates. But if I had to take a guess—"

Click.

The noise came from the main reception area. Someone walking through the front door.

As Zig started to turn, he had an actual smile on his face. A true dopey grin.

That is, until he spotted the two people—a man and a woman—

stepping across the threshold, joining them in the warehouse. Both redheads.

Mothertrucker, Zig was about to say, though he never got the word out.

Roddy was still in midturn, still gripping Elijah by the handcuffs.

"Yeah. I see him," Reagan said, lifting her gun. In one quick motion, she aimed at Roddy and pulled the trigger.

94

This was Nola when she was fourteen.

Royall didn't take Hartley's bait. More annoyed than anything else, Royall told him that this wasn't that absurd Demi Moore–Robert Redford movie—and if he wanted to place a real bet, with real money, he'd be happy to cover it.

With pocket queens, Royall figured his full house would be an easy payday. Too bad Hartley had quads—four of a kind. By the time the hand was done, Royall had lost nineteen hundred dollars, Hartley hiding his cards so well, Nola never got a good peek.

For another hour and a half, Royall tried winning back his cash. Nola got him halfway there. Then it got late. The pretzel bowl was empty. That was the night.

At nearly one in the morning, as the guys were wrapping up, Nola ducked out into the backyard to fish beer cans from the trash. Royall had a guy who'd drive them to New York for a piece of the five-cent deposit. He didn't like her doing it in the house, though—thought it made them look—

"*Cheap!* Jesus on a surfboard, is your dad cheap!" Trey teased from a nearby lounge chair, the teenager's thin frame looking like a needle. On the arm of his chair was his Sidekick, where a red notification light blinked in the dark.

Nola grinned at the crack at Royall, breathing an actual sigh of relief.

"You doing this for you or him?" Trey asked. At the foot of his chair were two empty beer cans. She thought he'd grabbed only one. He was faster than he looked.

"For *him*? Oh, shitty!" Trey laughed as Nola continued to rummage through the trash. He quickly felt bad, his tone shifting. "You should tell him to do it himself. Set him straight."

Nola didn't answer. She knew he meant well, but she also knew what would happen if Royall thought she was complaining.

"Here, I can— Lemme help," Trey added, hopping from his seat and heading toward her, the red light still blinking from the armrest.

"Your dad's gonna be looking for you," Nola warned, pointing over her own shoulder.

"He won't. He'll think I walked home," Trey said, reaching into the trash. "The real fun'll start when I text my mom that he left me behind and messed up his court-appointed night with me." The way Trey spoke . . . using words like knives to stab at his parents . . . It wasn't something she'd soon forget.

"He's a dick like that," Trey added, standing on the opposite side of the trash as he pulled out a can of Pabst Blue Ribbon and two bottles of Stroh's, which forever would be the smell Nola associated with tonight.

Across from him, Nola opened a plastic garbage bag to receive the recyclables. Trey threw the can inside, but as he went to hand over the bottles, he purposely missed the bag, letting one of the bottles plummet to the ground, where it shattered across the concrete.

"What're you doing!?" Nola asked.

Trey shrugged and shot Nola his own devil's grin, which lit her up in places she didn't realize lit up. Holding the second bottle with two fingers, like an arcade crane game, he cocked an eyebrow, about to let it go.

"Don't!" she called out, reaching to grab it.

She forgot how fast he was. He yanked the bottle up, out of her reach. Her hand gripped his wrist.

Too slow, he was about to say. He was fast for a drunk. But not nearly as fast as Nola.

Before he could get the words out, she snatched the bottle from his hand.

She held it up in victory. He playfully slapped it sideways, knocking it to the ground, where it shattered not far from the first one.

"Try it on purpose—it's better when you mean it," Trey said, reaching into the trash and handing her a new bottle.

She wanted to tell him he was a moron. Instead, for reasons she couldn't explain, she let go of the bottle, letting it smash.

Royall would definitely be pissed, but even she knew that's why it felt so good.

"Boy, am I clumsy tonight," Trey teased, dropping another bottle, then another Pabst Blue Ribbon can that hit with a hollow clink.

"I gotta say, I thought he was gonna bet you tonight," Trey added, stomping on the beer can to flatten it.

Nola stayed silent. Finally, she offered, "I appreciate you saying something to Hartley. You didn't have to."

"Eh, I was just protecting Hartley from you."

She liked that.

"Seriously, I'm glad you're safe," Trey added, standing there, staring at her. "The world needs pretty girls."

"And pretty boys," she shot back, blinking a few times, not sure where the words came from, wishing she could take them back, but not really. "N-Not pretty boys . . . *cute* boys," she corrected herself. "However you call it . . . you know what I mean." She stared down at the trash. "You should go. There's no more bottles to break."

Trey grinned, the red light of his phone blinking behind him, a one-second firework. "You really think that's why I keep coming to my dad's lame poker nights? To play with some bottles?" he asked, his eyes locking on Nola as he stepped toward her.

Before she knew what was happening, he was kissing her. He smelled like werewolf and tasted like Pabst Blue Ribbon, but as he put his mouth on hers, my God, everything crumbled and she was weightless, floating up, her feet leaving the ground.

The instant he touched her, she was tempted to push him away. It was instinct. But she didn't. Why say no to something that felt this good?

He pulled her close, and she could feel his stiffness pressing into her. Her hand reached down—another instinct—to feel it. His fingers skated along the waistband of her jeans, setting her on fire.

That was it.

They were all over each other within seconds—she undoing the belt on his jeans, he undoing hers, the rush of hormones overwhelming. Still kissing, they stumbled together toward a nearby folding lounge chair. They were moving so fast, still off balance, they fell to the ground. She landed on her back, his full weight on top of her.

Taking a breath, he pulled away, his face lit by the moon. She could see his bones moving under his skin. His iced-tea eyes curved into a grin.

You sure? You don't have to, he asked with a glance.

Nola froze. Years later, she'd replay this moment, knowing that this was the very last time Trey would ever speak to her. But on this night, as a teenage girl, all she kept thinking was how he tasted . . . and how good it felt . . . and how great it was to have someone look at you like that—with care and real affection, rather than anger and disgust.

Royall would kill her just for kissing him. And really, in those picoseconds when rash decisions get made, it was that thought that first motivated her. She had no deep attachment to Trey—she barely knew him. Yet as he kissed her again, his one hand gripping the back of her head, the other sliding into her jeans, skating against the edge of her panties, she wasn't thinking of Royall at all. He was gone for once, banished from existence. All that was left was this boy with the warmest eyes she'd ever seen, staring at her, staring through her, like she was revealed and he was mesmerized by what he saw. Nola didn't want much in life. But right now, she wanted this.

Do it, Nola said with a nod as Trey lowered his jeans.

She closed her eyes and tugged down her own jeans.

Today, Nola would say the details were lost to her, but back then, even with her eyes shut, she couldn't avoid the beer on his breath. She thought she hated that smell, but right now, as he entered her, as weightlessness again lifted her out of her body, there was no sweeter smell or taste in the entire universe. She opened her eyes to make sure it was real and spotted Trey staring down at her, his reassuring gaze promising she was safe. At that, she closed her eyes, finally able t—

"Boy, what the hell're you—!? NOLA!" a voice interrupted.

Trey jumped. No. He was yanked—flying sideways, off balance.

"Get off her!" Royall exploded, tugging the back of Trey's shirt, choking him as Trey scrambled to pull up his pants.

Nola did the same, still on the ground. *"Get outta here!"* she screamed. She wasn't talking to Royall. She was warning Trey.

"Sh-She was all over me!" Trey lied, climbing to his feet.

Royall started to yell something, but instead buried a punch into Trey's stomach, then his face, blood bursting from Trey's nose. *"That's. My. Girl!"* Royall exploded.

Trey was stumbling now, covering his face, just trying to—

"RUN!" Nola shouted as Trey took off, scurrying through the overgrown grass, hopping the fence into the neighbor's backyard.

"THAT'S. MY. GIRL!" Royall bellowed, spit flying from his lips, his nostrils flaring, throwing one last punch in the air. His face was purple, the web of veins swelling below his eyes.

Six feet away, Nola was still on the ground, near the flattened beer can. She was watching Trey run—watching the rage on Royall's face—watching him turn his attention toward her—and cursing herself for being so damn stupid, thinking she could actually have something good.

95

CameraWorld. That was the store Charmaine forgot.

"Mr. T!" she shouted through the phone at CameraWorld owner John Tang, a tall, handsome Asian man who used to wear his hair in a long ponytail.

"You know you can call me John."

"John. Of course. Sorry. How are you?" Charmaine asked, suddenly wondering if calling him *Mr. T* had been racist, or just annoying. "Terry Ainsley sends her love, by the way."

"She told me," he said, already sounding exhausted, "and also told me what you'd be calling about."

Back in the day, or at least in the days of real cameras, Charmaine and Zig had brought their undeveloped film to CameraWorld. They'd bought their original camcorder there. Most important, Camera-World was the place that transferred their old videos—their wedding to tons of birthday parties—from the camera's videotape to DVD.

"You're wondering if I converted any videotapes for Super-Stars—if I might have one of your daughter—"

"Maggie."

"—if I might have one of Maggie," Mr. Tang continued, his voice now calm, serene. "You know we closed the store years ago."

"I know, but I figured if you kept backups—"

"We never made backups. We'd never have the space to store

them all. Plus, a client's footage belongs only to the client, so, no, I don't have tapes of your daughter. I'm sorry."

Curling forward in her seat, elbows on her knees, Charmaine realized that was it. She'd hit the last dead end of all the dead ends. *I appreciate the time,* she was about to say.

"Of course, if you contacted the client directly . . ."

"What're you—? What client?"

"SuperStars," he said. "They were clients for years."

"Hold on," Charmaine blurted, popping out of her seat. "You're saying *you* don't have the footage, but . . ."

"Gloria Cash was the SuperStars owner. She'd record her videos, then bring a box of tapes over every Friday so we could transfer them to DVD."

"But she— I spoke to Gloria's daughter. She said she checked all the videotapes."

"I'm sure she did. But there's a reason people record over old videotapes. You can reuse them once you convert them to a more stable medium," Mr. Tang explained.

"So if I call her back, it might be possible that in addition to videotapes . . . she might also have some DVDs?"

"I'd certainly say it's worth a call, don't you think, Mrs. Zigarowski?"

96

The first shot hit Roddy in the stomach.

Zig had seen it before, with Afghan snipers targeting American troops. Instead of going for the kill shot, they'd aim for the knees or, more often, the belly—knowing it's usually a nonlethal hit, but also knowing exactly what happens when stomach acid and bile leak into the abdominal cavity.

The pain is unbearable.

"Roddy, get down!" Zig shouted, though Roddy didn't hear it. He was still in shock, blinking, standing there, staring down at the bloody wound blooming red from his stomach.

As the Reds entered the room, the color leaked from Roddy's face. His legs started to buckle, but he was on his feet—good sign, minimum blood loss—though he didn't realize he was still holding on to the handcuffs, still holding Elijah in place. With his free hand, Roddy reached for his own gun.

Across the room, Reagan pulled the trigger again.

The bullet burrowed into Roddy's forearm. A jolt of electricity ran to his elbow. Broken ulna, though it was nothing compared to the blazing flame that was now ignited in his stomach. As pain set in, he fought to stay on his feet, holding tight to the handcuffs, pulling Elijah closer, like a shield.

"Don't shoot! Don't shoot!" Elijah pleaded, trying to duck down, hands still cuffed behind his back.

Reagan marched forward, her gun still trained on Roddy. Seabass was in lockstep behind her, the two of them moving as a single unit, weaving methodically through the pallets of Push Packages.

In truth, Seabass's coloring was worse than Roddy's, but adrenaline kicked in quickly, and so did his training. As Reagan went right, Seabass swept left, aiming his gun at Zig and scanning the wider part of the room. The gauze still covered most of his cheek, but his bloody mouth guard looked shiny between his lips, a macabre smile, like he was enjoying himself.

"Roddy, I never take pleasure in someone's pain," Reagan warned, "but I have to say, I'm looking forward to making an exception."

Without warning, Reagan's eyes slid sideways and she aimed her gun at Zig. Seabass aimed his directly at Roddy's face, his finger gripping the trigger. That was their deal. Seabass gets the kill shot.

"DontshootDontshoot!" Elijah begged, still ducking down.

Roddy pulled Elijah closer, using him as a shield.

Next to them, Zig had his hands in the air, trying to process it all. Time skidded to a halt, making it feel like everyone was underwater. Elijah was still in midyell as Zig glanced back to the reception area, like he was waiting for someone else to enter. But no one was coming.

"Do NOT shoot! Do NOT!" Elijah yelled, still bent over, his body contorted. *"I can help! I can— I can— I know where the money is!"*

Seabass stopped, throwing a look at his partner.

Reagan's eyes narrowed. "What money?"

97

"*How* much?"

"Twenty-two," Elijah said.

"As in *million*? You have *twenty-two million dollars*?" Reagan asked.

"Not *on* me. But . . . well . . . *yeah*," Elijah said, trying to stall, trying to keep them talking, his wrists still cuffed as Reagan held a gun in his back, forcing them deeper into the warehouse.

Behind them, Zig and Roddy had their hands in the air, Seabass motioning to keep them up. It was Roddy who was moving slowly, his face ashen, lowering one arm to hold his bleeding stomach. Still, he was on his feet—alert, not disoriented. A good sign, Zig thought. No major blood vessels penetrated.

"He needs to rest—or at least sit," Zig said, though all it got them was another shove from behind.

"Where's the money now?" Reagan asked.

Elijah shook his head, eyeing yet another warehouse camera. *Not here.*

On their left, they passed an aisle filled with pallets of thermal burn creams and antimicrobial agents to be used on survivors of radiological or nuclear attacks. On their right was an aisle stocked with medical instruments—hacksaws and rongeurs, to file down bones during amputations—as well as stacked containers of sterile bred maggots to debride necrotic tissue and treat gangrene.

"At least get him some water," Zig added, though it got drowned out by the loud mechanical hum that filled the air. It sounded like an engine, though Zig knew the source as he eyed the metal door dead ahead. An orange-and-black warning sign read:

BIOHAZARD
NO FOOD OR DRINK
TO BE STORED IN FREEZER

"The original scene of the crime," Elijah said, motioning to the metal latch.

Reagan gave it a tug, and a cloud of cold air wafted through the plastic slats.

Five years ago, this was where arms dealer Salty and his daughter were reunited and ruthlessly murdered, their twenty-two million dollars stolen. The meeting was here because it was the only place in Grandma's Pantry without cameras. It was no different today.

"Everybody in," Reagan said, shoving Elijah through the slats, then grabbing Zig and doing the same. She was careful to hold him at arm's length—never let anyone get close enough to whip their head back in a head butt.

"You do realize, she's gonna slit your throat no matter what," Zig warned Elijah as they stumbled inside, Roddy right behind him, a cold frost biting them in the face.

The freezer was big—the size of half a dozen lanes at a bowling alley—with bright white walls and a matching resin floor, giving it the feel of a high-tech lab. It was divided into three aisles, all of them lined with padlocked metal cages holding lots of vaccines for everything from chicken pox to Ebola to yellow fever. Along the back wall, a maze of blue pipes squiggled toward a massive fan—the cooling system for the freezer and the source of the loud hum that was now a steady roar.

"Stay," Reagan warned, disappearing up the freezer's far-right aisle, scanning the room to make sure they were alone.

"Elijah, y'hear me?" Zig whispered, puffs of cold air rolling from his lips. His ears already hurt from the cold. A digital thermometer on the wall read three degrees Fahrenheit. "No matter what, she *will* kill you."

"That's what I would do," Roddy agreed, bent forward, eyes clamped in pain.

"You'd be surprised what people overlook when you give them money," Elijah shot back.

"I can hear you!" Reagan shouted from the aisle.

"Is that what you did with Mint? You gave him money?" Zig asked. "He somehow figured out you were the one who stole the twenty-two million, and then you what? You started paying him hush money to keep him quiet? Or better yet, he started asking for even more, and that's why you hired Zion to put a bullet in him."

"How many bad TV shows did you have to watch to put together those sentences? I know you want to see me as a murderer—"

"You just shot two people!" Zig shouted.

"And I'll have to live with that. But y'know what I'll never lose sleep over? Salty Trebbiano's dirty money. The man was a Nazi—I don't have a single regret taking it. You judge me all you want, but back at the bar, what I told you was the truth: I am not the scumbag in this story—and neither is Archie Mint. Whatever else happened, even his affair, Archie always had my back. I'd never hurt him . . . I wasn't sending him payoffs . . . and I certainly wouldn't lay a hand, or hire anyone, to hurt him or Rashida."

Roddy looked up, confused.

Zig was just as lost. It was their one immutable fact: Zion was the one who pulled the trigger. But if the Reds didn't hire him . . . and Elijah didn't hire him . . .

"Who the hell killed Mint?" Roddy asked.

98

Nola held her gun with both hands, low ready like a golf club, as she elbowed open the door.

Inside, the entryway was dark. Her eyes were still adjusting as the smell hit her. Fresh flowers. No surprise—though people would probably be less inclined to send them if they knew that flowers first became popular at funerals because they helped mask the stench of decomposition.

On her left, Nola eyed a DIY umbrella stand made from cinder blocks stacked sideways, three tall umbrellas tucked into the holes. She rolled her eyes, blaming HGTV. Same for the cherry floors.

By now, Zig and Roddy would be at Grandma's Pantry. In truth, Nola was planning to head there, too. As Vess had told her when she was leaving his office, that's where the evidence pointed—or at least the evidence for the missing twenty-two million. But from the moment this started, Nola never cared about the money. She cared about who killed Mint.

For days now, she'd been winding her way through the maze, checking for new paths, trying to figure out why someone sitting on twenty-two million dollars would hire a small-time scrub like Zion Lopez. But it was time to admit, she'd been looking at it wrong. Maybe the reason you hire Zion is because you *don't* have millions. So who'd that leave?

In her mind's eye, it went back to that photo from Zion's phone—of Mint and Rashida, wide smiles on their faces as they leaned close at the fancy restaurant. That wasn't an old photo; it was a recent one—one that Vess, the Reds, and Zion . . . everyone had a copy. Clearly, it was an important photo—yet no one had stopped to ask: Who would want it taken in the first place?

As she approached the living room, Nola glanced at the built-in bookcases stocked with kids' DVDs and far too many Tom Hanks movies. But what she noticed most of all was the silhouette of the thin woman sitting there, ankles crossed and with perfect military posture, on the chocolate-brown leather sectional.

Mint's wife, Tessa, raised her gun.

"Just so we're clear, Nola—when you break into my house, you realize I can shoot you."

99

"I'm not saying word one until you take the cuffs off."

Reagan didn't bother to reply. Heading down the middle aisle, she was still scanning the freezer. "Middle clear," she called to Seabass.

Left clear, Seabass motioned to her, joining her from the left aisle, looking worse than before, though the hostile cold reddened his nose and cheeks, pushing color back to his face.

"You hear what I said?" Elijah called out, his hands still cuffed behind his back.

They heard him.

"Elijah, they *will* kill you. They'll kill us all," Zig warned, blowing into his hands to stay warm.

"Elijah? That's your name?" Reagan asked, heading toward Elijah, in the corner with Zig and Roddy. "I'm trying to save you from an awful day, Elijah. So I'm asking this once. Where's the twenty-two million?"

Elijah didn't answer.

Reagan rolled her eyes, throwing a look at Seabass.

Picking up speed as he left the aisle, Seabass aimed his gun at the side of Elijah's head.

"He's going to shoot your ear off," Reagan explained, like she was offering coffee. "Then I'll ask you the same question again, and if I don't get the answer I want—"

Reagan never got to finish the thought.

When the autopsy was done, they'd say Seabass had an ischemic stroke, brought on by an arterial embolism from a bullet fragment that rode his carotid artery and caused a blood clot in his brain. But right now, his only hint was his left eyelid starting to droop, making it harder to see.

"Um . . . your boy don't look so good," Roddy said, Seabass already off balance, stumbling sideways, bumping into one of the metal cages, which rattled as he hit it. He was still trying to stay on his feet as momentum took hold.

"*Sebby . . . ?*" Reagan whispered.

Seabass's arm went numb; his eyes rolled back in his head. He was in free fall now, like some oversized opponent in a *Rocky* movie, heading face-first toward the canvas.

"*Sebby!*"

Seabass hit forehead first, with a sickening crunch that broke his nose and knocked out his mouth guard. Ribbons of blood sprayed across the white floor. But the only thing that Zig, that Roddy, that *all* of them were paying attention to was his—

"*Gun!*" Roddy shouted.

The pistol skittered across the floor, not far from Seabass's face-down body. Zig and Roddy both dove for it.

"*Don't—!*" Reagan warned, turning toward them, raising her own gun.

Zig and Roddy were already in midleap, arms outstretched like they were both diving for an out-of-bounds ball as they reached for the gun.

Roddy got his hand on it first. It was like grabbing a frozen pipe, his palm still covered in the blood from where he'd been holding his stomach. It made the gun slippery as he grabbed the barrel, then the grip, fighting to right it. He was still on the ground. The wound in his gut was on fire as he climbed to his feet. His hand wouldn't stop shaking. He lifted the gun . . .

. . . and pointed it toward Zig's face.

"I knew it—toldja he was nuts," Elijah said.

"R-Roddy . . . what're you doing?" Zig asked.

Roddy didn't answer, his hand shaking more than ever.

"Roddy, please—whatever you think this will get you—"

Roddy squeezed the trigger. Zig closed his eyes. As the shot exploded, his final thought wasn't of his daughter. It was of Charmaine, his ex-wife. Not on their wedding day or in some gauzy old memory. How she looked now, seasoned by life, the crow's-feet, the elevens, all of it. God, she was beautiful.

The shot was a deafening crack, reverberating off the metal walls.

To his surprise, Zig felt nothing. He opened his eyes, looking down, patting his own chest. It took him a moment to realize he hadn't been hit. Instead, the bullet . . . Zig glanced over his shoulder. Roddy was . . . he was aiming at something . . . No. *Someone.*

Behind Zig, Reagan was standing there, head tilted, a look of puzzlement on her face. She was holding her own neck, like she'd slapped a mosquito, blood seeping through her fingers.

Roddy had shot her in the throat.

She was still in shock, trying to breathe, though all she could muster was a hollow wheeze, the sucking sound from an empty drain.

"I'm gonna shoot your boyfriend next," Roddy said, aiming the gun at Reagan's chest and again pulling the—

Roddy never saw the massive forearm coming. Seabass was still on the ground as he swiped at Roddy's ankles, knocking his legs out from under him. As Roddy crashed to the floor, Seabass was all over him, flush with rage and adrenaline, swinging wildly, his meaty paw knocking the gun from Roddy's hands.

Don't touch her, Seabass yelled in his head, though nothing came out. He was white as bone, his lips blue, his vision a blur. Yet as he climbed onto Roddy's chest, he still knew how to do damage.

Bunching his fingers like a spear, he stabbed wildly at Roddy's belly, searching for— There. He jammed his fingertips into Roddy's bloody wound.

Roddy screamed, making a sound like a dog hit by a car.

"Get . . . off him!" Zig yelled, tackling Seabass from the side.

It was enough to knock Seabass off Roddy. That was all they needed.

Using momentum to his advantage, Roddy scrambled onto Seabass's chest, pressing his forearm like a baton into Seabass's neck and pinning him to the ground. From there, it didn't take much. Seabass was coughing—puffs of white filling the air—craning his neck in every direction. They thought he was trying to escape, but really, he was just trying to check on the only thing he actually cared about. Reagan.

In two seconds it was over, his eyes rolling backward, his head hitting the floor. Roddy was still sitting on his chest, cradling his own stomach as he tried to catch his breath.

"Her! Don't forget her!" Elijah shouted, still handcuffed, lying on his side by the door.

Zig turned, searching for Reagan.

She was gone—though along the white floor, a trail of blood ran up the far-right aisle . . .

"Take the gun, she dropped her gun," Elijah said. "When you find her, you can—"

"Elijah, shut your face, or I'm gonna shoot you, too," Zig said, grabbing the gun, its grip burning from the cold.

"Mr. Zig, I don't think he's breathing," Roddy called out, still huffing as he pointed at Seabass.

Zig nodded; he already knew it from Seabass's gray coloring. Picking up speed, he held the trigger on the gun and disappeared up the aisle.

She wasn't far.

One down; one to go.

100

"I want you out of here," Tessa warned.

Nola didn't move.

In a blink, Tessa was on her feet, racking the slide of her gun and chambering a round. Nola made a note, especially about her shooting posture. Two-handed Weaver stance, like a boxer—toes forward, elbows unlocked, to allow for a better pivot toward her blind side. Well trained. Unafraid. And strong enough to handle the kick from that Glock 22. But she wasn't driving her shoulder toward the gun. Definitely rusty.

"I said get out of my house," Tessa growled, a few strands of chestnut hair sliding down from her otherwise faultless bun.

Nola just stood there, keeping her own gun at low ready. Minimize confrontation. On the far wall was a framed antique buccaneer revolver. On the bookshelf was a fat 105mm shell, from a gunship, that'd been sawed off and turned into a beer mug. Otherwise, from what Nola could tell, no other hints of the Mints' military life. No unit plaques or framed berets. No shadow boxes with awards or medals. Instead, every frame in the room—on the glass coffee table, on an end table next to the sofa, on at least four of the bookshelves—contained family shots, smiling variations of Mint and Tessa with their kids, at Little League games, hiking at Arches National Park in Utah, swimming and laughing with a giant inflatable dragon, and at a junior high graduation. In one was a shot of Tessa holding a blue umbrella with clouds printed on it, her arms wrapped around Mint, him kissing her as she smiled like a chewing gum commercial.

"The affair," Nola said. "That's why you did this. You found out he and Rashida got back togeth—"

"Gun on the floor. *Now,*" Tessa growled. She sounded unshakable, but her eyes were dancing back and forth, dark circles like craters. No question, lack of sleep. Every few seconds, her lips parted, her mouth slightly open as her face got red. She was holding her breath, panicking, trying to get control.

"You were the one I saw in Black House. That was you with Zion," Nola said, tucking her gun into the back of her waistband. This was never about money. Never about that night at Grandma's Pantry. It was solely about Rashida.

"I said put the pistol on the floor!" Tessa barked.

"You were using Mint's account. Is that how you found out he and Rashida were—?"

"Don't. Don't say her name in this house," Tessa warned, her finger on the trigger. For sure rusty. Or something worse. Army training teaches you, don't touch the trigger unless you're willing to pull it.

"Mrs. Mint, I'm not your enemy."

"Why didn't you leave it alone? You could've just left it—"

"Mom, everything okay?" a soft voice asked.

On Nola's right, a twelve-year-old girl with a messy bird's nest of black hair and scabby knees and elbows stood there in the hallway. The daughter, Violet.

"VeeVee, Mom's talking—go back to your room," Tessa said, quickly hiding her gun behind her back. Nola did the same, angling her body, trying to look like whatever casual looked like.

The problem was, Violet had her mother's instincts. "Who's *she?*" the little girl asked, pointing at Nola.

"One of my friends. Go back to your room."

"Why do you have Daddy's gun?"

"It's my gun. I told you, we're friends. I'm showing it to her—she's thinking about buying one," Tessa insisted, adding that mom tone that says *I promise, we're fine.* "I was just about to show her Dad's guns. In the garage. Isn't that right, Nola?"

Nola turned, but didn't answer. At just the sight of young Violet, Nola felt something standing behind her, something old and forgotten. For half a second, she didn't recognize it, and then, like a remembered dream, it was clear as day. In life, we're taught that old wounds are the deepest wounds. But Nola knew . . . the deepest wounds are the ones you cause in someone else. Especially in someone young.

"Sure. The garage. We were going to the garage," Nola said, heading up the hallway, Tessa unsubtly pointing with her gun.

Violet watched as they both made their way to the garage. The girl's dark eyes searched you, frisked you. Nola liked that about her. "Mom, you need me to call the cops?"

"I'm fine, VeeVee. I'd tell you if I wasn't."

"No, you wouldn't," Violet said with a preteen's shrug, disappearing around the corner and heading back to her own room.

On the opposite side of the house, Tessa asked, "You like kids?"

"I don't," Nola said.

"You like them enough to spare her a confrontation. I appreciate that," Tessa said, her voice still fake-cheery as she stepped close to Nola and swiped her pistol from her waistband. She wasn't nearly as rusty as Nola thought.

Passing the kitchen on their right, Nola eyed the outdated glossy marble countertops and dark cherry cabinets, realizing just how long it'd been since she'd been in a suburban home. On the kitchen table was a glass bowl of truly perfect green pears, like something out of a magazine. But the way they shone . . . plastic. All for show.

"Door should be open," Tessa said, motioning for Nola to give the knob a twist.

The door swung wide, revealing a messy garage, centered around an abandoned workbench that was buried under computer boxes and air-conditioning filters. On the left was a spare freezer, on the right, four bicycles, including a pink one that was covered in Pokémon stickers. On the ceiling, Nola spotted a yellow-brown stain, the color of a bruise and the size of an amoeba-shaped pizza. *Roof leak*. Let it fester, and it could take the whole house down.

"You think I don't know who you are? The painter—from Grandma's Pantry," Tessa said, calmer now, more in control, as if seeing her daughter reminded her what she was fighting for. It was a bad sign. She pointed her gun at Nola's chest. "O.J. told me you were at the

funeral. That all those years ago, you were one of Archie's investigators," she added, her voice cracking as she said Mint's name. "He's the
one who sent you, isn't he? O.J. put you on this case."

"*O.J.?* Ma'am, listen to me—"

"Were you sleeping with my husband, too? Is that why you won't
leave this alone?"

"Ma'am, I wouldn't do that. What happened to your husband
was a tragedy—but your role in it . . ." Nola took a breath. "I don't
think you meant to kill him."

Tessa froze, tears pushing out from behind her eyes. "You don't
know anything about us."

"I know he and Rashida—"

"*I told you don't say her name in this house!* What that woman did
to us . . . what she cost us—I loved that man for over two decades!"

"That's why you hired Zion, isn't it? To get that man back."

"It was a robbery! Didn't you see the police report!?"

"You paid Zion to hide in your house—to put the scare in Colonel
Mint when he came home from the steak house—"

"Now you're just inventing theories. Look at the police report!"

Tessa kept raising her voice, still holding the gun, still pointing
it at Nola's chest. But the words she was saying . . . they sounded
stilted, like they were memorized or scripted. Right there, Nola's eyes
narrowed.

"Ma'am, I need you to answer this: After Colonel Mint was
killed—why'd you log back into Black House for that meeting with
Zion? You're a smart woman. You had to know people might be
watching."

Tessa stood there a moment, digesting the question. Between her
eyebrows, a tiny microwrinkle appeared, then was gone just as quick.
To the untrained eye, it looked like anger. It wasn't. It was confusion.

"Do you even know what meeting I'm talking about?" Nola
asked.

"And do you have any idea what my family's been through . . .
what you're putting us through?" Tessa challenged.

"You weren't at that meeting, were you, ma'am? That wasn't you I
saw in Black House," Nola said, glancing over at Mint's workbench,

at the piles of boxes, at the discarded bicycles, all of it chaos. It made
no sense. Back when Nola logged into Mint's Black House account,
there were *two* people there. According to Zion's computer, one was
definitely Zion.

So who was the other? On the ride here, Nola had been convinced it was Tessa. She certainly had the most to gain. By hiring
Zion to hide in the house and put some fear into her husband, she'd
scare Mint away from Rashida and send him running back to his
family. A desperate plan for sure, but isn't that what people do when
they're about to see the core of their family torn in half? Still, if Tessa
wasn't in Black House . . . if she wasn't the one who did this, who else
would possibly benefit from—?

"Mom, you all right . . . ?" The door in the corner flew open,
revealing a lanky seventeen-year-old with a long curved neck and
cropped blond hair, just like his dad. "Vi said there was some woman
asking questions abou—" Huck froze, spotting Nola.

"Huck, don't say a word!" Tessa warned.

"Mom, what's going on? Is she—?"

"Don't say a word!" Tessa roared.

"Of course," Nola muttered, not even realizing she said the words
out loud. She just stood there, staring at Mint's son.

101

Zig had no trouble finding her.

"Reagan, it's over."

She didn't hear him. The churn of the fan was deafening. *Vmm vmm vmm.*

There was no missing her, though, at the far end of the aisle, in the corner of the freezer. She was down on the floor, shivering, hugging the maze of blue pipes along the back wall, like they were the only thing holding her up. From the wound in her neck, a thin stream of blood ran down her arm, dripping from her elbow, dotting the white floor.

"He's dead, isn't he?" Reagan called out as Zig approached. She was asking about Seabass.

Zig didn't reply. As he got closer, a pungent smell of cleaning products hit him in the face.

"I need to know if he's dead!" she demanded, still not facing him.

Zig had presided over enough funerals to know silence was an easier answer.

"We were supposed to be in Brussels next week. For some reason, he thought Brussels would be nice," Reagan explained, the fan still churning. *Vmm vmm vmm.* "I told him we'd go after this."

Zig could only see her from behind, her body shaking, quivering. He couldn't tell if it was from the cold or her wound. Puffs of clouds left her lips. The way her body was curled, down on her knees, it looked like she was praying or crying. She wasn't doing either.

"Reagan, put your hands in the air," Zig said, his gun out, pointed straight at her.

She didn't reply. Hunched over, she was still hugging the thickest of the blue pipes that squiggled toward the industrial fan—the freezer's cooling system.

"Reagan, I need to see your hands."

She was panting now, her body moving side to side, like she was rocking an imaginary baby, matching the rhythm of the fan. *Vmm vmm vmm.* It was so loud, the cleaning smell so bad, Zig could barely think.

"It's over, Reagan. I know you know that."

Vmm vmm vmm.

"The fact you're still breathing—that means it didn't nick your carotid," Zig added, only a few feet away. "They'll stitch up your neck and—"

Zig froze, finally placing the smell.

Reagan's back was still to him, her body still moving—but not from the cold or her wound. Her hands moved side to side, faster and faster, like she was panning for gold. She was gripping her thin metal camping tool, its rings around each of her middle fingers. As she sawed back and forth—*zzzt zzzt zzzt*—its sharp teeth sliced into the length of the blue pipe.

Zig glanced upward, following the maze of pipes toward the humming fan, where a yellow-and-black triangle with a skull and crossbones confirmed the smell:

Danger—Ammonia

Mothertrucker.

Back at Dover, the morgue had the same industrial cooling system. In storage facilities all across the country, ammonia was favored as a cheap and environmentally friendly refrigerant with excellent heat-transferring properties. But as every business was warned, when a big enough leak combined with oxygen in the air, it'd create a chemical reaction—an explosive ammonia blast—capable of leveling an entire building.

It reminded Zig of a few years back, when an ammonia leak at a U.S. base in Kuwait ignited and took out the equivalent of a city block. Temperatures got so hot it melted soldiers' skin from their bones, killing anyone who was close enough t—

"Reagan, if that ignites—"

Reagan looked over her shoulder, her gaze locked on Zig, with more than just larceny in her eyes. She glanced at the opposite end of the aisle, where Seabass's crooked legs hadn't moved in minutes. Zig . . . Roddy . . . they had no idea what they took from her.

She started to speak. A leak of air crawled from her throat. "I will be your death," she told him, tugging the saw faster, the leak growing larger.

"Reagan, don't—"

She continued sawing the pipe. *Zzzt zzzt zzzt,* in perfect sync with the fan. The cylinder was already slit—ammonia gas filling the freezer. Zig thought about shooting her, but it was no different from the metal saw on the metal pipe—all she needed was a spark.

"Roddy! We need to get out of here!" Zig shouted, already running.

Up the aisle, Roddy turned, holding the wound in his belly. "Mr. Zig, is everything—?"

Behind Zig, Reagan sat there, hunched over, determined, as she sawed the pipe. *Zzzt zzzt zzzt.*

"Go! Get out!" Zig shouted, picking up speed, grabbing Roddy by the shoulder and spinning him around, both of them now running toward the red exit sign. *"Elijah, up! Let's go!"*

"Ammonia! I knew I smelled ammonia!" Elijah said, crinkling his nose, scrambling, trying to get to his knees, his hands still cuffed behind his back.

"Get up! Go! Get out!" Zig yelled, pushing Roddy toward the door and helping Elijah to his feet. Even with the fan, there was no missing the sound of her sawing. *Zzzt zzzt zzzt.*

"You shoulda shot her in the head!" Elijah said.

With a shove, Roddy hit the latch, pushing the freezer door open. Warm air slapped his face as he burst through the plastic slats.

Elijah and Zig were close behind. But as they were about to reach the door, Zig glanced back at Seabass's body, his legs askew, his face gray, his jaw sagging open as foamy red bile leaked from his ears and nose, canals that always flooded during a hemorrhage. Around his neck was a beaded chain. Dog tags. Someone who'd served the country.

"What're you doing?" Roddy asked from outside the slats.

Zig grabbed Seabass by the wrists, tugging him toward the door. *He's still someone's child. Someone's world.*

"He's gone! Let's go!" Roddy yelled.

Zig didn't care, now remembering how much modeling clay it took to rebuild the melted faces of the fallen soldiers from Kuwait so their parents could see their sons and daughters one last time.

With a tug, Zig pulled him to the door. *Seabass had served, too. Moving him would only take an extra second.*

In no time, Zig was through the slats, Seabass's body thumping down the threshold, sliding across the warehouse's polished concrete floor. The change in temperature brought a puddle of sweat across Zig's face.

"Mr. Zig, we need to *go!*"

Zig glanced back toward the freezer. Roddy was right—they needed to go. Even out here, the ammonia smell was worse than ever. But the thought of Reagan inside . . . If the ammonia exploded, she'd take out the whole building, maybe the whole block . . . plus all the supplies that help so many . . . and Zig and his crew, too. From where they were, at the back of the warehouse, they'd never make it out in time. But if he could stop her . . .

"Mr. Zig, this is not the time to do something stupid."

Roddy was right about that, too. But for two years now, since the day he left Dover, Zig had been working hard to show respect for the dead. And also for the living. If he was fast enough, he could save them all . . .

"Mr. Zig, do *not*—!"

Too late. Darting back into the freezer, Zig disappeared through the plastic slats. The smell hit him first—it was overwhelming—his face contorting at the ammonia. He put his nose into the crook of his elbow as he ran.

"*Reagan!*" he yelled, sprinting up the right-hand aisle.

She was exactly where he'd left her, by the pipes in the corner, still tugging on the camping saw. *Zzzt zzt zzt.* Her hands shifted back and forth, but she was moving slower now, at half speed. The wound in her neck . . . she was losing blood.

"Reagan, enough! Let's go!" Zig said, grabbing at her arm.

She ducked out of his reach, hitting him with a dark glare. Her skin was sallow, an unhealthy yellow. But what caught him off guard was the inferno in her eyes. "This is your suicide. You just don't know it yet."

Turning back to the pipe, she continued to saw.

Zig reached out again. In a blur, she spun around, her left hand letting go of the saw, her right wielding it like a metal whip, slicing a bloody slash across Zig's forearm.

It was a brutal hit, but as she wound up again, it left her exposed.

Zig plowed forward, tackling her, colliding chest to chest and never slowing down. Wrapping his arms around her, he lifted her off her feet, hiking her over his shoulder in a fireman's carry. So far, so good—keep everyone safe.

"Get . . . *off*!" she growled, thrashing, pounding at his back as he ran, the thin metal saw waving behind them like a flag. Reagan was still holding the saw with her right hand, fighting to grab the other side with her left.

Zig was moving too fast, barreling up the aisle, past the—

Reagan's eyes narrowed when she saw it. The vaccine cages that lined each aisle. They had metal doors. With a slash of her arm, she sent the saw whipping outward. If the saw's steel teeth hit the metal just right, a spark would—

"Reagan, no!" Zig shouted, jerking his shoulder to keep her off balance.

She lashed out again. And again, the saw flailed, never quite landing. She wound up again.

Zig was almost at the door. The ammonia smell was rancid, his eyes tearing, blurring everything in front of him. Just a few more steps. Get her outside . . .

Reagan jerked her arm, pounding down with one final shot. The flexible saw rat-tailed toward the cage, its metal teeth catching, taking a bite . . .

And then . . .

Nothing.

Thank God.

Zig was moving full speed, his head down as he rammed through the plastic slats. They parted around him, around Reagan, warm air waiting for them as they reentered the warehouse, where—

Boom.

The explosion was a lightning bolt. Zig saw it in his peripheral vision, felt it as the floor began to vibrate. Before he could even process what was happening, the heat shoved him from behind, pushing him, lighting his back ablaze, a firestorm of tendrils engulfing him and Reagan . . . He tried screaming, but it was like being in outer space.

I'm on fire.

That was Zig's final thought as his feet left the ground and the world went black.

102

"Huck, get out of here!" Tessa yelled at her son, her gun still on Nola, her finger tightening around the trigger.

"I saw you. In Black House. That was *you,*" Nola said, still locked on Huck as the walls of the maze came crumbling down. When a cheating husband returns to his family, his wife isn't the only one who benefits. His kids benefit, too. "You found your dad's Black House account. You saw his texts . . . that he was seeing Rashida. Then you started using that account—you knew how private it was. You were the one who hired Zion."

Huck shook his head over and over. He had the same open face, the same ice-blue eyes as his dad. He was taller, though, thinner, with bony arms like a scarecrow. Swaying in place, he kept running his hands over the lines of his own throat, like he was choking himself. Scared. No. Something worse.

"I-I was trying to help. This wasn't— Zion was just supposed to scare him . . . No one was supposed to get hurt—"

"Huck, shut your mouth!"

"I-I was trying to help . . . You have to believe me. *I just wanted to help!*"

"Huck!" Tessa screamed.

"That last meeting in Black House . . . when you saw us . . . I told Zion I was turning him in! He killed my dad!"

"I believe you," Nola said flatly. "It's over, though."

"Nonono, he's just a kid. He doesn't know what he—" Tessa cut herself off, still holding her pistol with two hands. "You can't prove he did anything."

"Ma'am, it's over. I need the gun," Nola said, stepping toward her, arm outstretched.

"Don't," Tessa warned. "I swear on my life, I *will* shoot you."

"You won't. You would've done it already. It's over, ma'am. I need your weapon," Nola said, taking another step forward.

"Mom, give her the gun. It's okay," Huck said. "I'll be okay."

"No . . . pleaseplease, Nola . . . blame it on me. *It was me!*" Tessa cried, blinking away tears, her whole body starting to shake as fear became panic. "I'll show you! I can prove it!"

"Ma'am, you can't."

"DON'T TELL ME WHAT I CAN DO!" Tessa exploded, snot running from her nose, her body teetering, coiling forward, like there was a black hole in her chest, about to collapse in upon itself. "You tell them what I said . . . you tell everyone it was me . . ."

Nola moved closer, extending her hand toward the gun.

"WHY AREN'T YOU LISTENING!? IT WAS ME!" Tessa insisted, her eyes darting back and forth. Her face was blank, like she was no longer in there.

Nola froze. She'd seen that look on other soldiers, including one who, in full panic, put their gun to their own head. Since the moment Nola arrived, she didn't think Tessa would pull the trigger. Now, she wasn't sure.

"Mom, what're you doing?" Huck asked.

"Protecting you. That's my job." Tessa's hands were shaking, vibrating, as she pointed the gun at Nola's chest—center mass—just like she was trained.

"Mrs. Mint—I'm not your enemy . . ." Nola said, raising her hands.

"Say the words," Tessa warned. "SAY IT WAS ME."

"Mom, please!"

"Say it was *me!* This is on you now!" Tessa said, still locked on Nola.

"Mom, put the gun down!"

"MA'AM," a voice called out. A new voice.

Tessa spun toward the source. Behind her, by the door.

Waggs stood there on the threshold, her palms open, facing them. Nola's first thought was that Waggs should've pulled her own gun. But she was trying to deescalate the situation.

"It's over," Waggs insisted.

Tessa shook her head, over and over. "N-No . . . if you . . . he can still—"

"Ma'am, we're done. The police are on their way," Waggs explained. "It's done. Your son—"

"WHY CAN'T YOU JUST SAY IT WAS ME!?" Tessa pleaded, screaming at Waggs, then Nola. She kept looking around at Huck, at the garage, at her husband's old tools, old bikes, at all these abandoned artifacts from her cratered life, as if nothing looked familiar.

"Mom, I'll be okay," Huck promised.

"You hearing what I said? Put down the gun," Waggs insisted.

Mucus and tears ran down in a waterfall, the black hole in Tessa's chest starting to swallow her whole. Her gun was still pointed at Nola, but Tessa didn't seem to notice. She was crying, huffing uncontrollably as she fought to catch her breath. Her face was red, approaching purple, and just like that . . .

Tessa's body teetered slightly, then went limp, sagging sideways, unconscious, a psychogenic blackout caused by extreme distress.

"Mom . . . !"

As Tessa's knees gave way, her head smacked into the side of the workbench—a dull, awful thud.

Huck raced forward, sliding down on his knees and wrapping his arms around his mom. For a half second, he tried holding her up, but she was out cold, her arms rag-dolling behind her, a thick gash across her forehead. Huck lowered her carefully onto her back, still holding her, hugging her. "Mom? Are you okay? I'm here . . . I'm sorry," he said, pulling her close as the pain woke her up. The blood flowed fast, pulsing from her forehead.

She was weeping now, sobbing, covering her face with her forearm so he wouldn't see her tears. Nola's first thought was that she wanted to paint this moment, to see if she could render the pain.

"What the hell is going—? *Mom!*" a girl's voice shouted.

Behind Waggs, the young girl burst into the garage, shoving Waggs aside as her own tears flooded her eyes. Tessa's daughter, Violet. She scanned the room, looking at her mom, back at Waggs, then to Nola.

"*You!*" Violet exploded, locked on Nola.

"Mom, I'm sorry," Huck continued, his voice a whisper. "Please, Mom—say something. I need to know you're okay. Please be okay."

"*What did you do!?*" Violet demanded, shouting at Nola. "*Why would you—? You could've left us alone!*" she screamed. "*Why'd you do this!?*"

103

This was Nola when she was fifteen.

She was trying on shoes—a pair of white Keds that she knew were bootleg for two obvious reasons: first, there was no blue Keds logo at the heel, and second, they were from Royall.

"Traded two cases of paper for 'em," Royall bragged, as if he'd gotten the better part of the deal. "They're your size."

They weren't. But there Nola was in the kitchen, down on one knee, lacing up the Keds, wearing an oversized Phillies sweatshirt even though it was June and ninety-three degrees. As she got up from kneeling, the blood rushed to her head and down she went, passing out, tumbling unconscious toward the kitchen floor.

"Nola!" Royall shouted, too late to catch her.

Her body started to curl as she hit the linoleum. Thankfully, it wasn't a bad fall. Racing to her side, Royall quickly tried to pick her up, yet as his hand grazed her stomach . . . *What in the—?* Nola had always been thin, built like a tomboy. But now, her sweatshirt . . . the way she filled it out . . .

"When'd you get so *fat?*" Royall asked.

Nola stayed quiet, unable to look him in the eye.

A pregnancy test later, Royall got his answer.

• • •

THE BABY WAS DUE THREE months later. This far along, abortion wasn't an option—and as a Catholic, Royall wouldn't've allowed it anyway. Instead, he did the only thing he could think of. He hid it.

It actually wasn't that difficult. The summer months meant Nola wasn't in school. As September rolled around, he kept her home. Nola didn't have friends. It wasn't like anyone missed her.

For a bit, he considered calling Acne Steve, to tell him what his son, Trey, had done—but Steve was still threatening to sue him for punching his boy. *Screw them,* Royall thought.

On September 26, while she was taking out the trash, her water broke. Royall rushed her to the hospital. The fourth question the intake nurse asked was, "Is this pregnancy the result of rape or incest?"

"No," Nola said.

"Teenagers," Royall clarified, rolling his eyes.

Six hours later, a baby girl was born, with a thick head of black hair, and fair skin like her dad, though her eyes were alert, just like her mother.

They immediately put the baby on Nola's chest. "Please . . . *Don't* . . . Just take her," Nola begged, trying to look away, trying to not get attached, but already starting to count the baby's eyelashes.

There were a few feverish moments where Nola considered keeping it. But the thought of Royall . . . of putting another child under Royall's care. No. She'd never do that.

Back in the hospital room, they gave Nola an adoption binder with family profiles and scrapbook pages. A Black social worker named Deeandra, who had a smile that was a hug, told her that in Pennsylvania, when you choose adoption, you control your journey, no matter your age. "Pick who you like."

Sitting there in her hospital bed, staring up at a game show that she didn't know how to turn off, Nola shook her head. She wanted no part of it.

Within hours, she tried sneaking out of the maternity ward, then begged the nurses to sign her out early. It was absolute torture to hear other babies crying in the nearby rooms.

The hardest part was when they cut off Nola's *Mother* hospital bracelet.

"The new family—if you want to meet them, they're coming today. Three P.M.," Deeandra told Nola, though again, the only thing Nola cared about was when the discharge papers would be ready.

To Nola's own surprise, however, a few minutes after three, she slipped out of her room and made her way down to the waiting room assigned to the adopting family.

Deeandra was already there, waiting in the hallway for Nola, a warm smile on her face.

Nola didn't say *thank you*, or ask how Deeandra knew that Nola would come.

For a minute, the two of them stood there. Finally, Nola asked, "Are they nice?"

"Go look."

Nola eyed the closed door like it was radioactive.

"You don't have to go in. Just peek," Deeandra added, motioning to the door's tall rectangular window.

Nola took a deep breath and approached slowly, knowing she was making a mistake. "They'll protect her, right?" she asked.

Deeandra grinned. "They're a military family. That's their specialty."

With that, Nola pressed her nose toward the thin vertical window. Inside, a young couple was beaming, both of them hunched over the stainless steel rolling cart with its clear plastic bassinet. Nola couldn't take her eyes off the mom. Short chestnut hair, perfect posture, eyes wide with the possibilities that only a new mother can see. She looked strong as she held their other child, a squirmy four-year-old boy with a long neck.

Since Mom's hands were full, it was Dad who reached down and cradled the baby. He was built like a bulldozer, bursting through his polo shirt, with crisp blue eyes and buzzed blond hair. Like Captain America, Nola thought, tears leaking out from her eyes as she stared through the glass window, where young Archie Mint continued to kiss his newly adopted daughter over and over again.

"Wanna go in?" Deeandra asked.

Nola shook her head no, telling herself she was finally doing something right, that this was the greatest gift she could ever give: a life away from Royall. It would be this thought, of this baby girl, that would sit with Nola . . . a thought so beautiful that even Royall couldn't jaundice it. Blooming over time, this thought would give Nola strength, would whisper to her, telling her to escape, and . . . eventually . . . would help her do just that—convincing her to run, to run as far as she could, on that night a year from now, when she'd finally fight back, leaving Royall unconscious, leaving him behind, running out of his life, and heading for her teacher's house, a place of safety.

In the years that followed, Nola would google the girl's name at least once a year, never quite sure what she was looking for. A few times, usually on birthdays, she'd be tempted to drive by her school, or even her home. Every birth mom wondered how her child was doing with their adoptive family. But when it came to Archie Mint, Nola wouldn't see him again in person until that night of the "break-in" at Grandma's Pantry.

After she got the job as Artist-in-Residence, Nola would spend every morning going over the nightly blotter reports from military bases and government facilities. Combing through them, she'd pick the most interesting one and race to paint it. It was the best benefit of the job: she got to choose where she went.

Usually, a 7C1—a simple burglary—wouldn't catch her attention. But when she looked at the report and spotted Mint's name as one of the investigators . . . what else was Nola supposed to do?

This was her chance. For so long, she didn't want to pry, didn't want to disrupt her little girl's world. But now . . . she had a chance to see her—or at least see Mint—up close. At the very least, she'd get to meet the man who was raising her daughter. She double-checked the location. Barely two hours away. How could she not check it out? Just to get even the smallest piece of info about the little girl she'd left behind. On that day, it wasn't dumb luck that brought Nola to Grandma's Pantry. It was something far more personal.

Back when she was enlisted, Army psychiatrists would say that Sergeant First Class Nola Brown was incapable of forming attachments—incapable of loving herself or anyone else—because of early neglect. They were wrong.

"I'd like to go now," Nola insisted, turning away from the glass window and heading up the hospital hallway.

104

By the time Waggs left, a crescent moon was winking from the sky.

"Seriously, I owe all of you beers," she called to the four cops trailing behind her as she stepped onto the Mints' manicured lawn.

Two of the cops were already on their radios, calling details back to headquarters as they headed to their cars.

Nola was gone, her car nowhere in sight. It didn't stop Waggs from scanning the cul-de-sac, with its waiting ambulance, two police cars, and a chubby neighbor standing there with a baby stroller, pretending to walk his equally chubby English bulldog, but really just gawking.

"Give them some privacy," Waggs barked at Stroller Man.

For half a second, the man reached for his phone.

"Take that phone out. Watch what happens," Waggs added.

Making a face, the man picked up his bulldog, put him in the stroller, and disappeared up the block. There was no baby in it. It was just for the dog.

Waggs glanced down at her phone. Her last text was fifteen minutes ago, to Zig: Where r u?

Still no reply. She tapped her keypad twice, texting him a quick ?? as if two question marks would up the ante. Still nothing. Heading to her own car, she was staring down at her phone as she slid inside.

"Nola, you think I don't see you there?" Waggs asked, glancing in the rearview.

Behind her in the back seat, Nola's pointy features looked even more pronounced in the dark.

"I didn't think you were the dramatic type," Waggs added, "but driving your car around the block so everyone thinks you're gone, then walking back here to surprise me in mine—that's a lotta extra steps."

"How's Mrs. Mint?"

"I'm not your chauffeur. Get in the front."

Nola sat there, stubborn as ever.

"Front. Seat," Waggs growled in a tone Nola hadn't heard before.

Grudgingly, Nola elbowed open the back door, stepped outside, then opened the front door and slid into the passenger seat. The way Waggs had parked, Mint's house and the heart of the cul-de-sac were behind them. *Smart,* Nola thought. If things went south and anyone ran, Waggs was ready to give chase.

With a tug, Nola pulled the door shut, never taking her eyes off the ambulance in the rearview—or the cops, whose headlights blinked to life.

"That's it? They're leaving?" Nola asked.

"You sound surprised."

Nola's eyes narrowed. "Mrs. Mint's head was bleeding when I left. Her son, Huck . . . he was the one who—" She cut herself off. At the very least, they should be questioning everyone for the next hour. "How'd you do it?" Nola asked.

"Charm and stunning looks. My alpha and omega."

"You told them it was federal."

"It *is* federal," Waggs shot back, pointing to the FBI badge on her waist. "This is an ongoing investigation with clear Bureau jurisdiction. But I also told them the truth. Tessa Mint just went through the very worst week of her life—she buried her husband, the father of their children—and she was so distraught, she blacked out, gashing her head on the edge of their workbench. Thankfully, I was there to stop the bleeding," Waggs explained as both police cars rolled past them.

Nola turned her head just enough so the officers wouldn't get a good look.

"Plus," Waggs added, "y'know how much paperwork you have to fill out to grab a complex case like a federal officer who might've knocked out a civilian? In cop terms, this whole thing is a bag of shit. And they'd much rather it be *my* bag of shit than *their* bag of shit."

As the cops disappeared around the corner, Nola was still glancing at the rearview. On the Mints' front lawn, two buff EMTs rolled an empty stretcher. Behind them was Mrs. Mint, following them to the open back doors of the ambulance.

Her forehead was bandaged, but she was walking on her own, leaning on her son, who had an arm wrapped tightly around her waist, his head dipped down toward her. Even from here, lit just by the streetlights, Nola could see them clutching each other like they'd never let go.

"They cleaned her wound and stitched it up," Waggs explained. "It's probably overkill, but since she blacked out, they want a CT scan, just to be safe."

Nola nodded, though she still hadn't made eye contact with Waggs. "I thought you'd take them out in cuffs," Nola finally offered.

"Isn't it nice when people surprise you?"

Nola didn't answer.

"To be honest, I thought about it—about the cuffs," Waggs explained. In truth, she was *still* thinking about it. Yet the more she played it out, the person who actually shot Lieutenant Colonel Mint and Rashida—a drug dealer named Zion Lopez—was already dead, no longer a threat to anyone. Could she still arrest Huck for hiring him—and making sure he, his mom, and his sister were all out of the house on that night when Zion came? Absolutely. Based on what Huck had said inside, he knew Zion was no angel.

For years, Zion had been selling K2 and cheap cocaine to the wealthy kids in Huck's high school. Yet as the students there knew, Zion's real specialty was his ability to move in and out of the school's hallways—in the middle of the day, with dozens of security cameras—without being seen. He'd be sitting at lunch in the cafeteria, right under the teachers' noses. That's what had caught Huck's eye, especially after he heard his mom crying one night about a flirty text that had popped up on Mint's iPad. Forget drugs. Huck wanted stealth—

someone who could shadow his dad and Rashida to confirm Huck's suspicions.

Still, as every drug dealer knows, the best business is repeat business, so when Zion brought back that photo of Mint and Rashida leaning close and eating dinner together, it didn't take much to convince Huck that maybe there was a way to get his dad to end the affair. *You really think you could scare him off?* Huck had asked.

Waggs could bring him in just for that. Part of her was wondering if she'd wake up tomorrow and regret *not* bringing him in. But at this exact moment, based on everything she'd seen, Huck was a kid who'd made a horrific mistake . . . an unforgivable mistake . . . one that would alter and haunt him for the rest of his life. But at the heart of that mistake—at the core of this entire investigation—did this seventeen-year-old boy ever—even once—want his father dead? Not a chance. Waggs would bet her life on that. Indeed, as far as she could tell, all Huck wanted was the same thing every teenager in that same situation would want: for his dad to stop causing his mom—and his family—so much pain.

"So that night at the steak restaurant, Rashida was already inside when Mint arrived?" Nola asked.

"Mint had forgotten his jacket in the car. As he went back outside and saw the valet stealing his ride, he—and Rashida—jumped into a nearby taxi. When Zion pulled the trigger, she was in the back seat, right next to Mint."

"Why didn't they just leave her body in the car?"

"They were panicking," Waggs explained. "Huck was actually in the neighborhood, waiting for Zion to call with a thumbs-up. So when Zion called in full freak-out, they knew they only had a few minutes. And Huck knew if her body was found with his dad's . . . if his mom found out the two of them were together . . . He said he was trying to protect Rashida's family, too, so he begged Zion and, well . . . Zion said for five grand, he'd take care of it. He told Huck to stay away, then called his cousin and they dragged Rashida's body into his cousin's car. Huck had no idea he'd drive it out to the airport and light it on fire later that night. Again, they were panicking."

Nola thought about that, telling herself that the actions of a teenager somehow made sense. "If it helps, you did the right thing."

Waggs laughed, a deep laugh that reached her belly. "Oh, that's very sweet that you think I feel guilty. You think I'm a better person than I am. The real truth is, my bosses would never let us prosecute a crap show like this. At best, they'd make a deal with Huck—have him pin the killing on Zion, and in exchange, as a minor, thank him with a non-pros," she said, referring to a non-prosecution agreement. "All I'm doing is saving myself the months of paperwork that'll leave me in the exact same spot I'm in now. I can live with it, though. As Huck's about to learn, the worst prisons are the ones we create for ourselves."

"You may be right."

"I'm definitely right," Waggs said, pulling a thumb drive from her pocket. "Huck gave me this. A screen recording from his last meeting with Zion on Black House. He was hoping to get Zion to confess on tape, that's why they were meeting. Zion wasn't that dumb, of course—but Huck was trying to get proof, to set things right, even if it meant turning himself in."

Nola nodded, still staring at the rearview, back at the manicured lawns that ringed the cul-de-sac. "One last question," Nola said. "The valet who stole Mint's car and broke into the house . . . Zion attacked him—"

"Zion mistakenly thought the valet was Mint. That's what you get for stealing cars."

"So in the end . . ."

"Wrong place, wrong time. For the valet, he just got hit by some bad luck."

"Like a lightning rod?" Nola challenged.

Waggs turned at the words. "Listen, I shouldn't've called you that."

"I don't need your apology."

"I didn't say you did. But if it makes you feel better, well . . . did you know that Ben Franklin originally did his kite experiment because he noticed that terrible fires were being caused when church steeples got hit by lightning? Thanks to him, the very first lightning rods were installed on roofs all around Philadelphia. When you think about it, those metal rods don't *cause* the problem—they take the beating, protecting everything close to them."

Nola sat there a moment, about to say something, then deciding against it. Turning back to the rearview, she eyed the EMTs as they helped Mrs. Mint onto the stretcher for her ride to the hospital.

"Really staying till the end of the credits, huh?" Waggs teased.

"If you want, I can leave."

"I'm just pointing out, you and Mint . . . you two must've been pretty close, huh? I mean, the way you threw yourself into this case. The way you're watching now . . . If I die, promise you'll avenge me, too."

Nola rolled her eyes. *Not funny*.

"What's interesting, though, at least to me, is five years ago, that time you spent with Mint at Grandma's Pantry . . ."

"Are you paying attention? This had nothing to do with Grandma's Pantry."

"I understand, and I clearly need more info from Zig, but I pulled the Grandma's Pantry files. Way back when, you were out there just a few days, barely a week," Waggs said calmly, eyeing her own rearview. "But the way you threw yourself into this case . . . jumping in like such a madwoman to solve Mint's murder . . . For you to take this all so personally, that's a pretty deep bond you two developed in such a short time."

Behind them, the EMTs pushed Tessa's stretcher into the ambulance, the legs collapsing. Huck was still holding his mother's hand, climbing in behind her.

"Mint was far from perfect, but it was one of my first cases. He was a good mentor," Nola explained.

"And that's why you came here? To help an old friend? Nothing more?"

"Nothing more," Nola replied, her tone flat, unwavering.

"Y'know, you're a frustrating demon, Nola Brown. But I will say, Mint and his family are lucky to have you. And as far as I'm concerned, so's my friend Zig."

There was a loud *thunk* behind them. The ambulance doors slamming shut.

"I really should go, Ms. Waggs."

"Yeah, I gotta run, too. They want me at the hospital and . . . hmm . . . now that I think about it, if you're headed that way . . . well . . . you wanna join us?"

Us?

Outside the car, the little girl appeared from nowhere, standing there, framed by the window. Nola was so busy studying the rear-view, she didn't see her approach, her bird's nest of black hair messier than ever. Mint's daughter, Violet.

"Personally, I hate other people's kids," Waggs explained, "but the EMTs said only one family member per ambulance, and I couldn't leave her home alone while her mother and brother were at the hospital."

Nola sat there, silent, staring dumbfounded at Waggs.

"It's just a fifteen-minute drive, but I'm not really from this area, so, anyway . . . was just thinking, if you're free . . ." Waggs added, a smile lighting her eyes. "You up for a ride to the hospital?"

Nola cracked her toes, her forehead filling with creases. She looked confused, like a rule had been broken, and if that rule was broken, then what else could give way?

"Nola, have you heard a word I've said?"

Nola nodded, slowly, then faster, like a translator was relaying a foreign language and she was a few seconds behind. It made Waggs realize that Nola Brown could deal with murder, with violence . . . even personal tragedy. But she didn't know how to deal with kindness.

"Don't look at me like that," Waggs added. "It's just . . . when you live in a ditch long enough, you start to decorate it. I thought you needed an upgrade, y'know?"

Nola sat there, turning back to the window.

Violet opened the back door and climbed inside.

"Ms. Waggs, I'm in," the girl said, her voice sounding wounded as she clicked her seat belt, holding the strap across her chest like a lifeline. She'd been through hell these past few days—her father dead, her mother now on her way to the hospital. Yet here she was, ready for whatever came next.

On their right, the ambulance blew past, Violet watching it race up the block. Nola tried to be subtle, taking a quick peek toward the back seat.

Violet's NASA T-shirt was faded and ratty, looking like something she'd slept in. Her jean shorts looked new; same with her sneakers, which, surprisingly, made Nola feel . . . *relieved?* . . . *proud?* . . . She didn't have the right word, but it felt good.

Within seconds, Violet had her phone out, thumbs furiously tapping and scrolling through some social media site that Nola had never been to in her life. The girl had an energy about her, like she was vibrating even when she was sitting still. She wouldn't look up—no eye contact—though Nola couldn't tell if it was from pain, shyness, or just being twelve.

"I'm sorry for yelling at you before," Violet finally offered, still staring at her phone. "Ms. Waggs told me . . ." She paused. "I didn't realize you were trying to help my mom."

"It's fine," Nola said, turning back to the front window and lowering her visor to quickly find Violet in the mini mirror. Nola had seen her before, always from afar. After her time with Mint at Grandma's Pantry, Nola would come by at least once a year, usually around Violet's birthday, sitting outside in the car but never going in—hoping to catch a glance, but really, just checking to make sure all was okay. Today, to have her this close, Nola had a chance to say something else . . . she *wanted* to say something else, but instead, she sat there, feeling equal parts alert and undone.

A deafening chirp pierced the air. Nola jumped as the ambulance flipped on its siren, flooding the car with swirling red lights.

"You got one of those in here?" Violet asked.

"That's just in the movies," Waggs said.

Violet nodded, appreciating being let in on the law enforcement secret.

For the next three minutes, that was the extent of their conversation. Waggs shot a look to Nola, trying to nudge her on. Nola barely noticed. She was still glued to the visor mirror. At one point, the car sped up, matching the speed of the ambulance. Nola shifted her head forward, then back, trying to get a better angle on the back seat.

"So, Violet, your mom said you like baseball."

"Yeah."

Waggs paused, an awkward silence filling the car. "You don't really want to talk baseball, do you?" Waggs asked.

"Not really."

"That's fine. What else you into? Movies? Bike riding?"

"Bike riding?"

"I dunno. Don't kids still ride bikes?"

"I like to draw," Violet offered.

Nola sat up straight, like a membrane had been pierced. Later tonight, she'd replay this moment, wondering if she embarrassed herself, if she was too enthusiastic, if she should've just stayed quiet . . . but right now, caught up in the moment, her glance slid sideways, toward the car's back seat—toward Violet, the two of them locking eyes as Nola quickly, impulsively, proudly blurted, "I draw, too."

"Cool," Violet replied with an indifferent shrug, turning back to her phone. For the rest of the ride, she didn't say another word.

But for Nola, it was enough.

105

"How's your ass?"

"Better than your colon," Zig teased, limping into the pale beige hospital room.

The bullet that tore through Roddy's stomach had also perforated his bowel, forcing the trauma surgeons to sew a colostomy bag to the left of his belly button. Only for a month, they promised. Same amount of time his right arm would be in a cast.

"At least I don't smell," Roddy said as the antiseptic and metallic stench of Silvadene burn cream filled the room. When the freezer exploded, Zig was lucky he was running, though he still took the brunt of it. Full-thickness burns—third degree—across his neck and back. Hair burned away, leaving the back of his head a mess of uneven patches. Plus bits of metal shrapnel, glass, and razor-sharp slivers of freezer door that lodged into his posterior thighs and rear end. The only unscathed part was the top of his left shoulder, from where he was carrying Reagan, whose body they never found in the rubble. Zig's doctors kept him for days to make sure there was no infection, but from the ginger way he was walking, full recovery would take weeks.

"I heard you're leaving," Roddy said, using the elbow of his cast to push the button and raise his hospital bed.

"Who told you that?"

"Josephine, the nurse—she's chatty. Plus, the clothes are kinda a giveaway," Roddy added, pointing to the khakis and polo shirt that Zig was wearing. Both bulged at the back from the thick gauze underneath. "And . . . y'know . . ." Roddy added, pointing to the half a dozen mylar balloons Zig was holding, ". . . all the pity presents."

"They're not pity—you earned them," Zig said, tying the balloons to the foot of Roddy's bed. Waggs had sent them to Zig, but for three days now, Roddy's room had been empty. No flowers, no cards, nothing.

"You're a good person, Mr. Zig—though I need to know: Were you always coming in to say goodbye, or only because you heard the FBI was here?"

"C'mon, what kinda monster you think I am?" After a pause, he added, "Though how'd you know I knew about the FBI?"

"Josephine. She said you gave her twenty bucks for a list of everyone who came to visit me."

"She really is chatty, isn't she?"

"Her brother and dad are both police. It's in her blood. Also, you're a mortician. No one likes morticians," Roddy said, glancing up at *Jeopardy!* on the muted TV. "That's a joke, Mr. Zig."

"I could tell," Zig said with a laugh. "But if we can get back to your visit with the FBI—"

"They found the money Elijah stole—the twenty-two million—most of it surprisingly still there, split among bank accounts in the Philippines, Burma, and the usual Caribbean islands. His lawyer's trying to make a deal, but the prosecutors aren't having it," Roddy explained. "What's interesting, though, is they finally got into Mint's Black House account—his bank accounts, too. Elijah didn't make a single payment to Archie Mint or Rashida Robinson."

"So that money Mint was getting . . . those $9,500 and $8,500 payments . . ."

"Mint was paying himself, for months now. Selling stocks, cashing in bonds—even took an early withdrawal from his 401(k)."

Zig nodded, putting the final pieces together. "Mint was getting ready to leave his wife."

"It happens in marriages every damn day. Raiding the family's accounts so when he started the divorce, he'd have money put away for his new life."

"Does Tessa know?"

"She does now."

Zig nodded. Since the moment they learned about Grandma's Pantry, they'd been convinced that the key to the case was figuring out who took the twenty-two million. O.J. thought the same, which explained why he and his Dover crew came racing to the crime scene, took over the investigation, and tried to keep things quiet. But as O.J.—and Zig—now understood, Mint's murder had no connection to Grandma's Pantry. They were two totally separate incidents—that is, except for the fact that Mint and Rashida were sleeping together then, and clearly sleeping together now.

In fact, when it came right down to it, the real reason O.J.'s forensic reports had made no mention of Rashida being in the car, well . . . it was no different than what motivated Mint's son in the first place. It wasn't some grand government scheme, but something personal and private—an infidelity that was about to tear the Mint family apart.

In the end, O.J. was simply trying to be a loyal friend, hiding Mint's second phone—and Rashida's location—in hopes of sparing his family the embarrassment of finding out that Mint was again cheating on his wife.

"You can be a great soldier and still be a bad husband," Zig finally said.

"Mhmm," Roddy agreed, glancing over at Zig, then back up to *Jeopardy!* "That's not really news to you, is it? The details about Mint's accounts . . . his divorce . . . Lemme guess—your friend in the Bureau, Waggs—she already told you what was going on."

"Roddy—"

"Did she tell you about the drug boss Zion worked for? Adrian Vess. Apparently, he's the one who hired the Reds to kill Zion. He didn't care about Mint—he just didn't like Zion freelancing, and even more, was worried about his empire crumbling if Zion ever got nabbed. Interestingly, a few days back, Vess was rushed to the emergency room. Said some berserker woman shot him in the foot and leg. Guy has nerve, though. He spends a decade shoveling drugs to kids, then files a police report—says that when he got back to his office, one of his paintings was missing."

Zig couldn't help but grin.

"Waggs told you that, too?" Roddy said.

"She was just—"

"I'd like to know what you're really doing here, Mr. Zig."

A Daily Double came up onscreen. "I told you, I came to say goodbye," Zig said, running his hand along the length of one of the balloon strings.

"Nola," Roddy said. "It always goes back to Nola for you, doesn't it? You think I'm still looking for her."

"Aren't you?"

Roddy liked that about Zig—always working the case.

"Roddy, if the agents told you something—"

"A few days back, they found an address. You have to understand, the Bureau doesn't care about Nola. Once they realized she didn't take the money, she became inconsequential."

"But not to you."

"Or to you."

"What'd you do with her address, Roddy?"

"I called in a favor—one of our dispatcher's stepsisters is a Pennsylvania detective. She and her partner went for a look."

"Please don't tell me they tried to confront her."

"Nola was living in an RV—an old Airstream trailer—in some kinda botanical garden. By the time they got there, Nola was gone, the place empty. They think she had a cat, though that was gone, too. From what they could tell, she cleared out in a hurry."

Zig exhaled loudly. "Of course she did."

"Mr. Zig, I'm the reason she ran."

"You don't know that."

"I don't blame her. When we were little, I used t— I was a shit to her. And not just to her . . . to everyone."

"Roddy . . ."

"Do you think people are capable of change?"

"Let's not get overdramatic."

"You were there. You saw me these past few days," Roddy said, his voice picking up speed. "You saw me lose my temper, the way I unleashed on Seabass. Did you know I broke my hand, fractured my knuckle from hitting him so much in the face? I even came after you. In Elijah's bar, I wanted to—" He stopped. "How can I be a good person if I still keep reverting to that old version of myself? It's like Mint—you can do all these good things, but no matter how good it looks on the outside, there's still something rotten lurking under the surface."

"Roddy, you're not like Mint."

"We're all like Mint."

"We're not," Zig insisted. "Everyone keeps a side of themselves slightly hidden, tucked away from the world."

"You don't."

"My wife didn't talk to me for three years. She probably still shouldn't. But for some people—in this case, for Nola—things just move slower than you want. But remember what you asked me when we were headed to Elijah's? *Who are you at your core?* The answer doesn't come from a single moment—and it certainly doesn't come from a third party."

"She's my twin sister."

"I don't care if she's Mother Teresa. The definition of you does *not* come from someone else. Especially her. I mean it. You don't need Nola Brown to figure out who you are. You saved my life twice, Roddy—at risk to your own. You're a good cop—and a good person as well."

Roddy cocked his head, looking unconvinced.

"There's a saying, Roddy: If gold rusts, then what can iron do?"

"I'm not sure what that means. Are you saying I'm iron?"

"We're *all* iron. And in those rare moments when we're gold . . . even then, we're not perfect. We're all a mess of failures and good intentions. Cut yourself some slack. When Nola's ready, she'll come around."

"She's never coming around."

"You're right. She may never come around," Zig agreed. "But

trust me on this, when it comes to forgiveness, you can't give it to anyone until you give it to yourself."

"Mhmm," Roddy said, letting Zig's words roll through his brain, still staring up at *Jeopardy!* "I like that iron and gold part. You get that from Facebook?"

"*The Canterbury Tales*. It's like the original Facebook, but with paper. And actual wisdom," Zig said, patting Roddy on the shoulder, like he was getting ready to leave.

"Y'know, Mr. Zig, there's still one last thing I don't understand."

"About the case?"

"About Nola," Roddy said, glancing over at Zig, watching his reaction, noticing Zig was now the one locked on *Jeopardy!* "Back when Mint first got shot, Nola rushed to the scene instantly. And she stayed committed to the case. That's a really good friend, don't you think?"

"I'm not sure what you're getting at."

"Just asking an honest question: When this started, I assumed Nola had a personal stake—that she was worried for her own life, or that something bad from her past was about to come out. But in the end, the reason she put herself at risk— It was just her friendship with Mint? That's why she was so concerned with everything?"

"Looks like that to me."

"And your friend Waggs agrees? She didn't tell you something different?"

Zig stood there, the balloons swaying slightly next to him. "That's all I know, Roddy. Though as far as I can tell, no one's really an expert on Nola."

For half a second, Roddy sat there, tempted to say something, but instead went with, "You're probably right." Up on the TV, one of the contestants punched the air, celebrating his correct answer for the second Daily Double.

"No sponge baths today—no matter how many times you ask," a nurse named Jarrika announced, shoving open the door. She was wiry, with wide eyes, a warm smile, and stray gray hairs like veins.

"Listen, I should get running," Zig said, spotting her rolling cart, which held a pink plastic basin filled with soapy water. Time to change the colostomy bag. "I'll speak to you later in the week," Zig added, heading for the door and flashing a thumbs-up.

Roddy gave his own thumbs-up, but he knew the truth. *You have a good life,* he thought as the door slowly shut and Zig disappeared.

"Aw, sweetie, someone sent you balloons," Nurse Jarrika said. "Those from your sis?"

Roddy sat up straight. "How'd you—?"

"Downstairs, at the check-in desk . . . They only give info to family, but as I passed, I heard this woman say she was your sis," Jarrika explained, circling to the other side of the bed, dragging her cart behind her. Along the wall, she gave a pump to the hand sanitizer, quickly cleaning her hands. "I gotta admit, she's like a clone of you, sweetie."

"W-Was she—? What else did she say?"

"Typical sibling. Wanted to know how you were. When you're getting out."

"And this was just now?"

"An hour ago . . . maybe a little less. Call downstairs—Gino spoke to her. But take it from me, I'm fluent in pushy family. She's worried about you," Jarrika teased, sliding on latex gloves and letting them snap like she was ready for surgery. "C'mon, let's get you clean."

Lifting the side of his gown, Roddy revealed the beige plastic bag attached to his belly. There was a stab of pain as she pressed the skin around the stoma—the fresh, tender hole—and freed the current bag, which had a pungent smell. To reassure him, Nurse Jarrika gently put her palm on his forearm. But at that exact moment, if she looked up, she wouldn't see pain or even embarrassment on Roddy's face. Instead, she'd see a lopsided but unmistakably wide grin.

Nola was here. Only for a few minutes, but she was actually here. *She's worried about you.*

That's something, Roddy thought.

106

"I really have to ride in this?" Zig asked.

Hector the orderly nodded, pointing Zig to the wheelchair, in no mood for a fight. "Hospital policy."

"What if I promise not to sue?"

"Those are always the people who sue," said Hector, a burly man with a bushy beard and a rainbow-striped button on his lapel that read: *Sounds Gay . . . I'm In!* "Don't worry—your manhood will survive."

"It's not my manhood I'm worried abou— Ahh . . . actually maybe it is," Zig said, gingerly lowering himself into the wheelchair. Between the burns and the shrapnel, sitting wasn't easy. "Just promise me there're no potholes."

"It's Newark, sir. There're always potholes," the orderly said, pushing him up the hallway to the nearby elevator.

A minute later, there was a ping, the doors opening on the ground floor.

"You got a ride?" the orderly asked.

"Uber," Zig said, pulling out his phone t—

"I got him," a female voice announced.

Zig looked up. Halfway down the polished hallway, she stood there alone, near the wall, like the last stubborn bowling pin refusing to fall. In the fluorescent light, she looked washed out and tired. But even from here, her dark eyes were knives. Nola.

"That your daughter?" the orderly asked.

Zig shook his head, blinking, like he still wasn't sure she was really there. *What're you doing?* he asked with a glance.

"It's a two-hour ride. Uber's a rip-off," Nola said. "Let's go. I'm double-parked."

"Not bad advice," the orderly agreed. "Anyway, on behalf of the city of Newark and our general counsel, you are officially no longer our legal responsibility. Also don't trip on the speed bumps outside."

Standing from the wheelchair, Zig was working hard to hide how much it hurt, not that Nola was looking. She was already outside, the revolving door still spinning as he followed her to her car, a beat-up gray Dodge with a dented roof that looked like it'd been repainted by hand.

As Zig tugged open the car door, he saw that the floor was littered with fast-food wrappers, Styrofoam coffee cups, and a swirl of plastic supermarket bags. Cat hair was sprinkled across the passenger seat, along with what looked like the top from a stick of deodorant. Nola wasn't just driving this car; she was living in it.

Sliding inside, Zig gripped the doorframe tightly, holding his breath to hide the fact that his legs and back were on fire.

"You're in pain. I'm sorry about that," Nola said.

"I'm fine."

"You smell like Silvadene. That's burn cream. The back of your hair is burned away." She waited for Zig to say something, but all he did was fidget with the cap from the deodorant. Shaking her head, Nola hit the gas, pulling out of the hospital roundabout. "Stop trying to fix everything—it's why you frustrate people, Mr. Zigarowski."

"Then I guess I'm on brand."

Leaving the hospital behind, Nola made a quick left onto Bergen Street, which was buried in a snarl of traffic. Up ahead, past the IHOP and KFC, a city worker in a cherry picker had his crane extended up to a broken traffic light. A motorcycle cop stood at the intersection, doing his best to direct the crush of lunchtime pedestrians and honking cars.

"Something tells me people in Newark aren't good at taking turns," Zig said.

Nola didn't even grin. Her jaw was clenched as she gripped the steering wheel like she was strangling it.

"Nola, I really do appreciate the ride, but I'm assuming you came here for more than just—"

"I didn't know about Elijah."

Zig turned, confused. "*Elijah?* Why would—?"

"Last time I saw you. At the funeral home. In the shower. You told me you were headed to see Elijah—to ask him about Grandma's Pantry," Nola said, still staring straight ahead. "But I'd never— If I knew Elijah was the one who stole the money all those years ago, I would've stopped you. When I heard the Reds were that close, I tried calling you. I wouldn't let you walk into danger like that."

In front of them, the traffic had barely moved, extending half the block. Nola was still murdering the steering wheel.

"And that's what's been weighing on you?" Zig asked. "That you weren't able to figure out, all by yourself, the case that stumped everyone for over half a decade?"

"You don't understand. I went to see him. When Mint and Rashida were killed, Elijah was one of my first stops. Even back in the day, he was top of the suspect list. Always a self-promoter, but smart. Didn't spend his money for years. Had a good alibi with his brother-in-law for funding his stupid bar. So when you said you were going to see him—" Nola stopped, eyes locked on the cherry picker. "I'm sorry you got hurt. Ms. Waggs showed me the reports. Third-degree burns . . . I could've— I shouldn't've let you go there."

Zig sat in silence, staring down at the deodorant cap like it was a manuscript of ancient wisdom. "You done?"

"I don't want to hear your stupid lectures."

"It's not a lecture, Nola. I appreciate better than nearly anyone what a powerful narcotic guilt is. And I know it's even more potent when you think I jumped into this case because of you. So let me just say it: I'm a grown man. When it came to Mint's case, I was the mortician of record—"

"The only reason O.J. brought you in—"

"Was to get to you—I'm well aware. But that doesn't change one immutable fact: this case smelled from the start. That's why, at the funeral, I followed the family into the gym. Whether you showed up or not, I would've looked into Mint's death."

"No. You wouldn't."

Zig thought about that, the car slowly inching forward. "Maybe I wouldn't. But I'm glad I did."

Nola turned at the words, annoyed. "You're really such a softball."

"No, Nola—I'm a friend."

Nola rolled her eyes as they approached the intersection. Slowly, KFC and IHOP gave way to mom-and-pops with dilapidated signs and metal bars across the windows. *Laisha Afrika Foods. Good Empire Check Cashing.* Most of them were closed or boarded up, this part of the neighborhood clearly struggling. Still, on the corner, Zig spotted two Asian men—father and grandfather—each on their own ladder, hand-painting a royal-blue awning with bright yellow letters. *Sammy & Sons,* plus a logo that looked like a wrench. A hardware store, Zig realized. Something new, even here.

"Nola, as a friend, can I give you a piece of advice?"

"If I say *no,* will you listen?"

"You don't like my advice, don't take it—but again, as a friend—have you thought about talking to your brother?"

"Stop."

"Nola—"

"*Stop.* I need you to stop, Mr. Zigarowski. You think you know Roddy—"

"I do."

"You don't. I can tell the two of you went through the grinder: you watched him get shot, and sure, that makes you feel bad—but that doesn't change who he is."

Outside, the traffic cop blew his whistle, waving them forward. With a tug of the wheel, Nola made a sharp right and punched the gas, sending them screeching around the corner, the hardware store fading behind them.

"Nola, at the risk of sounding prehistoric, have you ever heard of Liberace?"

"Famous piano guy. Matt Damon played him in that movie."

"Michael Douglas played him, but yes, the flamboyant piano player. Makes Elton John look like a yawn."

"Can you just skip to the inevitable moral lesson that you tack on at the end?"

"We've got a two-hour drive—it's either this, or I can start retelling old Girl Scout stories from when you were little."

Nola didn't answer. Zig was still playing with the deodorant cap, sticking his finger inside it, holding it up like a bobblehead.

"This is back in the eighties," Zig explained. "To celebrate fifty years of entertaining, Liberace did fifty shows across the country, culminating with two solid weeks at Radio City, which is no small feat. The first night at Radio City, he's sitting at the piano and starts telling the audience about this young couple who, fifty years ago, met at one of his very first shows. 'And so, ladies and gentlemen,' he says as the lights come up, *'here they are now!'* Ka-zam. The spotlight swings, revealing this sweet elderly couple in the sixth row. Everyone starts clapping, people are crying—it's one of those touching human moments that lets every person in the room experience the power of true love.

"But here's the thing," Zig quickly added. "The next night, he tells a similar story, of a couple that met at his show. *'And here they are . . .'* he says, pointing to a different old couple. The next night, there's a third new elderly couple. And the night after that . . ."

"The couples aren't real. They're plants," Nola said.

"Correct. This was before social media—no one was the wiser."

"It's a manipulative lie."

"No doubt—but every night, the audience ate it up, clapping, sobbing, leaving with tears in their eyes as they laced fingers with their loved ones, committed to being better people for just one night."

Nola turned with a look of annoyance. "Liberace's a lying manipulator—no different than my brother."

"Maybe. When Liberace died, though, his finances were such a mess, they didn't even realize he'd spent his life giving over six million dollars to fund scholarships for kids in the performing arts. Some of the endowments were permanent, and there were so many, even today, they still don't have an accurate count of how many kids he helped."

"That doesn't mean my brother's not a liar."

"I'm not saying it does. But we all have a person we were and a person we are. It's never a straight line between the two—and it's certainly never a predictable one. Just because you read the first few chapters doesn't mean you know everything that's coming. Keep an open mind. If you're lucky, there's a plot twist."

With a thump, the car hit a pothole. A blaze of pain shot up Zig's back, but he never took his eyes off Nola.

"Liberace still sounds like a pain in the rear," Nola said.

"Thousands of old women in sequined headbands and multiple rings disagree with you."

For a half second, Nola looked like she was about to smile. She didn't, but her hands did slide down the steering wheel to the five and seven o'clock positions. The shift in her posture was enough that Zig spotted, in her door's storage well, a plain manila envelope.

Squinting, Zig saw his name handwritten in black pen in the corner. "Nola, what's in the envelope?"

"I'll show you after."

"Show me now."

On their right, they blew past a dilapidated redbrick building, the roof sheared away, the zigzag of missing bricks resembling a crumbling smile. The place looked like it'd been hit by a bomb.

"I was— It's about Maggie," she said. Zig's daughter.

"Nola, what'd you do?"

"Ms. Waggs told me about the video . . . the one you were looking for . . . from the modeling agency . . ."

"If you found something—"

"A boyfriend. Liam Hudson. They called him Huddy, at least back then," Nola explained, eyes again straight ahead, hands back up to ten and two. "From what I could find, he was a new kid. Moved from Oregon. For some reason, everyone said he could do a lot of chin-ups."

"Did you know him, or—?"

"Just listen. He got there after I moved away. Apparently, at some point, Huddy asked Maggie out. They dated for a week or two, then he dumped her for Daniella Moran, a nasty little panty stain who's now a corporate lawyer in Philly. That's why Maggie was crying in the video. Every week, the head of the modeling agency would do 'open mics,' little interviews to give kids experience on camera, but really to get new sign-ups."

"We'd never let Maggie sign up there."

"She didn't seem to care—she went with Daniella," Nola explained, handing him the envelope. "You'll see in the footage. Daniella goes first and mentions her new boyfriend. By the time Maggie gets onscreen, the employee who's filming can tell something's wrong. He asks if she's okay, and the floodgates open about the breakup."

Reaching into the envelope, Zig pulled out a DVD in a cracked jewel case. He was calm, which was the giveaway.

"You already knew," Nola said.

Zig nodded, staring down at the DVD with the handwritten Post-it labeled *SuperStars Modeling*.

"Who told you? Ms. Waggs?" Nola asked.

Zig nodded again. "Though my ex-wife found it first, two days ago." Charmaine was smart. She remembered the old camera store in the same plaza. CameraWorld. That took her back to the source—the daughter whose parents used to run SuperStars and started this whole mess. When Charmaine first spoke to her, the daughter said she'd already looked through all the videotapes. But when Charmaine called back, the answer was a simple question away: *Among those old videos, do you happen to have a corresponding DVD?* That was it. "That's why the owners taped over the old video," Zig explained. "Once they had the DVD, the original tapes went back in the camera."

"So you've already seen it."

Zig nodded, eyes still locked on the DVD. "Charmaine emailed it last night."

It was two minutes and twenty-three seconds long, Maggie sitting on a sofa, wiping tears and snot on her sleeve as she told the story of how Huddy dumped her for Daniella—a detail that seemed to upset Maggie more than the actual breakup.

"Nola, do I even want to know how you got this?" Zig asked, holding up the DVD.

"You don't."

Zig laughed, tapping the jewel case like a drum against his own thigh. For years, just the sight of an old photo of Maggie, much less an actual video, would've ripped Zig apart. And sure enough, when he'd watched the video last night, hearing the story of her breakup with Huddy, Zig's eyes welled with tears. But they weren't tears of pain . . . or the even more ruthless tears of guilt for missing out on something as vital as his daughter's first boyfriend. To Zig's own surprise, it was actually . . . nice. It was nice having something new—a little piece of his daughter that came back when he least expected it.

"It was good seeing her again," Zig admitted, though it wasn't until this moment, as he drummed the jewel case, that he realized the full extent of it. This DVD . . . everything on it . . . it was a gift from a ghost, a gift from the past—wonderful for sure, but not nearly as vital as something in the present.

"It was thoughtful of you to do this, Nola. You didn't have to."

"You're getting sappy," she warned.

Of course he was, though he was done apologizing for it. All this time, Zig wasn't a broken man; he was a frozen man. Two years ago, he'd taken the job at Calta's Funeral Home to move on from Dover and dead soldiers, hoping it would help him come back to life. Yet it was time to admit, the only way to come back is to actually move forward. Otherwise, you just gather dust.

"By the way, not sure if you heard, but O.J. offered me a job," Zig added. "Wants me to leave the funeral home and come back to Dover. He said since we helped find the twenty-two million, he wants to bring me onto the investigative side. Have me look at bodies out in the field."

Nola sat there silent, unreadable.

"Know what else I heard?" Zig added. "That he offered you a job as well."

"Who told you that? Ms. Waggs?"

"She said your work on the Mint case was exceptional—O.J.'s words, not just hers—and that he'd be lucky to have brains like you on his team."

"I'd rather have ants eat my eyes than work for him."

"So how do you really feel?"

"Can you not be a sucker for once? O.J. is—"

"Let me tee it up differently for you: if *I* was there, and *you* were there, we cou—"

"Don't even think it."

"I'm not saying I'm taking the job, but if I did—"

"Don't. Think. It."

Zig tapped the jewel case against his leg, letting the car fill with silence.

"What else did Ms. Waggs tell you?" Nola asked.

"Nothing. That was it."

She glanced over at him, the two of them locking eyes.

"That was it," Zig said, holding up three fingers.

"Mr. Zigarowski, are you giving me the Boy Scout salute?"

"Old habits," Zig said, starting to laugh and waiting for her to join in.

She didn't.

Heading under an overpass and onto Oraton Parkway, they blew past a wide building with boarded-up windows. Zig thought it was a factory, but it was really a school.

"Nola, just think about the job, okay?"

"I'm not taking it."

Zig started to say something, but stopped himself. In half a mile, the road veered again, through a tollbooth that dumped them onto the Garden State Parkway. For the first minute or two, he searched the side of the road for green mile markers, to see how far they were from home. What caught his eye, though, was a sign for something called the Midwood Diner. Next exit.

Since his earliest days as a mortician, Zig knew that there are people you carry with you your entire life. They either help you or haunt you. But as the saying goes, you know you're on the right path when you stop looking back.

"You hungry?" Zig asked.

Nola thought about it. "I can eat."

107

Two weeks later

"Close your eyes."

"They're closed," Zig insisted.

"Really closed. Not that fakery where you peek," Charmaine said. Like any ex-wife, she knew his tricks.

"Char, why would I—? *Look! Closed!* Y'happy?" Zig asked, standing in the threshold of his front doorway. Outside, Charmaine was facing him, a big Lululemon bag at her side, resting on the doormat. As she opened it, Zig heard the jingling of the crystal and beaded bracelets on her wrist. Then a clink. Something glass.

"On three," Charmaine said. "One . . . two . . . *voilà*."

From the bag, she pulled out a vintage Waterford crystal decanter—etched glass, sterling silver collar at the top. Zig's eyes went wide. Growing up, he'd spent every Sunday watching his grandfather fill it with cheap scotch, trying to make it look fancy.

"Whoa. Where'd you find it?"

"In my bar."

"What're you talking about? You *stole* it?"

"Don't pick a fight," Charmaine teased, her crow's-feet deepening as she grinned. She looked stunning as the late summer sun waved goodbye to the sky, bathing her in golden light that made her green eyes glow. "I never stole it. You accidently left it behind. I just decided it liked me better."

"That sounds like kidnapping."

"Think of it as me making it a better offer."

"So like the U.S. government with World War II Nazi scientists."

"Personally, I tend to dial back Nazi metaphors, but if that's the hammer you need to make your point, so be it. And you're welcome. I refilled it."

She held up the crystal bottle. The liquid's pale bronze color gave it away. Balvenie 25 Year Single Barrel—the one his grandfather always talked about, but could never afford. The last time Zig got a bottle was a wild night in Vegas that they'd never talked about since the divorce. "To top it off, I pretend buy you those Winston Churchill lowball glasses that we should've bought in that antique shop in London."

Right there, Zig knew what to say. He had the perfect comeback on his tongue—loaded like a catapult—the retort that might make her blush, but would most likely make her lower her chin and cock her eyebrow in that way Zig could already feel in his pants.

Charmaine took a half step closer, handing him the crystal decanter. The thin neck and wide bottom of the bottle had always reminded Zig of *I Dream of Jeannie*. But right now, as he reached for it, it looked like an oversized pawn.

A light breeze blew through the porch, making the bamboo wind chime sway with a soothing timbre. Zig replayed his line again, but instead of cutting the catapult's rope, he holstered the comeback, putting it aside. Instead, he went with, "You're a good person, Charmaine. I pretend buy you something really nice, too."

Charmaine stood there a moment, her elevens shifting, like she expected something more—and was still waiting for it—even as she finally accepted that nothing more was coming.

She let go of the bottle as Zig gripped it with both hands. It was heavier than he remembered. "By the way, I'm sorry things have been hard with you and Warren. He's still a good guy. Give him a chance."

"We'll work it out. Or we won't," she said, truly at peace, still standing there in the fading sun, looking as beautiful as he'd ever seen her—but also, in the subtle tilt of her head, looking sad.

Years from now, Zig would remember this moment, remember this woman in his doorway, the sunlight on her cheeks, his fingertips anxiously tracing the etched patterns on this antique bottle. Over Charmaine's shoulder was her parked car, an old forest-green Subaru covered in yoga and *26.2* marathon bumper stickers. Over Zig's shoulder was a quiet house.

Most people think morticians are obsessed with death, or at least fascinated with it. For years, Zig's greatest fear was that death was all he was good at. Over time, especially lately, the universe seemed to be reminding him of that fact. But just being near Charmaine again—to feel the tug, the undertow of that old connection . . . just her smell of lavender and worn leather—nothing on this planet so instantly reminded him of one of the greatest, most rewarding things he'd ever accomplished—like his old life was right there, waiting to be reclaimed. All he had to do was ask.

Would it really be so bad to invite her inside?

Zig held his breath. Leaning toward her, he gave her a quick hug, adding a pat on the back. "It really was great seeing you again, Char." Lifting the crystal bottle, he added, "Thanks again for returning this to its rightful owner."

"Sure . . . no . . . of course. It was great seeing you, too, Ziggy."

"Send my best to Warren," he added, rubbing the back of his head to feel the patches of missing hair. Before Charmaine could react, Zig closed the door.

He loved her—he'd always love her. And maybe one day they'd give it a shot and try again. But not today.

Five minutes later, Zig was in his backyard, opening the roof of his hive, adding a fresh round of bee whiskey.

"I know, I know. Don't even say it," Zig said to his favorite girls.

Mmmmmmmm, thousands of bees sang back.

"You always liked her better."

Mmmmmmmmmmmmmm, the bees agreed, sounding stronger than ever.

"You gotta admit, she looked gorgeous, right?" Zig asked as he reached into the hive and pulled out a flat wooden frame. At the center of it was a smushed oval pattern, like a deflated basketball—a large cluster of larvae and eggs. Good sign, lots of activity.

As he pulled it closer, it wasn't hard to find the queen. He just looked for her attendants, a dozen bees, all of them pointing their heads toward her, grooming her, taking care of her—making sure she was safe. Queens weren't larger than other bees. Their giveaway was their shape—longer abdomen and legs; shorter wings. Plus, her back was bald and shiny.

"Looking good, your majesty," he said to Diana-28.

Some queens were skittish. Diana-28 moved slowly, poised and proud. The hive was thriving.

Sliding the wood frame back into place, Zig pulled out a different one. Similar oval, similar larvae and eggs, and yes, similar attendants. But at the center of this crowd? Diana-27. The old queen.

Back on the night Zig got out of the hospital, he was ready to squish Diana-27. According to the experts, when you have two queens, it's the only way for the hive to survive. Kill one to save the other. Otherwise, they'll battle to the death, potentially killing both in the process. Game of Combs, one of the websites warned. Bee-mageddon.

Yet on that night, when he opened the hive, to his surprise, the bees were doing . . . well. Every hive had its own personality, and somehow, some way, this one decided to work it out. Diana-28 was on the first frame; Diana-27 on the back one.

Not possible, Zig thought at the time.

When he posted the details of his two-queen hive on a popular online bee forum, most people told him it wouldn't last—that he should still squish the old queen. But a woman in Massachusetts told him that while it was rare, her two queens had lived together for over a year. "Bees don't read the same books we do," she wrote. "You don't have to choose."

Zig liked that.

"Okay, see you tomorrow, kiddos," Zig said, sliding the wooden frame back into its slot and putting the cover back in place.

Mmmmmmmmmmmmmmmmmmmmm, the hive sang, already drunk on bee whiskey.

When he was alone, Zig sometimes wondered what would've happened if he'd never met his wife . . . if they had never had a daughter. He'd play through the permutations, thinking how much easier his life would've been. In the end, though, even with the heart-ache, with the pain, with the loss—with the deafening, piercing regret that consumed his state of innocence and peace, ensuring he could never attain them again . . . If the only way for Zig to avoid all that was to erase those early years as a family, those moments of pure good . . . It wasn't a choice at all. He'd forever take the pain. He'd take all of it. Easily.

Sitting down in his favorite rusty lawn chair, Zig pulled out his phone and hit the button to dial a number. It rang once . . . twice . . .

"Please don't tell me you kissed her," Puerto Rican Andy answered.

"You really think I'm that predictable?"

"You told me she was coming over. Doesn't take a genius to guess the rest," Andy said. He lowered his voice. *"Humans do have a knack of choosing precisely those things that are worst for them."*

"That a Dumbledore quote?"

"All the best quotes are Dumbledore quotes. I'm proud of you, though. I thought for sure you'd screw it up."

Mmmmmmmm, the bees said.

"Yeah, yeah, yeah," Zig said. "Anyway, just wanted to see how you're holding up."

"You call twice a day. I'm doing okay."

It was a lie. Andy's voice was hoarse, his throat still healing. "You up for a visit?"

"Actually, if it's okay, Ziggy, can I rain-check?" He'd said the same yesterday, and the day before, and the day before that. "I'm just not the best company right now."

"Y'know, Andy," Zig said, lowering his own voice. *"Happiness can be found, even in the darkest of times, if one only remembers to turn on the light."*

"Sonuva—!" Andy let out a laugh, a loud rippling burst. "You're doing Dumbledore to me? To *me*? You just google that?"

"Memorized it last week. Figured it'd come in handy. Now, c'mon—I caused those stitches in your throat. Lemme make up for it. I got a fancy present for you."

The phone went silent. "How fancy?"

"Balvenie 25 Year," Zig said, glancing over at the crystal decanter sitting on a small three-legged plastic table that usually held a six-pack.

"Ten points to Gryffindor!" Puerto Rican Andy yelled, even though it hurt to yell. It'd hurt to drink scotch, too. After a beat, he added, "You understand that means—"

"I know what it means," Zig interrupted, hopping from his chair, grabbing the crystal bottle by the neck, and heading for the door.

"Let us step out into the night and pursue that flighty temptress, adventure! Guess who said that one: Harry, Ron, or Hermione?"

"Ron?"

"Dumbledore, man! I told you, Dumbledore always gets the best quotes!"

Zig laughed as the bees buzzed behind him. "By the way, Andy, I was thinking about work," he said, stepping out into the night. "When you're ready for it, what're your thoughts about Delaware?"

EPILOGUE

It took patience to find him.

Actually, that wasn't true. All it took was Nola's license plate, which gave him her car, which gave him her 2011 entry-level Dodge, an Avenger. From there, the Mopar system did the rest.

Tired of losing sales to LoJack, both Dodge and Chrysler introduced the Mopar tracking system in 2010, complete with silver and gold plans that gave you unlimited nationwide tracking, for both location and speed.

What most consumers didn't know, however, was that there was a base plan as well—no monthly fee—though good luck finding a dealer who'd tell you. As a result, to this day, there were tens of thousands of Dodge, Chrysler, and Jeep owners who had no idea their used cars were still sending trackable signals wherever they went.

From there, all it took was patience—and some friends in law enforcement. Fortunately, Roddy had both.

"And he's been here how long?" Roddy asked.

"I think at least . . ." Nurse Odessa flipped open the medical chart. She was a young oval-faced Honduran woman with hazel eyes and a trim figure, like a runner. "Yup, yup . . . he got here when my son was born, nearly two years ago."

Roddy nodded as they turned the corner in the empty, fluorescent-lit hallway. The only decorations were three framed portraits of white men in front of American flags. Secretary of Defense, Chief of Staff of the Army, and Sergeant Major of the Army. The photos were the only indication that this was a military facility—you'd never know it if you drove by.

From the outside, the Fairfax Manor Rehabilitation Center was like every other forgettable glass-and-concrete office building this close to Dulles Airport—designed to be overlooked. There wasn't even a sign out front. But again, Roddy knew where he was going.

"That kinda day, huh?" Nurse Odessa asked, eyeing Roddy's police uniform and the federal warrant he was still holding in his hand.

Roddy forced a grin that wasn't nearly as warm as he thought it was.

As they headed down the hallway, he saw that most of the rooms were filled. On their right was a Saudi Arabian professor getting chemo and state-of-the-art treatment in exchange for information about a former student who now lived in Tehran. In another room was an Asian woman—an Army Ranger out of North Carolina—who'd had four of her fingers cut off when the Chinese government accused her (correctly) of being embedded in a robotics plant in Beijing.

The U.S. government had facilities like this all over the globe. When undercover soldiers and secret squirrels make the wrong enemies, you can't just send them to emergency rooms or even military bases. Instead, you need a place that specializes in keeping them safe—and out of sight.

"*Mötley Crüe?*" Roddy asked, hearing the music at the end of the hallway.

"Def Leppard," the nurse replied as "Pour Some Sugar on Me" pounded in the distance.

According to some doctors—or at least the ones at Fairfax Manor—the best way to help someone with a traumatic brain injury was to play songs that remind them of something they love. A reason to come back.

"Apparently this was his band," Odessa explained, reaching the end of the hallway—room 113—as Def Leppard insisted they were sticky sweet, from their head to their feet.

"Yeah," Roddy whispered to himself, quickly pulling out his

phone. No signal, no surprise. Of course the military blocked it here. Still, cell signals were different from GPS, which explained why, when Waggs used Nola's phone to track her to various hospitals, it showed visits to three different patients in the past few weeks— all three with traumatic brain injuries. Otherwise, the patients had nothing in common. For Waggs and Zig, it was the one unanswered question: Why was Nola talking to people with brain injuries?

Naturally, Waggs tried going back further—there were plenty of places Nola drove in the past few months—but when Nola had come here, her cell signal faded a few blocks away, just past a Cracker Barrel off the highway. At the time, Waggs made a mental note, thinking Nola didn't seem like a Cracker Barrel type, but that was the end of it.

As a result, Waggs couldn't possibly know that instead of taking three car trips to three different patients, Nola had actually visited four. Roddy, though, thanks to the Mopar system, knew exactly where it was: right here, at Fairfax Manor. Patient zero. The very first person Nola came to see.

"Up and at 'em," Odessa announced, giving the door a shove. She didn't wait for a reply. Roddy knew there wouldn't be one.

The room was dated, painted a tranquil blue-green with laminate wood floors, making it feel more like a nineties Pottery Barn catalog than a hospital suite. On the wall was a framed and faded poster with neon video game lettering that read, *Good Health Is Contagious!*

Roddy didn't notice any of it. Trailing behind the nurse, he craned his neck at the unconscious man whose mouth sagged open like an empty Christmas stocking.

Propped up in his hospital bed, he had gray hair that needed a buzz, a pitted face, and a faded scar that split his bottom lip in a zigzag, from where it'd been torn open years ago.

"He looks old for liking Def Leppard," Roddy said.

"Def Leppard's *old*," Odessa clarified. The song was still playing on a nearby sound dock, punctuated by a choir of beeps and buzzing from the respiratory monitor and various other machines, including a tracheostomy tube in the man's throat and a PEG feeding tube in his stomach. His legs were wrapped in compression stockings to prevent an embolism. His face was gaunt from losing at least twenty-five pounds, making him nearly unrecognizable—key word being *nearly*.

The air in the room grew heavy, and Roddy felt a gash, a widening cut, like something was splitting him open. He recognized the man instantly. He remembered him, or at least a younger version of him, from that night all those years ago. Back then, the man's hair was less gray, and he certainly didn't have the zigzag scar, but, for Roddy, there was no forgetting that night, squinting down from the top of the stairs as the doorbell rang and this stranger stepped into their house—to take Nola away.

At the foot of the hospital bed, his name was written in faded black marker on a strip of white surgical tape.

Royall Barker

"Royall," Roddy whispered, not even realizing he was saying it out loud. The closest thing Nola ever had to a father.

He was supposed to be dead. Two years ago, Nola uncovered him running a corrupt military unit. When he tried to kill her, she shot him in the head. Everyone said he was dead. And yet, here he was, hidden away, mouth agape, feeding tube pumping, as "Pour Some Sugar on Me" played on eternal repeat.

Nola, that's what you discovered, isn't it? Roddy realized, snapping the last pieces into place.

For a moment, Roddy stood there, rewinding, trying to make sense of why the military would hide the truth about Royall, much less help him. Were they trying to protect him—or simply keep a lid on whatever embarrassing military secrets were still rolling around in his head?

As the rewind picked up speed, Roddy replayed the past two years, trying to picture Nola's reaction when she realized Royall was alive. Did someone tell her? Or could she feel it? Something that big . . . you'd feel it, wouldn't you?

Even here, even with Nola nowhere in sight, Roddy could sense an echo from her. He could feel his sister's rage, her fury, at knowing that Royall, the ultimate cheater, had even cheated death. Yet none of that compared to what really had been driving Nola these past few months. Those visits Waggs had been tracking—Nola's trips to various hospitals and patients—they had nothing to do with Mint, or Grandma's Pantry . . . nothing to do with Nola's anger or fury at the lies about Royall being alive. *That's your real secret, isn't it, sis?*

Those visits Nola took were about something more fundamental in her life, the one thing she'd never admit even to herself. Despite the self-protective walls she'd erected, despite the exquisite rage, worn as armor, to make her believe that she could take on anything, when it was late at night, in one of those quiet moments when the world made her feel like she was the only person still awake, there was still a little goblin lurking out there in the darkness that even the mighty Nola Brown was afraid of—the only goblin she'd ever been afraid of—the one she'd never been able to control: Royall himself.

That's why you went to see those victims with brain injuries. When it came to Royall, Nola was trying to answer the unanswerable questions: *Will he be like this forever—or is he going to wake up?* Which made Roddy wonder: *If he does wake up, what is she planning to do?*

"I take it he doesn't get many visitors?" Roddy finally asked, studying Royall's open mouth, his cigarette-stained lower teeth, like slanted books on a shelf.

"We don't do visitors. Just the one I told you about. The woman from the Army. She came here once. We had to ask her to leave—and no offense, but since your warrant is limited to a quick ID, I need to ask the same of you."

"Yeah, of course, my apologies," Roddy said, still standing there, taking a last good look at Royall.

On the nearby sound dock, Def Leppard sang that love was like a bomb and you should come and get it on. Roddy couldn't agree more.

For years now, he'd thought about searching for Nola, trying to track her down—to reconnect, to learn a little bit about her, and . . . he hoped, maybe . . . learn some more about himself—but the truth was, he never went through with it. It was the one white lie he told Zig. All these years, Roddy *thought* about looking for Nola, but he never did. Not until he had info about *her*—the most important *her* in his and Nola's life.

Back behind the funeral home, Roddy tried telling Nola, but she wouldn't listen. Replaying their short conversation, Roddy wondered if maybe Nola didn't realize who he meant, but c'mon, she was the one person both Roddy and Nola cared about.

In the end, that's what made him come searching for his sister. After years of digging, he'd finally found new info—an actual lead—about what really happened when his and Nola's mother was murdered.

Simply put, Roddy was searching for help. In the process, though, he'd found something far more important. He'd found insight. Now, when it came to Nola, he finally knew what was driving her.

The only question was: What would he do with it?

"By the way, who told you he likes Def Leppard?" Roddy asked.

"Excuse me?"

"The music. Who told you Royall likes this music?"

"Um . . . *he* did," Odessa said, pointing toward the bed.

Roddy cocked his head, confused.

"He woke up two weeks ago," the nurse added.

Roddy turned just in time to see the breathing tube in Royall's neck start to shake as he blinked himself awake.

"Who the hell're you?" Royall challenged, his voice an angry rasp as he covered the tracheostomy tube to speak.

"*Me?*" Roddy asked, standing there, his spidery fingers excitedly touching his own chest. "I'm nobody."

THE LONG WAY HOME

You made it, dear reader—welcome to the very end. This is the part where Barnes & Noble has graciously asked me to tell you a little bit more about this book you just finished. They said I could write about whether Zig and Nola are inspired by real people (they are, though they're amalgams of so many amazing heroes I've met at Dover and in the military), if a place like Black House really exists (all I'll say is, I didn't make up that idea), or whether the secret warehouses of the Strategic National Stockpile are real (they are, though I changed the location for national security purposes). But since I just told you those answers, I thought I'd take this space for something more personal. And so . . .

This marks the twenty-fifth anniversary of my writing life. That's a long time—and if you've been with me from the start, you're officially family. But as someone who loves history, I think it's important to look back and try to examine how we got from there to here.

In truth, it wasn't my best start. My first book got twenty-four rejection letters. There were only twenty publishers at the time, yet I got twenty-four rejection letters. That means some people were writing me twice to make sure I got the point.

I've told that story for years, but here's the part I rarely share: The first twenty-two letters were straight rejections. But two of the editors—#23 and #24—were actually interested in my first novel. I even came to New York to meet the two editors. At the time, my agent Jill Kneerim told me the meetings went well and that she thought my first book was going to sell. As someone who was in both college and law school debt, I was ecstatic.

From there, I was also told that editors #23 and #24 were both given a deadline—and that I should wait by my phone for the news (this was pre–cell phones). Naturally, I did exactly that. And then, at the appointed time, my phone rang. I can still fell the rush of adrenaline running through my twenty-four-year-old body. I picked up the phone, all excited to hear the good news and to hear that I was finally going to be debt free. Instead, as I put the phone to my ear, I heard these words from my agent, "Sorry, kiddo."

My heart sank to my feet. I was DEVASTATED. In two words, all my dreams evaporated. But here's my real secret. We all have our rituals. Here's one of mine: Every day that I sit down to write, I replay and recreate that moment.

I picture the phone I was holding at the time (one of those clear, see-through ones where you could see the wires inside, since that was high-tech back then). I picture the Formica desk on my left, with the swivel lamp every college kid had. I picture, on my right, the bed that was just a box spring and mattress, with no headboard. I picture the small terrace that overlooked the concrete parking lot below, and across the street, the fire station with its three doors that I mentally count to myself . . . 1 . . . 2 . . . 3. And then I say those words: "Sorry, kiddo."

Why? Because I never want to be anything but as hungry as I was at twenty-four years old. I never want to think I've made it, because if I think I've made it, I'm finished as a writer. And I never, ever, ever want to be anything but completely appreciative of this writer's life you've given me. For twenty-five years now, *every single time* I sit down to write, "Sorry, kiddo . . . sorry, kiddo . . . sorry, kiddo."

Which leads me to why I'm really taking you on this stroll down memory lane. The week after I got my twenty-third and twenty-fourth rejection letters, I started my second book, *The Tenth Justice*, which became my first published novel. The book sold to an editor named Rob Weisbach, for his imprint at William Morrow.

Here's why this is important. In that book, I created a character who was really my mother—the mother in *The Tenth Justice* was truly based on my mom. But when my first editor read it, he sent it back saying he didn't think the mother and father were realistic. He said they were *too crazy*. So I did what any young writer would do when they want to win an argument. I brought my parents to meet my editor.

They came up to the editor's office at William Morrow, and for the half hour or forty-five minutes, I sat there, silently smiling, as my mom and dad talked this poor man's face off. When they were done and had finally left, my editor turned to me and said, "Leave the parent scenes exactly as they are."

To this day, when I think of William Morrow, I think of that moment—the time I brought my parents to meet my publisher. From there, William Morrow launched my career. I planned to work with them forever, but a few years later William Morrow was sold, my editor shut his imprint, and I was forced to find a new publisher.

That is, until now.

Sometimes, dear reader, history feels like a game of dominoes. Other times, it feels like a selection process. Two years ago, we received a phone call that truly came out of the blue. It was from an editor who worked at . . . you guessed it . . . William Morrow, which means the book you now hold in your hands marks both my twenty-fifth anniversary as a published writer—and my return to the company that first gave me my chance when I was twenty-four years old.

I love when the universe works like that.

So here's to another twenty-five years together, dear reader—and more than anything else, let me tell you the most important thing of all: Thank you. Thank you for buying *The Lightning Rod*, thank you for sharing Zig and Nola with someone you love, and most important, thank you for coming with me on this long and winding journey home.

Keep being kind to each other.

Your friend,
Brad
Fort Lauderdale, Florida